The Yukon Grieves for No One

Lynn M. Berk

The Yukon Grieves for No One

References to real places, people, and organizations are used only to provide a sense of authenticity and are used fictitiously. Any other resemblance to real places, events, or persons living or dead is entirely coincidental.

For Toby
and
In memory of my mother,
who was unlike Lydia's in every way.

PROLOGUE

Breakup had come early to the Beaufort Sea. Warm southeast winds had already melted the ice in the shipping lanes and the ridge of pack ice was moving out. Icebergs still bobbed in the bay though, their shapes more fantastic each day as the sun and wind carved broad fissures and shallow caverns in every surface. The sky was deep blue. A single cumulus tower hovered over the village church.

The old man raised his face to the sun and smiled. "*Sixagiksuq*," he said out loud. Good weather. A perfect day for hunting seal. It was very early, but since there was no sunrise or sunset this time of year, that didn't matter at all. He had never been one to waste the morning.

The old man smiled again as he approached his aluminum skiff. While he was a traditionalist in most things, he firmly believed that this craft was an improvement over his old sealskin kayak. It required little maintenance, and the forty horse power engine carried him fast and far. He was getting too old to paddle all day. The boat had a seat, sparing his arthritic knees, and it was open, allowing him to move and stretch when his muscles cramped or his joints stiffened. He threw his rifle, his harpoon and rope, and his lunch bag into the bow. Grunting with the effort, he pushed the boat off the gravel shore and crawled over the gunwale. He touched a black button and the outboard caught on the first spark. As soon as the water was deep enough, he cranked the engine hard and headed north.

A neighbor had reported that there was a small herd of ringed seals on some ice floes near the *puktaaq*. Although there were scores of icebergs in the bay, the old man knew that, in this case, *puktaaq* referred to an enormous formation which floated midway between the village and the pack ice. Weeks of sun and warm wind had melted away all the sharp edges and now the two-story monolith was gently contoured, its slope a series of loose, soft folds. In recent weeks a large hole had appeared near the bottom of the ice, a window to the north side of the bay.

The old man wasn't interested in the puktaaq. He had caught sight of five dark forms wriggling on an ice floe a hundred yards beyond it. He turned toward the floe and backed off the throttle to quiet the engine. As he reached for his rifle, he saw something through the hole in the puktaaq—a brief movement, a flash of color. This worried him. What if someone beat him and took all the seals or scared them off? He peered through the hole again. At first there was nothing, and then he saw a flash, a surface reflecting sunlight. He heard a sharp crack at the same time something hit him hard in the chest, knocking him backwards. As he lay folded between the stern seat and the outboard motor, he saw a dark stain spreading over the front of his gray sweatshirt. He touched the spot. It was sticky. He rubbed his fingers together. He noticed that his own blood didn't feel any different than seal blood, or caribou blood, or the blood of a snow goose. Not surprising, he thought, but interesting.

He closed his eyes. He didn't feel much pain, but he was very tired. He wanted nothing more than to sleep. Then he heard a loud rumble; it was the unmistakable sound of an outboard. Someone was coming to help him. He willed his eyes open and watched as a large boat headed directly for him. It was coming fast. Too fast. He caught the barest glimpse of the single occupant before the bow of the big boat drove into his midsection. "*Naluabmiu*," he said as his skiff was torn apart. White man.

The old man knew that the Beaufort Sea was barely above freezing. He knew that hypothermia would take hold of him quickly. He knew was going to die. But the sensation was not unpleasant. As he slowly sank into the black water, a great sense of calm and peace came over him. His mind emptied, his muscles relaxed, and for the first time in years there was no ache in his knees.

CHAPTER 1

"Crap!" said Lydia Falkner when the engine of her Honda Civic made a horrible clanking sound just south of Dawson City, Yukon Territory. "Shit!" she said when the car went utterly silent. The Civic rolled to a stop. Lydia got out and gazed morosely at the pool of oil that was collecting on the gravel shoulder. She wrenched open the hood, scowled at the labyrinth of hoses and cables, and slammed the thing shut again. With an enormous sigh of resignation, she began to trot back to the automotive shop she had passed a few minutes before.

Lydia's jeans and waffle soled hiking boots were ill-suited for jogging. The denim chafed her inner thighs and the boxy boot toes kept catching on the rocks that littered the edge of the road. She ran head down, watching the shoulder, trying to avoid a tumble. By the time Lydia saw the bear, she was less than thirty feet from him. He was digging for grubs or insects in a small stand of dead aspen below the berm. Dirt and wood chips flew as he uprooted old stumps and tore into rotten logs. Lydia halted so abruptly she nearly pitched forward. Standing absolutely still, she held her breath and stared. It was a young grizzly, less than three years old. He was still brown, although his ear tips, the top of his head, and his hump were turning blond. His fur looked soft and fluffy, as if he'd just had a bath.

The breeze was carrying Lydia's scent in the other direction, and the cub didn't notice her until he sat back on his haunches to sample a morsel he had just unearthed. He blinked, dropped his lunch and, with some effort, rose up on his back legs to get a better look at this intruder. Pawing the air, he stretched his neck, peered at Lydia, and sniffed. Then he dropped to all fours and took a few tentative steps up the slope in her direction. Lydia Falkner, the staunch non-believer, clasped her hands together and whispered fervently, "Oh, Lord, I pray that this cub has separated from his mother."

A squirrel began chattering hysterically somewhere behind Lydia. A rivulet of cold sweat crawled down her spine. Turning slowly, she scanned the area for momma bear. But except for a red squirrel skittering up and down an alder branch and two silent ravens perched shoulder to shoulder on a mossy log, the meadow was devoid of wildlife.

Lydia turned her attention back to the cub. He was watching her intently, still trying to figure out what she was. In an effort to appear larger, Lydia drew herself up and held her arms out sideways; then she moved backward, one long step followed by another, and another. She spoke; her voice was loud and firm. "Go home now. Get lost. Skedaddle." The cub cocked his head to one side. He sniffed the air again and took two more steps in Lydia's direction. She suppressed a groan.

Then, as if he'd suddenly remembered an appointment on the other side of the road, the bear turned, scrambled up the embankment, and stepped into the northbound lane of the Klondike Loop Highway. Brakes squealed as a camper van with Ohio plates stopped dead in the middle of the pavement. A woman opened the door and climbed out of the driver's seat, video camera in hand.

"Hey, get back in the car," yelled Lydia. "That's dangerous!" The woman gave Lydia a withering look, stood her ground, and put the camcorder to her eye.

In the meantime, a teenaged boy had opened the passenger door and was standing on the running board. He began motioning to the cub. "Here bear, here bear, here bear," he called in a high pitched voice. Then the kid made kissing noises in the air. By now six other vehicles had stopped and traffic in both directions had come to a halt. Ignoring the cars, the excited exclamations, and the clicking of cameras, the cub strolled across the road. He turned and gave Lydia one last look before he disappeared into the ditch on the other side.

"Stupid tourists," muttered Lydia as traffic began moving again. She took a few deep breaths and resumed her trek, walking slowly and watchfully toward the big white Quonset hut with the gas pumps out front. When she finally entered the building, she pushed back the damp strands of hair clinging to her forehead and smiled. This was a real repair shop. The workbench was littered with dog-eared, oil-stained manuals and there was a reassuring pile of used parts on the floor. A young guy who had *Rodney* embroidered on his shirt pocket agreed to drive Lydia back to her car and attempt a diagnosis. He helped Lydia climb into the passenger seat of an enormous wrecker.

"Jeez," said Lydia. "You could tow a bus with this thing."

"I do," said Rodney grinning. "Lots of 'em. But up here we call 'em RVs."

"Tourists are a pain," said Lydia, as if tourists had been the topic of conversation all along.

Rodney looked at her and frowned. "What's wrong with tourists? They're our bread and butter up here."

"Yeah, but doesn't it bother you to have a bunch of Americans clogging up your roads and harassing your wildlife?"

"Nah," said Rodney. "Tourists don't do much damage. Tourism's a pretty clean industry when you think about it. No oil slicks or nothin'."

"Maybe so," said Lydia, "but over in Alaska the big cruise ships are ruining the air in Glacier Bay."

"Yeah," said Rodney, "but that won't happen here. We don't have much coastline. That's one reason the Yukon will never be the big tourist draw Alaska is. I wish the provincial government would do more to promote tourism." He grinned broadly. "It's great for us mechanics."

Lydia grimaced. "Yeah, I'll bet. I'm not exactly a tourist, but

I think I'm about to make a major contribution to the Canadian economy."

Rodney pulled over in front of the Civic, the big red wrecker dwarfing the little blue car. After poking and prodding the engine and examining the puddle in the gravel, he announced, "She's thrown a rod. That's definitely gonna cost ya."

Lydia groaned. It was true; bad things really did come in threes. First there had been that cold, curt message on her computer monitor. *In this time of budgetary crisis, the English Department must reduce its full time teaching staff. I regret to inform you that your contract will not be renewed in the fall.* Two days later Lydia had been awakened by the sound of two backhoes chugging and clanging in the empty lot next to her tiny, rented house. Longmont, Colorado was getting yet another strip mall. And now this.

Lydia gave the Honda's left front tire a vicious kick. She felt abandoned and betrayed by her rusty, battered sedan. She knew this wasn't fair; the Civic had served her well for twelve long years. Despite her insistence on driving it over ill-maintained forest service roads, despite her tendency to procrastinate on oil and air filter changes, despite many long trips from Colorado to the Yukon Territory, the Civic had always been reliable. But Lydia's finances were precarious now, and it made no sense to put a rebuilt engine into this automotive geezer. Besides, she wouldn't need a car for the next few months. "Screw it," muttered Lydia, half to herself and half to Rodney. She sold him the car for parts.

Now without wheels of her own, Lydia exercised her only transportation option. She hid her shotgun behind her back, plastered a huge smile on her face, and stuck out her thumb. She figured that a bespectacled, forty-four-year-old woman, neatly dressed in blue jeans and a gingham shirt, a few strands of gray hair in her chestnut braid, should have no trouble cadging a ride from a tourist family.

Within minutes, an RV pulled over and stopped. Lydia couldn't believe her eyes. This forty foot behemoth was towing a full-sized pickup truck and in the bed of the pickup was a Harley Davidson touring bike. As Lydia stared open-mouthed, a curly white head popped out of the passenger window. "Need a ride into Dawson?" it asked. Lydia closed her mouth and nodded. The head disappeared and a hand reached back and unlocked the side door. Lydia pulled it open, quickly threw in her gun case and backpack, and stepped into automotive splendor. The passenger, who introduced herself as Mrs. Audrey Earhart from Battleground, Indiana, cheerfully waved Lydia onto the vivid pink, vinyl bench in the breakfast nook.

The RV was so long that conversation with its owners was nearly impossible. Lydia and Mrs. Earhart managed to exchange a few pleasantries and then tired of shouting. Mr. Earhart drove in placid silence. Lydia longed to look out the window and watch the countryside pass. She wanted to peer over the rail of the Klondike Bridge; she wanted to see the turnoff to Midnight Dome, the round wooded mountain that embraced the back edge of Dawson; she wanted to catch a glimpse of the enormous landslide scar that hung dramatically above the town, a stark white fan gouged out of the deep green slope. Most of all, she longed to watch the Yukon River as it rushed madly past the Front Street dike. Unfortunately, the vehicle's side windows were covered with Venetian blinds and all the blinds were canted downward. Lydia lifted a couple of the pale pink slats behind her, but all she could see was the white stripe that marked the edge of the lane.

Mr. Earhart stopped for gas a few miles outside of town and then headed for the river crossing where the Earharts were going to catch the George Black. This small automotive ferry would carry them across the mighty Yukon, up the Top of the World Highway, and into Alaska. As Lydia climbed out of the vehicle, Mrs. Earhart explained that they were anxious to get to Alaska so they could see real live Eskimos.

"But," pointed out Lydia, trying not to show her annoyance, "you already have. That young woman who just pumped your gas is probably a full-blooded Inuvialuit."

"Inoovult? What in heaven's name is that?" Mrs. Earhart had made a fatal mistake. She had asked a college professor a simple question, but college professors never have simple answers. Standing in the road next to Mrs. Earhart's open window, Lydia leapt into full pedagogical mode.

"Well," she said, conscious that she was using her teacher voice, "there are lots of different groups of Eskimos, and, while they have some cultural similarities, they're distinct communities. Canadians use the word *Inuit* as a generic term instead of *Eskimo*. Anyhow, the Inuvialuit are the Inuit who live in northwest Canada, and in Alaska there are the Inupiat, the Yupik and —." Lydia's voice trailed off when she saw the vacant look on the face of her interlocutor. She decided to show Mrs. Earhart some mercy and let the whole thing drop.

After thanking the Earharts and shouldering her backpack and shotgun, Lydia hiked over to Dawson Dolly's. As she passed a small knot of tourists on Front Street, someone made a snotty crack about gun nuts. But the cashier at Dolly's didn't bat an eye. He simply stowed both gun and backpack behind the counter, while Lydia stood in the doorway looking around for her friend Anna.

Anna was a server at the restaurant, one of the two in Dawson that offered year-round employment. The place was hopping. When Lydia finally caught Anna's eye, Anna rushed over and gave her a bear hug. Then she put her arm around Lydia's shoulder and ushered her to a quiet table out on the patio.

"I can't talk now," Anna said, "but I get a break in half an hour. I'll bring you something to eat in the meantime." Ten minutes later Anna brought her a plate of spaghetti covered with a pesto sauce so green it glowed.

Lydia was famished. Within minutes she had devoured the pasta, the sauce, and even the parsley garnish. She was sitting back and listening to a couple exclaim over their macadamia encrusted halibut when Anna slipped into the chair across from her. Lydia gave her old pal a broad smile. Anna was one of those people whose very presence electrifies the air. She was a small, energetic woman with short dark curls, lively brown eyes and an infectious smile. She was an anomaly, a sophisticated urbanite who had abandoned

New York City to settle down in this small sub-Arctic tourist town, a place that boasted a population of less than 2,000 in winter and temperatures that dipped to 45 F below zero. Lydia and Anna hadn't seen each other at all over the last three years, but they were thoroughly at ease. As Lydia's mother had said of her own best friend, Anna was like an old, comfortable shoe.

Anna couldn't contain her curiosity. She planted both her elbows on the table and leaned forward until she was almost nose to nose with Lydia. "I'm thrilled to see you, but why did you decide to come back up? Your phone message was pretty damn cryptic."

Lydia's shoulders sagged and she looked away from her friend for a moment. She blinked hard and made eye contact again. "I recently had one of those life-changing experiences they talk about." Anna raised her eyebrows and leaned even closer.

"I lost my job," said Lydia bitterly. "They fired my ass."

"Why?" asked Anna. "What'd you do? Pick your nose in class? Sleep with a student? Tell the provost to go hell?" She knew that Lydia had been teaching at Mountain View Community College for eight years.

"No. My behavior was impeccable. My dean just decided that she didn't want to pay full time faculty anymore. More than half of us were let go; *non-renewed* was her euphemism. We were all replaced by part-timers who get a lousy two thousand dollars a course."

"That's really crappy. But there's no teaching jobs up here. Believe me, if there were, I wouldn't be doing this."

"I know," said Lydia. "I didn't come up here on a job search." She took a deep breath. "My financial situation isn't good. I'll probably have to sell the cabin. It's my only real asset." Using a fingernail, she began to scratch at a piece of vegetable matter that had dried on the table top.

Anna gave Lydia a pained look. "That would be a real shame. Do you really think it'll come to that?"

"It might. I've tried to get a teaching job for the fall, but no luck so far. If I'm really frugal, I've got enough money to see me through December. By then I'll probably be willing to tend bar or, God forbid, waitress." Anna flipped her a perfunctory bird. "Anyhow," Lydia continued, "if I *am* going to sell the cabin, I have to fix it up. Three years of neglect probably hasn't enhanced its curb appeal." Lydia finally dislodged the crust and flicked it to the floor.

Anna touched her hand. "I'm glad you can joke about it anyway."

"Actually, I can't." Lydia blew her nose into a paper napkin and breathed out through pursed lips. "I have to get the documents for the cabin. When I left, I left almost everything. Frank Johnson retrieved our files and our books and took them to his place. I wrote him that I'd be coming up to get the papers. I hope to God he still has them."

"Damn. If you sell the cabin, I'll hardly ever see you," said Anna. "This is awful."

"Believe me. I don't like it either." Lydia paused. "But fixing up the place is only one of the reasons I came. I need to confront my ghosts. After Dad died, I wasn't sure I would ever come up here again, but lately I've been thinking about the cabin, the river, the fireweed. I had to come back and see it." She looked at the ceiling. "Not just see it. I need to smell it, touch it, hear it." Then she fixed her eyes on Anna. "I'm going to stay up there all summer. It'll take me at least a month to clean up the property and make repairs."

Anna looked dubious. "Oookay. Remember, you'll be alone up there now. Are you sure you want to be that far from civilization?"

"God, you sound just like my mother," said Lydia. "I'm sure. I've thought about nothing else for the past three weeks. Fixing the place up will keep me plenty busy. And I won't really be alone. Frank'll be next door."

Anna leaned back in her chair and snorted. "Next door! Twenty miles away is more like it."

"Yeah, but he'll be there. That's the main thing. We'll look out for each other the way we used to before, before Dad died." Lydia closed her eyes. It took an act of will to peel the lids open again. "Look, I need to get some sleep. It's been a hard day. Can I have the key to your place?"

Anna laughed. "It's not locked, you numbskull. What you think this is, Manhattan? You've been gone too long."

CHAPTER 2

Fifteen minutes after climbing the stairs to number 3-B in the Blue Moose Apartment complex, Lydia collapsed on the daybed in the back room and slept for thirteen hours. When she awoke, it was mid morning and it was hot and stuffy in the tiny room. Lydia crawled out of bed and into her jeans. Further activity was impossible before coffee.

Unfortunately, Anna did not share Lydia's passion for a strong, well-brewed cup of java. All Lydia could find in her tidy but seldom-used cupboard was a box of coffee bags. She hadn't even known such a thing existed. Apparently, they were to be dunked in boiling water like tea bags. Lydia was not in the mood for games.

Sleepy and surly, she went in search of real caffeine. She headed for a favorite cafe a few blocks away. Dawson's unpaved streets and wooden sidewalks were already filled with tourists, who were gawking at the Gold Rush era architecture. A few of the town's buildings were untouched historic relics. Ramshackle and unpainted, they leaned at crazy angles as they sank, millimeter by millimeter, into the permafrost. Most, however, were in good repair and brightly painted. One wore a coat of deep red and sported a bay window trimmed in navy blue. Its neighbor was pale yellow with forest green doors and window frames. On the corner, purple steps, a purple banister, and a purple front door welcomed visitors to a tiny dove-gray bungalow. Porches and balconies were supported by elaborately carved spindles and roof lines dripped with gingerbread trim.

The cafe was in one of the restored store fronts. It was already crowded when Lydia pushed open the door. She glanced around for an empty table, then broke into a huge grin. It was inspired by the sight of a shock of white hair and a flannel-clad back hunched over an enormous plate of fried eggs and toast. Lydia loped across the restaurant shouting, "Frank!" She flung her arms around the blue plaid shoulders.

The white head turned abruptly and yelled, "What the hell?" Then recognition dawned. "Oh, Lydia, it's you. Sit down." The man named Frank turned his back to her and speared an egg with a fork. A vivid yellow puddle spread across his plate.

Lydia lowered herself into the chair across from him. "No 'Hi, how are you' or 'Gee, it's great to see you' or 'I've missed you?'" she said, the reprimand undercut by her smile.

"Hmfff," replied Frank. He picked up his coffee mug, slurped, then bit off half a slice of buttered toast and chewed vigorously. Lydia laughed out loud and shook her head. She ordered a cup of coffee from a harried waitress and sat back and waited.

Frank Johnson was Lydia's closest neighbor on the Yukon and a dear friend. He lived upstream on a homestead he had built with his own hands. Frank was in his mid seventies, tall, thin, and slightly stooped. He looked frail but he wasn't. Beneath the flannel and denim was a body well conditioned by a lifetime of physical labor. Frank routinely carried his fifty-five pound solo canoe overhead on three mile portages; he could hike for ten hours straight, up hill and down, over boulders and scree, through streams and muskeg; he had even been known to hitch himself to a homemade sledge and pull three hundred pounds of timber over the snow to his workshop. Frank's massive hands were knotted and scarred from years of tree cutting, log splitting, and cabin building.

Frank was dressed in the same clothes he had been wearing when Lydia had last seen him—stained, mail-order blue jeans, well worn high-top work boots, and a long sleeved flannel shirt, frayed at the collar and cuffs. Frank always wore a long sleeved plaid flannel shirt—indoors or out, summer or winter, picnic or funeral. He had three identical shirts in different colors which he rotated every fourth day. Every couple of years he would order another three flannel shirts and the cycle would begin again. Frank was also sporting a baseball cap. The once forest-green cotton was now the color of canned peas, but Lydia could still read the words *TREE HUGGER* stenciled across the front. She had given Frank that hat for his birthday three and half years ago. It looked as though he'd worn it every day since.

As she watched Frank devour his eggs and toast, Lydia was overcome with affection and nostalgia. Frank had been the Falkners' mentor and guide to life on the Yukon. He had taught both father and daughter how to hunt in the sub-Arctic, how to fish the rushing waters of the river, how to can salmon, and how to bake in a wood burning oven. He had helped Otto Falkner design his log cabin and had contributed free labor. Frank had every skill needed to live in the wilderness.

Frank was also an old curmudgeon. He was blunt and tactless and had few conventional social skills. His discourse was so enigmatic, his remarks so oblique, that conversation with him was an exercise in code-breaking.

Frank was comfortable with very long silences. Lydia would wait him out; she knew he'd talk eventually. They'd kept in touch by mail and Frank knew that Lydia needed the papers for her cabin and why. She hadn't expected to run into Frank in Dawson. He didn't come to town much.

Lydia anchored one elbow on the table and rested her chin on her hand as she scrutinized Frank's face. That's when she realized that there was something wrong. His eyes held little expression, and he chewed mechanically as if he weren't really tasting his food. One foot was beating a tattoo on the floor. Finally Frank dragged his last sliver of toast through the egg yoke that had pooled in the center of the plate. He pushed his chair back and looked at her. He cleared his throat twice and then spoke in a low voice.

"You can't do it," he said. He folded his arms on his chest and stared at her grimly.

"Can't do what?"

"You can't sell that place." His voice was even lower now.

"Frank, I may not have any choice."

"Otto and me, we built it. He loved it. You'd be betraying his memory if you let somebody else have it. A stranger." Frank's ice-blue eyes bored into hers.

Lydia sighed deeply. She should have seen this coming. "Frank, believe me, I don't want to sell it but I'll probably have to. I've been fired and I don't have a lot of money saved up. It's the only thing I have of value *to* sell."

"Value!" Frank spit the word out. Now he was yelling. "Value isn't about money. The river, the land, they have value. Money isn't worth shit."

Lydia groaned inside. There was no way to make Frank understand. Frank had never had a regular job or a checkbook or health insurance. Existing beyond the margins of society, he lived on the fruits of his own labor. He hunted, fished, gardened, and on rare occasions sold the exquisite boxes he made in his workshop. In his younger days, he had built cabins and outbuildings for cash.

In a placating tone, Lydia said, "I hope I don't have to do it, Frank. Believe me, I'll do everything I can to hold on to it. But I came to clean the place up, just in case. If there's any way to keep it, I will. I promise."

Frank shook his finger at Lydia. "Don't betray your father; don't betray the land." He lowered his eyes, looked away from her, and clutched his empty coffee cup hard. "Too much betrayal going on up here as it is." He fixed his gaze on the yellow stain in the middle of his plate.

"What are you talking about?"

"Nothin'," he mumbled. "Nothin'. Forget it."

Lydia leaned forward and put her hand on Frank's arm. "Frank, what's wrong? Has someone betrayed you somehow? Hurt you?"

Frank shook his head. "No, not me. Everyone. Everything."

Lydia was growing exasperated. "Good God, Frank, stop talking in riddles. What do you mean?" Frank shook his head firmly, clamped his lips shut, and signaled the waitress for more coffee.

"Please, Frank, talk to me." He shook his head again and put his two hands palm out in a halt gesture.

Lydia knew there was no point in pursuing this. If she did, Frank would get up and leave. She accepted a refill and they sat in silence as the air conditioner tried to combat the heat generated by two waffle irons, three toasters, a large grill, and twenty patrons.

Finally, Frank offered the barest hint of a smile and his body relaxed a bit. He broke the silence. "I have a present for you. I made it myself. I think you'll like it."

"What is it?" asked Lydia.

"Come up to the homestead and see for yourself. It's a gift that will speak to you."

Oh, great, thought Lydia, more riddles. But to Frank she said, "That's terrific. I can't wait to see it." She gently touched his arm. "I'll get up to your place as soon as I can. I still have to buy a boat and get supplies. It could be a week. But I promise to come see you as soon as I get my stuff to the cabin."

"I know you will," said Frank. He gave her a real smile this time. He pushed back from the table, stood up, and unfurled his lanky frame. "I gotta get on the river. Buck's alone up there." Buck was Frank's dog. Lydia stood, too, and they looked at each other awkwardly for a few seconds. Then, in one long step, Frank came around the table and embraced her. He held her tight, then wordlessly he dropped his arms to his sides. He looked embarrassed.

Lydia took his hand and squeezed it. "I've missed you, Frank. I've missed you a lot."

Frank nodded. "That goes for me, too," he said. "And Otto. I miss Otto something fierce." He abruptly turned away from Lydia and cleared his throat. Then he reached behind his chair and grabbed a three foot length of plastic pipe that had been leaning in the corner. From under the chair he pulled a paper bag. Lydia could see a package of hacksaw blades peeking over the top. Frank tucked the pipe under one arm and grabbed the bag with the same hand. With the other he waved goodbye and disappeared through the front door.

After polishing off a short stack, three strips of bacon, and two more cups of coffee, Lydia began boat shopping. She needed something solid but cheap. She also needed a motor powerful enough to handle a seven mile an hour current. She pored over the *For Sale* ads on the bulletin board at the General Store, scanned the classifieds in the *Yukon News*, and asked everyone she knew for leads. Two days later she found a well-used but sound sixteen and a half foot aluminum skiff. It had once been bright yellow, but the finish was flaking badly now and it looked as if it had a case of mange. The mottling did nothing to hide the dings, dents, and abrasions that the craft had suffered over its countless trips up and down the great rivers of the north. It came with a used twenty-five horse power outboard, two bright orange life vests, and two cheap wooden paddles. She loved the whole ensemble.

Now Lydia had to provision herself for a life (or at least a few weeks) on a remote sub-Arctic river. The Yukon was once a busy superhighway. In 1898 thousands of miners reached the Klondike gold fields by poling their handmade boats and rafts downriver from Lake Bennett to Dawson. Paddle wheelers began to run the river as early as 1869 and continued carrying passengers and freight until 1955. For almost a century, small communities and isolated homesteads grew up along the banks of the Yukon. But when the commercial sternwheelers began carrying construction material for the building of the Alaska Canada Highway, they carried the seeds of their own demise. People no longer wanted to travel by river when it was easier and cheaper to travel by road. Most of the old river towns were abandoned over time.

Otto Falkner's log cabin was about sixty miles upstream from Dawson and there were no communities and very few homesteads between his property and town. Buying supplies was a serious and expensive business. Four hundred and seventy-three dollars later, Lydia felt equipped to face the wilderness.

The next day Anna and her Corolla hauled Lydia's boat and supplies to Dawson's floating pier. After a number of false starts and some ear-splitting curses, Anna managed to back the borrowed boat trailer into the water. Lydia, holding the bow line tight against rushing current, slid the skiff into the river. She secured the craft to two giant cleats on the pier. It took twenty minutes to load the boat. Then Lydia stepped gingerly into the stern, adjusted her hat, and pushed the starter button with her thumb. The engine spit, sputtered, and coughed, but the spark finally caught. Anna released the lines and the skiff lurched forward, its bow waving merrily in the air. Anna waved, too, and Lydia, grinning from ear to ear, gunned the engine, leaving an impressive rooster tail in her wake.

Local wags often note that the Yukon is too thick to drink and too thin to plow, an allusion to the huge quantities of silt the river carries as it makes the journey from its headwaters in British Columbia, through the Yukon Territory, into Alaska, all the way to the Bering Sea. Like all big rivers in the far north, the Yukon is ever-changing. In periods of low water, new islands break through and are quickly dotted with cotton grass sporting fluffy white heads, deep green alder saplings, and soft delicate reeds called horsetails. Then in the spring, rising water whittles new channels and the process starts all over again. The rushing waters of the snowmelt will often undercut a high riverbank until the overhang becomes so heavy that it topples into the river; the mud and sand are carried downstream and deposited in another spot. So each year the river widens and narrows in an inevitable yet unpredictable cycle.

Lydia headed her mottled yellow craft upstream. Just outside of Dawson she passed the confluence of the Yukon and the Klondike. The water's surface swirled and churned as the currents of these two fabled rivers mingled. It was hard to imagine that just a few miles from here lay the legendary Klondike goldfields, stomping grounds of Sam McGee (prior to his unorthodox cremation) and Dangerous Dan McGrew. Beyond the goldfields stood the deep dark forests where the descendants of Buck, Jack London's magnificent sled dog, still heed the call of the wild.

At the first bend of the river Dawson fell from view and Lydia was alone. The morning mists were burning off. It was going to be cool and sunny. The soft purr of the motor, the hissing of the river silt as the bow sliced the water, and the breeze playing with her hat brim were as hypnotic as a mantra. Lydia settled back in her seat, turned her face to the sun, and felt every muscle in her body relax. There were no deans, no telephones, and no shopping malls on the Yukon River. Nobody except Anna, Frank, and her mother knew that she was here.

Even in the short trip to Otto Falkner's cabin, now Lydia's, the Yukon River cut through an astonishing variety of terrain. After the confluence with the Klondike, the right bank of the river flattened out and Lydia could see meadows dotted with drooping bluebells, bright yellow marsh violets, pale pink wild roses, and the delicate but deadly purple monkshood. The meadows eventually gave way to stands of tall straight birch trees, the white bark scarred almost black where branches had broken off in high winds and heavy snows. The banks of the river and even its islands provided an excellent environment for water loving cottonwoods and alder trees. At times chalky white cliffs towered over Lydia's boat and at one point she glimpsed eight white specks moving along a ridge, a flock of mountain sheep. She chastised herself for not leaving her binoculars accessible.

At noon Lydia headed for one of the many islands that dot the river. Nestled between two broad channels, this island was large and wooded at the center. She ran the bow of her boat aground and hopped over the side. Immediately her feet sank into the mud to the very tops of her shoes. Not quite quicksand but a long way from terra firma, the mud of these islands was dangerous stuff. The more you trampled an area, the more the mud sucked.

Lydia tied the bow line to a heavy piece of driftwood and headed for the stunted alders and cotton grass in the middle of the island, where the ground would be firm enough to hold her weight. After checking for fresh bear tracks, she found a piece of driftwood on which to stretch out and devour the feast Anna had pilfered from Dolly's gourmet larder. She was savoring the smoked salmon, sourdough bread, and Greek olives when a sea gull waddled over to her and inspected the crumbs on the ground. The bird offered her an unblinking stare, flapped his heavy wings, and snatched an entire piece of fish from her fingers. He was airborne before she could react.

As Lydia reclined against the smooth, gray log, she noticed a canoeist paddling rapidly downstream in the opposite channel. It was unusual to see someone on the river alone in an unmotorized craft. While there were few rapids on the Yukon, the fast current made solo landings tricky. But this canoeist had no intention of landing. He was stroking hard and every pull of the paddle was smooth and efficient. The canoe was forest green with *Mohawk* written in white script just below the gunwale. Mohawk solos had a reputation for being light and maneuverable, but they were made in Florida and it was unusual to see one on the Yukon.

This fellow was traveling light. Lydia saw only a long gun case and a waterproof bag strapped to the thwart. She waved, but her dark green shirt and tan pants provided excellent camouflage. He didn't see her. As the canoe shot past, she noticed that the paddler was fairly young, tall, and bearded. He was wearing an expensive fishing shirt with lots of pockets and zippers, the kind so often featured in the L. L. Bean Catalog. Lydia turned her attention to the remaining smoked salmon.

Half an hour later she was back on the river. The hypnotic drone of the engine and the soporific effects of the lunch were beginning to take a toll. She reached for her thermos of coffee before she realized that, in the chaos and excitement of packing the boat, she had left it on the front seat of Anna's car. Damn. It had been four hours since she'd had her first and apparently last cup of coffee; this was going to be a hard day. Twice she caught herself before her chin reached her chest. Lydia didn't realize she had dozed until a deep thud announced that the boat had hit one of the thousands of uprooted tree trunks that are carried downstream by the mighty current. The bow glanced off the obstacle with no ill effect and she was thoroughly awake.

As Lydia approached her cabin, familiar landmarks began to

appear. A pile of rotting boards marked what remained of an old mining shack; a stark white moose skull still lay unmolested in the weeds, its eye sockets and molars lined with soft green moss; an ancient cottonwood, festooned with elaborate, grotesque burls, dropped white fluff into the amber waters of the Yukon. Lydia's chest began to tighten. What would she find at her place? What if bears had broken into the shed, or worse yet, the cabin? Would the creek, her primary water supply, be dry? How would it feel to walk through the door, knowing that her father would never again cross that threshold?

Finally Lydia saw the thirty foot flagpole that Otto had erected above the river. It looked naked without its Maple Leaf flag. Lydia cut the motor and ran the boat onto the riverbank at the sandy spot that served as a launch. She pulled it aground as far as she could and tied it to a tree. She would scout the place out before she brought any supplies up to the cabin. She loaded the shotgun and slung it over her shoulder. The bank was a tangle of scrub alder and lustrous purple foxtail grass. She cursed as her pant leg was captured by a patch of devil's club, a mean-spirited plant with woody spiked stems and huge prickly leaves.

Pushing back underbrush with each step, Lydia climbed the steep hill and stepped into the meadow that served as her front yard. The grasses were high but the path to the front door was unobstructed. And there stood the cabin, the place that had been her summer home for eleven years, the place that had precipitated her parent's divorce, the place where she had scattered her father's ashes, the place that she loved above all other places. She stopped a moment and caught her breath. She felt excitement, emptiness, fear, and great calm, all at once and then each in its turn.

Lydia walked slowly toward the building. Everything looked fine. The front windows were opaque with dirt and mold but they had been spared the ravages of bears and high winds. The front door was also intact, right down to the large sliding bolt that kept it firmly closed but not locked. It was customary in the northern wilderness to make a cabin accessible to the errant traveler. Many property owners stocked their empty cabins with some canned food, a bit of split wood, and matches, just in case. Lydia had asked Frank to do exactly this when he had closed the cabin for her three years before. Access to four walls and a fire could mean the difference between life and death for a broken down snow machinist or a trapper stranded in a blizzard.

Lydia took a big breath, released the bolt, and pushed open the heavy plank door. It took a moment for her eyes to adjust to the gloom. When the interior finally came into focus, Lydia gasped and whispered, "Oh, my God." A kitchen chair lay upside down in the entryway. The mattress had been hauled down from the loft and dumped in the middle of the cabin, its blanket, sheets, and pillow heaped in a corner. Every horizontal surface was littered with beer cans, crumpled cellophane bags, and bits of hot dog bun. The coffee table was stained with mysterious gobs of rust and green. Clots of mud mixed with grass and gravel dotted the linoleum floor.

Lydia's knees felt weak. She laid the shotgun down, leaned against the wall, and slid until her butt hit the floor. Through clenched teeth, she shouted, "Goddam you. Goddam you, whoever you are." She felt violated. This place had always been her special refuge. It had no phone, no Internet access, no television, and no regular radio reception. The nearest post office was sixty miles away. The rhythm of life was dictated by the seasons, the weather, and the migration of geese and salmon. It was Lydia's sanctuary.

She hauled herself to her feet, picked up the gun, and placed it behind the door. Then she stood in the middle of the cabin floor and turned a slow three-hundred-sixty degrees. She took a deep breath and did it again. And again. The third time Lydia was able to look past the trash, the mattress, and the overturned chair. There seemed to be little real damage. The two fresh cigarette burns were barely visible on the battered old end table. The crushed potato chips and cookie crumbs in the fold of the futon cushion could be brushed away. The stains on the coffee table were nothing more than ketchup mixed with pickle relish and mustard. Her grandmother's old oak rocker sat garbage-free and unsullied.

Lydia pursed her lips and blew out air as she walked into the kitchen area. Its centerpiece was an ancient, wood-burning cook stove, Lydia's most prized possession. Like all such stoves, it was made of cast iron but every exterior surface except the cooktop had been enameled in an iridescent eggshell white. The edges of the oven and firebox doors were trimmed in light blue. Squat and chunky and at the same time elegant and imperious, it was the Queen Victoria of stoves. However, at the moment its dignity was compromised by spattered tomato sauce, clumps of dried oatmeal, and a pyramid of crusty pots and pans. A deep sink stood next the stove, its stark white porcelain set off by a bright green pitcher pump, the only indoor plumbing on the premises. The sink currently held every plate Lydia owned; dirty cups and silverware had been thrust into every available gap.

Lydia picked her four inch paring knife out of a crevice. It was gouged and pitted. Some idiot had used it to open tin cans. She shook her head in disgust as she sat down at the kitchen table. It was then that she realized that the intruders had indeed inflicted real damage, damage that could not be repaired. A deep, ragged **KZB** had been carved into the top of the pine table, a house warming gift that had been built by Frank Johnson. "Fraternity boys!" she yelled. "I should have guessed."She stood up and rubbed the letters hard with her palm, as if to wipe them away.

Then Lydia's gaze moved to the big spruce rafters overhead. With some trepidation, she approached the wooden ladder standing in the middle of the room. She climbed three rungs and peeked into the sleeping loft, which spanned only half the building. Furnished with two painted crates, two footlockers, and a mattress, this had been Lydia's bedroom when she and her father had shared the cabin. Lydia was thankful that, apart from the mattress, this room had been spared altogether. The kids had probably been too drunk to climb up there more than once.

Calmer now, Lydia backed down the ladder, jumped to the floor, and began to poke through the debris. It was recent. She didn't mind the clean up so much, but since anything that couldn't be burned had to be hauled back to Dawson, this pile of bottles and cans was an unwelcome sight. She'd have to cram all this trash into sturdy plastic bags and take it to town in a couple of weeks. "Fraternities bite," she said aloud.

Lydia returned to the river and proceeded to carry her supplies from the boat to the cabin. Finally she was able to unearth her new cleaning supplies and get down to the business of digging the place out.

As she picked through the detritus left on the floor, Lydia had to smile at the collection of items the boys had left behind—a **KZB** baseball cap, one muddy boat shoe (size thirteen), a set of optically worthless binoculars (a promotional item from the Seattle Mariners), a new Swiss Army knife too small to be of any real value on a canoe trip (it had no can opener, which explained the abuse of her paring knife), a half empty bottle of bourbon, and an unopened, giant-economy-size package of sour cream and onion potato chips. She rescued the knife, the chips, and the bourbon and threw everything else into three large trash bags which she hauled out to the shed. Then Lydia hoisted the musty, beer stained mattress to her shoulder and pitched it into the yard. She would sleep on her camping pad in her down sleeping bag.

After pulling a bucket and some old scrub brushes from under the sink, Lydia unpacked a big jug of detergent and a package of new sponges. For the next three hours she wiped off shelves and carefully stowed the contents of the bags and boxes. Finally she tackled the floor. The activities of the frat boys had left a slurry of dirt, crumbs, and spilled beer. Lydia got down on her knees and scoured with the biggest brush. Two back-breaking hours later it was possible to stride across the linoleum without sticking to it.

By ten o'clock that evening the cabin, while not spotless, was tolerable. Lydia stood in the entryway for a moment admiring her handiwork and then opened the heavy front door. As she stepped over the threshold, she was aware of movement in front of her. She stopped in mid stride. On the other side of the clearing stood a huge dog. But how did a dog . . .? Then Lydia gaped in amazement. This wasn't a dog. It was a wolf, a large male, completely black except for the eyes, which were amber orbs with jet centers. Even though it was summer, his coat was thick and luxuriant; the tip of his long tail disappeared among the downy white heads of the cotton grass. The wolf's eyes locked on hers and he stood absolutely motionless as if taking her measure. They stared at each other for fifteen or twenty seconds. The wolf showed no sign of fear or even curiosity; his gaze was utterly impersonal. And then, as if dismissing her, he turned, raised his tail, and slowly, imperiously, walked into the brush.

The wolf had been the climax of an exhilarating and exhausting day. Lydia began to prepare for bed. She washed her face and hands at the pump and headed for the latrine. Thank goodness the outhouse had been spared during the fraternity bacchanal. The boys had even made some improvements. The toilet seat was free of spider webs and a fresh roll of very soft toilet paper was nestled in the holder. Two superhero comic books graced the magazine rack. As Lydia sat on the high wooden throne, flipping through *Aquaman*, she could hear the rapid *hoo*, *hoo*, *hoo* of a boreal owl somewhere deep in the woods.

Half an hour later, Lydia climbed the ladder to the loft and stripped off her clothes. Before settling into her sleeping bag, she dug her sleep mask out of her pack. She was no longer accustomed to a world in which sunset and sunrise were only three hours apart. Once the mask was in place, she concentrated on the silence. Apart from the hypnotic rush of the river in the distance, there was no sound at all, not even a breeze rustling the cottonwood leaves. As Lydia lay in her bag, the brown, swirling current of the Yukon moved hypnotically behind her closed eyes until she slept.

CHAPTER 3

The next morning dawned cold and cloudy. The light admitted by cabin's grimy panes was gray and feeble. "Damn," muttered Lydia, as she fumbled for her glasses, "I've got to get those windows washed." She perched her glasses on her nose, stood up, and as she stretched, her eyes moved around the loft. At first glance the room looked stark and unadorned but the beauty was in the details. Frank Johnson's exquisite handiwork was everywhere. Spaced at precise intervals on the back wall were the birch clothes pegs that Frank had turned on his foot powered lathe. She could still remember his drilling ten perfect holes with his old fashioned brace, leaving ten perfect corkscrews of black spruce on the plank floor. Her gaze moved to the mirror hanging over her footlocker. Frank had fashioned its frame out of willow branches, which he had stripped of bark to expose the bright, white sapwood. Each branch sported a series of small, heartwood depressions, which he had then excavated with a penknife, creating copper colored diamonds in bas relief.

It was damp in the cabin. Lydia began to shiver and grabbed for her clothes. Her flannel shirt felt clammy against her skin. As she sat on a footlocker to pull on her socks and hiking boots, she remembered why she was here and that, someday soon, she would probably have to sell this place to someone who couldn't possibly love it as much as she did.

In a deep funk, Lydia climbed down the ladder and shuffled toward the kitchen. Standing over the big porcelain sink, she dashed two handfuls of cold pump water on her face and brushed her teeth. Then she disassembled her braid and pulled a hairbrush through her thick, unruly hair. She started to re-braid, but whenever she finished two or three plaits, she'd lose control of one of the strands and have to start over. Neither her brain nor her hands were working. She gave a disgusted snort and pulled her mane back in a single bushy pony tail.

Unwilling to wield an axe until she had some caffeine in her system, Lydia pulled some kindling and a few small sticks out of the emergency wood supply. Once she got a small blaze started in the stove's fire box, she pawed through the cans on the shelves, looking for coffee. There wasn't any. She smacked herself on the forehead. She had forgotten to buy coffee, the most essential item on her shopping list. First the missing thermos, now this. Lydia looked at her watch and calculated; she hadn't had a cup of coffee in over twenty-six hours. At this point she would have settled for coffee bags.

With a disgusted snort, Lydia sat down at the pine table to plan her day. First and foremost she had to motor up to the Johnson homestead. She needed to resolve things with Frank, settle their differences about the cabin. Frank's approval mattered a great deal to Lydia and she couldn't bear the thought of his being disappointed in her. Frank was stubborn and it wasn't going to be easy to make him see her point of view. But there *was* a bright side. Frank, too, was a caffeine addict and he would have coffee, a pot on the stove and a case of two pound cans on the pantry shelf. Lydia fried up two eggs and washed them down with spring water.

Frank's homestead was only twenty miles upstream from Lydia's cabin and a few miles below (she couldn't believe the irony) Coffee Creek. Coffee Creek was aptly named. Stained by tannin, it ran a rich dark brown. Until recently Coffee Creek's most famous denizen had been Coffee John, a colorful Yukon character who made his living carving intricate and whimsical bears and walking sticks for tourists. When Frank had written Lydia a few years earlier to tell her about John's death, he had also explained that John's cabin and outbuildings stood just as he had left them, a memorial to the man and a tribute to his chosen lifestyle.

Lydia collected her hat, her life vest, and her canteen and headed down the bank to the yellow skiff. She was actually glad that the day was overcast; it made for cooler traveling and the cloudiness would increase her chances of seeing wildlife. Sure enough, within her first five minutes on the river, she spotted a female moose and a young calf browsing on the margin of an island. It was clearly this year's baby, all knees, ears, and nose. The adult moose followed the approaching boat with her eyes. Lydia backed off the throttle until she was almost dead in the water.

She watched the cow just as intently as the cow was watching her. She knew that the mother wouldn't hesitate to attack if she feared for her baby's safety. Lydia had her hand firmly on the throttle and, at any sign of forward motion on the part of this massive animal, she was set to gun the motor. But then the calf buckled its front knees and lay down in the mud. Lydia relaxed her throttle hand. The mother had somehow signaled to her offspring that this intruder was not a threat. The baby dozed and the mother returned to her grazing as Lydia eased slowly past.

Once the moose was out of sight, Lydia cranked the engine. Now her bow was cutting through water that looked like *cafe au lait*. At Whitehorse the Yukon is a clear river but about seventy-five miles south of Dawson, the aptly named White River enters from the southwest. Its glacial silt is chalky and where the two rivers actually converge, the swirling current looks like the melted remains of vanilla ice cream and chocolate syrup. Within minutes Lydia's boat was riding through this confection.

When she passed the log jam that marked Thistle Creek, Lydia began to watch for Frank's flag. The huge red maple leaf was clearly visible above the alders and cottonwoods along the shore. She landed and pulled the boat up on the bank. The song of an invisible warbler heralded her arrival. As she ascended the path to Frank's cabin, she let out a loud "hello." She was greeted by silence. She approached the cabin and called again. No answer. It was unlikely that Frank had gone back to Dawson since his old aluminum boat was clearly visible in the weeds. She pounded heavily on the front door. No sound emanated from within. She walked over to the privy and shouted. She stuck her head into the workshop. Finally she returned to the cabin, pushed the door open, and entered.

Frank's cabin was large but the roof was low and the windows small. Lydia peered into the gloom and saw that the place was in its usual disarray. Magazines and books were piled on every flat surface, dirty dishes were stacked in the sink, and wads of crumpled paper dotted the floor. In the midst of the chaos on a lovely, old desk made of cherry sat Frank's 1950 Smith Corona manual typewriter, the most cherished of his possessions. The typing table was uncluttered and the typewriter was dust free. Five unopened reams of expensive bond lay under the desk.

Frank Johnson had worked for decades to end corporate logging along the Yukon River. In the old days, he had taken direct action—lying down in front of bulldozers and crashing shareholder meetings at Boise Cascade and Weyerhaeuser when someone else could come up with a proxy, plane fare, and a sport coat. These occasional forays into the halls of corporate North America would have been funny if Frank hadn't been so deadly serious about his mission. The ill-fitting, borrowed sport coat, the wild hair, and an ear misshapen by frostbite gave him away on sight. More than once he had been spotted and stopped by building security before he even made it to the elevators. If Frank did manage to infiltrate the meeting, he rarely got more than a few sentences out before he was hustled out of the room. Once though, he did manage to deposit a big gob of chewing gum on a corporate lawyer's well-shined shoe.

In the past five or six years, Frank had given up the more strenuous forms of activism. Now he wrote. Reams and reams of paper fell from the carriage of his ancient machine—leaflets, letters-to-the-editor, position papers, articles that were submitted to newspapers and magazines but never published. Frank wasn't writing today though. And he wasn't baking, reading, or drinking home brew. He wasn't anywhere in the cabin.

Then Lydia heard a faint noise, high and shrill. She opened the back door and the noise grew louder. It took her moment to locate the source. There next to Frank's trash pile lay his dog, who had been named for the magnificent beast in the *Call of the Wild* but was his opposite in every way. Whereas Jack London's Buck was large, muscular, and highly intelligent, Frank's Buck had been from puppyhood small, lethargic, and slightly addled. The original Buck had led miners and dogs over the treacherous Chilkoot Pass; Frank's Buck could barely find his way out the front door to pee. London's Buck had been a stately St. Bernard-shepherd mix; this Buck's lineage appeared to contain nothing but short, squat breeds with stub noses and a tendency to yip. Lydia whistled but Buck didn't come. His howls became more insistent, more desperate.

Lydia sprinted the thirty yards to the trash pile, stepped over the low split-log fence that surrounded it, and crouched next to the frenzied animal. She wrinkled her nose at the sour, moldy smell of decaying vegetable scraps. As she looked down to put her hand on the dog's head, she saw why Buck was howling. There, covered with brush, empty cans, old newspapers, and lettuce leaves was a human arm.

Lydia leapt up and screamed. Buck howled louder. She retreated a few steps, turned away from the sight, and took a couple of gasping gulps of air. Turning her head slowly, she looked again at the red plaid sleeve and the large hand that protruded from the opening. She realized that bits of denim and the toe of a boot were also visible under the debris. The head was completely covered with newspapers. With shaking hands and a churning stomach, she returned to the pile and lifted one sheet of damp newspaper and then another from the invisible face. As she removed the last page, she confirmed what she had already known. This body belonged to Frank Johnson.

Abandoning the distraught dog and the dead man, Lydia ran blindly across the small meadow and back into the cabin. She collapsed into Frank's easy chair and put her head to her knees as she alternately sobbed and fought off waves of nausea. She sat there a long time, clenching the upholstered arms and swallowing the acid that rose into her throat. She tried to collect her wits but she couldn't wrap her mind around what she had just seen. Absurd scenarios flitted across her consciousness. Frank had an accident while throwing things on the pile; Frank had just learned that he had a terminal illness and had killed himself; Frank had died of natural causes and some passerby had attempted to bury him. But there was only one plausible explanation; someone had killed Frank and tried to conceal the body. Nausea gripped Lydia once more. She ran for the front door and vomited in the yard.

After the heaving stopped, Lydia remained on her knees, not wanting to move at all. But she had to go back to the trash pile; she had to know how Frank had died. She closed her eyes, drew her lips tightly together, slowly rose and walked around the building. It took every ounce of will she possessed to put one foot in front of the other.

When Lydia reached the body, she stood for a moment and looked into Frank's eyes. Even in death his gaze had a piercing intensity. She knelt by the old man and gently covered his face with a piece of newspaper. She held her breath as she removed the rest of the newsprint and random debris from his torso. It didn't take a medical examiner to determine what had killed him. There was a ragged hole the size of a quarter in his chest; the flannel was stiff with dried blood. This was the work of a shotgun or large bore rifle. It was unmistakably murder. It was also preposterous. People who lived alone in the bush weren't murdered. They died of alcoholism or lung cancer; they fell off their snow machines and died of hypothermia; they went through the ice and drowned during spring breakup; more than occasionally they took their own lives. But they weren't murdered.

The flies discovered Frank's exposed wound. Stepping daintily over the stained shirt, a small horde began to probe the bloody hole. Lydia couldn't bear it. She returned to the cabin and pulled a ragged patchwork quilt off Frank's bed. Sobbing softly, she laid it over his body. As she stepped back, she averted her eyes. That's when she caught sight of Frank's *TREE HUGGER* hat lying in the weeds behind the trash pile. She could barely see through her tears as she ran for the river. Buck followed her, barking frantically.

Lydia was about to push her boat into the current when Buck's cries finally registered. He was on his belly now, whimpering and scratching the dirt. Lydia realized that the dog probably hadn't eaten in days. She ran back up the bank and into the cabin. It took her a few minutes to find a bag of dried dog food and a soup pot. She carried both items to the porch and emptied the bag into the kettle. Buck immediately drove his nose into the pellets.

Lydia ran back to the river, shoved the skiff into the water, and almost pitched headlong into the stern as she threw herself over the side. When she regained her equilibrium, she mashed the starter button. The engine whined, spit, almost caught and then died. In a panic, she grabbed the backup starter rope in both hands and she pulled with all her might, once, twice, three times. She was panting and her arms burned with the effort. Finally the engine fired and she took off at full throttle down the river.

The three and a half hours it took Lydia to reach Dawson passed in a blur. She couldn't focus; she couldn't think; she felt as if her head were disconnected from her body. She had been traveling in a light mist for ten minutes before she even noticed that her shirt was wet. Near Sixty Mile River a black bear was digging in a shallow gully. Sometime later a red fox trotted along the bank with a snowshoe hare in its mouth. With the grace of prima ballerinas, coal black ravens rode the thermals high above the river. She saw it all and remembered none of it.

Finally, the edge of Dawson came into view. Lydia passed the Klondike and made for the floating pier. At the last minute, she was forced to throw the engine into reverse and wait as a bevy of tourist canoeists was being hauled onto the dock by their outfitter. She wanted to scream at them as they chatted and laughed and clogged up the landing area. But finally she was ashore. She began to run. Her lungs were on fire by the time she burst into the Royal Canadian Mounted Police headquarters shouting, "There's been a murder."

After much loud talking and banging of interior doors, Lydia was escorted to a small room containing a metal table and three hard chairs. Across from her sat an officer whom she vaguely remembered meeting at a party some years before. He was short, plump, and nearly bald. He threw a yellow legal pad on the table and pulled a black and gold fountain pen from his pocket. Lydia was surprised to encounter a policeman whose taste ran to Mont Blanc. As if reading her mind, the Mountie explained that the damn tape recorder was broken yet again. He introduced himself as Wilbur Rogers and began to ply Lydia with questions. It was clear that he had known Frank Johnson.

After determining her full name, her permanent address, and her relationship to the deceased, he let Lydia begin her story. Her voice shaking with emotion, she described looking for Frank, hearing Buck's howls, and finding the body in the trash pile. She described the debris which had been deliberately piled on the corpse and the wound in Frank's chest. As the gold nib of Roger's fountain pen flew across the page, Lydia could see her own words etched in his thick black strokes. It was chilling.

"Was there putrefaction?" asked Rogers. "A strong smell? Flies?"

Lydia grimaced and thought a moment. "There was garbage in the pile. Rotting vegetables. I don't think it smelled any worse than that. There were flies everywhere but I don't think Frank's body had"—she could barely get the word out—"decomposed."

"What about animals? Were there any signs that the body had been molested?"

"No," Lydia said. "I didn't see anything."But she knew it was only a matter of time before the ravens, wolves, and coyotes would find Frank.

"Did you see anyone on the river near Mr. Johnson's place?"

Lydia shook her head.

"When was the last time you saw the deceased?"

Lydia described her encounter with Frank at the cafe and repeated his riddling comments.

When she was done, Rogers shook his head slowly. "That's not much to go on. Did you see the gift he mentioned when you were in the cabin?"

"No," said Lydia, shaking her head. "But when I went in the first time I was looking for Frank, and the other times—." She paused and her eyes filled. "Oh, God, the other times I couldn't see anything." Lydia put her face in her hands. Rogers continued, undeterred by her tears.

"Can you think of anything else at all that might be relevant?"

Lydia blew her nose and thought a moment. "Yes," she exclaimed. "I completely forgot about the mess at my place." She described what she had found when she had first entered her cabin. At Roger's request, she wrote out the Greek letters that had been carved into the table.

"You'd better save your trash and let us look through it," he said when he finally put his pen down. Lydia nodded.

After two exhausting hours, the Mountie seemed satisfied that Lydia had told him everything she knew. "Look," he said, "I don't know who will be in charge of this investigation, but whoever it is may want to interview you further."

Lydia gave Rogers Anna's telephone number and address. "But I want to go back up to my cabin tomorrow."

Rogers nodded. "That's okay. We just need to know where to find you." She drew him a crude map on the piece paper he tore from his legal pad. Rogers looked at it and smiled. "Oh, yeah, I know that place. Nice piece of construction. Mr. Johnson helped build it, didn't he?"

Lydia nodded but her thoughts were elsewhere. "Please get up to Frank's as soon as you can. I'm so afraid something will happen to him."

"Ma'am, the worst has already happened."

CHAPTER 4

Lydia left the RCMP detachment and walked down Front Street through a light drizzle. She stumbled almost blindly up the staircase to Anna's apartment, praying that she would be home. She was and she was astonished to find Lydia at her door. "What in the hell are you doing here? You just left yesterday. What's wrong?" She grabbed Lydia's forearm and pulled her into the living room.

Lydia collapsed on the couch and the story poured out of her. When she had finished, she closed her eyes and exhaled. She felt hollow. Anna was incredulous. "Who would want to kill Frank? He was as harmless as they come; he wouldn't—." Her eyes narrowed. "He was harmless unless you were a logger, or a pulp mill, or a corporate executive with interests in the forest," she said softly.

Lydia sat bolt upright. "Oh, God! I forgot about Frank's environmental crusades." She paused and frowned. "But his anti-logging activities are all so old. Could they really be a motive for murder?"

Anna shrugged. "I don't know but I think the Mounties should hear about it." She handed Lydia the telephone.

After leaving a lengthy message for Wilbur Rogers, Lydia realized that she was hungry. She smiled ruefully to herself as she also realized that she still wanted a cup of coffee. She and Anna walked the two blocks to Dawson Dolly's where they ordered halibut, fresh peas, and yellow rice. Because of the rain, they sat inside. The restaurant was small and noisy. Pots banged in the kitchen and dishes clattered as the waitresses cleared the tables. Next to them a young man shouted into his cell phone. He was pissed at his wife or girlfriend, and he didn't care who knew it. Three tables away a young couple, probably tourists, wrestled with two bored and whiny toddlers, identically dressed. As soon as one baby had been bribed into silence by a cookie, the other one erupted. It seemed to be a continuous cycle.

To distract herself from the din, Lydia stared at the building across the street. Its wooden siding had been painted a deep gold over which someone had printed in thick, ornate, black letters:

I wanted the gold and I sought it;
I scrabbled and mucked like a slave.
Was it famine or scurvy-I fought it;
I hurled my youth into a grave.
I wanted the gold, and I got it.
Came out with a fortune last fall.
Yet somehow life's not what I thought it,
And somehow the gold isn't all.

This was, of course, the first verse of *The Spell of the Yukon*, the most famous of Robert Service's gold rush poems. It always reminded Lydia of her cousin Kenneth, who had scrabbled and mucked in an investment brokerage firm, sacrificing his marriage, his children, and his own health for the next big commission. Frank Johnson would never have understood a man like Kenny. He was baffled by those who grubbed for gold or glory. Life was to be savored. The only meaningful work was work that produced something—a cabin, a piece of furniture, a carboy of home-brew. Lydia was sure that Frank had died with very few regrets.

She was glad to be with Anna right now. Anna's toughness and directness were reassuring. Anna was often described as *cute* by people who didn't really know her. Those who were quick to stereotype were ultimately caught off guard by her incisive wit, her sharp tongue, and her spine of steel. The two women had known each other since graduate school at the University of Michigan. Although Lydia had come from a small, northern Michigan town and Anna had grown up in Brooklyn, they had bonded upon their first meeting in a Henry James seminar. Somehow the indirect, reticent, small town WASP and the outgoing, assertive, urban Jew found common ground in their acute differences. They were both older than the other graduate students in the program and that served to strengthen the relationship.

"What are you going to do now?" asked Anna.

"What do you mean?"

"You can't go back up to the cabin," said Anna. "There's a murderer on the loose."

"I have to go back up, Anna. I've got so much to do up there. I'm sure the killer is long gone."

Anna fixed her large brown eyes on Lydia. Her nostrils flared. "Oh, sure. Let's just assume he's in Indonesia or Mongolia. Damn it, Lydia, why do you insist on pushing yourself this way? Just because your mother is afraid of everything doesn't mean you have to prove that you're different every goddam minute of every goddam day."

"That's not what I'm doing," said Lydia through tight lips.

"Yes, it is," said Anna. "You're afraid of fear so you keep testing yourself." She adopted the cadence of someone reciting a litany of grievances. "You were afraid of whitewater, so you made yourself raft down the Colorado River; you were afraid of riding your motorcycle in the rain so you took a three week bike trip in the Pacific Northwest; you were afraid of grizzlies so you went camping in the Kenai Peninsula when the salmon were running."

"What's wrong with trying to overcome my fears?" said Lydia angrily, her upper teeth biting hard into her lower lip on the *f*.

"Yeah, yeah, yeah," said Anna. "And just how smart is it to try to overcome a fear of killers?"

"Give it a rest," said Lydia. She immediately regretted her words and her tone. She touched Anna's arm. "I'm sorry. I know you're looking out for me. But you sounded so much like my mother just then. I'll buy a lock and, remember, I have my shotgun. Besides, the area will be crawling with Mounties for the next couple of days."

"I still think you're just being macho. It's stupid to take the risk."

"I'm going back in the morning, Anna. It'll be fine."

But Lydia wasn't so sure it would be fine and she knew that Anna was right. Lydia *was* afraid of fear and her biggest fear was becoming like her mother. Jean Falkner was a small, frail woman who eschewed all things physical and who saw the world as a dangerous place. She never went anywhere, never took risks, and hated to sweat. Lydia had vowed never to be like her. At an early age, she attached herself to her father and insisted that he teach her to hunt, to fish, to canoe. Lydia got her first rifle when she was only thirteen and by fifteen was a better shot than her dad. As a teenager, she threw herself into the world of the physical; she ran, she lifted weights, she took long hikes in the Michigan woods. As soon as she got her driver's license, she bought a 90cc motorcycle. The little bike didn't go over fifty miles an hour but it gave Lydia untold freedom, not to mention a cool reputation among her peers. But even the Honda didn't completely quell her fear that she might someday turn into her mother.

That night Lydia dozed fitfully on the daybed. The next morning, she ate breakfast with Anna and bought four pounds of coffee, a sturdy lock, and two new bits for her hand drill. Then she headed back to the Dawson pier. For the second time in three days, Lydia steered her boat upstream. But this trip held none of the joy and anticipation of her first journey. The tension in her back did not melt away and she had a kink in her neck that kept her from looking over her right shoulder. She tried to focus on the blue sky and the gentle slap of the water on her bow, but she kept seeing instead Frank's body among the old newspapers and cabbage leaves. She knew she was clenching her teeth and she couldn't help it. Before she reached Indian River, she felt the familiar physical precursors to a headache and by the time she caught sight of her own flag pole, she had a full blown migraine. She could barely see as she hauled the boat onto the bank. Then she dragged herself up to the cabin and collapsed on the futon.

Lydia must have slept hard for at least three hours when she was roused by a loud knock on the door. She couldn't remember where she was, couldn't remember where the door was, couldn't imagine who was pounding on it. Then she heard a shout. "It's Sergeant West of the Yukon Royal Canadian Mounted Police." For a moment she thought the voice had said, "Sergeant Preston of the Yukon."

Unfortunately, the officer who stood in the entryway was no radio-serial hero in a smart, red uniform. He was older than Lydia, very tall and almost bald, his few remaining pale hairs plastered to his head in a pathetic comb-over. He hunched slightly when he walked, which, along with his long nose and receding chin, made him look like an albino buzzard. His eyes were gray and he was dressed in a perfectly pressed gray uniform shirt. Everything about him was pallid and tentative. His voice was high and nasal and when he said, "Hello, how are you?" it sounded like a whine.

West lowered himself into one of the kitchen chairs and asked with genuine perplexity, "Why would a woman live alone in a place like this?"

"Because she likes it," retorted Lydia. They lapsed into a strained silence with Lydia looking directly at West and West looking down at his well polished boots. Finally Lydia looked down at them, too—boots so shiny she could see his knees reflected in the leather. Then she exploded. "For God sake, what did you guys find out about Frank? Did you find any evidence? Did you find the gun? Do you know who did it?"

West gave her weak smile and patted her right hand, which was lying on the table. She glared at him and snatched it away. He was visibly flustered. He shoved his hand into his pocket and muttered, "Sorry, I didn't mean—." His words trailed off and he seemed to lose focus. Finally he gathered himself and answered her questions. "Mr. Johnson was killed by a slug from a twelve gauge shotgun. It's clear that he was shot a few feet from that trash pile. The body is being shipped to the coroner's facility in Whitehorse. One of the constables has taken the dog to the Humane Society in Dawson."

Lydia blanched at this piece of news. She'd been so focused on Frank that she hadn't given any thought to the fact that Buck was alone on the homestead. "Look," she said to West, "about the dog.

When you get back, will you please call the Humane Society and tell them I'll take him if nobody else adopts him. Please tell them not to put Buck to sleep."

West nodded. Then he picked up his shiny snap briefcase and took out a legal pad and a ball point pen. "Ms. Falkner, did Mr. Johnson perchance own weapons?" Lydia couldn't believe that a Mountie stationed in the Yukon Territory could ask such a stupid question.

"Of course, Frank owned weapons," she snapped and under her breath added a sarcastic, "perchance."

West should have known full well that everyone who lived in the bush had a shotgun or a high powered rifle, usually both. Bears were sometimes a nuisance and on rare occasions a real threat. River residents hunted geese, moose, and caribou for food. Lydia explained that Frank had always kept his rifle in a corner of the living room and his 12 gauge shotgun behind the back door.

But Sergeant West shook his head. "The rifle was there but we didn't find a shotgun. It's possible that Mr. Johnson was killed with his own gun, which the murderer then took with him."

Sergeant West had little to say about the murder itself. He politely asked Lydia a few questions about her movements on the day Frank was killed, but it was clear that he didn't consider her a serious suspect. When he asked her if she had seen anyone else on or near the river, she remembered the paddler in the Mohawk canoe. West was interested and made copious notes in his neat Catholic school handwriting. Lydia saw that his nails were perfectly manicured, not a common affectation among men in the far North.

West pointed to the graffiti on the pine table. "The fraternity boys did that, eh?"

"Yes," said Lydia.

"I was a Kappa Zeta in college," he said with some pride.

"Well, I wouldn't brag about it. Your fraternal brothers are thoughtless vandals."

West bristled, pursed his lips, and started to speak. But no words came and he slumped even lower in his chair.

"What else do you need to know?" asked Lydia, anxious to get this fool out of her cabin.

"What can you tell me about Mr. Johnson's family and friends?"

Lydia knew that Frank had one grown son Jesse, who, three years ago at least, was living in Inuvik, up in the Northwest Territories. Frank's late wife Maggie had been a lot younger than he was, and after living fifteen years in the Yukon bush, she had wanted out of the oppressively dark cabin, out of the wilderness, and out of the marriage. Maggie was Inuvialuit and after she and Frank had divorced, she had taken Jesse back to her parents' place in the Mackenzie River delta just outside of Inuvik. Maggie had died of cervical cancer a few years after the move.

Lydia remembered Jesse as a handsome, shy, dark-eyed teenager, who loved hunting and fishing a lot more than the home schooling his mother inflicted on him. After the divorce, Jesse visited Frank occasionally and at least three times a year Frank made the trip up the Dempster Highway to see his son. These trips were legendary in Dawson because they always began with Frank's attempts to borrow a car or a truck. The Dempster is a 737 kilometer (456 mile) dirt road that meanders through the remote wilderness of the northern Yukon and Northwest Territories. The road ends sixty miles from the Arctic Ocean. Not surprisingly, people were unenthusiastic about loaning Frank a vehicle for such a journey. After years of listening to Frank's tri-annual wheedling and pleading, the citizens of Dawson put their collective foot down and told Frank he had to take the bus. But Frank didn't much like being packed in with strangers for the overnight ride and Lydia wasn't sure how often Frank had seen Jesse in the last few years.

All of this flashed through Lydia's mind, but West didn't need these details so she simply said, "Frank's ex-wife is dead, and I think his son Jesse lives in Inuvik. I haven't seen Jesse in four, maybe five years. I don't know anything about their recent relationship. I know that they were close when Jesse was growing up. Frank pretty much knew everybody on the river from Minto to Circle and he knew most of the year-round residents of Dawson, too. His closest friends were my late father and Mick and Mack McDougal, who live between Mayo and Keno."

Satisfied, Sergeant West stuffed his notes into the briefcase and pulled a business card out of his shirt pocket. Lydia took it but pointed out to him with an edge in her voice that she had no telephone, so contact would require a sixty mile trip one-way up and down the Yukon. West shrank further into his gray shirt, clasped his hands to his chest, and explained in his high thin voice that the RCMP patrolled the river regularly and if she remembered anything else or learned anything else, she should hoist a red flag and the police boat would stop. When he shook her hand goodbye, Lydia wasn't surprised to find it damp and clammy.

Stooping to avoid whacking his head on the low door frame, Sergeant West exited the cabin. As he started across the meadow, Lydia remembered the trash she had been asked to save. With malicious satisfaction she ran after him, shouting, "You forgot to take out the garbage." The two of them carried the reeking bags to the police boat and piled them in the bow. Lydia even talked him into to taking the mattress.

As the RCMP boat roared away, Lydia returned to the cabin and lowered herself into her grandmother's chair. As she rocked, she tried to make sense of what had happened. She couldn't imagine anyone hurting Frank. Sure he had been gruff and cranky, but he was also kind and gentle. His generosity was legendary. He never turned a traveler away from his door and freely shared his food, money, beer, and opinions. Homesteaders who were too old or sick to hunt and fish could depend on Frank to supply them with moose steaks, dressed wild geese, and smoked fish. Everyone on the river had been treated to Frank's splendid home brew. Why had this happened? There had to be an answer.

Lydia stood up and walked across the room. An old photo of her mother, father, and a much younger Lydia sat on a shelf in the kitchen. She picked up the picture and stared at it. She gently touched her father's face. Then she threw her head back and shouted at the rafters. "First Dad and now Frank. Frank and Dad. I can't stand this. I can't stand it."

Still clutching the photo, she bolted out of the front door, across the front meadow, and down the bank. When she reached the water's edge, she threw herself down in the damp sand and fixed her eyes on the river. The never-ending rush of the water, the symmetry of the eddies, even the water bugs that danced on the surface were strangely comforting. She stared for a long time and was gradually able to match her breathing with the hypnotic rhythm of the current. Calm returned. She took a deep breath, stood up, and walked back up to the cabin.

"To hell with window washing," she said out loud as she replaced the photo on the shelf. "I've got to do something diverting or I'm going to drive myself crazy." Fishing. That was it. There was nothing more diverting than casting and retrieving a line, and if you caught a fish, so much the better. Lydia actually smiled at the prospect. She put on sunscreen and a broad-brimmed hat and threw the canteen and a couple of apples into her daypack. Then she trotted to the shed and grabbed her medium-weight graphite rod, her battered metal tackle box, a net, and a stringer. This fishing equipment had been sitting idle for three years, but Lydia was relieved to note that the monofilament line had not degraded, that the reel still turned smoothly, and that mice had not snacked on her net.

She headed for her boat and then remembered. There was a murderer out there. Somewhere. She went back to the cabin and picked up her shotgun.

Lydia was on the river within minutes. She headed for a spot she had fished many times before. It was a pretty, slow flowing creek about thirteen miles upstream, a place where she could anchor the boat, cast for grayling, and do a little skinny-dipping if she felt like it. As her bow sliced through the roiling brown water, she settled back on her seat, periodically scanning the shore for wildlife.

She was rewarded when a pair of disembodied antlers appeared above a tangle of scrub alder. Keeping a safe distance from the apparition, Lydia slowed down and watched the rack move along, sometimes disappearing in the brush but always reemerging. Then the bushes thinned and two huge eyes appeared and blinked at her. Finally a long thick nose and a broad expanse of chest pushed through the branches. The creature stepped daintily into the open, its massive body supported on long skinny legs that looked inadequate to the task. He was the biggest moose Lydia had ever seen. It was clear that this fellow was king of this particular patch of earth, and he wasn't going to be intimidated by a fragile slab of aluminum and its contents, which he outweighed by a factor of four. As Lydia backed off the throttle, he batted his two inch eye lashes, twitched his nose to unseat a swarm of mosquitoes, then lowered his head and resumed browsing.

From that point on Lydia kept her eye on the bank but saw only sand pipers, crows, and sea gulls. When she was just a few miles below her fishing creek, something in the weeds caught her eye. The sun was glinting off a shiny surface, a piece of metal from the look of it. As she approached the shore, Lydia could see that the metal was attached to something else, something long and straight, not a product of nature to be sure. The bank was low and Lydia was able to run the bow of the skiff onto a mud flat. She climbed out, secured the bow line, and then made her way through the mud and the horse tails.

There, obscured by waving sedges and cotton grass fluff, was a long gun. It was lying partially submerged in the river, its barrel wedged under a small log. The sun had been reflecting off the stainless steel swivel that attached the sling to the stock. At a glance Lydia knew it was Frank's shotgun, an old Ithaca Model 37. There was no other gun like it. The thirty inch black barrel was unmodified but the breech had been intricately engraved by an old hunting buddy of Frank's. The scene pictured a hunter stalking a caribou. The tiny man looked a bit like Frank.

Lydia squeezed her eyes shut and forced air over her top lip. She was going to have to raise that distress flag after all. She decided it would be unwise to touch the gun, so she marked the spot by tying a red bandana to a low hanging branch. With a deep sigh, she pushed the boat off the mud flats and headed downstream.

An hour later Lydia ran a red plastic tablecloth up her flagpole. She hoped that the cops would see it before the wind tore it off. She worried that a storm would come up and wash the shotgun downstream. She prayed that the weapon would be covered with fingerprints or DNA or something that would lead to the immediate arrest and conviction of Frank's killer. Hope, anxiety, and a little bit of fear skirmished in her consciousness.

CHAPTER 5

It wasn't until noon the next day that an RCMP officer bellowed *hello* from the top of the riverbank. Lydia trotted out to meet him, hoping that the greeting hadn't come from Sergeant Louis West. It hadn't. Corporal Al Cerwinski was big and jovial, his voice a deep baritone. His uniform was well rumpled and his boots were worn and scuffed. Lydia liked him instantly. She shook his beefy hand as she explained why she had hoisted the distress flag.

"Wow," said Cerwinski, looking grave. "You've had a tough week. How are you holding up?"

Lydia swallowed hard. "I'm doing okay."

"This has got to be a nightmare for you," said the Mountie. He paused. A look of unease crossed his face. "I hate to ask, but would you mind taking me to the gun? I might miss it if I go up there alone."

"I wouldn't mind at all," said Lydia. "Let's go right now. We'll take my boat. It has less draft than yours." Cerwinski nodded.

The trip upstream was short. At first Cerwinski was subdued and professional, but as the two chatted about Dawson, mutual friends, and fishing, the Corporal began to relax. Soon his eyes were dancing and the corners of his mouth turned up in a wry smile.

"What's so funny?" said Lydia smiling back.

"Do you know the name of the snake that joined the Canadian Police Force?" With an indulgent smile, Lydia shook her head. "Mountie Python," Cerwinski shouted with glee.

"Oh, no," groaned Lydia. She made a show of pressing her lips together and covering an ear with her free hand. But Cerwinski was gratified by her reaction. He segued into stream of Ole and Lena jokes, a few funny lawyer stories, and a couple of inoffensive Polish jokes, to honor his ancestry he said. By the time the red bandana came into view, Lydia had almost forgotten the purpose of their journey.

But as soon as they climbed out of the boat, the jokes stopped and Cerwinski was all business. He spent half an hour closely examining the ground around the weapon but found nothing significant. He took some photos of the gun as it lay there and then donned latex gloves and pulled it from under the log. "Wow," he murmured softly. "I'd hate to think that this beauty committed murder, but it sure looks like it." He took a bright green plastic bag from his satchel and carefully rolled the Ithaca Model 37 in it. The 12 gauge looked like a Red Rider BB gun all wrapped up for Christmas.

When they got back to the cabin, Cerwinski accepted Lydia's offer of coffee. They sat facing each other across the pine table. It didn't take long for Lydia to discover that Cerwinski was a Yukon boy, born and bred in Haines Junction. He had moved to Dawson two and a half years earlier. An avid fisherman and canoeist, he was delighted to be living along the Yukon River and its scores of tributaries. He confirmed what Lydia had suspected, that Sergeant West was not a Yukon boy.

Cerwinski was happy to pass along the station-house gossip. "Yeah, old Louie is from Lotus Land."

"Lotus Land?"

"Sorry," said Cerwinski, grinning. "Vancouver. He's been in Dawson less than a year. We heard he wound up here because he screwed up a high stakes case in the city, money laundering or something. He wanted a low profile post and he sure enough got it. Unfortunately, he's the senior officer. He hates it here and frankly most of the constables hate having him here. All he does is whine." Cerwinski affected a nasal falsetto. "There's no real movie theaters in Dawson, there's no Indian food, there's no place to buy decent brandy, blah, blah, blah." His voice returned to normal. "Louie won't last. I'm sure the constables at the detachment will manage to—how shall I put this—facilitate his move back to the big city. What about you? How did you wind up living on the river?" It's amazing what a difference a turn of phrase can make. This was so close to West's utterly offensive question and yet so different.

Lydia smiled. "It's a long story. Do you really want to hear it?"

He settled back in the chair. "If you've got the coffee, I've got the time."

"Well, it was really because of my dad. He lived in Michigan but he always wanted a cabin on the Yukon River."

"That's an unusual fantasy," said Cerwinski. "Most people just want a nice house in the suburbs."

"Not my dad. When he was young, he worked on the Klondike Loop of the Alcan Highway. He became fascinated by the Yukon River. He and a buddy once spent three months canoeing the whole length of it, all the way to the Bering Sea. It was one of the high points of his life. So, when he decided to build a cabin, it had to be on the Yukon."

"So what did your mum think about this idea of a cabin on the Yukon?"

"She didn't like it. In fact, she hated it. She only came up once and she was afraid of it all—the bears, the river, the isolation. She just hated it. She begged Dad to sell the place and Dad refused. They were divorced a couple of years after the cabin was finished."

"That's too bad," said Al. "That must have been hard for you."

"Not really," said Lydia. "I was expecting it. My parents never had much in common. I was an accident and my parents got married without knowing each other very well. They were very different, and I don't think they were ever truly happy together. But Mom was afraid of being alone and Dad would never have left her to fend for herself. But in the end she left *him*. I'm sure it was a big relief for both of them."

"How did your dad manage to build a cabin up here when he lived in Michigan?"

"He was a high school physics teacher, so he had three months off every summer. Frank Johnson helped him build the cabin. It took them two years."

"What about you? Did you spend summers up here, too?"

"I did. I was in grad school at the time and didn't have any financial support in the summer months, so I was able to come up and help."

"Up from where?" asked Al, accepting a second cup of coffee.

"Ann Arbor, Michigan and then Longmont, Colorado. I got a job at a community college near Longmont after grad school," said Lydia. "I wanted to work in the Yukon but there was no way to get a teaching job up here. I like Colorado, but I've always spent my summers in the cabin with Dad."

"Where are your parents now?"

"Mom still lives in the upper peninsula of Michigan, in the little town where I grew up. She remarried and seems happy. I like her new husband. I see them now and then." She clasped her hands tightly in her lap. "Dad was killed on the river three years ago."

"Oh, I'm sorry." Cerwinski paused. "Can I ask what happened?"

Lydia looked down and bit her bottom lip. "Sure, I'll tell you." Her voice was husky.

"You don't have to."

"I know. It's okay." Lydia took a deep breath. "Dad and I were in our boat heading back to this cabin. We'd been at a blues festival in Eagle. We got a late start, and we'd only been on the river a couple of hours when a storm came up. We were stupid not to get off the water, but we really wanted to make it home. At first things were okay, but then the wind started blowing incredibly hard. There was no place to land. I was in the bow; Dad was in the stern. Suddenly we hit a huge standing wave and the boat flipped over. I saw Dad's orange vest and then it disappeared. Poof. He was gone. Completely gone."

"Jesus," said Cerwinski, "you must have been terrified."

"I was. I have no idea how far the river carried me. It was impossible to swim in the current but finally I managed to get into an eddy and crawl to shore."

"What did you do then?"

"There wasn't anything I *could* do except hope and pray that someone would come along. I was exhausted and chilled to the bone, but my life jacket, wool shirt, and rain suit kept me warm enough to prevent hypothermia. I got through the night." Lydia paused and looked down at the table.

"You really don't have to do this," said Cerwinski.

"I know," said Lydia, "but I want to." She met his eyes again. "I just kept praying that Dad had managed to get to dry ground. The rain stopped early in the morning and eventually a couple of fisherman came by. I flagged them down and we went to search for Dad. We finally found him. He'd been caught by a sweeper, a big cottonwood that had toppled into the river. He was wedged face down under water by a heavy limb. He was dead."

Cerwinski's eyes reflected genuine sadness. "I'm so sorry." He paused and then said softly, "I think I would be angry at the river for killing someone I love."

Lydia shook her head. "I never hated the river for killing my father. I don't see the Yukon as malevolent or benign. It doesn't gloat and it doesn't grieve. It's simply indifferent. I scattered Dad's ashes in the river in front of our place; I knew that's where he would want to be. But even though I didn't blame the river, I couldn't stay in the cabin. I went back to Colorado. Frank Johnson cleaned out the place for me. This is my first time back in three years."

"What made you come back?" asked Cerwinski.

"I just got fired and might have to sell the cabin."

"You don't strike me as the kind of person who would get fired."

"Lots of people get fired when colleges trade good teaching for making money," said Lydia, and she launched into her tirade against the corporatization of higher education.

When she was done, Cerwinski grinned. "Whew, I wouldn't want to be on the wrong side in a debate with you. You'd chew me up and spit me out." He pushed up his sleeve and glanced at his watch. "Oh, damn, I gotta go pretty soon." He seemed distressed at the prospect of leaving. As he rose, he looked intently at Lydia. "Be very careful. I doubt that the murderer is anywhere in the area, but we don't know for sure." He pointed to the shotgun behind the door. "Keep that loaded and at hand."

"I will," said Lydia.

"If you have a friend that might be willing to come up and stay for a few days, that would be good, too. I'd be glad to deliver a note if you'd like to invite someone."

Lydia thought for a moment and realized that she very much wanted to do that. Cerwinski waited patiently while she scrawled a quick note to Anna, who had some vacation days coming. Besides, it wouldn't hurt Anna to get away from her on-again, off-again boyfriend, a short order cook named Bryan. Bryan also worked at Dawson Dolly's and he dogged Anna's every step. Bryan had a lot of *issues* with his parents, with his ex-wife, and with the eight-year-old son that he sometimes failed to support. Anna knew that she was wasting her time with him, but she maintained that the sex was terrific and that Bryan was hard to get rid of. Lydia folded her note, scrawled *Anna Fain at Dawson Dolly's* on the outside, and handed it to Cerwinski.

"Hey," said Cerwinski, "I know Anna. I usually take my coffee break at Dolly's. Anna always saves me the biggest piece of blueberry pie."

Lydia frowned. "Really? I thought cops ate doughnuts."

"That's a vicious American stereotype," replied Corporal Cerwinski. Then, after a very silly joke about carrier pigeons, he went on his very merry way.

The next day, Lydia washed all the first floor windows inside and out and chopped enough wood for two weeks worth of cooking. She was sweeping out the shed when she heard the whine of an outboard. Lydia dropped her broom and ran for the riverbank. As she reached the edge, she tripped on an old mooring wire and rolled ass over head down to the water's edge. When she stopped rolling, her nose was planted between Anna's two well worn boat shoes. She looked up at Anna's trim, perfectly tanned legs.

"We have to stop meeting like this," whispered Anna.

"Screw you," said Lydia as she turned over and sat up.

Much to Lydia's astonishment, Anna was carrying a shiny new shotgun. She was holding it awkwardly in one hand with the barrel pointed directly at Lydia's head. "Jesus," said Lydia as she stood up and snatched the gun out of Anna's hand. "Don't point a gun at anyone you're not prepared to shoot."

"But," protested Anna, "it's not—."

"Loaded. Yeah, I know. You'd be amazed at how many people are killed by unloaded guns. Where'd you get this, anyway?"

"My old boyfriend Hank bought it for me. I have to confess that I'm not a very good shot. I always flinch when I pull the trigger."

"A lot of help you'll be."

"Well, I figure if the bad guy comes, I'll just blast away in his general direction. Besides he won't know that I can't shoot straight."

"Yeah," said Lydia, "not until you put your first slug into your own foot."

"All right, all right," said Anna, "maybe this will help." She pulled a cooler out of the boat and opened it to reveal an apple pie, a huge sirloin steak, two enormous potatoes, and two six packs of Molson. The beer had been sitting in melting ice for the last few hours and the translucent green bottles were cold, wet, and inviting.

Lydia laid the shotgun on the ground, and with two quick flips of her Swiss Army knife, she snapped the caps off two bottles. Standing on the grassy bank, heads tipped back, eyes closed to the searing sun, the women downed the Molson. Then Lydia picked up the gun while Anna hoisted the cooler. Together they trudged up to the cabin where they each had a second, more leisurely beer.

"I'm glad you came to your senses," said Anna. "You really shouldn't be alone up here."

"Well I'm not alone now," said Lydia. "Thanks so much for coming. And thanks for the backup artillery. I think." She leaned over and gave Anna a hug.

"But," said Anna, her face now serious, "I can only stay a couple of days, then you'll be right back where you were."

"I know," said Lydia. "I'll cross that bridge when I come to it. Right now, I think we should burn that steak."

Hoping to save the pile of newly split wood for the stove, Lydia insisted that they forage for firewood. Fortunately, the creek bank was littered with small trees which had been uprooted during runoff. Wielding the bow saw with more energy than skill, Anna cut small cottonwood trunks into foot long sections. Lydia, using a large flat log as a chopping block, split them in half with an axe. In half an hour a fire roared in the stone ring which the two women had constructed in the front meadow. Lydia found an old grate in the shed and propped it on rocks over the flames.

When the logs had been reduced to shimmering orange, Lydia dropped two foil wrapped baking potatoes into the coals; a little later, she the plopped the enormous sirloin on the grill. The embers immediately began to pop and sizzle as the fat dropped into the fire. The two women sighed in anticipation. All but the most committed vegan would have been tempted by the smells that were wafting toward the river. Since bears were most assuredly not vegans, Lydia propped Anna's shotgun against a nearby spruce.

By the time the potatoes were baked through and the steak had turned juicy pink inside, Anna had spread a blue checked table cloth in the meadow and anchored it with four pieces of split wood. In the middle she placed an old coffee can filled with fire weed; then at each end she carefully positioned one of Lydia's chipped dinner plates and a mismatched knife and fork.

All conversation ceased as they tackled the outsized sirloin. Over apple pie and coffee, Lydia grew pensive.

"What are you thinking about?" Anna asked suspiciously.

"I think we should go up to Frank's place and look around."

"Wouldn't that be disturbing a crime scene? I don't want to spend my best years in a Yukon jail."

"No one will know and Frank deserves better than that idiot West."

Anna shrugged. "Okay. What the hell. If we get caught, I'll just say it was all your idea, which will be God's truth." She jumped up and began stacking plates and gathering silverware.

Lydia thought she was tough enough to return to the scene of Frank's murder. She thought she had worked through the worst of her grief. But when she and Anna started up the bank toward Frank's gazebo, she found herself clutching her elbows with opposite hands and squeezing her arms against her body. Her pulse began to race.

"I'm not sure I can do it," she said. She sank down on the bank and fixed her eyes on the roiling current. Anna sat next to her and put a reassuring arm around her shoulder. The two sat quietly on the damp ground amid the buzzing mosquitoes and soft, green horsetails.

Finally, Lydia groaned and got up on one knee. "Okay. I'm ready."

"You never give in, do you?" said Anna. It wasn't really a question.

Lydia stood, turned, and headed toward the well worn path. Despite her resolve, her legs felt like alien appendages, nerveless, wooden. It was as if someone else's body were carrying her up that embankment. Anna followed close behind. A flock of crows squawked at them from a cottonwood tree, and a cloud of white butterflies rose up in front of them. Lydia could feel the fragile wings as they softly brushed her fingertips. When Lydia and Anna reached the cabin, everything looked normal, mundane, peaceful. There was no yellow crime scene tape, no printed notice, no indication whatsoever that the authorities had even been there.

At the front door, Lydia paused for a moment, breathed deeply, and then grabbed Anna's hand. She led her around the building and across the little meadow to the spot where she had found Frank's body. Her relief at finding all the trash gone—every cabbage leaf, can, and newspaper—was overwhelming. She released Anna's hand and almost mustered a smile.

They returned to the cabin. Lydia pushed open the back door

and stepped across the threshold. "Hey," said Anna, who was peering around Lydia's shoulder, "it's dark in there. We'll never find anything."

"Not to worry," said Lydia. She pulled a Coleman lantern from a hook by the door and found a box of matches by the wood burning stove. The instant she touched a match to the fragile silk mantels, the room was ablaze with a harsh, white light. Lydia stood in the middle of the floor and turned around slowly. The place looked exactly as it had the last time she had seen it. If the Mounties had made a mess while searching, it had been subsumed in the original chaos. Somehow she found the familiar disorder comforting. The knot in her stomach began to dissolve.

Anna, however, was incredulous at the state of the cabin. "My God. Did the Mounties do this?"

"No," said Lydia. "Frank did." She walked over to Frank's old wooden filing cabinet, which was squeezed between two massive bookcases. "If Frank's murder has anything to do with his environmental activities, there might be something in here that will give us a clue. Frank documented everything he worked on. Everything. I'm surprised the Mounties didn't cart this back to Dawson."

It was immediately clear why they hadn't. The drawers were all locked and the entire cabinet, which was made of one-inch white oak, probably weighed two hundred pounds empty. But Lydia knew something the Mounties didn't. She reached under the drawer of the cherry typing table, ripped off a piece of duct tape, and came up with a small silver key. Anna's jaw dropped.

"Frank told me where he kept this years ago," explained Lydia. She put the key in the lock and then turned to look at Anna. "We probably shouldn't be doing this."

"But we're going to do it anyway, right?"

"Right."

Lydia opened the top drawer and pulled out the first folder. It was labeled *KNOTHEADS 1992-94* in Frank's spidery script.

Anna frowned. "What in the hell are knotheads?"

"You know. *Knothead.* A polite word for stupid jerk."

"Yeah, but why would Frank have a folder about stupid jerks."

Lydia laughed. "Knotheads is what he called loggers, because of the knots in timber."

"Oh, of course," said Anna, rolling her eyes.

"That's the point," said Lydia. "Frank didn't want his filing system to be obvious. He had this strange paranoid streak. His really important documents aren't even in here. The deed to this property is hidden in a book on cabin building and he used to keep Jesse's birth certificate behind that picture." Lydia pointed to a black and white photo of a little boy of about six. He had thick dark hair in a bowl cut and a body that was just beginning to lose its baby pudginess. A huge grin exposed two missing front teeth. In one hand the little boy held a rod and reel and in the other a salmon that was almost as big as he was.

"And you won't believe where Frank kept his money," said Lydia.

"I suppose a bank was out of the question."

"Absolutely. He kept it taped to the lid of his flour bin."

Anna snorted. "And I'm supposed to assume there's a perfectly logical explanation for that, too."

"Certainly. Money is dough. Flour. Dough. Get it?"

Anna shook her head. "I wouldn't want to have to dig this place out. Poor Jesse." She opened the second drawer. It, too, was devoted to Frank's environmental activities. Anna picked up the last file in the drawer. "Wow. This stuff goes back to 1965."

"Oh, yeah," said Lydia. "Frank kept everything he ever wrote and took detailed notes at every meeting he attended." She waved her hands over the filing cabinet. "And it's all here."

"Great," said Anna. "And we get to paw through every damn page looking for—. Hell, we don't know what we're looking for."

"I don't think we need to worry about the second drawer," said Lydia. "I can't believe that Frank's murder is connected to anything that happened that far back."

The third drawer contained personal papers. There were short notes from Frank's ex-wife Maggie, old correspondence with a home schooling organization, and a few letters from Frank's mother, long dead. In a file labeled *Falkner's Mansion*, Lydia found the ownership papers for her own property. She bit her lip as she pulled out the folder and laid it aside. The fourth drawer was crammed with Jesse's home schooling materials—everything from psychedelic finger paintings to typed essays on the history of the Canadian fur trade.

"Hey, what's that?" said Anna, peering into the drawer. At the very back lay a lumpy parcel wrapped in newspaper. A limp bow had been fashioned out of twine. Anna reached around Lydia and grabbed the package. She peered closely at the wrapping. "Lydia, your name is on it."

Lydia took the parcel and sank into a chair. "Oh, my God. This is the present Frank told me about. He said he made it." She covered her mouth with her hand.

"Open it," demanded Anna.

Lydia's hands shook as she tore the paper away. Nestled in a square of plaid red flannel was an exquisite knife. It was about the size of a paring knife, but this was no conventional kitchen implement. Its blade was straight, sturdy, and about three inches long. In tiny script letters, it was inscribed with Frank's name and a date. The handle was off-white and a tiny pair of caribou antlers had been scrimshawed between the two rivets. Lydia picked the knife up and wrapped her fingers around it; the grip had been carefully shaped to fit her small hand. The balance was perfect. She opened and closed her fist around the handle a couple of times, savoring the feel.

"It's beautiful," said Lydia. "It's simply beautiful. It looks like ivory. I wonder if it is." She ran her index finger over the tiny black antlers. "Frank only gave knives to his very closest friends. My dad had one and now I do, too." Tears came to her eyes.

"Look," said Anna, pointing to another flannel lump lying in the newspaper. "There's something else in there." Lydia picked up a soft package just a bit bigger than the knife. She opened it to reveal a simple hide sheath. The leather had been lightly tanned so the sheath was rigid enough to hold the knife but still supple. The only adornment was a small bone button that, along with a leather loop, held the flap closed. Lydia put the sheath to her face. It was soft and still carried a faint animal smell, earthy but pleasant.

Anna tapped her foot impatiently. "Come on. It's beautiful, but we've got work to do."

"Okay, okay." Lydia gently slid the knife into its sheath and the sheath onto her belt. "This is the best remembrance of Frank I could have." She stroked the leather again.

"Come *on*," said Anna. She began piling the folders from the top drawer on Frank's desk. "Hey, this is weird," she said, pulling out the last two files. Unlike the other folders, these were crisp and new. She held up the top file. "This one is labeled *Rudolph* and it's not dated."

Lydia took it from Anna and flipped through the contents. "It looks like information about the migration routes and habitats of the Porcupine herd."

"I didn't even know porcupines came in herds," said Anna. Lydia turned and stared at her, waiting for a grin or a smirk. But Anna was serious. Lydia hooted.

"Caribou, you knothead, not porcupines. Don't you know *anything* about your adopted homeland? It's a caribou herd named for the Porcupine River up in the northern Yukon."

"So why did Frank call the file *Rudolph*?" asked Anna.

"Because caribou and reindeer are the same animal."

"Okay, Miss Know-it-all. *Why* does Frank have a file on caribou?"

"I have no idea. Let's look at that one later."

Lydia set the *Rudolph* folder aside. The tab on the second file read *Rosemary's Baby*. It was empty.

"How odd," said Lydia. "Who is Rosemary's baby and why does Frank have a file folder for it?"

"Rosemary's baby is the spawn of the devil," replied Anna smugly. "Everyone knows that."

"Yeah, sure, but why would he use it to label a file?"

"You're the one who's supposed to understand his filing system." Anna frowned. "Did Frank actually go to movies?"

"Not as far as I know. He probably read the novel. During the winter, he read four or five books a week."

Anna grimaced. "These days I'm lucky if I read four or five books a year."

Lydia and Anna sat down at Frank's kitchen table to examine the contents of the *Knothead* files. After two hours of turning pages and scanning contents, Lydia was convinced that there was nothing helpful in any of them. "Throw me that Porcupine herd file," she said. Anna tossed Lydia the pale yellow folder.

Lydia opened it and flipped through the pages. There were three long articles on caribou, four very detailed maps showing the Porcupine herd's migration patterns, a stunning aerial photo of the animals moving across the tundra, and a short, upbeat newspaper article about Yukon school kids who had "adopted" and named four electronically tagged caribou. As part of their science curriculum, these fourth graders were monitoring the movements of Donner, Blitzen, Dasher, and Vixen during the spring migration.

Lydia picked up one of the articles and scanned the title page. She smiled. "This is by a Dr. Geraldine Rudolph of the University of Alaska-Fairbanks. I guess *Rudolph* was a double code word." She glanced at the two remaining articles. "These were written by Dr. Rudolph, too." She peered closely at the title page of one of them. In one corner Frank had scribbled, *Check out Bluenose herd.*

"Hmm," said Lydia. "I've never heard of the Bluenose herd. I wonder where they live."

"Well, I certainly don't know," said Anna.

Lydia picked up the large color photo of the migrating Porcupine herd and stared at it. A caption indicated that the picture had been taken in Alaska on the north slope of the Brooks Range. The well worn mountains had a light dusting of snow and the treeless tundra glowed in shades of reddish brown and gold. The landscape was dotted with countless glittering lakes and ponds and was bisected by a wide, braided river. Long gravel bars divided the main channel into a series of narrow, intertwining waterways. But the dominant feature of the photo was tens of thousands of caribou, all of whom seemed intent on crossing that river.

"God," said Lydia. "What an extraordinary event. I'd give anything to see an aggregation of caribou."

"Not me," said Anna. "Too damn many mosquitoes. Why do you think Frank has all this stuff anyway? He must have gone to a lot of trouble to get it. How did he know about this Rudolph person, for God sake?"

"Frank spent a lot of time in the library when he came to town. I'll bet one of the librarians helped him find what he was looking for and made him copies. But why does he care so much about the Porcupine herd?"

"Maybe he wanted to protest the oil drilling in the Alaska National Wildlife Refuge," said Anna. "Isn't that supposed to be a big threat to caribou?"

"I never knew him to get involved in environmental fights in the U.S."

"Then maybe he was planning a trip to see the migration."

"I doubt it. Frank flew only when it was absolutely necessary. He didn't like planes much."

As Lydia started to close the file folder, she noticed a small piece of notebook paper stuck in its crease. She picked it up and peered at it. "This is interesting. Here's a name, Evelyn Avingaq, and a phone number. I've never heard of her. The phone number seems to be in the territories but it's not a Dawson exchange."

"You should call this woman when you go back to Dawson," said Anna. "She might know why Frank had a burning interest in caribou." Lydia scribbled the phone number on a piece of Frank's bond and put it in her pocket. She returned the original scrap to the file and leaned back in her chair, staring at the ceiling.

"You know, you're right. Frank did have a burning interest in caribou for some reason. The question is why. This folder is new. Caribou captured his attention recently. Let's take this file with us."

"Sure. I've always wanted to engage in evidence tampering."

"Hey, it's only one file," said Lydia as she returned the rest of the folders to Frank's cabinet and returned the key to its hiding place.

"I'm sure the authorities will be impressed with your logic," said Anna. "I'll see if I can find a plastic bag to put this stuff in."

Anna was headed toward Frank's pantry when she stopped to look at a glossy brochure on the kitchen counter. She picked it up and grinned at Lydia. "Hey, look at this. It's a promotional pamphlet from an outfit called Holiday Cruise Lines. Do you suppose that Frank was getting ready to book a cruise up the Inland Passage?" She laughed and handed Lydia the brochure.

It was standard promotional material, including photographs of a loaded buffet table, a lithe young couple cavorting with a beach ball in an on-deck pool, and a handsome gray-haired couple in evening attire dancing under a full moon. "I don't think Frank's wardrobe would pass muster," Lydia said. A wave of sadness washed over her. She put the brochure back on the counter.

Anna finally found a plastic bag and Lydia carefully wrapped the *Rudolph* folder and her property deed. She blew out the Coleman lantern and Frank's cabin was immediately enveloped in a deep gloom.

"Ouch," yelled Anna, as she banged her hip on the cherry desk.

"Wait a minute. I'll open these curtains." Lydia pulled two stiff and tattered green rectangles away from the front window. "Now you can see where you're going."

The two women stepped onto Frank's broad front porch. As Lydia waited for Anna to close the front door, something caught her eye. "Hey, take this a minute." She handed off the bag, went to her knees, and reached under a split-log bench. She came up with two pieces of crinkled paper. "Look at this," she screeched.

"What, what?" asked Anna.

"These are empty potato chip bags, sour cream with onion."

"Who cares?"

"Those frat boys were eating these. Same brand even. I found a full bag on my floor. Those guys were here."

"You don't know that. Maybe Frank liked potato chips."

"No way. He would never eat this crap." She stuffed the bags in her pants pocket. "I'm showing this to Cerwinski. Or you are when you go back to town."

"You think Frank was killed by fraternity boys? Wow. That's a great plot twist. I can see the headlines now." She paused, composing in her head. "Kappa Zetas Accidentally Slay Elderly Pledge." Her voice trailed off. "I'm sorry. That wasn't the least bit funny."

Lydia waved the apology aside with a flick of her wrist. "I didn't say those boys did it. I have no idea. But if they were here, the police should know about it. Even if they didn't do it, maybe they saw something." Her voice grew soft. "If they can help us, I forgive them their trespasses."

CHAPTER 6

It was a quick trip back to Lydia's cabin and that six-pack of chilled Molson. "You know," said Anna, peering at Lydia over the top of her beer bottle, "I think we should both go back to Dawson tomorrow. You can crash at my place. You've got some important stuff to tell Cerwinski and we need to call this Evelyn person. And, frankly, I don't like the idea of you, or me for that matter, being up here. We're assuming there's only one bad guy. What if there's more? What if two shotguns aren't enough? And I really am a lousy shot."

Lydia drew her lips together, but she nodded, a look of resignation on her face. "Yeah, you're probably right. Besides, I'm really curious about Evelyn whatshername and I would like to get Cerwinski's take on my theory about the frat boys."

"Good," said Anna with a sigh of relief. "It's settled then. Let's leave first thing in the morning and take my boat; it'll be a lot faster. I'll bring you back up whenever you want. And since you took the trouble to install that new deadbolt, how about locking the door?" Lydia complied.

They spent the rest of the evening eating peanuts and playing an old Trivial Pursuit game Lydia had found in a footlocker. The game moved slowly since each of them had significant gaps in her trivia expertise. Anna could answer most of the popular culture questions but was lousy at science and geography. Lydia, on the other hand, knew what two countries were joined by the Harwich-Ostende ferry and how many equal sides there are on a scalene triangle but had no clue as to Kojak's first name or the identity of the Chinese cook on the Ponderosa. They could both recite the names of the three Bronte sisters, but neither of them knew what sport Boris Onishchenko was caught cheating at during the Montreal Olympics.

When, at 9:00 PM, it became clear that the game might never end, Lydia and Anna decided to settle it by sudden death. They would take turns choosing the hardest questions they could find and the first person to answer correctly would win the match. Anna began. "Okay, you'll never get this. Who shot J.R.?"

Lydia groaned. "What kind of clue is that? Who the hell is J.R.? There must be millions of people with those initials." She paused. "Wait. Wait. I've got it! T.R. shot J.R. in the BR and took him to the ER, then the DR. sent him to the OR." She gave Ann a self-satisfied smile.

"You are a media illiterate. Didn't you ever watch *Dallas* when you were a kid?"

"Never. So who did it?" Lydia looked at Anna expectantly.

Anna turned the card over and frowned. "I can't tell. Somebody wrote *TV rots the brain* on the answer." She handed the card to Lydia.

Lydia touched the words with her finger and smiled. "My dad wrote that. He didn't approve of television. We didn't get one until I was almost sixteen. Mom insisted."

"No wonder you're so lousy at this game."

Lydia yawned. "Too lousy to soldier on. I'm going to bed." She threw the tokens into the box and closed the board with a *thwack*.

Lydia had climbed half way up the ladder to the loft when she turned to Anna, her face stern. She raised her index finger. "Keep that shotgun handy," she said, "but for God sake, don't point it at the ceiling." Anna raised her middle finger in response.

Later—maybe minutes, maybe hours—Lydia was awakened by a noise. Her eyes flew open and she lay absolutely still. She heard it again. A sharp crack followed by a rolling boom. Thunder. Heaving a sigh of relief, she rolled over and settled back into her sleeping bag. But then she heard something else, a distant scraping sound and a thump. She sat up and listened hard. There were two more thumps and a faint metallic bang. Adrenaline shot through her system. Heart pounding, Lydia crawled out of the bag and crept to the loft's small window. She braced herself on the wall and peered through the lower pane. The coming storm had turned the sky an inky blue-black, but the sun had not set and Lydia had a clear view of the meadow. It was empty. She knelt on the floor with her chin on the window sill and watched. A few moments later a figure emerged from the scrub alder at the top of the riverbank. The tall, lean frame was swathed in dark, loose clothing and the face was invisible under a broad-brimmed hat. The intruder carried a shotgun over one shoulder. He stood still and slowly turned his head to the left and then the right, taking in the creek, the cabin, and each of the out-buildings. Then he lowered the gun and gripped it with both hands. He began walking toward the cabin. There was someone behind him.

Lydia gasped silently, ducked down, and collapsed against the wall. Her pulse was racing and her hands shook. Her own shotgun lay on the footlocker at the head of her sleeping bag. She crawled silently across the pine planks and seized it. Its weight steadied her hands. Then, moving on her forearms and belly, she slithered to the edge of the loft. Lying in the crease between the floor and the low gable, she peeked into the space below. Her eyes met those of the man who was peering in the front window. His face was thin and the hair beneath the hat was dark and curly. The man in the Mohawk.

Frank's killer! The words were in Lydia's throat but she couldn't utter them. Finally she was able to scream, "Anna, get down on the floor and lie flat." She racked the gun and pointed it toward the window; her finger disengaged the safety.

Anna screamed back. "What? Why?" Lydia could see the man waving his empty hands at her and shaking his head *no*.

"Just do it," yelled Lydia. She heard the thump as Anna hit the floor. The man at the window disappeared. When Lydia saw him again, he was standing ten feet beyond the pane. He had a child in his arms.

Lydia lowered the gun. "Holy shit," she muttered.

The man had cupped one hand around his mouth and was shouting toward the cabin. The blood was pounding so hard in Lydia's ears that she couldn't hear him. She sat up and tried to quiet the noise in her head. Now Anna was yelling, too. "He says he means no harm. He says he needs a place to camp. He has his daughter with him."

Lydia stood up and re-engaged the safety on the shotgun. She held the weapon horizontal against one hip as she descended the ladder and walked to the door. When she opened it, the man was standing on the stoop. His strange garb was nothing more ominous than a rain hat and an oversize, waterproof jacket. His gun was lying in the grass three yards away. He still held the little girl in his arms. She was sobbing.

"I'm so sorry we frightened you," he said. "A storm is coming up, and I didn't want to stay on the river with Molly in the boat. She's only six." He was having trouble catching his breath and his forehead was beaded with sweat. He took in a lungful of air. "I've been trying to find a decent camping spot for half an hour. I wanted to see if anyone was awake. If no one was, I was going to pitch my tent without bothering you."

Lydia stood mute, staring at the man as she clutched the doorframe. His resemblance to the guy in the green canoe was fading. This man was clean-shaven, his hair was much shorter, and he looked bigger. When Lydia finally spoke, her voice was thin and strained. "I almost shot you."

"I know," said the man. He swallowed hard.

"You better come in," said Lydia. "The little girl is upset and she looks cold."

"Can I bring my gun in? It's starting to rain."

Lydia nodded. "I'll get it." She stepped into the meadow and picked up a battered old 12 gauge. She opened the door wide and followed the man with the child into the cabin. She placed his shotgun behind the front door but kept hers at her side. When she offered the uninvited visitors the big oak rocking chair, the man accepted gratefully. He took off his rain gear and removed the little girl's yellow slicker and matching boots. Then he held the child tightly and rocked. The motion and rhythmic squeaking soon calmed her. She stopped crying and looked over at Lydia who was sharing the futon with Anna, the gun propped between them.

"What's your names?" the child asked.

"I'm Anna."

"I'm Lydia. And you're Molly, right?"

The little girl smiled and nodded. "Yes," she said. "I'm Molly Maguire." She reached up and touched the man's cheek. "This is my daddy. His name is Tom Maguire. We live in Anchorage. Where do you live?"

"Anna lives in Dawson and I live right here in the summertime," replied Lydia.

"Oh, that's so cool," said Molly. She looked up at her father. "I want to live in a cabin, Daddy. Can we?" Then she cast her eyes around the room. "Where's your TV?"

"I don't have a TV. I don't have any electricity. You can't have a TV without electricity."

Molly's face fell. "Oh," she said, "I need 'lectricity."

"Where were you going?" Anna asked Tom.

"We're on our way to Fort Selkirk," Tom explained. "I wanted Molly to see the old RCMP cabins. The Weather Channel said it would be clear and warm for the next couple of days. They lied."

"I have to get my weather report by sticking my head out the door," said Lydia.

Molly was craning her neck toward the kitchen. Her eyes were fixed on the row of canisters sitting under the window. "Do you have any cookies?" she asked.

Lydia laughed. "I do, indeed." She glanced at Anna and moved the shotgun in her direction.

Tom noticed. "I promise I'm harmless," he said.

Molly chattered happily as Lydia went to the kitchen and

opened the smallest canister. After piling a mound of store bought cookies on a plate, she poured apple juice into a glass. She managed all of this without taking her eyes off the man in the rocking chair.

The sight of treats energized Molly. She hopped off her father's lap and grabbed the plate and the glass. She sat cross-legged in front of him and began disassembling Oreos. After licking off the creamy filling of each cookie, she passed the soggy chocolate portion up to her dad. He ate them without protest.

After his fourth naked Oreo, Tom turned to Lydia. He cleared his throat before he spoke. "If you don't mind me asking, why were you laying on the floor with a shotgun pointed at my head?"

"Because I heard your boat land," Lydia replied.

"But most people just wait at the front door if they hear visitors coming," said Tom. He smiled at her.

Lydia didn't smile back. "I was afraid you were a bad guy," she said.

"A bad guy! Why?"

Lydia took a deep breath and let it out slowly. She could hear cottonwood leaves rattling in a stiff wind and the rat-a-tat-tat of light rain on the tin roof of the cabin. "Because there's been a murder in the neighborhood."

Tom's eyes widened. "Good God," he said softly. "That's awful. Who?"

"A man named Frank Johnson. He had a homestead near here."

"Was he a friend of yours?" asked Tom.

"Yes," replied Lydia, "he was."

"I'm so sorry," said Tom. "I bet you're really going to miss him. There's not a lot of company out here on the river."

"I will miss him," said Lydia. "And the worst thing is that I've been gone three years and only got to see him once before he died. And that was only for a few minutes."

"That's a real shame," said Tom, shaking his head. "I hate to sound like a—oh, what do you call it—a ghoul, but do you have any idea who killed him?"

"No."

"And the Mounties don't either," added Anna.

"That's frightening," said Tom. "But why would anybody kill a homesteader? I assume he didn't have a lot of money or valuables or anything like that. Do you think he might have pis...." Tom stopped mid-word and looked down at Molly. "Do you think he might have made somebody mad?"

Lydia shrugged. "I have no idea."

Tom looked down at Molly again. Then he stroked her auburn curls. "I'm not sure it's a good idea to camp in your meadow after all. Maybe it would be better for us to go on. If there's a murderer on the loose—." He let the thought hang.

Lydia frowned and shook her head. "No way. I won't let you back on the river in this weather. You and Molly can spread your sleeping bags in the kitchen.

Tom Maguire seemed unsure about the offer, but when rain began to pound overhead, he nodded. "Thanks so much. I really do appreciate it."

"Good," said Lydia. "I only ask that you let me take your gun to the loft with me."

"Sure," said Tom. He stood up and put on his rain coat and hat. "I'll go down to the boat and get our things."

By the time Tom had returned with two waterproof stuff sacks, Molly was fast asleep on the rag rug in front of the futon, a small white mustache on her upper lip and a damp mound of black crumbs clutched in one hand.

CHAPTER 7

Lydia slept long and hard. When she finally rolled out of her sleeping bag the next morning, she was greeted by an accusation from below. "You're a great big sleepy head," said Molly Maguire.

Lydia put her glasses on and peered down into the kitchen. Anna and Molly were sitting at the pine table eating canned peaches. Tom was at the stove making pancakes in Lydia's cast iron skillet. The smell of fresh coffee wafted into the loft. She smoothed the creases out of her sweat pants and put on a clean T shirt. Anna greeted her at the bottom of the ladder with a cup coffee.

"I can't remember the last time somebody made me breakfast," said Lydia. "This is great."

Tom grinned. "It's one of the skills you learn as a single parent." He motioned Lydia into a chair and delivered a platter of pancakes to the table. "I took the liberty of looking on your shelves for a topping." He produced a tin of maple syrup. "This okay?"

"Perfect," said Lydia.

As soon as Lydia sat down at the table, Molly hopped off her own chair and dragged it next to Lydia's. She sat so close that Lydia could smell the sweet scent of shampoo in the little girl's freshly combed hair. Molly was dressed in blue jeans and a red Mickey Mouse sweat shirt. Mickey was wearing a top hat and carrying a cane as he strutted across Molly's tiny chest.

"Do you like Mickey Mouse?" asked Lydia, gently poking Mickey's shiny black nose.

"Oh yes," said Molly. "I love Mickey. And you know what?" She paused for effect.

"What?"

"I saw him. I saw the real, live Mickey Mouse. He looked right at me and he waved. It was so wonderful." Molly closed her eyes and reveled in the memory.

"Come on, Pumpkin. You need to eat something," said Tom as he plopped a child size pancake on Molly's plate. "Dig in," he said to Anna and Lydia.

The three adults dug in. Molly pushed her pancake around her plate awhile and then scraped the syrup off and licked the spoon. She watched Lydia eat for a moment and then tugged on her sleeve. "Did you know I have a cat named Kitty and a canary named Tweetie? Mrs. Dancer takes care of them when I'm at Grandma's. Did you know that I'm going to be in the first grade? I was in *kindygarden* last year. I just loved Miss Laros. She let us have a snack every single day."

By the end of the meal Molly had eaten little but had told all assembled about the class hamster Squeaky, who had pooped on her desk; about Jeremy, who was mean; about Bart, who picked his nose and ate it; and Isabel, who was her *bestest* friend in the whole world. She also warned them that Mr. Conklin would chase you if you stepped on his grass even a teensy weensy bit.

Tom shook his head and grinned. "She learned to talk when she was twenty months old and hasn't stopped since."

"She's delightful," said Lydia.

Tom wiped his mouth and stood. "You've been so kind. I can't thank you enough. I think we'd better get back on the river now. I'd like to get to Fort Selkirk this afternoon."

"Just a minute," said Lydia. She opened the cookie canister and put a handful of Oreos into a small plastic bag. She handed them to Molly.

"Ooo, my favorite," squealed Molly. She gave Lydia a hug.

Lydia and Anna walked the Maguires down to the river. As Tom tinkered with his outboard, Molly pleaded, "Can't we stay longer, Daddy. I just love Lydia." As an afterthought she added, "And Anna."

Tom laughed. "Maybe we'll come again sometime."

"A more orthodox visit, I hope," said Lydia. Tom smiled and nodded as the spark caught. Molly turned in her seat and waved a frantic goodbye.

Lydia and Anna returned to the cabin to pack for their trip back to Dawson. Lydia climbed to the loft and opened a footlocker. But she didn't examine the contents. Instead her eyes went to the sharp angle where the floor met the steep roof of the cabin. She took a few steps, ducked to avoid the low roof, kneeled, and then stretched out flat on her belly. She slithered to the edge of the loft and fixed her eyes on the front window.

Anna looked up. "What's this? A new yoga pose?"

"I'm reliving that moment when I actually thought I was going to shoot someone."

"Good grief, why?"

"I'm trying to figure out if I could have done it, if I could've pulled that trigger."

"And?" asked Anna.

"The answer is *yes* and that scares the hell out of me."

Anna was silent for a moment. Then she spoke softly. "Lydia, this is one fear you should never overcome." Lydia nodded silently as she stood up. She returned to the footlocker and tried to fold her T shirts and jeans neatly into her duffle bag, but her hands were unsteady and the result was anything but tidy.

The storm had left the air hot and muggy. Lydia's German ancestry made her susceptible to sunburn, so she covered up. Her envy of the barelegged, bare armed Anna was ill-concealed.

"I'm Sephardic" said Anna with annoying smugness. "Mediterranean genes. I never burn." Lydia cursed at her while she stood at the kitchen mirror and slathered sunscreen all over her face.

Anna's boat was fast but, nonetheless, Lydia felt like a frustrated commuter on a watery interstate. She resented it every time a knot of canoeists forced Anna to back off the throttle. The landmarks that had thrilled her just a few days ago now held no more attraction than the average billboard. The local wildlife seemed to be hibernating. Time crawled.

When they finally reached Dawson, Anna moored the boat while Lydia headed for the RCMP headquarters. A young officer with freckles and a Beaver Cleaver haircut sat at the front desk. "Corporal Cerwinski, please," said Lydia. The kid pushed a button and in two short minutes Cerwinski's smiling face appeared in the doorway. He escorted her into his small office and offered her a cup of what he assured her would be the world's worst coffee.

Lydia hesitated. "No," she said at last. "I do have some standards."

When Cerwinski went to get himself some in a mug that read *Catfish: It's Not Just for Breakfast Anymore*, Lydia glanced around the office. It was surprisingly tidy given Cerwinski's own rumpled appearance. The papers on the desk were piled in two perfect squares, the pens, pencils, and one pair of scissors were arranged neatly in a large cup, and the stapler and scotch tape stood at a perfect right angle to the in-box. The only decoration was a series of color photos on the wall—Cerwinski grinning, his fingers laced through the gills of a hefty king salmon, Cerwinski grinning as he held a string of grayling aloft, Cerwinski and two other guys grinning down at an enormous wall-eyed halibut lying on a dock. Almost subconsciously Lydia noted that there were no pictures of wife, girl friend, or kids. She perched herself on the hard wooden chair across from Cerwinksi's desk.

When Cerwinski returned with his coffee, he settled into his ancient, leather desk chair. As he leaned back, it protested with a series of sharp squeaks and low groans. With eyes downcast and her hands folded demurely in her lap, Lydia told the Corporal that she and Anna had gone up to Frank's homestead to look around.

"You shouldn't have done that, you know," Cerwinski said, his face serious. "It's against the law to enter a crime scene."

Lydia bit her lip in a show of contrition. "We figured as much, but there wasn't any official notice and that guy West seemed so damn ineffectual, I couldn't believe he'd find anything. And," she paused and looked Cerwinski straight in the eye, "we did."

Cerwinski sat up straight. His chair squealed. "What? What did you find?"

"A couple of things," said Lydia. She revealed the location of Frank's hidden key and described the contents of the oak file cabinet. She handed him the Porcupine herd folder. "We think this is important, but we don't know if or how it's connected to Frank's death."

"That damn West," Cerwinski grumbled as he placed the manila folder in the exact center of his desk. "He should have found that key." He gave a disgusted snort.

Then Lydia pulled the crumpled chip bags from her pocket and shared her theories about the fraternity boys. "Now that's interesting," Cerwinski said, and he grinned his now familiar grin. "Lydia comes through when the chips are down."

Lydia groaned, but then her face grew serious. "You know, something just occurred to me. If this thing is related to Frank's environmental activities, why didn't the killer try to jimmy the file cabinet? It didn't look damaged at all." She paused and then her eyes lit up. "If those boys interrupted him, he may have decided it wasn't safe to hang around. Maybe he didn't have a chance to break into it."

Cerwinski nodded vigorously. "And maybe that's why he tried to bury the body in the trash pile. He didn't have time to drag it all the way to the woods or into the cabin. He certainly didn't want anyone stumbling on it. We may have something here." Then Cerwinski took a deep breath and shifted his weight in his chair. His face tightened. "Look," he said, his voice low. "I do have some less-than-good news. West is in charge of Johnson's murder investigation."

"Oh, hell," muttered Lydia.

"Hell, indeed," said Cerwinski. "Louie has very little interest in anything that goes on around here and will put in a minimum of effort, I'm sure. I'll do what I can to help, but I have to maintain a low profile. I can help with the frat boys though. I do a lot of canoeing and know most of the outfitters in the Territory. I'll make some phone calls and see if I can find out who rented canoes or boats to these guys. They would have had to leave a deposit on a credit card and an address and phone number. I'll ask about the Mohawk, too, just in case somebody does rent those. I should be able to have this information by tomorrow afternoon. Stop by before five and I might have some news."

Then Cerwinski's face registered a *eureka* moment. "Hey. I've got an idea. I get off work in a few minutes. Why don't you and Anna come over to my place for dinner tonight? My grandma was Polish and I make mighty fine pirogies. I can also promise you cocktails and excellent coffee."

Lydia said she'd have to check with Anna and she'd call him back as soon as she got to the apartment. As she left the station, she had to resist an inexplicable desire to skip. She walked very fast instead, swinging her arms so vigorously that other pedestrians were forced to the inside of the boardwalk. Her euphoria was short-lived when she remembered the circumstances under which she had met Cerwinski. She was immediately overcome with guilt.

Anna, however, was not the least bit conflicted. "Thank goodness. Now I don't have to make dinner. You've just been spared an Anna Fain classic, tuna casserole with canned peas and crushed potato chips."

"Thank you, Jesus," said Lydia as she flopped on the couch.

"Don't get comfortable," said Anna. "We've got a dinner invitation. We've only got a couple of hours. You need to call Cerwinski and we need to get gussied up."

"Gussied up? You think I got a silk sheath and a strand of pearls stuffed in this bag?" Lydia pointed to her army surplus duffle, which lay on the floor at her feet.

"Okay, a clean T-shirt then," said Anna. "You've got a coffee stain on that one." She pointed to a faint spot above Lydia's left breast.

After calling Corporal Cerwinski, Lydia began rummaging through her bag. She pulled out a relatively new shirt sporting a bright red, Mountain View Community College logo. The drawing outlined a jagged mountain peak with an elegant Victorian building nestled at its base. This rendering was a gross misrepresentation of MVCC, a series of squat concrete buildings standing on a dusty plain, twenty-five miles from the mountains. "Does my esteemed sartorial consultant approve of this?" Lydia asked, holding the shirt up for inspection. Anna nodded.

Lydia stood up, pulled off her plain gray athletic T, and threw it on a chair. She dragged the MVCC shirt over her head and then studied her image in the mirror which hung over Anna's couch. "Oh, hell, I might as well go all the way," she muttered. As Anna looked on with a bemused smile, Lydia pulled the sturdy rubber band from her braid and un-plaited it. Her thick chestnut hair fell below her shoulder blades. Normally she kept it constrained in the braid or two long pigtails but tonight she would release it from bondage. She found her brush in a side pocket of the duffle bag and pulled it through her mane until it was subdued enough to fall across her shoulders in a series of soft waves.

Anna emitted a low wolf whistle. "Wow. You'll knock Cerwinski's socks off. You should wear your hair down more often."

"Actually, it's a real pain in the butt," said Lydia. "I oughta just cut it off. And what makes you think that this has anything to do with Cerwinski?"

"Of course, it doesn't," said Anna. "And I'm the queen of Romania."

CHAPTER 8

Lydia had assumed that Cerwinski lived in a small bachelor apartment. She was surprised when the address turned out to be a nicely landscaped frame house not far from Jack London's historic cabin. She nudged Anna. "Do you think there's a wife or an ex-wife? Those flowers don't look like the work of a cop who spends all his time off fishing." Lydia pointed to a walkway lined with huge ceramic pots filled with red and yellow roses. Anna shrugged.

As she mounted the front steps, Lydia spied a BMW motorcycle in the driveway. It was a horizontal twin, probably forty years old. The highly polished black tank and shiny chrome headlight housing reflected the afternoon sun. There wasn't a speck of dust or a drop of oil on the machine. Lydia offered an appreciative, "Mmmmm," as Anna dragged her up the last step.

Cerwinski opened the front door before they could ring the bell. He was wearing rumpled khaki shorts and a T-shirt that featured a school of shimmering fish swimming up a series of interlocking blue ribbons; a silver moon illuminated the clouds and mountains in the background. The legend below the picture read, "Salmon chanted evening." Lydia recognized the shirt as the work of Ray Troll, an Alaskan artist who specialized in whimsical fish art.

Seeing Al Cerwinski out of uniform for the first time, Lydia noted that he wasn't fat at all, just big and tall. Although his size was undoubtedly an asset in his work, his square face was so open and cheerful that it was hard to imagine him intimidating a perpetrator. His light brown hair was just long enough to curl a bit and was thinning at the crown.

Al carried a martini glass in each large hand and presented the drinks to his guests. "Never let it be said that anyone ever went thirsty in my house," he said as he waved his arm through the front door. "Come in and partake of Polish soul food." The smell of sauerkraut wafted through the front hall.

The house, like Cerwinski's office, was tidy and uncluttered. The wooden floor was polished to a bright shine and the leather chairs and couch were Scandinavian in design. In front of the pass through to the kitchen sat a simple Shaker style table with four matching chairs. Even though the sun wouldn't set until after midnight, track lights illuminated the table and the sitting room area, creating soft shadows in the rest of the room. The wall opposite the couch was filled with beautifully matted and framed nature photos and specimens of Gwich'in beadwork, each lit with a small spotlight. In front of the couch lay a large wool rug woven with intricate black and red geometric patterns. A small collection of Inuit soapstone carvings had been carefully arranged on the long coffee table.

Al seated his guests on the couch and passed around the hors d'oeuvre, brie mixed with roasted garlic on homemade rye bread. This, thought Lydia, might be the perfect man. Anna must have read her mind because she leered at Lydia and kicked her under the coffee table.

As they settled back into the couch cushions, Al addressed his guests with an impish smile. "Since I'm Polish and we're having Polish food, I thought it was only fitting that we start with a Polish joke."

"No," said Lydia, covering her ears. "Spare us, please. The food smells so good. Don't ruin my appetite."

Al turned to Anna and dismissed Lydia with a wave of his hand. "English professors have no sense of humor." Anna nodded happily in agreement, so Al continued. "Did you hear about the new automatic Polish parachutes?" Anna shook her head. "They open on impact." Al slapped his open palm on his knee.

Anna grinned and gave Al a thumbs-up while Lydia pleaded in

her most pathetic voice, "Please, please. Not on an empty stomach."

"Point well taken," said Al, "and the food is ready." He stood up and escorted Anna and Lydia to the dining room table. The two women sat and Al disappeared into the kitchen. A few seconds later he reemerged holding a platter piled high with pirogies swimming in butter. This was followed by another plate of potato pancakes and a huge bowl of apple sauce, chunky enough to be homemade.

"Hey," Al said. "It may not be nouvelle, but you won't be hungry for two days. I guarantee it." Anna and Lydia applauded.

There were three kinds of pirogies. Some were stuffed with cheese, some with meat and onions, and some with sauerkraut. The potato pancakes were fried to perfection, crisp and light brown and the applesauce was the perfect complement, tart and slightly sweet.

It took almost an hour to polish off the food. Conversation all but stopped in the feeding frenzy. Then Al disappeared again and returned with a strawberry rhubarb pie and coffee. "I'll never get into these jeans again," said Lydia aloud. To herself she said, "This *is* the perfect man."

They took their pie and coffee into the living room and Al put an old Bob Dylan recording in the CD player. While Dylan moaned softly about the girl from the North Country, the three chatted about the influence of American culture and politics on contemporary Canada. Anna took the position that, except in French and indigenous communities, the two cultures were so similar that influences didn't matter. But Al pointed out that most Americans assumed that every North American who was famous belonged to them, despite the fact that Michael J. Fox, Matthew Perry, and Keifer Sutherland were all Canadian.

"Wait a minute," said Anna. "Are you trying to tell me that all the good looking men are Canadian?"

"Definitely not," said Lydia, getting into the spirit of the debate. "Dan Akroyd's Canadian and so are Martin Short, and Jim Carrey."

"Come on," said Al. "It's not just actors. There's famous Canadians in other fields, too, like Margaret Atwood, Joni Mitchell, and John Kenneth Galbraith."

"Yeah, yeah, yeah," said Anna. "Big deal."

Al kept going. "There's lots of famous dead Canadians, too. Guy Lombardo, Fay Wray, and Jay Silverheels, just to name a few."

"Fay Wray," said Anna, wrinkling her nose. "What did she ever do besides scream on cue and get carried up the Empire State Building. And who the hell was Silverheels before he changed his name?"

"Surely you know about Tonto, the Lone Ranger's faithful Indian sidekick," said Lydia.

"And he really was First Nation," added Al. "From Ontario."

Lydia turned to Al. "You forgot to mention Pamela Anderson, the poster girl for silicone from *Baywatch*."

"Hey, I didn't say all famous Canadians were smart or talented. And besides, those are real."

"Of course, they are," said Lydia.

"Okay, okay, I concede," said Anna, throwing up her hands. "Canadians rule."

But Al wasn't finished. "Hey," he said, "there are Americans who even believe that Wayne Gretsky was born in L.A."

Anna gave Al a blank look, but Lydia picked up on the theme. "Professional hockey is the perfect case in point. America isn't just influencing Canada; it's buying it. Hockey is dying up here because Canadians can't compete with the huge American markets. When the Colorado Avalanche won the Stanley Cup, everybody in Denver was so excited that their team had won. But it wasn't their team, a team they had built over the years. They had simply bought the Quebec Nordiques, lock, stock, and barrel."

"What's the Stanley Cup?" asked Anna.

Finally, the food, liquor, and Bob Dylan began to take their toll and everyone started yawning. Cerwinski reiterated that he should have some information about the frat guys by late the next day, and Lydia agreed to stop by the station at 4:00 PM. She and Anna walked slowly back to Anna's place, savoring the evening.

"He really is an unusual guy," said Anna. "He's sweet, he can cook, he's funny, and he's a great housekeeper." She ticked off each of Al's qualities on her raised fingers. Then she stopped walking and stared intently at Lydia. Her eyes danced.

"Oh, my God," Anna said, slapping her own cheeks. "How could I have missed this? It's as clear as the nose on your face." Lydia looked at her quizzically. "Al's gay. The great ones always are." She burst out laughing as Lydia punched her in the ribs.

"Sorry," Anna said, rubbing her side. "I couldn't resist. But I do think you should go for it. Al is a terrific guy."

"I don't know. I think I'm too tired and stressed right now to work on a relationship. I'll settle for friendship in the short term."

Anna shook her finger at her friend. "You've been celibate too long. It's time to take the plunge again."

Lydia scowled. "What's the point of having a boyfriend in the Yukon? I'll never be able to get a teaching job up here." The very thought of job hunting destroyed her ebullient mood. "Damn it," she muttered.

When Lydia stopped by the station the next afternoon, Corporal Cerwinski had news. "No word on the Mohawk, but I didn't have any trouble finding the outfitter who rented those kids their canoes. Your vandals were eight college guys in four boats. They're from Seattle and go to the University of Washington. I called the guy whose credit card they used for the rental. They were definitely at Frank Johnson's place, but they thought it was Coffee John's. They had stopped because they had read about John in some tourist guide and wanted to buy carved walking sticks. They didn't realize that he'd died."

Lydia nodded. "Frank used to complain that a lot of people mistook his place for John's. John's cabin is invisible from the river, so folks would float right past without even realizing it."

"According to the kid I talked to, a guy named Randy Dexter, they never knew that they had the wrong cabin. Dexter said they pounded on the door a long time and no one answered. They saw a canoe on the bank and a boat in the weeds and assumed someone would be back soon."

"What color was the canoe?" asked Lydia.

"Green."

"Holy shit," said Lydia.

"These guys were novice canoeists and didn't notice if it was a solo or a tandem," added Al.

"What else did they tell you?"

"They said they sat on the porch and ate lunch, but after half an hour or so they got tired of waiting. They tried to look in the front windows but the curtains were drawn. Then they left."

Something clicked in Lydia's memory. "Curtains!" she shouted. Al almost overturned his coffee cup.

"What about curtains?"

"Frank never drew those curtains, but I know they were closed when Anna and I went back to look at the files. I opened them so Anna could see her way to the door. I even noticed how brittle they were when I touched them. I'll bet they were closed when I found the body, although it didn't register at the time. Did those boys try the door?"

"They said they did and it was locked."

"Oh, my God. I'll bet the killer was hiding inside the cabin while those kids sat on the front porch. For one thing, Frank never locked his front door, even when he left the homestead for extended periods, and for another, the door was unlocked when I discovered the body. It must have been the killer who closed the curtains and locked the door."

"Hell," said Al dispiritedly. "West never bothered to look for signs of a landing before he landed himself and left boat scuffs and footprints all over the place. I'll send another boat up there to look for signs of that canoe, but I doubt that they'll find anything. It's rained too much since then."

Al paused and seemed to be making a mental note. Then he continued. "The coroner's report supports your conjecture, by the way. Johnson was probably killed the same day the boys showed up at his homestead; that's two days before you found his body.

This was also the same day that the boys partied at your place. Randy Dexter told me that shortly after they left Johnson's, the weather turned really foul. They decided that it was dangerous to stay on the river and when they saw your flag pole, they landed and took refuge in your cabin. They got blasted and you saw the aftermath when you showed up. They left the next day, the same day you came upstream, but they stopped at that wilderness camp near Indian River, which may be why you never saw them on the Yukon."

"But I did see the guy in the green canoe," said Lydia. "If the boys got hung up by bad weather, so did he. If I'm right, he killed Frank, holed up somewhere, and then paddled on after the weather broke."

Al nodded, his face grave. "It's certainly possible. Ever since you told us about him, we've been trying to find someone else who saw that boat. Nothing. Not one single soul saw that green Mohawk after you did."

"Damn. I wish I'd gotten a better look at that guy," said Lydia.

"We don't know that he's our man either. But whoever he is, he's the only suspect we've got." The very word made Lydia shudder.

Al changed the subject. "By the way, the brothers of Kappa Zeta Beta expressed heartfelt regrets about trashing your place and said they would reimburse you for your time and any damage."

"No, they've already paid their debt, but tell them if they ever come back to the Yukon, they could bring me another issue of *Aquaman* and a few rolls of that nice, soft toilet paper.

It was early evening when Lydia finally sat down to call Evelyn Avingaq, the name on the scrap of paper in Frank's folder. Everybody in the Yukon and the Northwest Territories had the same area code so it was impossible to ascertain a location. Lydia knew only that this was not a Dawson phone number. She punched the numbers in slowly, not altogether sure what she was going to say this woman she had never met, had never even heard of. At the other end of the line, a phone rang for a long time. When somebody finally answered, it was almost impossible to hear over the unmistakable din of a crowded bar. Lydia had to shout, "Evelyn Avingaq, please" into the receiver twice before the person on the other end could understand what she was saying.

"I'll get her," the guy yelled back.

Almost a minute later a soft voice said, "Hello, this is Evelyn," and Lydia could hear the click of the extension being disconnected. "Sorry to keep you waiting. Who is this?"

"Hi. My name is Lydia Falkner. I'm a friend of Frank Johnson's. I got your number from him."

"Okay," replied Evelyn with some wariness in her voice. "But why are you calling me?"

"Actually, I, ah, he, um. Frank. Oh, damn." She paused and took a very deep breath. "I don't know how to say this except to come right out and say it. I have terrible news. Frank has been murdered."

Lydia heard a gasp at the other end of the phone and then, "Oh, my God, it's our fault." There was a click and a dial tone.

"Damn," said Lydia as she hung up. A few minutes later she dialed again. Evelyn answered on the first ring.

"Please talk to me," Lydia begged. "I need your help. Frank needs your help."

Evelyn spoke softly but firmly. It was clear that she had been crying. "Why should I talk to you? Why should I trust you? I don't know who you are or what you want."

"I'm an old friend of Frank's. I live downriver from him." Lydia paused and closed her eyes a moment. "I found his body, Evelyn. I found his body."

"Oh, my God," Evelyn whispered. Then Lydia heard only ragged breathing on the line.

"Please, please," pleaded Lydia. "Frank meant a lot to me. I need to find out what happened. I have a friend who's a Mountie and he'll help. Why do you think this is your fault?"

"I can't tell you. You sound nice enough, but I don't know who you are," said Evelyn.

"Please talk to me."

There was a long pause at the other end of the wire. Then Evelyn said, "No, I can't take the chance." Her voice was low, almost a whisper.

Lydia gazed at the ceiling and took a deep breath. "Okay, look. I'll come to you. You can see me face to face. Decide whether or not to trust me. If you don't like what you see, I'll turn around and come home. I won't bother you again."

There was another long pause. "Oh, I don't know, maybe." Evelyn's voice broke. Lydia could hear her blowing her nose and then she was back on the line. "Maybe that would be okay. But I'm not promising to talk to you. I'm not promising anything. Besides, I doubt that you're going to want to come all the way up here."

"I don't even know where *here* is," said Lydia. "All I have is your phone number."

"I'm in Eagle Plains. Up on the Dempster Highway. I work in the restaurant here in the summer."

Lydia groaned to herself as she scanned her mental map of the Yukon. She remembered that Eagle Plains was about halfway up the Dempster Highway, almost at the border of the Northwest Territories, way the hell north and a million miles from nowhere.

She also knew she had to make a decision before Evelyn changed her mind. "Okay. Okay. I'll come up there," she said quickly. "But I don't have a car, so I'll have to borrow something. I'm not sure how long that'll take."

She smiled to herself as she remembered Frank trying to wheedle a pickup out of his friend Mick. "Don't worry about it," Frank had assured the big Scotsman. "The Dempster is smooth and well graded. It's a good road. It won't be hard on your truck." Of course, when Frank returned the Ford Ranger, it had a cracked windshield, one punctured tire, and a long crimp in the exhaust pipe.

Lydia agreed to call Evelyn the minute she located a vehicle. Then she hung up the phone, moaned out loud, and headed for Anna's refrigerator. When Anna got home from work an hour later,

Lydia was into her second Bass Ale. Anna may not have been a good cook but her taste in liquor was impeccable. She snagged a bottle of Bass for herself and joined Lydia on the couch.

"You won't believe what I just agreed to do," said Lydia, grimacing.

After she had explained the situation, Anna turned her attention to the transportation problem. "I know my Toyota couldn't stand that trip. The suspension is already shot and the transmission is on its death bed. We've got to borrow something. Who do we know who has an extra vehicle?" She scrunched up her face and closed her eyes.

"That looks like constipation, not concentration," noted Lydia.

"Wait," said Anna. "I've got it. Al Cerwinski. He rides that motorcycle everywhere. I'll bet you he'd let you use his SUV if you ask him nicely."

"I can't ask that. I hardly know him."

"Of course, you can. Come on. Call him. Be assertive."

But instead of heading for the phone, Lydia lay down on the couch and plopped a pillow over her face.

"Umm, what just happened here? I thought you were calling Al. Have you suddenly developed narcolepsy?" Anna grabbed the pillow and threw it on the floor.

Lydia sat up. "Look," she said. "Al's a cop. He's sweet, but he's a professional. He doesn't know I copied down that woman's phone number. He's not going to appreciate my meddling in this case even if he does think West is a screw up."

"Hey, you're not really meddling. You don't know what you'll find. Besides, you don't have to tell him much. Just tell him you're just going up to see a friend of Frank's, offer her comfort, give her a shoulder to cry on."

"I don't know. It seems dishonest to me."

"Oh, come on. Sometimes that Midwestern righteousness of yours is a real pain in the ass."

Lydia groaned. "Okay, okay. I guess you're right. I really am going up to see a friend of Frank's, and I'll certainly try to comfort her if she'll accept comfort from me, which is doubtful."

"That-a-girl," said Anna, smiling broadly.

Lydia found Cerwinski's home phone number in her notebook and dialed. She was ready to hang up when he finally picked up the receiver. "Sorry," he said, "I was just finishing a shower."

Lydia had a vision of Al standing naked in his bedroom, dripping water on the hardwood floor as he pressed the receiver to his ear. She grinned and then squeezed her eyes shut to banish the fantasy. In her most businesslike voice, she explained that she was going up to Eagle Plains to talk to a friend of Frank's. "And I have a huge favor to ask," she said. She almost lost her nerve and paused a bit too long. Anna punched her in the arm.

"What's the favor?" asked Al.

"I don't have a car and I was wondering if I could borrow your SUV for the trip. Anna's car would never make it. It's okay to say no." Anna rolled her eyes in exasperation. Lydia talked faster. "It's a dirt road and it's a long way and I'll understand if you don't want to lend it to me." Anna scowled and shook her head vigorously.

"Sure, you can have it," said Al. "I ride the bike in the summer. The Explorer could use a good outing. I've even got a spare jerry can for gas."

Lydia relaxed and smiled into the receiver. "Thanks so much. I'll take good care of it."

"Tell you what," said Al. "I'll take the car in and have the oil changed and the tires checked first thing in the morning. I'll bring it to Anna's place around ten. Will that work?"

"That would be fabulous." Lydia hung up the phone with a big grin on her face.

"See?" said Anna. "See? How hard was *that*?"

Since Eagle Plains was a long day's drive and she would get a late start, Lydia decided to spend one night on the road. She borrowed a tent and sleeping bag from Anna, threw a few clothes into a day pack, and was in bed by ten.

When Lydia arose at six the next morning, she was famished. Without much hope, she opened Anna's refrigerator and surveyed its meager contents. There were a couple of potatoes that had already sprouted thick white roots; a piece of pizza, the cheese hard and oily and the pepperoni curled up into perfect little cylinders; a Styrofoam take-out box containing something which may have once been half a sandwich but was now a fuzzy green triangle with brown trim. Anna was an immaculate housekeeper, but since she rarely cooked, she rarely inventoried her refrigerator. Perishables tended to perish. Lydia did, however, manage to find a couple of eggs, half a red onion, and a tomato that was mushy on only one side. She wiped the dust out of a small frying pan and made herself an omelet.

As usual, there was no coffee on the premises and after breakfast Lydia was forced to stroll over to Java City for her morning fix. She was on her second cup of something called Guatemala Antigua when Al walked in carrying a large metal thermos. "Hey," he said. "I was just getting ready to bring the Explorer over to Anna's. It's oiled and aired. You can take it now. Just let me get my thermos filled."

The clerk, or *barista* according to the tag on her uniform, poured the house blend into the battered thermos while Lydia finished her coffee. Then Lydia and Al walked outside to examine the vehicle. The Explorer was white, immaculate inside and out, and sported a CD player. "I threw in a bunch of CDs," said Cerwinski. "A drive like this requires music. I hope you like my selections."

Lydia opened the door and thumbed through the jewel boxes sitting in a box on the front passenger seat. There was BB King, Bonnie Raitt, Marcia Ball, Muddy Waters, and her favorite artist, Big Momma Thornton. "Jeez," said Lydia, "you remembered that I was a blues freak."

"And," Al grinned sheepishly, "since there's no place to eat on the Dempster before Eagle Plains, I packed a cooler for you. My mother was here a week ago and she bought more food than I can eat in a month. I'm simply sharing the wealth." He pulled a small flip top Coleman from the back seat. He opened it up and pointed to a mound of zip lock bags on ice. "There are two roast beef sandwiches in that one and half a chicken in this one. The one on the bottom is fresh fruit." He picked up a paper sack. "There's four bottles of water in here and a couple of bags of trail mix."

"Thank goodness you didn't leave me to forage in Anna's refrigerator," said Lydia. "This is wonderful."

"And now for the pièce d'resistance." Cerwinski handed her the thermos. "You certainly can't make this trip without stimulants." Without thinking, Lydia stood on her toes and kissed him quickly on the lips. She flushed red and clutched the thermos to her bosom with both hands.

Al gave her very broad grin. "That's the kind of gratitude I like." He took one hand, helped her into the driver's seat, and saluted as she drove off. Anna was still sleeping when Lydia returned, so Lydia left her a note with Evelyn Avingaq's phone number and headed out of Dawson on the Klondike Loop. With a slight pang of regret, she drove past the spot where her Honda Civic had died and turned north onto the Dempster.

CHAPTER 9

The Dempster Highway is the northernmost public road in North America, although the word *highway* overstates the case. It's a wide, dirt road that culminates as a strip of pavement in the town of Inuvik, Northwest Territories. Eagle Plains, the first gas stop on this 737 kilometer journey, is at the 369 kilometer mark. Any vehicle attempting the trip must be equipped with a large gas tank or carry extra cans of fuel.

The road is reasonably well maintained but its condition varies according to the region and the season. The area is relatively arid and, unless it's raining, the road is very dusty. The dirt sifts in through the doors and windows, coats the dashboard and the inside of the windshield, and eventually clogs the air cleaner and the lungs. Sometimes the road surface is alarmingly soft, which can send a vehicle fishtailing toward a ditch. When it rains, the surface becomes as slick as ice; when it rains heavily, it turns into a mud slough. Fortunately, traffic is usually light on the Dempster and one can drive for hours without seeing another car. Many tourists are deterred by a sign in the visitor center in Dawson warning that vehicles traveling the highway should carry not one, but two, spare tires.

As the Explorer wound its way through stands of spruce, aspen, and birch, Lydia relaxed into the seat and tried to forget the purpose of her journey. Periodically she could see the North Fork of the Klondike River, the sun reflecting off its surface and illuminating the dust motes in the air. The road rose and fell with the curve of the hills, snaking through borders of vibrant pink fireweed, a beautiful plant that seemed undeserving of the appellation *weed*, but which bursts forth wherever the earth has been disturbed by construction or fire.

Lydia extracted Big Momma Thornton's *Stronger Than Dirt* from its jewel box and inserted it into the CD player. The familiar strains of *You Ain't Nothin' but a Hound Dog* rolled from Al's quadraphonic speakers, but Big Momma's version was no teeny bopper dance number. Her sexy voice was alternately raspy and smoky, underscoring what Elvis had only hinted, that this wasn't rock 'n roll at all; it was dirty blues. When Big Momma growled, "You can wag your tail but I ain't gonna feed you no more," she wasn't talking about steak and potatoes. Lydia cranked up the volume and roared the lyrics along with Willie Mae Thornton while she kept time with one hand on the arm rest. But a sharp, unexpected slide in a patch of deep sand eliminated the percussion section.

Soon the Tombstone Mountains loomed in the distance. This was a magnificent range of jagged gray peaks and sheer granite cliffs. The steep slopes close to the road were called Golden Sides, named for the thick yellow lichen that clung to the rock, nectar to barren-ground caribou. And sure enough, as Lydia stopped to enjoy the extraordinary view of the river valley, she saw five caribou grazing on the hill just above her. All were in the process of losing winter fur, which left their flanks looking like ragged patchwork quilts. Each animal sported a fringe of long white hair growing from its throat to its chest, a wispy beard misplaced by Mother Nature. Towering antlers inscribed two enormous Cs on top of each head. These antlers branched into fingers at both ends, while another branch, broad and flat, jutted out over each patrician nose. This elaborate headgear made the caribou look awkward and front heavy, but their footing on the steep and rocky cliff was sure.

Lydia had never been past the campground at Tombstone and she was interested in seeing what other treasures the Dempster had in store. She stopped at Two Moose Lake and was pleased to see exactly two moose browsing in the shallows. Both were cows and they gazed at her impassively, their muzzles streaming water and dripping with aquatic weeds. There were scores of waterfowl floating in the middle of the small lake.

Lydia walked over to the wooden viewing platform as a large white truck drove into the little parking area. A man got out and stretched. He joined her at the wooden rail. "Hi," he said. "Cool birds, eh?"

Lydia nodded. "This pond has everything–harlequins, northern shovelers, mallards. And look at that!" She pointed at three red-throated loons who seemed to be engaged in some sort of courtship ritual. Two of them were clearly a mated pair; they swam only a few inches apart; when one bird turned left, the other turned left; when one bird dived, the other dived; when one dipped its head under its right wing, so did the other one. These motions were almost but not quite synchronous and Lydia felt like she was watching a parody of *Swan Lake*. The third loon seemed to be a hanger-on. He stayed a few feet away from the pair, hanging back as if he longed to, but didn't dare, join in their ballet.

"I guess he's the one who never gets the girl," said Lydia grinning.

The guy smiled back. "Poor little fellow," he said. "He probably gets beat up on the playground, too. So what are you doing on the Dempster? Going up to Inuvik?"

Lydia shook her head. "No. Just going to Eagle Plains to visit somebody."

"You're a good friend to go all that way," said the guy. He checked his watch. "Well, I gotta get back on the road." He waved goodbye, returned to his truck, and took off in a spray of sand. Lydia resumed her journey a few minutes later.

When she crossed the bridge over Engineer Creek, Lydia knew she was close to her immediate destination, a small territorial campground. Above her loomed Sapper Hill, a geological marvel marked by a series of ragged, narrow limestone ridges that ran both horizontally along the top of the hill and vertically up the hill. The whole thing looked a like giant birthday cake on which the decorative white icing had gone askew. The tiny camping area was nestled below this frothy formation. Lydia turned in and was pleased to find that the place was mostly empty. Two sites away, a tent had been pitched beside a truck that said *Great North Construction* on the side; it was the truck from Two Moose Lake. A small rental RV occupied the space across from Lydia. Through the open blinds she could see an elderly couple changing bed sheets with fluid and perfectly coordinated motions.

The campground had provided nicely raked tent pads, which meant Lydia wouldn't have to spend the night trying to avoid roots, rocks, and sticks. She pulled Anna's tent from its sack and laid it out in the middle of the smooth dirt. One by one, she unfolded three long flexible poles and threaded them through the nylon sleeves. Hooking the end of one pole into a grommet on the floor, she bowed the pole until the other end reached a grommet on the opposite side. She did this three times and as the third pole flexed into a large arc, the pile of wrinkled blue fabric turned magically into shelter. After unrolling the foam sleeping pad, Lydia crawled into the blue dome and pulled the down bag from its stuff sack. She laid it out flat, fluffed it up, and surveyed the cozy interior with satisfaction. She loved sleeping in a tent. As flimsy as those nylon walls were, they provided psychological if not physical protection from any evil that might lurk in the forest.

Satisfied with her accommodations, Lydia exited the tent on her hands and knees butt first and stood up slowly. Her muscles protested as she assumed an upright position. I need more exercise and less food, she thought, as she began to rummage through the cooler. It wasn't until she pulled out a roast beef sandwich that she saw the two bottles of pale ale hidden under the mound of plastic bags. That Al Cerwinski really was a prince. She pulled one out and popped its cap. Then she threw her legs over the bench and anchored her elbows on the table. Lydia made short work of both the sandwich and the beer. When she finished, it was almost 10:00 PM. She crawled into the tent, undressed, put on her eye mask, and was asleep in five minutes.

When Lydia crawled out of her sleeping bag early the next morning, the ground fog was so thick she couldn't even see the RV parked across the road. The weather was damp and cold. It had been warm inside the tiny tent and now Lydia was shivering in her jeans and T-shirt. Since driving in this soup was out of the question, she walked over the to the kitchen shelter in the hopes that someone would have coffee brewing on the wood burning stove. Someone did. It was the guy in the construction company truck. He smiled with recognition. He was more than happy to share his coffee with Lydia, especially after she offered him a substantial share of Cerwinski's roast chicken.

Lydia introduced herself. The guy's name was Greg Rymer and he was from Inuvik. He was a little younger than Lydia, very good looking, and quite talkative. He said he was going home after having spent a few days in Whitehorse buying hardware and lumber for the construction business. He explained that he made the trip twice a month since it wasn't cost effective to bring in the small, heavy items by cargo plane. "I also shop for my family when I'm down there," he said. "I buy staples, clothes, tools, school supplies for the kids, stuff like that. Everything is so damn expensive in Inuvik."

"So why do you even live in Inuvik? Wouldn't it be easier just to move south?"

"Yeah, but the money is incredibly good up there. I can make twice what I can make in Whitehorse in a season. That's hard to walk away from."

"Money isn't everything," said Lydia, flashing on her own dwindling bank account.

"No," replied Greg, "but it's high on the list."

Lydia shrugged. "Thanks a lot for the coffee. I'd better get going." She took her last swallow and returned to the campsite to strike her tent. By the time she had finished packing up, the fog hung in feathery wisps over the trees and on the mountain slopes.

Lydia fired up the Explorer. The wipers cleared two perfect half moons in the condensation on the windshield. Visibility was fine. She exited the campground and turned north. At first the landscape had a soft, undulating quality, as if someone had gently tossed a gray-green blanket over the wilderness. Soon Lydia reached the Northern Ogilvie Mountains, a limestone range that was bare and rounded, in stark contrast to the jagged peaks of the Tombstones. Since limestone is easily sculpted by wind and water, the road here was lined with wonderful ridges and outcroppings, resembling the battlements of a medieval castle. Small trees clung precariously to the cliffs. After following the Ogilvie River for many miles, the road began to climb, following a high ridge with spectacular views in all directions. The stands of spruce and aspen gave way to tundra. The only tree of any size was the occasional black spruce, the one species that could gain purchase in the permafrost. The queen of flora at this latitude was lichen, tiny moss-like plants that grew in clumps of red, bronze, and gold on the rocky slopes.

The white construction truck passed Lydia and the driver honked and waved. She honked back. The truck was traveling fast and Lydia slowed down to let the dust clear.

It was late afternoon when Lydia finally spied the corrugated buildings, tall antennas, and huge satellite dishes that constituted Eagle Plains. These were the first real buildings she had seen since the ranger station at Tombstone. The service station was in one of the detached metal structures, while the long, low green building that ran parallel to the road was home to the hotel, restaurant, bar, laundry, and store. There was a small campground next to the hotel where a couple of RVs huddled together in the lee of the building.

Over the last two days Lydia had passed a few carefully graded wide spots in the road, places that had been marked with bright orange wind socks for the benefit of small aircraft. Eagle Plains, however, had an actual gravel runway. The sign on the garage advertised aviation fuel as well as unleaded, diesel, and propane. Lydia pulled up to the pump. She still had to translate liters into gallons before she knew what the gas was costing her. She did the calculation on a scrap of paper and looked at the numbers in astonishment.

"Good grief!" she exclaimed to the teenage attendant who was standing by her window awaiting instructions. "I drink wine that's cheaper than that."

The boy shrugged. "Fill 'er up, ma'am?" he asked, already knowing the answer. Lydia nodded.

After the tank was filled and the windshield washed, Lydia drove to the front of the main building. The parking lot was dusty and deeply rutted. A *PLEASE REMOVE SHOES* sign greeted her when she opened the heavy glass door. After stowing her boots in one of the cubby holes provided, Lydia walked to the gift shop. It was strange walking around a public building in her stocking feet. She called to the desk clerk, a young First Nation woman with enormous eyes and thick black hair down to her waist. "I'm looking for an Evelyn Avingaq."

The young woman pointed to her left. "Evelyn's in the restaurant. She's the waitress with red hair." Lydia was surprised at that piece of information. She had been sure that Evelyn was Inuit; the last name certainly was.

The restaurant was a combination cafeteria and sit-down cafe. A young woman was serving a table of tourists, parents and two whiny kids. She was indeed a red head. Her hair had been dyed the color of old bricks and each ear sported as many earrings as the lobe could support. She was wearing bright blue eye shadow and heavy black eye liner. Her jewelry and make-up contrasted sharply with her crisp white blouse and khaki pants. Lydia chose a table close to the window and grabbed a menu. She was hungry. In a few minutes, the redhead approached her.

"Hi, what would you like?"

"Are you Evelyn?"

"Yeah, I am." Evelyn's beautiful, dark eyes scrutinized Lydia. "You must be Lydia. I can't talk to you now. I don't get a break until five-thirty. Why don't I bring you something to eat in the meantime."

"That would be great. Bring me a burger and fries. And a cup of coffee if it's drinkable."

"It's not bad," said Evelyn. "I made it myself."

Lydia sat back and covertly watched the young woman wait table. Evelyn was in her early twenties, slim, and very pretty. She moved with great efficiency; not a motion was wasted. The tourist family was a demanding bunch. The steak was too rare, the fries were cold, the cold slaw was yucky, yadda yadda yadda. Lydia was pleased to see that Evelyn was polite but unapologetic in dealing with this difficult clan. One of the kids knocked a glass of milk to the floor, which precipitated two tantrums, one on the part of the kid and another on the part of the father. When the kid jumped out of his chair and soaked his socks with the spilled milk, two more tantrums ensued.

Lydia turned her head away. "Family World, the theme park," she muttered to herself.

"What do you mean?" asked a voice behind her. It was Evelyn with her order.

Lydia smiled up at her. "Oh, just that there's this repertoire of family scenarios that every family seems doomed to repeat. So I always think of families as theme parks where there's a limited number of rides. Some are great fun and some make you sick to your stomach."

Evelyn nodded gravely. "Well *that* family makes me want to barf," she said softly. "Here's your food. Let me know if you need anything else." Evelyn placed Lydia's plate in front of her and, with a look of resignation, walked over to assist in the great spill crisis.

Lydia grinned when she looked down and saw gravy on her french fries. This was one Canadian culinary habit she still wasn't used to. As Lydia ate, she looked out the big window at the multi-hued tundra that stretched out below her. She longed to go for a hike, but she knew that those low rolling hills were muskeg, unstable, lichen-covered dirt clods sitting in water. Since the permafrost was only a few feet from the surface, the land never really drained. It was the Arctic hiker's persistent dilemma—do I step over the tussocks and stay ankle deep in water or step from tussock to tussock and risk turning an ankle? Anna once described hiking in muskeg as walking across a wading pool covered with basketballs.

Lydia was lost in reverie when Evelyn slipped into the chair across from her. "I'm on break now," she said. Her face was gray, her eyes expressionless, her body tense. She was massaging the right side of her neck with her fingertips. "Let's go outside where it's quiet."

They got up and Lydia retrieved her shoes from the rack. Evelyn steered her out the back door of the restaurant. There was a sturdy, old-fashioned playground set behind the building, an incongruous sight in the middle of the Yukon wilderness. Evelyn headed for the swings. Her tiny butt fit easily into the small, U shaped seat, but Lydia had to shimmy between the chains.

They sat without speaking for a long time. Finally Lydia broke the silence. "Look, Evelyn, I drove all this way. It took me almost two days to get here. I have a lot invested in this trip. Please trust me."

Evelyn began to cry. Lydia could barely understand her when she said, "I don't know what to think. I don't know who to trust. I can't believe Frank's dead. I just can't believe it."

Lydia reached over and touched Evelyn's hand. "I know it's awful. I can't believe it either. Ask anything you want about me, about my relationship with Frank. Anything."

Evelyn wiped her eyes with her fists. She swallowed hard. "Okay, tell me something about him that only a close friend would know."

A small smile played on Lydia's lips. "He loved Limburger cheese and mustard sandwiches. And," she added, "he always put salt in his beer."

Evelyn looked at Lydia and her face brightened. "I guess you really did know him."

"I knew him very well, but," Lydia paused and peered intently at Evelyn, "you haven't told me how *you* know him."

Evelyn looked up. Her eye shadow was smudged and her mascara had run down both cheeks. "Frank's son is my boyfriend."

Lydia sat bolt upright in her swing. "My God, you know Jesse."

Evelyn nodded.

"I don't believe it," said Lydia. "The Mounties have been looking for Jesse for days. Just to tell him about Frank and to get some background," she quickly explained in response to Evelyn's look of alarm.

"Well, they didn't look very hard. He's in the Inuvik phone book."

"Damn," said Lydia, her voice thick with disgust. "West isn't even pretending to work on this case."

Evelyn threw Lydia a puzzled look but didn't ask her to explain. "So do you know Jesse?" she asked. Her voice had lost its flatness.

Lydia nodded. "I've known him since he was a kid."

"You should have told me that on the phone." Evelyn gave Lydia a sheepish look. "I wouldn't have been such a pain in the ass."

"But I didn't know *you* knew Jesse."

"Good point," said Evelyn. She flashed Lydia a real smile this time.

"Can you tell me anything that might help us figure out who killed Frank," asked Lydia. "Anything at all?"

Evelyn gazed at her own knees for a moment and then answered. "Jesse and me, we told Frank some stuff that we shouldn't have. It's all our fault." She began to weep again.

"Evelyn, I'm sure it's not your fault." Lydia paused for a moment as her own eyes filled. Then she touched Evelyn's hand again. "Are you in danger? Is Jesse?"

Evelyn took a deep breath and wiped her eyes with a paper napkin she took from her pocket. Her face was covered with blue and black smudges. "I don't know. Like I said, we gave Frank some information and I think he did something that got him killed. But I don't have any idea what he did."

"What information did you give him?" asked Lydia.

Evelyn stared at her for a long time. "Okay, I think I can trust you. It's not like it's really a secret anyhow."

Lydia was incredulous. All this reluctance and it wasn't really a secret anyhow?

"Let me start at the beginning," said Evelyn. "It's a long story."

"That's fine," said Lydia. "I've got all the time in the world."

Evelyn sat in thought for a couple of moments and then she began. "I used to work for a small tourism company in Inuvik. The owner, a guy named Matthew Reston, was Inuvialuit and he put together some awesome tours so that the people who come up the Dempster could experience native culture. One of our most popular trips was a flight up to Nuvaktuk."

"What's Nuvaktuk?" asked Lydia.

"It's a tiny, traditional Inuvialuit village. It's right on the Arctic Ocean, but it's called the Beaufort Sea up there. The people live on whale hunting, fishing, and caribou. Matt wanted tourists to be able to see native culture without threatening it."

Lydia nodded and Evelyn continued. "Matt took just a few people at a time up to Nuvaktuk in a small plane. They only stayed a couple of hours and they weren't allowed to wander off on their own. They got to see the fish camps and some traditional cabins, things like that. They spent a little money on handmade crafts and some of the locals got jobs as guides."

"That sounds pretty responsible to me," observed Lydia.

"It was and the people in the village were glad to have the money. But then Matt died in a plane crash a couple of years ago. His son Curtis took over Aurora Tours. Matt and his wife got divorced when Curtis was young. He grew up in Edmonton and never spent much time up here. Even though Curtis is half Inuvialuit, he doesn't like native people. He always acts like he's better than the rest of us."

As she warmed to her subject, Evelyn's voice grew stronger and she became more animated. "Curtis is a total greedhead. He doesn't know anything about the Arctic and doesn't give a damn about it. For him Aurora Tours is all about money. He doesn't know the meaning of *low impact tourism*." Evelyn articulated the words very carefully.

Lydia nodded. "So it's environmental. It makes sense that Frank would get caught up in something environmental."

Evelyn nodded, too. "Right after he takes over, Curtis starts getting real secretive about certain parts of the business. There's only two actual offices in the place and he made one of them off-limits to the staff. No one has a key but Curtis. That meant that all three of us staff members had to squeeze into the reception area."

"That's odd," said Lydia.

"Real odd. But that's not all. When Matt was alive, I helped him plan new tours, make arrangements, and line up other tourist services if we needed them. I loved doing that. And then one day Curtis goes, 'Evelyn, I've changed your job description.' From then on all he'd let me do is type letters and file. He treated me like a stupid temp. That lasted for about six months and then he ups and fires me. For no reason. This was a big blow because me and Jesse are saving for a house. I hear a couple of days later that Curtis hired some high school drop-out to fill my job. Thank God he didn't fire Jesse, too."

"What does Jesse do at Aurora Tours?"

"He's the company coordinator for Nuvaktuk," Evelyn said. "He trains guides, coordinates with the locals, plans itineraries, stuff like that. He goes up there a lot. Well, one time he noticed some construction along the water. It looked like a big dock. But Nuvaktuk doesn't need a dock. Everybody just pulls their boats up on the shore."

"So what was this thing?"

"A cruise ship pier! Can you believe it?"

"How can they bring cruise ships into a tiny village like that?" asked Lydia.

"It'll destroy it," said Evelyn. "It's insane. There's only one tiny hotel in Nuvaktuk, no real restaurants, and no shops. The tourists who fly in just want to put their feet in the Arctic Ocean and leave. It doesn't make any sense at all to bring cruise ships in there."

"So why are they doing it?"

"We don't know. But we do know that it's Aurora putting in that pier."

"But I thought Aurora did small time tourism."

"It does. This has to mean that Curtis is working with some cruise ship company, but we don't know which one."

"Whoa," cried Lydia. "Wait a minute." She stared straight ahead, bit her lower lip, and frowned. "My friend found a cruise ship brochure in Frank's cabin. What was it advertising?" She paused again. "Holiday Cruise Lines. That was it."

"Never heard of it," said Evelyn, shaking her head.

"Me neither, not until then."

"Well," continued Evelyn, "I'm sure that the cruise ship pier is the reason Curtis fired me. I think he didn't want me to see any of the papers about it."

"But why? Putting in a cruise ship pier isn't illegal, is it?"

"No," said Evelyn. "Not if the Nuvaktuk governing council approved the project and they must have since the pier's partly built."

"So you told Frank about the pier."

"Yeah, and he was really pissed off. Frank is super protective of native culture. He was really surprised that the council had approved the thing. He said it didn't make any sense to bring a bunch of rich tourists into Nuvaktuk by boat just so they could wander around the village for an hour. He thought there was something more going on. He told us that he'd check around and see what he could find out."

"So what *did* he find out?"

"That's the problem. We don't know. Frank was in Inuvik for over a week and he flew up to Nuvaktuk twice. But then he left town without telling us anything."

"Does this guy Reston know that Jesse is Frank's son?" asked Lydia.

Evelyn shook her head slowly. "I don't think so. Most people up here don't even know Frank. He didn't come up very often and he didn't stay very long when he did. As far as I know, the only other person in Inuvik who really knows him is his brother-in-law, Jesse's Uncle Moses."

"I remember Frank talking about Moses. I'd always assumed they were just old friends. I didn't realize they were related."

"By marriage," said Evelyn. "Moses is Jesse's mother's sister's husband." She ticked off the possessives on her fingers as she spoke. "Jesse's aunt died about six months ago; she had cancer, too, like Jesse's mom."

"Do you think Frank might have told Moses something?"

"I doubt it," said Evelyn. "If he didn't tell us, I don't think he'd tell anybody."

Lydia squeezed her temples with her fingers and thumb as a wave of fatigue and melancholy washed over her. She opened her eyes wide, sat up straighter in the swing, and tried to focus. "So what about the police in Inuvik? Shouldn't you tell them that you think Frank's murder is connected with something going on in Nuvaktuk?"

Evelyn shook her head. "Two people in the Inuvik RCMP detachment are related to Curtis. We don't know if we can trust them or not."

"That's bad," said Lydia. "Is Jesse still in Inuvik or has he gone down to Dawson to talk to the police?"

Evelyn gave Lydia a guilty look and her eyes filled with tears. "I haven't called Jesse yet," she said softly.

"Oh, my God," said Lydia. "He doesn't know." Fatigue was replaced by astonishment.

"No," said Evelyn, choking back a sob. "I couldn't call him and tell him this on the phone. It would have been terrible for him." She took a deep breath. "I had to hear what you had to say before I talked to Jesse. I'm driving up to Inuvik tomorrow." Tears were streaming down Evelyn's face now and her knuckles were white as she clutched the chains. "Jesse adored his father. I have to be there with him when he gets the news. I have to. Except for Moses, I'm the only person he has left."

The two women sat in silence for a long time. Evelyn studied her blue fingernail polish and Lydia fixed her eyes on the mountains in the distance. Then Lydia hauled herself out of the swing and stood directly in front of Evelyn. "I'm coming with you to Inuvik," she said too abruptly and too forcefully. Evelyn looked startled. Lydia started talking fast. "I mean if it's all right with you. I don't want to intrude on you and Jesse, but I do want to do anything I can to help find Frank's killer, and if Aurora is based there, it's probably a good place to start. And I'm not pretending to be a cop or anything, but I'm hoping I can find out something that will help the Mounties or at least my Mountie friend because the guy who's really in charge is an idiot." She stopped and took a deep breath.

Evelyn didn't respond at first. Lydia was afraid she had offended her and was greatly relieved when she heard Evelyn say, "Sure, it would be all right. I really believe that you care about Frank. And I think it would comfort Jesse to have you there. After all, you knew him in the old days."

Lydia smiled to herself. The *old days,* all of four or five years ago.

Evelyn continued. "And, Lydia, you found the body. As awful as it is, Jesse will want to know about that. He'll want to know everything you know."

Lydia said, "Good. I really do want to see Jesse. Is there a phone I can use to make a call in the morning? I need to check in with the owner of the car I'm driving, but I don't want to bother him at work."

"There's a pay phone in the hotel," said Evelyn. She glanced down at her watch. "Damn it!" she said. She leapt out of the swing and was already headed for the building when she called over her shoulder. "I gotta get back to work. I'm already five minutes late. Look, why don't you spend the night in my room."

"Oh, that's okay, I've got a tent."

Evelyn stopped and snorted. "Are you kidding? The wind will blow you all the way to the Arctic Ocean. It never stops up here. Besides, you'll never get your tent stakes into the gravel; it's like concrete. Stay in my room." She trotted back to Lydia and took a brass key out of her pants pocket. "It's number seven. Just leave the room unlocked after you go in."

Lydia accepted the key and followed Evelyn into the building. Evelyn turned into the restaurant while Lydia removed her shoes and headed for the bar and lounge. The room was large and low with a lovely old wooden bar at one end and huge windows on two sides looking out at the Eagle Plain. As she entered, she realized that the walls were covered with large, black and white photos. It was clear that they were very old. Curious, she walked over to examine them. The first photo she encountered was the head and upper torso of a man whose eyes were open and empty and whose teeth were bared in a chilling expression somewhere between a smile and a sneer. The man was unquestionably dead. Lydia recoiled and then looked again. The bartender walked over and smiled at her.

"What kind of bar puts pictures of dead men on its walls?" said Lydia, grimacing. "This is bizarre."

"Oh, this guy is our one claim to fame. He put this part of Canada on the map," said the bartender, tapping the dead man's head with his finger.

"Ah hah," said Lydia, "another famous Canadian. So who was he?"

"He's always been called the Mad Trapper of Rat River. No one is completely sure of his real name. Maybe Albert Johnson. Maybe not."

"So why is he famous and why is he dead?"

The bartender pointed to a legend typed on an old manual typewriter and taped beneath the photo. "This is really the end of the exhibit. If you start over there, you can get the whole story." He pointed to the wall opposite the bar.

Lydia walked around the room's perimeter reading the cards and examining the photos. It was a classic Yukon story. In the winter of 1931, the RCMP had gone to the Mad Trapper's cabin to complain about his trap tampering. The Mad Trapper shot a Mountie. The Mounties came back later and blew up his cabin with dynamite. The Mad Trapper held them off for fifteen hours with a rifle and then fled into the wilderness. The last photo showed the final shootout between the Mad Trapper and the Mounties. It was an aerial shot, taken from the monoplane that had been tracking Johnson for days. It was a startling and beautiful picture, the black figures of the men arranged in random patterns on the stark white snow with little hint of the violence that was ensuing.

The Mad Trapper was no hero. He had stolen pelts from the traps of his Indian neighbors; he had wounded one police officer and killed another. But Lydia couldn't help but admire the determination and resourcefulness of a man who had survived for weeks in the rugged Richardson Mountains at temperatures of fifty below zero with only a tarp for shelter. This may have been the story of a killer, but it was also a story of incredible human strength and endurance.

There were a lot of people like the Mad Trapper in the far North, people who could endure anything except authority and interference. Frank was a little like that. Lydia smiled to herself. Albert Johnson, huh. Who knows? Maybe Frank and Albert were kin.

Lydia sat down at a table and ordered a bourbon on the rocks. She leaned back in her chair and tried to enjoy the magnificent view. But she couldn't concentrate. There were too many inexplicable events, too many mysteries, too many unanswered questions. Lydia knew she was walking into something ugly and she felt fear. It wasn't the kind of fear she had experienced that awful night on the Yukon when her father had died. That had been an unbearable combination of helplessness, hopelessness, and loss that lay in her guts and gripped her heart. What she was experiencing now was a focused, almost rational emotion. There was a murderer out there and it seemed fairly clear that he (she?) had killed Frank because of something Frank knew. And now Lydia was trying to found out what Frank knew. Then she'd know it, too. Ergo. "Stop it. Don't go there," she said to herself. She finished her drink in three gulps and went to find Evelyn's room. She flopped on one of the single beds and was asleep almost instantly. She didn't hear Evelyn enter at the end of her shift.

Lydia was awakened by the soft purr of a vacuum running in the hall. She looked at her watch. It was 7:00 AM. She rubbed her eyes, swung her legs over the edge of the bed, and sat up. Mornings were not Lydia's best time and she hoped that she could get some breakfast before she had to talk to anybody. Evelyn didn't stir as Lydia dressed in the dim light that filtered in through the curtains. She opened and closed the door as quietly as she could and hurried off to the restaurant to enjoy her first cup of coffee.

Lydia couldn't believe that she had agreed to drive another two hundred miles up the Dempster. This would mean a round trip of almost a thousand miles on a dirt road. She promised herself that after breakfast she would call Al and get his permission to double the trip mileage on his car. Besides, she wanted to tell him about his idiot colleague's latest screw up. She hoped Al was an early riser.

After a restrained breakfast of coffee, raisin bran, and a banana, Lydia found the telephone. Al answered on the second ring, his voice thick with sleep. Lydia forged ahead without apology. By the time she had finished telling him about West's failure to check directory assistance, he was thoroughly awake. "That dumb fuck," he shouted over the wire. Then he immediately apologized. "Sorry. I hope I didn't offend you."

Lydia hooted. "Not at all. West *is* a dumb fuck." She then explained who Evelyn was and why she wanted to take his SUV to Inuvik.

Al offered a low whistle upon hearing Lydia's summary of Evelyn's story. "We definitely need to talk to Jesse Johnson. Ask him to call us, or better yet, come down to Dawson. Maybe he'd be willing to ride down with you. I hate to send a constable up there, since we're so short-handed." Lydia agreed.

By the time she returned to the room, Evelyn was up and dressed and was heading off to the restaurant kitchen to pack some food for the trip. Forty minutes later the two women pulled out of the parking lot in tandem. Evelyn was driving a Toyota Corolla that was even older than Anna's.

The day was gray, cold, and windy. When they passed the

turnout for the Arctic Circle, Lydia saw the milk spill family huddled in front of the large wooden marker. Dad was video taping mom and the kids, who were bunched up together, trying to keep warm. No one was smiling and no one was admiring the view.

The sky darkened as Lydia and Evelyn crossed the border into the Northwest Territories. From here on, all water flowing west went into the Pacific and all water flowing east emptied into the Arctic Ocean. The plateau was high, very rocky, and there were no trees at all. Great gray clouds loomed on the horizon and it looked as if it might snow. The wind was fierce. Lydia found it eerie and beautiful. Two magnificent long tailed jaegers swooped and dipped in front of the cars, their white and black markings complementing the stark, almost monochromatic landscape. The road began to descend, the wind abated, and the temperature rose. Trees began to dot the landscape and the world looked like summer again.

A few hours later, Lydia and Evelyn reached the confluence of Arctic Red River and the mighty Mackenzie, the second largest river in North America. As they lounged beside their vehicles, waiting for the auto ferry, Lydia noticed that the banks of the Arctic Red River were dotted with white canvas tents. She pointed. "Why are all these people camping here? Is it a festival or something?"

"No," said Evelyn. "Those are Gwich'in fish camps. First Nation people catch the fish and then dry them. It's a big part of their winter food supply."

As if to illustrate her point, a fisherman stood in his boat and started hauling in a drag line. On each hook a long sheefish struggled and arched its shimmering body. In an unbroken rhythm, the man unhooked each fish in its turn and threw it into the boat. Soon the bottom was alive with flapping, writhing strips of silver. Then the fisherman stowed his line and, still standing, motored downstream to avoid the broad wake of the on-coming ferry.

This ferry served both the Dempster Highway and the local village of Tsiigehtchic (known as Arctic Red River to non-Gwich'ins who had no hope of mastering Athabascan phonetics). Since the village generated local traffic, the boat carried a significant number of pedestrians. As it slowly moved toward Tsiigehtchic, Lydia and Evelyn stood at the rail eating peanut butter and jelly sandwiches and listening to three elderly women chat among themselves. Concentrating hard on the steady stream of Gwich'in, Lydia realized that she couldn't even tell where one word ended and another began. It was a lovely language filled with *j, ch, gw* sounds and words that resembled *chit* and *chew* but weren't. Some of the vowels were pronounced so far back in the throat that Lydia couldn't mimic them.

Lydia had always been embarrassed by her own monolingualism, and Evelyn admitted that, like many of her generation, she only knew a few Inuvialuit words. Evelyn pointed out that in general the Athabascan Indians were more protective of their traditional culture than the Inuit were. "A lot of Gwich'in still speak their language and they're more likely than we are to pass on the old ways to their children. Inuit are usually very willing to accept new ways of doing things; we're real practical," she said. "Hell, the happiest day of my grandfather's life was the day he could get rid of his sled dogs and get a snow machine."

The rest of the trip passed uneventfully and it was early evening when the Explorer and Corolla passed the local campground and reached the faded sign that said **Welcome to Inuvik**. Lydia followed Evelyn as she turned up the main street of town. When they passed a crew of workers who were assembling bleachers in a grassy park, two young guys hooted, whistled, and waved at Evelyn.

Lydia was astonished at how modern and almost urban Inuvik was. With its population of over 3,000 people, it was the second largest community in the Northwest Territories. Over lunch Evelyn had explained that almost forty percent of its population was non-native. Inuvik had none of the feel of a native village either. Most of the buildings were new and modular and the main street was wide and paved. The centerpiece of the main drag was a huge metal structure that served as department store, hardware emporium, and fast food court. There were also a number of restaurants, a couple of hotels, and a myriad of tourist shops, most selling the predictable schlock, but in some of the windows Lydia could see fine carvings of bone and ivory.

Despite the relative newness of the community, the contrasts between the traditional and the modern were palpable. Standing on a corner, waiting to cross the street, was a middle aged Inuvialuit woman wearing the traditional long-waisted dress of Arctic natives; next to her was a much younger woman in a skimpy halter top and ragged cut offs. On a bench in front of the library sat an old man in a traditional summer parka of cotton cloth trimmed with fox fur. His face was deeply furrowed and the color of tea. Lydia could imagine him on the seal hunt, crouched in the boat, harpoon in hand. On his knee he held a small child who was dressed in purple denim Oshkosh by B' Gosh overalls and tiny shoes bearing the Nike *shwoosh*.

Lydia followed Evelyn as she turned up a side street and parked in front an apartment complex. The buildings were long, two stories high, and the exterior of each unit had been painted a different primary color. It made the buildings look a bit like large nursery schools. Evelyn noted that during the long winter these splotches of color broke the monotony of whiteness. She led Lydia up the stairs and knocked on a bright blue door. It was answered by a handsome dark-eyed man.

"My God, it's Lydia Falkner! This is amazing. What are you doing in Inuvik? And Evelyn! I thought you weren't coming back up until next week." He looked at one woman and then the other. "I didn't even know you two knew each other." He smiled broadly as he embraced each woman in turn. His grin faded when he saw the look on Evelyn's face. He grasped her shoulders. "Something's wrong. What is it?"

"You're right," Evelyn said, turning her head away from Jesse, her voice cracking. "Something terrible has happened. Let's go inside. Please."

Jesse paled as he opened the door wide and led them into the small living room. "What happened? What's going on?"

Evelyn sat next to Jesse on the couch and put her hand on his knee. Lydia sat stiffly on a straight wooden chair. "Jesse, Jesse," Evelyn whispered, drawing the name out as if it were hard to say. She stopped, took a deep breath, and forged ahead, "Jesse, your father is dead."

Jesse sat utterly still and stared blankly at Evelyn. Then he shook his head and said, "No. No. It can't be. He's perfectly healthy."

Evelyn took both his hands in hers. "He was murdered, Jesse. Lydia found him."

His eyes searched Evelyn's face as if looking for some sign of a hoax. "What do you mean?"

"Somebody shot him, out at the homestead. Somebody killed him." Tears were streaming down her cheeks now.

Jesse emitted a groan as if he'd been socked in the stomach. "Oh, God," he said, his voice almost a whisper. "I did this. It's my fault. I shouldn't have told him." He was looking at the wall now, but his eyes were unfocused and his lips were quivering. Evelyn put her arms around him and he began to cry—dry, wrenching sobs.

Wanting to give Evelyn and Jesse a few minutes alone, Lydia got up and went into the kitchen. She put her hands on the edge of the sink and gazed out of the window. The normalcy of the scene was reassuring. A middle-aged couple sat on a wooden bench and chatted, their faces animated, their gestures exclamatory. A young woman pulled a laughing toddler across the grass in a bright red wagon. On the sidewalk a group of pre-adolescent girls was jumping rope. When the twirlers launched two long ropes in opposite directions, Lydia recognized the game as one from her childhood, double Dutch. The jumper, timing her entry perfectly, skillfully hopped over one rope and entered a blur of spinning hemp. Her long ponytail flying, she jumped constantly, never once brushing a rope. When she was winded, she exited gracefully and the next jumper entered the arc.

As Lydia turned away from the window, she could hear the soft murmur of Evelyn's voice on the other side of the wall. She couldn't make out the words, but the rhythm was slow, calming. Lydia opened the cupboard and picked up a water glass, which she filled from the tap. She returned to the living room and handed the glass to Jesse, who was sitting up now, wiping his eyes, and breathing hard. Jesse accepted the glass, stared at it a moment, and then put it down on the coffee table. As Lydia sat, he turned to her and spoke, his voice soft, strained, and ragged. Lydia had to lean forward to hear him.

"Lydia, where did you find him? What happened? Do you know who killed him?"

Lydia told her story. As she talked, Jesse's face grew grayer and grayer. At the end of her narrative, he put his head in his hands. When he finally looked up, he repeated his earlier words. "I did this. It's my fault." Jesse had his mother's beautiful eyes and thick, straight hair, but his long, expressive face and tall, rangy body were Frank's. It almost made Lydia weep to watch him.

"You don't know that, Jesse," said Lydia with a faint shake of her head.

Jesse responded with a slow nod. "Why would a stranger kill an old man who lives alone on the Yukon? Dad found something out and somebody knew it."

Jesse pulled a bandana out of his pocket and blew his nose and wiped his eyes as Evelyn gently rubbed his back. Finally he turned to Evelyn. "Maybe Dad knew he had dangerous information and that's why he didn't tell us about it."

Evelyn nodded and softly touched his cheek. "That would be just like Frank, to protect us."

Jesse emitted a sound that was both a curse and a wail. "Damn! I have to have a funeral. I don't know how to arrange a funeral. I don't know anything about funerals. When my mother died, my aunt took care of all that. I don't know how to do any of it." He gave Lydia a panicked look. "Will they even let me have a funeral if my dad was murdered?"

"Yes," said Lydia, "but maybe not right away. Don't worry about it now. It doesn't matter when you have the funeral. I'll help you when the time comes."

Jesse looked utterly drained and Evelyn didn't look much

better. "Look," said Lydia. "I've got my tent and a sleeping bag. I'll stay in that provincial campground on the edge of town. You guys get some rest, and let's meet in the morning for breakfast."

They both nodded. "There's a little cafe across the street from the Mad Trapper Saloon. We'll meet you there at nine," said Evelyn. That Mad Trapper got around.

After a restaurant meal of undercooked fish and overcooked vegetables, Lydia found the campground. It was almost 9:00 PM. Near the registration booth, a family was roasting marshmallows over an open fire and singing camp songs. In a large, grassy spot near the bathrooms, a group of teenagers was playing volleyball over a makeshift net while a pack of younger kids chased each other in a spirited game of tag.

Everybody found it hard to go to bed on these endless, summer nights and the activity in the campground showed no signs of abating. Lydia, however, was exhausted. She drove to the far edge, to an isolated and wooded site near the Mackenzie River. She could still hear the singing and laughing, but the distance reduced it to a pleasant, indistinct burble. She got out of the car and grabbed the tent and sleeping bag from behind the driver's seat. It was a windless, cloudless night, so she pitched the tent without its rain-fly and used only four stakes to secure the floor. She crawled into her nylon cave, slipped off her shoes and her jeans, and curled herself into a fetal position. She fell asleep listening to the faint, sweet harmonies of *The Lion Sleeps Tonight.*

CHAPTER 10

When Lydia awoke, the campground was alive with activity (again or still, she couldn't be sure which). She could smell frying bacon and hear the gravel crunch as kids rode their bikes up and down the road. She tried to hear the CBC news report on somebody's radio, but the commentator was periodically drowned out by a raven croaking raucously nearby. Lydia stretched, sat up, and glanced at her watch. "Oh hell, it's eight-thirty," she said out loud. She pulled on her jeans and her shoes, and after a dash to the bathroom to wash her face and drag a brush through her hair, she was on her way back into Inuvik.

Evelyn and Jesse were already sipping coffee when Lydia entered the cafe. She ordered an onion bagel and the biggest cup of coffee they served. Jesse shook his head when he saw the sixteen ounce cup. "Still haven't kicked the habit, I see," he said. Lydia, her dad, and Jesse's had spent many afternoons lounging in Frank's gazebo, swilling cup after cup of coffee, devouring Frank's homemade molasses cookies.

"Nope, it's my only true addiction." She chugged the rest of the paper cup and began to tear it into tiny pieces. When she'd made a small neat pile of debris, she turned to Jesse, who was picking at a piece of buttered toast.

"Jesse, think hard. Is there anything your dad said to you when you last saw him that seemed weird?"

Jesse gave Lydia a wan smile. "Come on, Lydia. Dad, weird? You know how he was. He said weird stuff all the time. I wracked my brain all night, but I couldn't think of anything that stood out.

He was really torqued about the pier, but we all were. I can tell you that just before he went home, he started acting different."

"Different how?" asked Lydia through a mouthful of dough.

"Well, there were a couple of things. One was that he was quieter than usual. Dad liked to tell me stories, but the day before he left, he didn't have much to say. He didn't seem mad or anything. It was like his mind was somewhere else. We went fishing that afternoon, after I got off work. You know how Dad loved fishing."

Lydia nodded. Frank was the most passionate fisherman she had ever known. A fifty mile an hour wind and squadron of five pound mosquitoes wouldn't get him off the river if the fish were biting. And when the salmon were running, Frank could cast for twenty hours straight.

Jesse continued. "It was clear his heart wasn't in it. When he caught this nice Dolly Varden, he unhooked it and threw it back. A couple of those would have been dinner for me and him, but he threw it back. Dad was not a catch and release fisherman. He didn't even hold the damn thing up for me to admire; he just threw it back."

"You're sure that was the day before he left?"

Jesse didn't hesitate. "Yeah, I'm sure. And that was another strange thing. He flew back. He didn't take the bus. He had a round-trip bus ticket, but he flew. You know how Dad hated to fly and he'd already flown up to Nuvaktuk twice. I couldn't believe that he was flying all the way back to Dawson."

"Do you know which day he flew home?" asked Lydia.

"Yeah," said Jesse. "It was June twelfth. Moses drove him to the airport."

Lydia blinked back tears. "He got back to Dawson the same day I did. I saw him for the last time the next day."

Jesse touched Lydia's hand. "But you saw him, Lydia. You saw him before he died."

Suddenly Evelyn groaned and grabbed Jesse's other hand. "Oh, God, we have to tell Moses."

Jesse nodded glumly and swallowed hard. "Yeah, we do. He's

gonna be upset, real upset." Jesse ran his fingers through his hair and clutched his skull with both hands.

Evelyn pushed her chair back and stood up. "Let's go," she said. "I think we should do it right now."

Lydia had only finished half her bagel and had been contemplating another sixteen ounce cup of coffee. With a small sigh, she pushed her plate away and stood up. "I'm ready," she said without meaning it.

Jesse and Evelyn walked Lydia to the north edge of town where a cluster of house trailers huddled together on the delta plain. Most of the mobile homes were well maintained, and pansies and marigolds bloomed in front yard planters. Jesse turned up the driveway of a double-wide with pale yellow siding. Sitting in the long driveway was a perfectly restored 1966 step-side Chevy pickup truck with the spare tire on the side. It had been painted a dark green and polished to a deep shine. Lydia could see herself in the fender. "Oh, wow. What a beauty."

"Moses's winter project," said Jesse. "He bought it from some guy about four years ago. He just finished restoring it with his brother's help. They take turns driving it, but the brother usually keeps it in his garage. I guess it's Moses's turn to play with it today." Lydia was very familiar with the concept of the winter project. Without one, denizens of the far North tended to drink too much, eat too much, and brood too much during the long, dark winters.

Jesse knocked once on the mobile home door, and it was answered immediately by a Gwich'in man who must have been about sixty, although his thick black hair didn't contain a trace of gray. He was tall and lean and stood ramrod straight in the door frame. The weathered face and strong, calloused hands spoke of a life spent outdoors, a life of hard physical work. Jesse addressed the older man in grave tones. "Moses, this is my old friend Lydia Falkner. She lives on the Yukon near my dad." He turned to Lydia. "Lydia, this is Moses Charlie, my uncle."

Jesse put his hand on his uncle's shoulder. "Can we come in, Moses? We have something important to tell you."

Moses nodded. He shook Lydia's hand as she came through the door and said with great formality, "Welcome to my home Miss Falkner. I'm very glad to meet you." He pointed to a tidy but sparsely furnished living room. "Please sit down and make yourself comfortable."

As Lydia walked into the room, she became instantly aware that something was strange. Not only was there very little furniture, but those few pieces were oddly arranged. On one wall there was a couch, a coffee table, and an end table. The opposite wall was empty except for a gooseneck reading lamp and a small low table of the sort one might place next to an easy chair. The table and lamp were too far away from the couch to be of use to its occupants. There were a few small pieces of intricate Gwich'in beadwork on the wall over the couch, but in the middle of that space was an empty picture hook. The bright rectangle around the hook contrasted with the faded paneling. Lydia turned toward Evelyn and noticed that Evelyn was looking around the room and frowning. Jesse's eyes were fixed only on Moses.

Moses led Lydia and Evelyn to the couch and went into the kitchen to get two straight backed chairs. He seated himself in one and motioned Jesse into the other. But instead, Jesse sat crossed-legged on the floor at Moses's feet, facing him. He put his hand on the older man's knee as his eyes filled with tears. "Moses," he said in a small voice. "Frank is dead."

Moses stared in disbelief and his response echoed Jesse's of the night before. "Dead? He was fine when he left here. He looked completely healthy. How could he be dead?"

For what felt like the hundredth time, Lydia told her story. Moses never took his eyes off her face as she spoke. He hardly blinked. He didn't move. It was unnerving. Moses's own face registered little, but when she had finished, she saw that there were unshed tears in his eyes.

"Moses, do you have any idea what Frank was doing while he was up here?" asked Evelyn. "We think that his death has something to do with this cruise ship stuff at Nuvaktuk, but he never told us anything."

Moses shrugged. He thought carefully before he spoke. He seemed to be a man unaccustomed to long stretches of discourse. "Just before Frank left, he found out something that was even worse than cruise ships coming in there. But he wouldn't tell me what it was. He said something to me about betrayal, but that's all he'd say. Then he left." Moses looked at the ceiling, then closed his eyes as if the act of speaking had worn him out.

Lydia addressed Moses. "A friend and I went through Frank's files to look for some clue as to why he'd been killed. We didn't really find anything except a new folder with some papers in it about the Porcupine caribou herd. That might be significant, but we don't know how. We also found a brochure for Holiday Cruise Lines on the counter. Have you ever heard of it?" Moses shook his head, shrugged again, and said nothing.

The four sat in silence so long that Lydia became uncomfortable. She finally rose and said, "I think I'd better go. I have a few things I need to do." Everyone stood. Moses accompanied them to the door and shook Lydia's hand. "Goodbye, Miss Falkner," he said with his careful, elegant diction. "I wish we could have met under different circumstances."

Lydia nodded and squeezed the calloused fingers. "Me, too, Mr. Charlie."

As soon as Moses had closed the door, Evelyn grabbed Jesse's arm. "Did you notice?"

"Did I notice what?"

"The diamond willow chairs were gone."

Jesse frowned. "Maybe they were in the bedroom."

Evelyn shook the elbow she was holding. "Jesse, they wouldn't *fit* in the bedroom. They're gone."

"What are you talking about?" asked Lydia.

Evelyn explained. "Frank made Moses and Catherine two chairs out of diamond willow a long time ago. They were beautiful and worth a lot."

"They used to sit across from the couch, didn't they," said Lydia, "on either side of that little table?" Evelyn nodded. "What do you think happened to them?"

"Moses must have sold them. I bet he's hard up for money and he sold them."

Jesse stared at his girlfriend. "I think you're right. You know what else? That big piece of beadwork is gone, too—the one he had over the couch."

"This is awful," said Evelyn. "I can't believe that Moses needed money so bad he'd sell his treasures."

"Why would Moses need money?" asked Lydia.

"Probably because of Aunt Catherine," said Jesse. "She was sick a long time. He must have had a whole lot of expenses."

As they passed the pickup, Lydia cast a quick appreciative glance and then stopped and stared hard. To the surprise of her companions, she turned abruptly, walked around the bed to the passenger side, and peered in through the window. When she looked up, her face was grim. "There's a *for sale* sign on the dashboard, Jesse."

It was a somber party that walked back toward the main street. When they approached a coffee shop, Lydia stopped and looked through the plate glass. "Hey, this place has Internet access. We can find out where Holiday Lines is located and what kinds of cruises they do."

The shop was nearly empty and a computer was available. Her companions weren't interested in coffee, but Lydia was unable to ignore the lure of an Italian espresso. She plunked down enough money for the drink and an hour's worth of Internet time. Pulling up one of the standard search engines, she typed in *Holiday Cruise Lines.* More than twenty links popped onto the screen. The URL for the Holiday Cruise Lines homepage was halfway down. She clinked on the link and a lovely white ship filled the top half of the screen. The rest of the page was devoted to links to various cruise packages.

Lydia started surfing. "Whoa," she said in a low voice. "This is a large operation. Its home base is Miami, Florida, for God sake.

They have three different trips to Alaska, so they obviously operate up here." She clicked on an icon and then yelped. "Jeez! Look at this. They actually go through the Aleutians. I didn't know there were any cruise ships operating in that area."

Jesse's eyebrows rose. "They must offer some incredibly expensive trips."

Lydia nodded. "Look here. They're billing themselves as the only cruise ship line that takes passengers to the *True North*. This says they already stop at Kodiak Island and Dutch Harbor and are planning trips to Nome and Barrow. I guess if they're going as far as Barrow, they could go all the way to Nuvaktuk."

Evelyn and Jesse peered over her shoulder at the screen, and the three continued to read in silence. Every time the cafe door opened, Jesse looked up anxiously. Finally, he said, "Look, I'm not comfortable doing this in public. I know it sounds paranoid, but I don't want anyone from work walking in here and it's getting close to lunchtime." Lydia immediately cleared the history file and logged off. She had forgotten about her espresso. She reached for the tiny cup. The coffee was cold. She drank it anyway.

"I can follow this up in Dawson," said Lydia softly as she pushed back her chair and picked up her daypack. "But I bet a hundred bucks that this is the cruise line that's building that pier."

Lydia had her hand on the handle of the door when Jesse grabbed her arm and pulled her back into the room. He led her to the window and pointed. "Curtis Reston is walking down the other side of the street," he said in a low voice. "See the guy smoking the cigar?"

Lydia peered through the glass. "I see him." She had been anticipating a creepy looking fellow in ill-fitting clothes with oily, slicked-back hair. Instead, Curtis Reston was handsome, had an excellent haircut, and was tastefully dressed in well pressed khaki pants, a brown suede sport coat, and shiny brown loafers with tassels. He walked with a confident air and smiled and nodded at the people he passed on the street. He was accompanied by a tall, slim blonde woman, who looked straight ahead and smiled and nodded at no one.

"So that's our villain," said Lydia. "He looks like your average business man."

"A lot of them do, I guess," said Jesse. The three didn't exit the coffee shop until Curtis and his companion had entered a building.

As they walked back toward Jesse's apartment, Lydia asked, "Those bleachers I saw last night, what are they for?"

"Those are for the Great Northern Arts Festival and Northern Games" said Jesse. "It's an annual event up here."

"What kind of arts festival?"

"It's all native art," explained Evelyn. "Beadwork, ivory carvings, woodworking. The artists come and show their work and sometimes demonstrate how the things are made."

"So there'll be artists there who work in ivory."

"Sure," replied Evelyn. "Why?"

Lydia's hand went to her belt. But she wasn't wearing her belt. In her haste to get dressed, she'd left it in the tent.

"Damn it," she muttered.

"What's the matter?" asked Jesse.

"Your dad made me an ivory knife, Jesse. I found it in a package addressed to me in his filing cabinet just a few days ago. I always wear it on my belt. But this morning I was in such a hurry, I didn't put my belt on. I'd like to show it to a knife maker. I'll go back to the campground and get it if it's okay with you guys."

"Oh, please do," said Jesse. "I'd love to see it."

"We'll wait for you at the apartment," said Evelyn.

"I'll hurry," said Lydia.

"Take your time," said Jesse. "The festival goes on into the night. I'll try to rest while you're gone."

Lydia pulled into the campground twenty minutes later. Except for two bicyclists who were setting up a tiny backpacking tent, the place was empty. Lydia crawled halfway into her own tent, retrieved the belt, and snaked out again. As she stood and began threading the belt through the loops on her pants, she became aware of the sound of a large outboard on the other side of the trees. The engine throttled back and a few moments later a boat bottom scraped the gravel on the river bank. Lydia heard male voices and then the sound of something being thrown on the ground. Maybe these guys had a big catch. It was worth taking a quick look.

Buckling her belt as she walked, she entered the small grove of alders next to her tent site. Standing in the shade of the scrub trees, she watched three men unload wooden boxes from a large fishing boat. The short fat guy on the boat picked them up easily and, one by one, handed them to a tall, skinny man, who was standing in the shallows. This guy in turn handed them to a medium sized man, who was stacking them neatly on the bank. As the tall man thrust the last box toward his companion, he lost his grip and the box landed on the foot of its intended recipient.

"You stupid pig," yelled the victim as he hopped around on one foot. He had a thick Slavic accent. "You broke my toe." Hoping to avoid a hospital run, Lydia turned and quietly headed back to the SUV. There was, after all, a phone in the campground and this wasn't exactly an emergency.

As Lydia steered the Explorer toward the main road, she realized that an RV was coming way too fast through the narrow gate. She swerved onto the grass to avoid grazing it. "Idiot," she muttered to herself. At least the injured fisherman would have a ride into town if he needed one.

When Lydia reached the apartment complex, Evelyn and Jesse were seated in front of the building on a concrete bench. Jesse was slumped against Evelyn, his face empty, his eyes glassy. Lydia sat cross-legged on the grass in front of the couple. "Couldn't rest, huh?" she said to Jesse. He shook his head.

Lydia reached toward her belt and pulled the knife from the sheath. "Here it is, Jesse. It's a beautiful thing." She handed it to him.

The instant Jesse touched his father's creation, his whole demeanor changed. He sat up straight; his eyes brightened; his face regained expression. He caressed the handle, and then gripped it firmly a couple of times; he traced the scrimshaw antlers with the tip of his finger; he tested the sharpness of the blade with his thumb. Then Jesse held the whole thing to his cheek for a moment and wordlessly handed it to Evelyn. Her eyes filled as she held it in her palm and then returned it to Lydia. Lydia slipped the knife back into its sheath and pulled the tiny bone button through its tiny loop.

"When Frank told me he had a present for me, he also said it would speak to me. But I have no idea what he meant," said Lydia. "I'd like to talk to somebody who knows about knife making. Maybe I can find someone at the arts festival who can help me understand."

"I'll take you over there," said Evelyn. She checked her watch. "In fact, the events just started." She touched Jesse's cheek. "Why don't you try to sleep again?"

Jesse nodded. Then he turned to Lydia. "I will ride back to Dawson with you like you suggested. I'd rather talk to the Mounties in person, and I want to get Buck out of the pound and bring him up here."

"Great," said Lydia. "I'll be happy to have the company. What about you, Evelyn? Will you go back to Eagle Plains tomorrow?"

Evelyn shook her head. "It's been a long time since I've had any time off. I need to buy some things and visit my aunt and uncle. I want to see Moses again, too. I'll go back down in a couple of days." She kissed Jesse goodbye and he trudged slowly up the apartment stairs.

Lydia and Evelyn walked south, dodging noisy, rambunctious children, who grinned at them and poked at each other. They passed knots of oh-so-cool teenagers, who sauntered self-consciously and seemed oblivious to everything except the voices on their cell phones and the tunes on their MP3 players.

The Great Northern Arts Festival had the feel of a small town fair. Kids and dogs darted in and out of the bleacher uprights while parents stood in small groups, talking and laughing. There were hot dog vendors, cotton candy booths, big tubs of cold soda, and a seal meat concession where women in long, greasy aprons were deep frying blubber in large vats of smoking oil.

Some sort of odd sporting event was transpiring on the low stage. "Good grief!" Lydia exclaimed. "What *is* that guy doing?" She was referring to the teenager who was on the floor beneath an oval ball, which had been suspended from a small gallows style post. With his right hand anchored on the stage, the boy thrust his right leg and entire torso high into the air. At the same time he held his left foot in his left hand. Straining hard, he managed to kick the ball, which must have been suspended more than six feet above the ground.

"That's called the high kick," explained Evelyn. "That ball is an inflated seal bladder. They keep moving the bladder higher and higher, and the person who can kick it at the highest point wins." The announcer reported that the next event would be the knuckle hop, followed by the ear pull and leg wrestling. As intrigued as she was by the names of these competitions, Lydia was anxious to find a knife maker.

After paying a token entry fee, Lydia and Evelyn strolled into a giant room two walls of which were lined with glass cases. These were filled with small artistic creations. There was jewelry made of ivory and silver, fountain pens inlaid with wood and stone, and bone-handle knives with thin stone blades. The larger pieces sat on folding tables in the middle of the room—eagles carved from five thousand-year-old mammoth tusks; figures of seal hunters, bears, and whales fashioned from iridescent, green soap-stone; exquisitely detailed ivory otters, walruses, and caribou. Every inch of available wall space was covered with paintings, photos, and beadwork.

While it was all native art, it wasn't all traditional. There were oil paintings of snow machines and float planes as well as caribou and sled dogs. Elaborately beaded moccasins were displayed next to a soft, caribou-skin motorcycle jacket trimmed with red and blue glass orbs so tiny that Lydia couldn't imagine a needle small enough to penetrate the holes.

Then Lydia caught sight of a large piece sitting alone on a table.

Her hand went to her sternum and she held her breath. A long white walrus tusk had been carved into a sled, driver, and dog team along its horizontal plane. The plump, smiling driver was dressed in a fur parka, the bottom, collar, and cuffs of which were trimmed in fur; each hair was a single, fragile piece of ivory. The sled dogs were in mid stride, visibly straining in their traces. The lead dog's mouth was open and you could almost hear him barking orders to the others. The man and his team looked straight ahead with wide, black eyes made of whale baleen. The sled and dogs ran along the bottom of the tusk on a field of unbroken snow.

"Incredible," exclaimed Lydia.

Evelyn nodded. "You won't see anything this good anywhere else. These are the best artists in the North. I know this guy. He works construction in the summer and does this in the winter. This piece probably took him three months."

Lydia pulled herself away from the magnificent carving, took her knife out of its sheath, and approached a young woman who sat behind a large display of knives and ivory pendants. "Hi," she said. "My name is Lydia and I have a favor to ask. This is a knife a friend made for me. Can you tell me what it's made of and if there's anything unusual about it?"

"Hi," said the artist. "I'm Sherry." Sherry was Inuit. She was pretty and plump with an easy smile. When she accepted the knife, Lydia noticed that her hands were small and her fingers long and slender, the perfect tools for the dainty scrimshaw work displayed in the glass case in front of her.

Sherry looked at Frank's knife closely. "It's lovely," she said. "Whoever made this was an excellent craftsman."

"Yes, he was," said Lydia. "He died before he could tell me anything about it."

The artist looked closely at both the blade and the handle. "Well," she said, "the blade is made from a chainsaw bar. It's been very carefully honed. The handle is walrus ivory and the guard is brass." She pointed to the piece of metal between the blade and the handle. "The rivets are brass, too. I'm not sure what else I can tell you."

"My friend said something about how this knife would speak to me," said Lydia. "Do you have any idea what he meant?"

Sherry screwed up her face and thought a moment. "Well, northern natives do have a tradition of story knives. Women and girls use them to tell stories by drawing pictures in the dirt. These are often ivory, sometimes whale baleen. I've never seen a traditional story knife with a metal blade though."

Lydia shrugged. "Oh, well. It was worth a shot." Then she pointed to a sign over Sherry's table. It read ***Only fossilized ivory has been used in the creation of these pieces***.

"What does that mean?"

"Well," said Sherry, who seemed pleased to have been asked, "ivory is either fossilized or new. New ivory is sort of a misleading term; it's anything less than a hundred years old. All mammoth ivory is fossilized since mammoths have been extinct for a long time. Walrus ivory is another matter; it can be either new or old."

"Can you tell whether this is old or new ivory?" asked Lydia, holding up her knife.

"It's probably old ivory," said Sherry, peering closely at the handle. "New ivory is whiter than that. Was the craftsman Inuit?" Lydia shook her head.

"Then it's very unlikely that it's new. There aren't many walruses in northwest Canada, so most new ivory comes from Alaska. Only Alaskan natives are allowed to hunt walrus and work the new ivory. The laws are strict. Inuit can't hunt walrus just for the tusks. That's called head-hunting and it's highly illegal. If they're going to hunt walrus, they have to use the whole animal—tusks, skin, flippers, everything. Because of all the laws governing new ivory, most commerce is in fossilized ivory."

"So is walrus ivory worth a lot?" asked Lydia.

"The right piece can be very valuable," said the artist. "Most of the trade is in chunks and pieces. Choice bits go for three to four hundred American dollars a pound. Of course, a whole tusk is worth more. If you could find a nose plate with both tusks attached, that could fetch five or six thousand dollars. There's a lot of fossil ivory in the ground, but it's getting harder to find whole tusks, much less matched sets. So, of course, there are poachers. A few years ago they busted a group of people in Alaska for trading tusks and *oosiks* for drugs."

"Oosiks?" said Lydia.

"Oosiks. Walrus penis bones. A two foot oosik is worth quite a bit." Evelyn giggled and Sherry threw her a disapproving glance. "A lot of knife makers use oosiks for handles, and some people just want them for the novelty."

"I imagine policing the ivory trade is pretty difficult," said Lydia.

"Yes, and unfortunately walruses clump together in colonies so it's damn easy to wade in and slaughter them in large numbers. Occasionally poachers go in with chain saws and cut off their heads. It's terrible." She pointed to a small stack of pamphlets on the display table. "Take one of those. It'll tell you all about it."

Lydia picked up a pamphlet. The walrus on the cover was an endearingly ugly fellow with loose wrinkled skin, a bristled muzzle, and tiny eyes. Lydia read aloud to Evelyn. "'Male *odobenus rosmarus* can weigh up to sixteen hundred and fifty pounds. The tusks on a Pacific bull can reach forty inches.' Wow. Those are some mighty big boys."

Lydia thanked Sherry for her help, shoved the pamphlet into her pocket, and put the little ivory knife back in its sheath. "Well," she said to Evelyn, "that was interesting but not very helpful. If my knife is a story knife, I can't hear the story. Even in death Frank is speaking in riddles."

Lydia and Evelyn exited the hall and rounded a corner, nearly tripping over two rows of people kneeling on athletic mats which had been placed end-to-end in the dirt. They seemed to be preparing for some sort of game as they faced each other across the expanse of blue plastic. Many of the participants wore conventional T shirts, but some were sporting black felt vests with the words *Team Gwich'in* embroidered in red on the back. Behind the players seven men sat quietly, each of them holding a thin drum made of taut animal hide.

On a signal from one of the men, the drummers began to beat the skins, each with a long, narrow stick. The players on one side of the mat began to sway and chant as they thrust their hands under the long yellow blanket that lay in front of them. Lydia could see movement under the blanket but had no idea what was going on. At a second signal, the participants revealed their closed fists and began moving their hands and arms. Everyone had a different style; some produced large, fluid arcs; others kept their hands close to their bodies in small delicate motions. A few of the men grasped their own forearms and kept them chest high. The long, black hair of one young woman brushed the shoulders of her neighbors as she swayed to the beat. One old man tucked his fists beneath his chin and flapped his elbows like a bird.

As the drummers began to pound faster and faster, a man on the other team clapped once and held his right hand out flat; then he made a series of gestures with his fingers that Lydia couldn't follow. Colored sticks were shoved across the blue mat.

"What are they doing?" asked Lydia as they headed for the street. "I don't understand it at all."

"That's stick gambling," said Evelyn. "It's an Indian game but up here everybody does it."

"It looks complicated," said Lydia.

"It's not hard to learn," said Evelyn. "Each member of the team that's *up* hides some sort of token, a stone or a coin maybe, in one hand and the captain of the other team tries to guess which hand each player has the token in. The captain chooses which person and which hand with set of hand signals. That's the complicated part. If the captain's right, that player is out of the game. If the captain's wrong, the other team gets a counting stick. As soon as one team has all the sticks, that round is over. The movements and drums are part of the ritual, but it doesn't affect who wins."

"It sure is wonderful to watch," said Lydia.

"Yeah," said Evelyn, "it's very cool, but it's a betting game and the stakes can be high."

Lydia told Evelyn goodbye at Jesse's front door and spent the rest of the day wandering around Inuvik, trying to be a proper tourist. Her heart wasn't in it. Finally she stopped at the Mad Trapper Saloon for a beer and a burger. She found a quiet table away from the jukebox and settled into the wooden chair. Just as the bartender arrived to take her order, shouting erupted from one of the booths along the wall.

"Hey! This isn't what I ordered. I said *rare*! I want it *rare*. What's the matter? Don't you speak English? R-a-r-e!" The patron, whose back was to Lydia, spelled the word slowly, his voice thick with sarcasm.

The young waitress took two steps backwards. "I'm sorry, sir. I'll return it to the kitchen. I'm sure the cook will make it right."

"He better make it right. And take these fries back, too. They're greasy as hell." The back of the booth was high, but Lydia could see the man's arm as he picked up two plates and thrust them at his server. As the woman walked rapidly toward the kitchen, clutching a plate in each hand, Lydia heard the patron say, "What a dumb broad," to his companion. The waitress hunched her shoulders. She had heard it, too.

The bartender sucked in a large breath. "Always the asshole," he muttered.

"You know that guy?" asked Lydia.

"Oh, yeah," replied the bartender. "He's a local bigshot. Comes in here a lot. Treats everybody like crap. We're all used to it and try to ignore him, but Janie's new and she's never seen him in action before."

Lydia placed her order and then got up to find the bathroom. She made a deliberate detour past the angry patron's booth and glanced at him as she walked by. She gasped silently when she realized that the man sitting on the wooden bench was Curtis Reston. The icy blonde woman Lydia had seen with him on the street was seated across from him.

When Lydia returned to her table, Reston was still talking

loud. Now he seemed to be complaining about his own workers. "Those guys are already two weeks behind," Reston growled. The blonde said something inaudible. Reston responded with, "Fuckin' Eskimos. They'd rather hunt whales than work construction. But I haven't got time to screw around. I don't know how long I can keep everybody in line. We've already had some problems."

Reston stopped talking when the waitress appeared at his side with his order. With eyes lowered, she sat it gently on the table and began to walk away. "Wait a minute!" he demanded. There was a pause and then he erupted again. "Jesus Christ! I said rare, not breathing. Can't you people do anything right?" Lydia heard him slam his knife and fork down on the table. "Let's get outa here," he said. "The food stinks and the service sucks. I don't need this shit."

Reston stood up, walked around the booth, and offered his female companion his hand. She arose and, knees primly together, exited the booth. Neither of them even glanced at their waitress as they marched toward the front door. The tassels on Reston's loafers danced as he walked.

Her face collapsing, Janie slid into the booth, put her arms on the table, and laid her head on her arms. The bartender slid in next to her and squeezed her shoulder. She picked up her head, wiped her eyes, and let him lead her back into the kitchen.

Lydia considered Reston's words. Was he talking about the pier at Nuvaktuk? What did he mean by *keeping people in line*? Was he threatening local council members? Had Frank found out? Was Frank one of the problems he was talking about? Lydia's heart pounded as she began to formulate a plan. By the time her food arrived, she had decided that she would get into Curtis Reston's office. If there was anything in there linking Reston to Frank's murder, she'd find it. She'd do what the Mounties couldn't.

The decision made, Lydia tackled her dinner with enthusiasm. The hamburger was medium rare, just as she had requested, the beer was cold, and the fries were delicious and not the least bit greasy.

As soon as she finished eating, she headed for the pay phone on the street in front of the bar. She dug Jesse's phone number out of her pocket and punched in the numbers. Jesse answered on the second ring. Lydia didn't even identify herself. "Do you have a key to Aurora Tours?"

"Yeah," he said warily. "Why?"

"I'm going in there tonight. I want to look around." She told Jesse what she had overheard.

"Are you crazy, Lydia? You can't just walk in there. What if Reston or somebody else spots you?"

"Reston won't spot me. I just saw him leave the Mad Trapper with a woman. He's got plans."

Jesse gave a big sigh. "I can't let you do that alone. I'm coming with you."

"No," Lydia snapped. "This was my idea and I won't let you take the risk. I'm going alone. I'll come over and get the key right now. And I could use a small flashlight if you have one." She hung up in the middle of Jesse's protestations.

Jesse was standing in front of his apartment building when Lydia drove up. He handed her a brass key and a pen light through the open car window and then leaned his head in. "Remember that Curtis Reston is a mean son-of-a-bitch."

Lydia nodded. "I'll return to this to you in the morning. Okay?"

Jesse nodded and then shook his head. "I don't like this one bit."

"You don't have to like it," said Lydia, as she put the car in gear, "but I have to do it."

CHAPTER 11

Lydia couldn't depend on the cover of darkness, but the only street activity was in the vicinity of the Mad Trapper. Reston's office was blocks away. Lydia parked the Explorer on a side street and strolled over to the main thoroughfare. Aurora Tours was sandwiched between a defunct pizza parlor and a small gift shop, which had been closed for hours. Lydia approached the office casually, stopping to gaze for a moment at the T shirts and fake ivory pendants in the gift shop window. After a quick glance up and down the street, she inserted the key into Aurora's front door and slipped inside.

The blinds on the large plate glass window were half closed, providing Lydia some light and allowing her to move around the room without being observed from the street. It was a standard tourism office. Brochures were displayed in metal racks on a counter just inside the door, and colorful posters featuring various Arctic destinations were tacked to the back wall. A receptionist's desk containing a computer, monitor, printer, and combination telephone and fax machine sat next to the counter. Lydia opened the desk drawers. They contained only paper clips, staples, pens, and printer paper. There were two other desks in the room and they were similarly equipped. A Xerox machine sat along one wall. There were no filing cabinets.

Lydia noted the two interior doors at the back of the reception area. One was white metal with a shiny brass deadbolt. Both the door and the lock looked new. Lydia tried Jesse's key in the lock; it didn't fit. The other door had *Curtis Reston, President* stenciled on the frosted glass window. It was unlocked. Lydia pushed it open and entered the President's inner sanctum.

The office window was curtained, but even in the gloom Lydia could see that Curtis Reston was a man with expensive taste and a good interior designer. The walls were covered with delicate pen and ink drawings of Arctic animals. A thick wool Persian carpet covered the center of the hardwood floor. In the middle of this field of deep red, gold, and green sat a massive cherry desk flanked by a matching credenza and a low bookcase. Two oxblood leather chairs and a table were arranged in front of the desk. A leather couch sat against the opposite wall.

Lydia inspected the contents of the table. An inlaid wooden box sat at one end. When Lydia opened it, the pungent smell of tobacco filled the room. Each cigar wore a ring identifying it as the handiwork of a cigar factory in Havana. The table also sported a crystal tray holding two snifters and a crystal decanter filled with amber liquid. Lydia resisted a strong temptation to sample the brandy.

Then Lydia saw what she'd come for—a tall, cherry filing cabinet. She pulled the flashlight from her pocket and tugged on the top drawer. It moved silently on its runners. She opened all four drawers and noted that each file folder was carefully alphabetized and neatly labeled. It appeared that none of the documents was more than three years old. Lydia left the files in their hanging folders and, standing beside the cabinet, she skimmed the contents of every one. In the bottom drawer of the last cabinet she found two unlabeled folders. One of them contained two very interesting business letters. The first was on heavy ivory bond. The letterhead was elegant; *Holiday Cruise Lines* and a Miami address appeared across the top in a thick art deco font; at the bottom an exquisite line drawing of a ship steamed across the page. The letter was dated May twenty-second.

Dear Mr. Reston, she read.

Please let us know how the plans for the construction project

> *are developing. As you know, we won't be taking possession until next year, but I'd like to see substantial progress before September 1. I would appreciate getting monthly reports from you until then.*
>
> *The Board of Directors has ratified my decision to offer you the special concession. We will supply the equipment but you will be in charge of hiring personnel and running the operation locally. Your assurances that the local native council will not be an impediment were greatly appreciated.*
>
> *Sincerely,*
> *Herman M. Evangelist, Director and CEO*

The second letter was clearly a response to the first. It was a photocopy. A muddy gray aurora borealis surrounded the words *AURORA TOURS*, which had been rendered in absurdly large type.

> *Dear Mr. Evangelist:*
>
> *The pier in Nuvaktuk should be completed by early September. I am looking forward to handling the concession. We are very experienced in this area and I think you will be very satisfied with the results.*
>
> *Let me reiterate that our contacts on the council will keep the Eskimos from interfering with the project.*
>
> *Sincerely,*
> *Curtis Reston, President Aurora Tours*

"What a slimebag," muttered Lydia as she laid the letters on top of the filing cabinet.

She tackled Reston's desk next. The top was bare except for a small lamp of green glass and an elaborate telephone. There were only two drawers. One held a sealed box of cigars. The other was crammed with old telephone messages, pens, rubber bands, scraps of paper, and a spiral notebook of the sort college kids had used in her day. Lydia pulled it out, opened it, and flicked on her flashlight. The notebook appeared to be some sort of financial ledger—names in alphabetical order on the left, numbers on the right. The headings above the numbers were cryptic—LA, IR, PO. All the entries had been made by hand in pencil.

Lydia frowned as she tried to make sense of the numbers. They were clearly dollar amounts, some small, some large, followed by a percent figure. In some cases, these numbers were followed by a far larger number and a date. It took Lydia a few minutes to realize what she was looking at. The leftmost numbers were loans and the percentages were interest rates, exorbitant rates, usurious rates. The rightmost number was the final payoff. Curtis Reston was loan sharking. Lydia flipped through the pages. There must have been thirty names on this list. And then on the last page, she saw a name that made her cry, "No!" It was Moses Charlie.

Lydia grabbed the notebook and the two letters and headed for the reception area. She closed the blinds tightly before she photocopied the pages. When she returned to Reston's office, she left his door open. As she was slipping the notebook back into the desk drawer, she heard a faint noise on the street. She stood motionless, trying to identify the source. Then she heard the knob rattle as someone unlocked the front door of Aurora Tours. She heard the door open and then the sharp click of heels on the tile floor of the reception area. Then there were additional footsteps, slower and softer but heavier.

Lydia jammed the photocopied pages into her shirt pocket and looked around frantically for a hiding place. There was nowhere to go. She ducked down and crawled head first into the chair hole under Reston's desk. She reached out and pulled the desk chair in after her. Lydia's skull was jammed against the desktop, one leg was cocked under her, and the other knee dug into her chest. She tried desperately to quiet her breathing.

Whoever had entered the reception area had stopped moving at the door of Reston's office. Then an overhead light went on directly over the desk. The footsteps resumed but were soon muffled by the Persian rug. Lydia heard a soft thump and the creak of leather as the intruders settled into the two chairs in front of the desk. One of them stretched out khaki clad legs until Lydia was able to see the tassels on the shiny brown loafers. There was the clink of crystal and the sound of brandy being poured into glasses.

"Drink up," Curtis Reston said.

There was a pause and then a thin female voice said, "I don't like brandy. Don't you have anything else?"

"Nope," said Reston. "I guess you're going to have to fuck sober."

"Don't be crude, Curt."

Reston snorted. "Oh, yeah," he said. "We both know what a prude you are."

"It's late. Your wife will be getting suspicious. We need to hurry."

"Yeah, I guess we'd better get to it."

Lydia listened as the couple stood up. She heard footsteps as they approached the couch. She heard the squeak of leather as they settled in. Then there was a sharp slap on the wooden floor. Someone had stood up.

"What are you doing?" asked the woman sharply.

"Something's wrong," said Reston. "I'm sure I closed the office door before I left tonight. I wonder if someone's been in here."

Lydia clenched her jaw. The knot in her chest grew to the size of a grapefruit.

"Forget it, Curt. Forget it," said the woman. "Concentrate on this." Lydia heard the distinct sound of a zipper. She heard the jingle of a belt dropping to the floor. Within seconds, Curtis Reston was moaning. Lydia heard a loud thump as he collapsed back onto the couch. Reston's moans were punctuated with high squeals and it sounded to Lydia as though he were kicking the arm of the couch. A series of low *uh, uh, uhs* was followed by a long guttural cry. Then Reston fell silent except for some very heavy breathing.

"You owe me," said the woman.

Reston muttered something incomprehensible.

It took Reston a good five minutes to reassemble himself. He and the woman bickered loudly throughout the whole procedure, which gave Lydia a chance to take a couple of deep, calming breaths. By the time Reston finally locked the front door behind him, Lydia's extremities were completely numb and the top of her head was raw. Her wrists gave way when she tried to crawl out of the chair hole, but she managed to propel herself forward on her forearms. Using the desk chair as an anchor, she pulled herself to a kneeling position. Finally enough feeling returned to her legs to allow her to stand. When she attempted to walk, it felt as though joy buzzers had been attached to the bottoms of her feet. She finally made it to the reception area. After peering carefully through the window in the front office, she reached for the front door knob. Her hands were shaking so hard she could barely turn it.

In less than ten minutes, Lydia was pounding on Jesse's front door. He opened it almost instantly. "Shhh," he said as pulled Lydia inside and pointed to the closed bedroom door. "Evelyn's asleep. I don't want to wake her."

Lydia pulled the photocopied pages from her pocket. She ironed the creases with the flat of her palm and handed Jesse the two letters.

He read Evangelist's letter without comment, but his face darkened as he read Reston's response. "What's this crap about the *Eskimos* not interfering with the project? He's part Inuvialuit, just like me." Then Jesse shook his head. "I take that back. Curtis isn't Inuvialuit. There's nothing Inuvialuit about him except a few liters of Matt's blood in his veins."

"That's not the important thing, Jesse. Curtis says he's keeping people in Nuvaktuk in line and I think I know how he's doing it." She handed Jesse the photocopied ledger. "He's loan sharking."

After Jesse had scanned the first page of names and numbers, he looked at Lydia. "This is a whole lot of money."

"Keep going," said Lydia, her voice grim.

When Jesse read his uncle's name on the last page, his eyes grew large. "That son-of-a-bitch." His voice was hoarse with anger. "I can't believe he sucked Uncle Moses in. I'd like to rip his head off."

"Yeah, me, too," said Lydia. "I'm sure we'll have to stand in line. Do you know any of the others on the list?"

"Oh, yeah," said Jesse. "A few are from Nuvaktuk. I don't know if they're on the governing council or not, but I'll bet they are. I recognize some Inuvik names, too. There's a woman from Dawson." Jesse gave a bitter laugh. "At least Curtis is an equal-opportunity asshole. Whites, Gwich'in, Inuvialuit. He snared them all."

"Do you have any idea what kind of concession Reston is talking about? It sounds like something big."

"I have no idea," said Jesse. "And I don't think anybody in Nuvaktuk does either."

"Look," said Lydia. "I'll give these copies to Al Cerwinski and he can take it from here." She paused and bit her lip. "He is going to be *so* pissed at me." She blew out air. "I hope to God he can do something with this information. It's not going to be worth anything in court."

"It's gotta be worth something," said Jesse. "Curtis is ripping people off. That can't be legal."

"No, it's not. But neither is breaking and entering."

"You didn't break, Lydia. You only entered. That makes it only half as bad."

Lydia smiled. "Let's hope the Mounties see it that way." Then she grew serious again. "Don't say anything to anyone about any of this. Not even Evelyn."

Jesse glanced at the bedroom door. He took a couple of deep breaths. "Okay. I'll keep my mouth shut."

Lydia yawned and Jesse put his hand on her shoulder. "You're beat," he said. "Crash on my couch tonight. No point in driving back to the campground."

"You're right," said Lydia. "No point at all." Jesse found her a pillow and blanket.

Lydia lay on the couch fully clothed. It was a cheap Danish modern affair, and the seat was hard and very narrow. There was no room for her arms and little enough for her butt. She closed her eyes and tried to relax. Sleep did not come. She employed every breathing technique she knew, but her efforts were no match for the mix of adrenaline, anger, and anxiety that was percolating through her nervous system. Finally she allowed herself to succumb to sleeplessness. She tossed and turned and pounded her pillow. She fell into a fitful doze about an hour before Jesse arose to make coffee.

After breakfast Lydia called Al and told him that Jesse was coming back to Dawson and would talk to the Mounties then. She and Jesse stopped at the campground to retrieve her tent and then headed south on the Dempster. They stopped again about 2:00 for lunch at James Creek. This lively little stream danced through rocks and fireweed before it tumbled through the culvert under the Dempster Highway. There was an unofficial camping area just off the road, a lovely spot that looked like it got some use from local fishermen. There was no picnic table, but the gravel by the river was level and someone had brought in a steel trash barrel.

It wasn't until Lydia walked around to the back of the Explorer to open the tailgate that she realized just how filthy Al's car was. The entire back including the rear window was completely caked with mud. The *Fish Happens* bumper sticker was utterly invisible, and the license plate had been transformed into a clay tablet, its numbers and letters an indecipherable cuneiform. The spare tire looked like an enormous chocolate donut. She fervently hoped that the car wash would be open when she hit Dawson.

Lydia pulled out the cooler. She and Jesse plopped on the creek bank and stretched their legs into a patch of fireweed that was just coming into gaudy bloom. As she munched on her sandwich, Lydia noticed a pile of neatly stacked flat rectangular stones on the bank of the river. The effigy was about two and a half feet high and looked like a granite stick figure. There were two bandy legs, a short, fat torso, one long stone serving as two short arms, and a large square head.

"What's that?" asked Lydia.

"That's an *inukshuk*," said Jesse. "The Inuit have made them forever. They're used to mark special places. Sometimes they're used like cairns to mark routes through the wilderness. If you think about it, there aren't a lot of landmarks on the tundra. Everything is pretty flat and there aren't any trees, but you can see the inukshuks from a long way off. Sometimes an inukshuk will have a hole in it and if you look through it, you can see the next inukshuk, which will have a hole in it, and so on and so on." Jesse inscribed a spiral in the air. "People also use them to mark special spots, like a place where somebody died or where something good happened, maybe a place where a kid shot his first caribou or a good fishing hole."

As if summoned by Jesse's words, another SUV pulled into the spot and four Gwich'in teenagers tumbled out with fishing rods and tackle boxes in hand. They grinned and waved and headed for the big culvert which carried the creek water under the road.

It was late when Jesse and Lydia arrived at Eagle Plains. Evelyn had given them the key to her room and they agreed that they would share it, propriety be damned. Jesse passed out on his bed fully clothed before Lydia had finished washing her face and brushing her teeth. As he slept, Lydia gazed down at him and saw Frank—the square chin, the long face, the big strong hands.

Lydia drove hard the next day and they were in Dawson by 8:00 PM. The carwash was closed.

CHAPTER 12

After depositing Jesse at the home of a friend of his, Lydia drove directly to Al's. He opened the door before she had even mounted the porch steps. He took one look at her face, put his arm around her shoulder, and led her into the living room. After gently pushing her onto the couch, he disappeared and returned with a cup of steaming coffee and a piece of German chocolate cake.

"Don't talk. Relax for a few minutes. Eat. Drink. Then you can tell me about your trip."

Gratefully Lydia balanced the plate on her knee while she inhaled the aroma of strong, well-brewed coffee. She took a long sip. "Ah, the nectar of the gods," she murmured. She ate and drank slowly, putting off the inevitable confession.

"Okay," said Al at last. "The price of the car rental is a story."

Lydia wiped the chocolate from her lips and began. By the time she finished describing her break-in and what she had found, Al's face was grim. When she handed him the ledger, he stared at her silently. She refused to look away. Finally she said, "The last entry is Frank Johnson's brother-in-law."

"Jesus," Al said. He lowered his head to examine the pages.

When he was done, he looked up at Lydia and grimaced. "I don't know what in the hell to say about this. It was a stupid and dangerous thing for you to do, but you know that. If you'd been caught, you'd be in a territorial jail, but you know that, too. The fact that you used my car only makes it worse." Lydia put her hand to her mouth. That she hadn't thought of.

Al forged on. "We can't use the evidence you copied, but you probably know that. On the other hand," and with this his face relaxed, "this ledger might be gold. Maybe some of these names do belong to Nuvaktuk council members. Maybe Reston was sucking these people in and then blackmailing them. Maybe Frank Johnson found out about it through his brother-in-law." He paused dramatically. "Maybe that ledger is a motive for murder." Then he smiled. "Maybe it's a good thing you have a larcenous streak."

Lydia took a deep breath and smiled back. "I was afraid you were going to kill me."

"The thought crossed my mind," said Al, "but we don't have the death penalty in Canada."

Lydia tried to stifle a huge yawn. She realized it was after midnight and she was bone tired. "I'm exhausted," she said. "I've got to get back to Anna's."

"Look," said Al, "I have a nice spare room with a comfortable bed. Why don't you spend the night here? There's clean sheets and plenty of hot water. I promise to be a perfect gentleman and make you a breakfast fit for a queen in the morning."

Lydia nodded. "That's an offer I can't refuse. Please lead me there now, because I'm going to be asleep on my feet in two minutes." He took her hand and helped her off the couch. He didn't let go of it when he led her down the hall into a combination study and guest room.

"I'll go get your things out of the car," said Al. Lydia nodded. He released her hand and she collapsed onto the navy blue bedspread. She was half asleep by the time he got back with her duffle bag. She felt him throw an afghan over her and pat her twice on the back. His hand lingered after the second pat. Then he turned out the light and left the room.

When Lydia awoke, sun was pouring in the window and she could smell onions frying. It took her a minute to remember where she was. She stretched luxuriously, yawned, and reached for her glasses. She stood up, stretched again, then looked in the small, framed mirror next to Al's desk. The image that blinked back at her made her groan. The face was creased and puffy and there were dark smudges under the bleary, blue eyes. The hair was matted and greasy and the pieces that had escaped the rubber band stuck out at unbecoming angles. Lydia looked down and noted that her T shirt was badly wrinkled and none too clean. She pulled her toiletry kit out of her duffle bag and headed for the bathroom.

Cerwinski's guest facilities seemed palatial after Anna's daybed and tiny tin shower. The frosted shower door was etched with a school of fish, species indeterminate, which swam across both panels. The shower itself was large and featured a detachable, pulsating shower head. The hanging wire shelf was well-stocked with toiletries and implements, but apparently balding men don't buy hair conditioner.

Lydia stripped and tiptoed into the hard spray, a luxury she rarely enjoyed in the Yukon. When she emerged from the stall, she found two fluffy towels neatly folded on a wire rack. After drying off with one, she wrapped it around her body tucking the corner in at the top and wound the other one around her head. Then she padded off to the guest room. Al, who was just emerging from the kitchen, caught a glimpse of her and gave an appreciative wolf whistle.

After donning clean underwear, a clean T-shirt, and yesterday's jeans, Lydia dragged a comb through her hair, a painful operation after days of driving with an open window. Periodically she found it necessary to grab a fistful and focus on a single, intransigent snarl. As she did battle with her comb, she looked around the study. There were no loose papers, no books, and no office supplies cluttering up the desktop. The computer table held only the machine, the monitor, the keyboard, and the printer. The wastebasket was empty. One wall of the room was lined with floor to ceiling bookcases and all of the books had been arranged by topic and then alphabetically by author. Lydia shook her head in amazement.

Finally the comb passed through her hair without protest and she felt well enough assembled to face her host. As she walked into the dining area, Al was placing a big platter of scrambled eggs on the table. "Dig in," he said as he poured her an enormous cup of coffee.

Lydia dug in. "Oh, wow. This is good," she said with her mouth full. The scramble went well beyond eggs; it contained red and green pepper, pungent white onion, zucchini, fresh cilantro and basil, and thin slices of chorizo. She declined a second helping. "Hey, I can scarcely get into my jeans as it is. This endless commute is doing bad things to my waistline."

"Speaking of waistlines," said Al, "didn't you tell me that Frank Johnson never ate junk food?"

"He didn't," said Lydia. "He wouldn't touch anything with preservatives or chemicals except chewing gum."

"Well, that's odd because the constables found an empty cellophane bag in his trash pile under the body. It said *plantain chips*. I don't know what they are, but the bag looked like a potato chip bag."

"I think plantains are some kind of banana, but I've never seen plantain chips in a store in the Yukon. Have you?" asked Lydia.

"Nope. I think it's safe to say that Frank Johnson didn't leave it there."

"You think the murderer did?"

Al shrugged. "It's certainly possible."

"So, I wonder where a person buys plantain chips," said Lydia. "Someplace tropical, I assume. Let's check it out on the web." She paused. "Hey, Holiday Cruise Lines is based in Miami; that's sort of tropical."

"Let's go," said Al. They pushed back from the table simultaneously and almost sprinted down the hall. Lydia pulled up a spare chair and they sat shoulder to shoulder at the small computer table. Their arms and thighs touched and Lydia was acutely aware of the heat from Al's body. When Al touched the *on* button of his monitor, the screen flickered, went blue, and then Lydia found herself eye to eye with an enormous king salmon; it stared blankly at her for a few seconds and then slowly morphed into a large mouth bass; the bass broke into pieces and reassembled as a brook trout; the brook trout came apart like a puzzle and reappeared as a blue fin tuna.

Al typed *plantains* into his search engine. A huge number of sites popped up. Then Lydia saw what she was looking for. "Hey," she said, as she pointed to the bottom of the screen. It was a link to a site called *What's Doing in Miami*. Al clicked on it. The page featured the usual array of urban attractions including a description of dinner at Los Ranchos, a Nicaraguan steakhouse, featuring churrasco steak, gallo pinto, and fried plantains.

"Did anybody notice where those chips were made?" asked Lydia.

"I don't know. I'll call the station and check." Al sucked on his top front teeth. "How odd that this entire investigation seems to be hinging on cellophane chip bags."

He logged off and picked up the phone. He spoke to someone for a few minutes and then it was clear that he had been put on hold. His next words were, "That's great. Thanks a lot."

When Al hung up, he had a smile on his face. "Bingo. Those chips were distributed by an outfit called International Products; the address is a post office box in Miami, Florida. It's no smoking gun, but it's a nice little piece of circumstantial evidence."

"I hope something uncircumstantial crops up soon," said Lydia. "Frank deserves justice and it's damn slow in coming."

"Welcome to my world," said Al. His voice was flat.

"Well, I'd better call Anna and let her know I'm reclaiming the daybed," said Lydia. "Can I use your phone?" Al handed her the receiver and went to pour himself another cup of coffee.

Anna answered the phone on the fifth ring and sounded upset. She explained that she and Bryan were in the middle of a huge argument. From Anna's point of view, they were in the process of breaking up—this time it was for real—and Anna was not fit company for anyone. If Lydia could find another place to stay for a few days, that might be better.

Lydia hung up and said, "Damn it," not realizing that Al had returned with another cup of coffee for her.

"What's the problem?" he asked. She explained and he broke

into a smile. “The solution is obvious. You’ll stay here.”

“Are you sure?” said Lydia. “I’ve got other friends I can stay with.”

“I’m sure,” said Al. “I’d enjoy the company.” His smile faded. “Besides,” he said, “you’ll be safer here.”

Lydia stared at him a moment. “Do you really think I’m in danger?”

“Probably not,” said Al, “but it doesn’t hurt to be careful. Reston is clearly a crook. He might be something worse.”

Lydia breathed out. “Okay. I will stay. And thanks.”

“It’s settled then,” said Al. “I’ve got to get to work. Help yourself to anything you need. I should be home by seven, and I’ll bring something for dinner.”

Lydia spent the next few hours job hunting in cyberspace. By late afternoon she was thoroughly discouraged. She needed a beer. She strolled over to her favorite watering hole, a small tavern that did not cater to tourists. The room was dark after the glare of the sun. As she hitched herself up on a barstool, she became aware of a man who had just walked in. He was squinting at her and looked very familiar. He walked over to the bar.

“Hey,” he said. “I remember you. You’re Lydia, right?”

Lydia nodded and furrowed her brow. “I know I’ve met you, but I don’t remember where.”

“It was a few days ago up on the Dempster. I’m the guy in the construction van. Greg Rymer. I remember your name because I had an old girl friend named Lydia. Can I join you? And let me buy you a beer.”

Lydia smiled with recognition. “Sure, you can join me and I’d love a beer. Chilkoot Lager, please,” she said to the bartender. Greg ordered a Yukon Red. The bartender took two mugs from the cooler and filled one from an ancient brass tap and the other from a bottle. He pushed the mugs across the bar as Greg straddled the stool on Lydia’s left.

“What are you doing here anyway?” asked Lydia. “Last time I saw you, you were on your way to Inuvik. I thought you lived there."

"I do. Well, maybe I do. I'm not sure at this point. My wife and I are having marital problems. I'm not sure I want to stay in Inuvik just now. Things have been pretty ugly and my wife is related to half the town. On the other hand, I hate to be very far from my kids, so it's a dilemma. What about you? What are you doing here? I thought you lived on a homestead upriver somewhere."

"It's just a cabin. I have to say that, even though I've been in the Yukon for weeks, I haven't spent much time up there."

"How come?" asked Greg.

"A friend of mine died and there have been a lot of things to take care of."

Lydia was half way through her Harps when Anna walked into the gloom of the tavern. She looked angry and exhausted. Her hands were clenched. She collapsed on the barstool at Lydia's right.

"You need a beer," observed Lydia. Anna nodded.

Greg pulled his top lip tight across his teeth. "'The problem with the world is that everyone is three drinks behind,'" he intoned.

Anna scowled at him. "What's that supposed to mean?"

"Sorry," said Greg. "That's just a line from an old Humphrey Bogart picture. I'm a big Bogie fan."

"Me, too," said Lydia. "Introduce yourselves while I flag the bartender. Then Anna will only be two drinks behind, like the rest of us."

Lydia raised one finger and pointed to her glass. The bartender nodded and few moments later another icy mug slid down the wooden bar.

"So," said Lydia turning to Anna. "What is going on?"

"Oh," said Anna, her voice tight, "we're in about round ten of a fifteen round fight. How any man can be such a son-of-a-bitch and such a baby at the same time is beyond me. This is it! This really is it!"

"Yeah, yeah, yeah, I've heard that before."

"No, I'm serious. He's refusing to give his ex-wife anything for his little boy. I can't forgive that. Somewhere in his little pea brain he cooked up the notion that child support is immoral. He says he's sure that his ex-wife is going to live off it, and it'll sap her will to work. I can't make him see what a sexist and stupid idea this is. He's being a total schmuck."

Greg was listening intently. "Man, that really sucks. I think if a guy brings a child into the world, he has an obligation to support that child, no matter what. Children shouldn't be the victims of their parents' mistakes."

"Absolutely," said Anna emphatically.

Greg leaned forward, his right ear approaching Lydia's nose. "I'm in the process of getting divorced, but my wife will have no issues with me over child support. I guarantee it. I know that single mothers have it tough. Besides, I want my kids to have the best life they can." He nodded at Anna.

"Well, you clearly don't have much in common with Bryan the bastard, that's for sure," said Anna.

"Hey, a man has responsibilities," Greg said, leaning so far toward Anna that Lydia was forced to push herself back from the bar.

Greg's behavior was starting to irritate Lydia. While she agreed with him, his remarks were a little too pat, a little too glib. He sounded like he was using someone else's words, quoting from *Ms.* magazine or *Redbook*. Then came the epiphany. Greg was making a move. Lydia groaned inwardly. Anna attracted men like a picnic attracts ants. Lydia wasn't sure she had the strength to shepherd Anna through yet another tumultuous romance, especially one with a man who was still married. And Bryan's body wasn't even cold yet, for God sake!

Lydia had to admit that Greg was good looking. With his boyish face, big blue eyes, and soft blond curls, he looked like a grown up version of one of Raphael's cherubs. Although he had to be almost forty, he was sporting a *Nine Inch Nails* T shirt and was wearing his Toronto Blue Jays cap backwards. Soon Anna and Greg were deep in conversation, both leaning in front of Lydia, oblivious to her presence. Lydia excused herself abruptly. Neither of them noticed. Lydia pushed her arms through the straps of her daypack and jogged all the way to Al's house in an effort to work off her annoyance.

After starting a fresh pot of coffee, Lydia perused his book shelves for something diverting and decidedly unromantic. Fifteen minutes later she was so engrossed in a novel called *Love Is a Racket* that she didn't hear Al drive up. It was only when he slammed the front door that she realized he had arrived. She jumped up to help him with the plastic grocery bags he was carrying.

"Given your recent road food diet, I figured you might like something with a few vitamins in it." One by one, he pulled out those white cartons with wire handles that signal Chinese take-out. For the next hour Al and Lydia feasted on garlic eggplant, moo shoo vegetables wrapped in paper thin pancakes, and broccoli and pea pod stir fry.

They cleared the table and loaded the dishwasher together. It was Lydia's first chance to inspect Al's kitchen. It was a cook's paradise. Copper clad sauce pans and cast iron skillets hung in descending order of size from a rack suspended over a large maple butcher block. A magnificent set of knives sat in slits cut into the block. The large gas stove was equipped with a griddle that lay between the burners. There was an abundance of cupboard and counter space. Lydia laughed out loud when she saw Al's spice rack.

"What's so funny?" he asked.

"Your spices," she said. "They're all alphabetized."

"So?"

"Do you alphabetize your canned goods, too?"

"Only the soups," said Al.

"You're not serious."

Al opened a cabinet door and there they were in perfectly straight rows. Bean soup was on the far left, followed by beef and chicken broth, clam chowder, minestrone, mushroom, split pea, and tomato. Lydia looked away from him before she grinned and rolled her eyes.

When the clean-up was complete, Al and Lydia retired to the

living room. With small glasses of plum brandy in hand, they sat on the couch in the living room and listened to Al's collection of Robert Johnson recordings.

As Lydia settled back to the plaintive strains of "Crossroads," she studied her companion. There wasn't anything particularly distinctive about Al. He was attractive enough but not truly handsome. His nose was a little crooked, like it might have been broken when he was a kid. His ears were large and it was clear that he'd be bald someday. He had a small scar on his chin. Al's eyes were his one stunning feature. They were large, expressive, and changed color constantly. When he wore a green shirt, they were emerald; when he wore brown, they were hazel; navy rendered them blue-gray. Despite his compulsive housekeeping habits, Al's clothes were always a little rumpled, a little wrinkled, as if he hadn't removed them from the dryer in time.

Al was watching Lydia as she examined him. "So what's the verdict? Do I pass inspection or not?"

"With flying colors," said Lydia, blushing. "But you know, you've learned a lot about me and I don't know anything about you. Tell me about your life, what your family was like, whether or not you always lived in Haines Junction. That kind of thing."

"Okay," said Al. "I'll make you a deal. If you ask questions, I'll answer them. Just don't make me tell my life story all in one take."

"Deal. Ready?" Al nodded. "Question one. What's your whole name? What's Al short for?"

"Do I really have to answer that?" asked Al, making a sour face.

"That's the deal," replied Lydia sternly.

Al sighed. "Okay. My whole name is Aloysius Steven Cerwinski. Now do you see why I go by Al?"

"Good grief! How did a nice Polish boy come by a name like that?"

"Well," said Al, "I must confess that I'm only three quarters Polish. My paternal grandmother was Italian, and she begged my parents to name me for the patron saint of Catholic youth, the inestimable Aloysius Gonzaga. She thought it would keep me on the straight and narrow. When I was just a wee lad, she'd sit me on her knee and explain how my namesake had lived a clean and austere life, and how he always kept his eyes downcast in the presence of women in order to avoid temptation. And, as I'm sure you've noticed, I always try to follow his example. Grandma's ghost haunts me still."

Lydia laughed. "Okay, next question. How old are you?"

"Forty-eight."

"Do you have any siblings? I know your mom is alive. What about your dad? Where does your family live?"

"Yes, yes, in Whitehorse, Toronto, Watson Lake, and California."

"Aw, come on. You can be more forthcoming than that."

"Okay, okay." He sighed dramatically and downed a healthy slug of plum brandy. "My parents are divorced. My dad lives in Whitehorse, but my mum got tired of the winters and moved to San Diego about five years ago. She's got a brother there. I have two sisters, both younger. One is an emergency room nurse in Toronto and the other is a lawyer in Watson Lake."

"Were you close to your sisters growing up?"

"Yeah, we were close. Still are actually. I'm especially close to the nurse, Louise; we're only two years apart in age." Lydia smiled to herself. That explained a lot. He seemed like a man who had experienced positive relationships with women.

"Have you ever been married?"

"Nope. Came close once but she decided she couldn't handle being married to a Mountie. She was a pediatrician; almost everybody in her family was a doctor of one kind or another. A cop was just a little too blue collar for her, I guess. She was a nice person and she dumped me in the sweetest way possible. I don't hold any grudges. Besides," said Al, smiling wickedly, "the guy she did marry let her put him through the last two years of dental school, then he dumped her for a twenty-year-old hygienist."

"No grudges indeed," said Lydia. "How did you get into police work?"

"Well, actually it was a result of smoking pot."

"What!"

"Indirectly anyway. I was attending the University of Alberta and got caught smoking a joint in my dorm room. They kicked me out of school even though I was in the middle of my senior year. I knocked around awhile and just couldn't find anything I really wanted to do. A buddy of mine was applying to the RCMP Training Academy in Regina and suggested I do it, too. So, I did."

"They took you despite the pot episode?" said Lydia, incredulous.

"I was very lucky," said Al. "This was in the days when colleges dealt with their student problems internally. They never reported me to the police, so there wasn't any record. And I discovered I really liked the police academy. They had a special program for people who were willing to work in small communities and in the bush. That sounded just right to a boy from Haines Junction, so I signed up."

"It must be really hard to do police work in a place where everybody knows everybody. If you thought Frank's killer was local, what would you do?"

"Actually, there are ways in which investigations are very easy up here because there are no secrets. If Frank's killer was from Dawson, we'd probably know his name by now. The northern grapevine is phenomenal. On the other hand, it can be hard on cops. If just one officer lets something slip to a spouse or a drinking buddy, it's all over town in a day. I'm actually a bit worried about that. Reston's got local connections. If he is involved in Frank Johnson's murder, this is bad news. Reston may know that you were Mr. Johnson's good friend; he might even know that you found the body."

"So you really are worried about my safety," said Lydia.

"Just a little. But I think you're okay here. I'm pretty sure that Reston or anyone who's working for him will think twice before he messes with a Mountie."

Lydia found Al's concerns unsettling. She took a deep breath and exhaled hard. "Just be cautious and alert," said Al. "Don't go anywhere with someone you don't know and stay out of Reston's way." He wagged his finger at Lydia and mustered a small smile. "And please, no more B and E."

"I'll try to be good," said Lydia.

"It'll be over soon," said Al. "The Mounties always get their man." He put his arm around her and gave her shoulder a gentle squeeze. Then he laid his arm on the sofa back behind her. Lydia could smell a hint of aftershave, not sweet, not strong, faintly woodsy. She thought about closing the gap between them, about snuggling up in the crook of his arm. But what if his gesture reflected concern rather than sexual attraction? What if he wasn't interested? What if she made a fool of herself?

Finally Al dropped his arm and reached for the stereo remote. "I'm tired of Delta blues. How about some Eric Clapton?"

"Okay," said Lydia. Her shoulders sagged. During the endless guitar solo in *Layla,* she inhaled Al's scent, felt the heat of his body, and pondered opportunities missed.

When Lydia awoke the next morning, it was almost nine o'clock and Al was gone. The note on the dining room table said that he had to conduct a couple of interviews and wouldn't be back until evening. He had, however, left a fresh pot of coffee on the stove.

After downing two cups of something strong with a hint of chicory, Lydia wandered over to Anna's to see if she wanted to join her for breakfast. Anna was up but still in her pajamas and still in a foul mood over Bryan.

"I don't want to do anything. I just want to veg out and indulge my misery," said Anna petulantly. "I'm going to lie on my bed, eat bonbons, and watch soap operas."

Lydia could hear the television blaring in the next room. "Come on," she said. "You need to get out. Bryan isn't worthy of misery."

Anna glared at her. Then she gave a reluctant nod. "You're right. You're absolutely right. Give me a few minutes to get dressed." She trotted off to the bedroom and, over the sound of the television, Lydia could hear the banging of the closet door and the scrape of drawers. She had just settled back into a chair with the newspaper when she heard a screech and then a shout.

"Lydia, get your ass in here. Now!"

Lydia ran into the bedroom. Anna was standing in her underwear and pointing at the television screen. A commentator was sitting at a standard television news desk. Behind her was the standard bank of video monitors. One monitor read *Environmentalism: A Dangerous Business?* while an old black and white photo of Frank Johnson's face filled another screen. With just the right mix of professionalism and sadness in her voice, the anchor was explaining that Frank James Johnson, age seventy-four, had been found murdered on his homestead on June eighteenth. After a description of the murder scene, the commentator continued. "His body was found by a neighbor, Ms. Lydia Falkner, who owns a cabin downriver from Mr. Johnson. She had gone to visit her friend. While there are no suspects in the case, it is believed that the murder is connected to some kind of environmental activity in which Mr. Johnson was engaged. Both Mr. Johnson and Ms. Falkner are environmental activists who have been working together on various issues."

The commentator went on to report the story of a Greenpeace activist who had drowned under mysterious circumstances. When the network broke for commercials, the well coifed reporter was replaced by loud abrasive pitchman waving a cell phone and promising free long-distance with no roaming charges.

Lydia spoke through tight lips. "I don't like this. I don't like this one bit."

Frank's murder had been reported by the local media shortly after the event, but those stories had indicated only that a neighbor had found Mr. Johnson's body and had alerted the authorities. Lydia's name had not been mentioned. She stared blankly at the pitchman, who was now assuring viewers that they would never be frustrated by static or a fading signal.

"That's just ridiculous," said Anna, grabbing a pair of blue jeans off the chair. "You haven't even lived here for the last three years. TV news is so bogus."

"Anyone watching that would think that Frank and I were

working hand-in-glove until the day he died. I hope to God they don't get this show in Inuvik."

"So what are you going to do?" asked Anna as she stepped into her pants.

"I'm not sure," said Lydia. She threw herself on Anna's bed and closed her eyes. She lay silent for awhile and then sat up and frowned. "It's ironic. I wasn't working with Frank before he died, but I just realized that I have been working with him ever since."

Anna smiled. "You just figured that out? I've known that ever since we rifled his files. But let me repeat, what are you going to do now?"

"I don't know, but I'm convinced his murder is somehow connected with caribou."

"Maybe." Anna didn't sound so sure.

Lydia was quiet for a long time. The she smiled. "I've got it! I'm going to Fairbanks."

"Fairbanks! Why?"

"To see that professor, Dr. Rudolph. The caribou expert. Frank was reading her research. Remember? It was important to him for some reason."

Anna frowned. "Yeah, but Frank was pissed off about that cruise ship dock up north, too. Maybe that's the key to this thing."

Lydia nodded. "Yes. Maybe. And maybe there's a connection between the two. I don't have the resources to find out any more about the cruise ship dock, but I can find out everything there is to know about caribou."

"Isn't that a long way to go just to get some information?"

"Hell, I drove all the way to Inuvik for information. And I want the chance to pick Rudolph's brain. That's hard to do long-distance. I'm going back to Al's to find her phone number and make an appointment. Come with me. Then we'll go to breakfast."

"Okay," said Anna. "At least I won't be here when Bryan makes his rounds."

"Hey, what happened with you and that Greg guy, anyway?" asked Lydia.

Anna's eyes lit up. "Oh, we had a really nice talk. He's great. Doesn't share any of Bryan's sexist tendencies. And he's so funny. We're going out tomorrow night."

"That's nice," said Lydia without enthusiasm. She was even less enthusiastic when they ran into Greg on the street. He was dressed in gray sweats, high-top athletic shoes, and wore his Blue Jays cap backwards just as before. He had a basketball tucked under one arm and kept bouncing up and down on his toes.

"What's up?" he said. Then he turned the full force of his charm on Anna. "You look great. Red is definitely your color. What's the word on the boyfriend?"

"He'll be out of the picture by the end of the day," said Anna.

"Cool," said Greg. "That makes *my* day." He gave Anna a big, boyish grin.

Anna touched Greg's arm. "Hey, we're going over to a friend's house, why don't you—." Lydia kicked her in the ankle and shook her head just slightly.

Anna backtracked. "Well, actually we're in kind of a hurry, so maybe we better go alone. I'll see you tomorrow night. About eight?"

Greg nodded and raised an imaginary glass to Anna. "'Here's lookin' at you, kid.'"

"Why didn't you want him to come?" asked Anna when Greg was out of earshot.

"For one thing, it's Al's house not mine and he doesn't know Greg from Adam. And second, I really don't want people knowing about any more of this than they already do. I feel pretty exposed right now."

"You're right, of course. I'm sorry."

"No harm done," said Lydia with more generosity than she felt.

When they were settled in Al's study, Lydia pulled Frank's Porcupine herd file from a drawer in Al's filing cabinet. "If I'm seeking Rudolph's expertise, I should know a little about her before I call." She skimmed the title page and the abstract of the first article. "Not much of a bio here. She's an Associate Professor at the University of Alaska and teaches in the Biology Department. Her specialty is the *population dynamics and behavioral ecology of ungulates.*"

"Ungulates? I thought we were interested in caribou."

"Caribou are ungulates, you idiot," said Lydia, smacking her friend on the head with the file folder. "God, how'd you ever pass the verbal portion of the Graduate Record Exam."

"There weren't any questions about caribou on the GRE," snapped Anna.

Lydia read a little more. "Wow. She's been tracking the Porcupine herd for years. She's got scads of data."

"Call her already," said Anna.

"Okay, okay," said Lydia. "Why don't you go in the other room so I won't be distracted?" Anna made a face but she left the study.

Lydia brought up Professor Rudolph's professional web page on Al's computer and located her office telephone number. Dr. Rudolph answered on the first ring. Very briefly, Lydia told her that she was a fellow academic who needed to find out everything she could about the migration patterns of caribou.

Rudolph was curt. "Yes, I can see you, but it has to be this week."

"I should be able get up there in the next two days," said Lydia.

"That will be fine," said Rudolph. She sounded anxious to get off the phone.

A quick call ascertained that Lydia could catch an Air North flight early the next morning. She confirmed this with the professor and went into the living room to tell Anna about her travel plans.

"Great. Can we please get some breakfast now?" Anna pointed to her watch. It was almost noon.

That evening Lydia told Al about the news story and her decision to go to Fairbanks. His question echoed Anna's. "Why don't you just call this professor?"

"I really don't like phones. I guess I'm a little like Evelyn Avingaq in that regard. I've got the time. What the hell."

"I certainly can't argue with your impeccable logic. But be careful. You can be sure that someone will tell Reston about that TV report." He put his hands firmly on her shoulders and his eyes turned from gray to blue as they gazed into hers. He didn't remove his hands when he said, "By the way, we've had little break in the case. It seems that someone licked the inside of that chip bag to get the last crumbs. We've got ourselves a DNA sample."

"That's fantastic!" cried Lydia. "So now all you have to do is put it in your database and out pops the killer's name, right?"

"Wrong," said Al. "It's unlikely that our guy's DNA is in the system. We need a suspect first. But if we find him, we can place him at the scene and that's a breakthrough."

"Breakthroughs are good," said Lydia.

"Yes, indeed" said Al. Then he looked down at Lydia with a half smile and dropped his hands from her shoulders to her waist. "And speaking of breakthroughs." He planted a gentle kiss on her lips. "I hope you don't mind. I've been wanting to do that for a long time."

"Me, too," said Lydia.

"Really?" said Al.

"Really. Let's try for another breakthrough." She tipped her head up, put her hand on the back of his head, and pulled it toward her. This kiss was hard and went on for a long time. Al's hands ran over Lydia's shoulders and up and down her back, as he pulled her tight against him. When he ran his tongue along her lips, she greeted it with her own tongue.

"Wow," breathed Lydia, gently pushing Al away and looking into his eyes. "Apparently your patron saint is lying down on the job. What happened to austerity and downcast eyes?"

"I always *was* a disappointment to my grandmother," muttered Al as he traced Lydia's nose and chin with his index finger. Then with one hand, he reached behind her and gently unwrapped the rubber band from the end of her braid. With both hands, he carefully unplaited her hair. He threaded his fingers into her mane and gently combed it over her shoulders. "Your hair is so beautiful," he murmured as he stroked it. "Beautiful."

He buried his face in her neck as he pulled her tight again. She could feel every curve of his body as his erection pushed into her belly. "Are you willing to go for the ultimate breakthrough?"

"Yes," said Lydia.

With arms still wrapped around one another, Lydia and Al headed for the bedroom. After they crossed the threshold, Al pushed the door closed with his foot. "My grandmother's ghost is not allowed in here," he whispered.

Lydia awoke very early and, lying with her fingers interlaced behind her head, she watched her sleeping companion. Al was the first man that Lydia had slept with in over three years. Her last relationship had been a long term one and a good one. Sam had been a professor of psychology at the University of Colorado in Boulder. He had shared Lydia's passion for the mountains, her interest in hiking, fishing, and canoeing, even her love of old movies. He was also a very successful academic, which led to his being offered a department chairmanship at Ohio State University. It was a very good job and Sam wanted desperately to accept the offer. Lydia had done her time in the Midwest and wanted just as desperately not to return. With regret, she had refused to accompany Sam to Columbus.

Lydia hadn't been looking for a new relationship. Hadn't even been sure she wanted one. There were so many ways in which being one was easier than being two—no need to consult, no need to coordinate schedules, no need to consider another's emotional needs. She had gotten used to doing what she wanted, when she wanted, how she wanted. But last night had been satisfying in every way. It had been good to feel connected again, to feel another's touch, another's breath in her ear. Al was an attentive lover and Lydia had been surprised at the intensity of her own physical release. She hadn't realized that she had been wanting it, needing it. She felt more relaxed and more content than she had in a long time. It had been a breakthrough in so many ways.

Al snored softly as Lydia got up and dressed. An hour later

she was on the tarmac at the Dawson airport boarding a twelve passenger turbo-prop bound for Fairbanks. She stowed her day pack in the open overhead shelf and settled back into the small seat. A mother and baby were seated directly in front of her and Lydia eyed the infant warily as his mother put him over her shoulder. He was bald, had a single bottom tooth, and the front of his tiny striped T shirt was damp with curdled milk. Lydia liked kids but she disliked flying with them. She was just about to look around for an empty space far from this urchin when he gave her an enormous smile and gurgled at her. Lydia couldn't help smiling back. The baby giggled and Lydia giggled. The baby laughed and Lydia laughed. Lydia was astonished to find herself talking in a high pitched voice, making silly faces, and offering her index finger to the tiny curling fist. Finally the baby dozed off and her demeanor returned to normal.

Lydia enjoyed flying in small planes, where you could actually watch the landscape as it passed beneath the wings. When the turbo-prop banked and turned, she could see a long swath of the Yukon River, its mysterious brown currents boiling to the surface, a giant witch's cauldron. Before the plane had finished its arc, it bisected the Klondike, and Lydia caught a glimpse of the endless rows of gray, dredge tailings along its banks. Then the plane abandoned the two legendary rivers and turned northwest to follow the Top of World Highway as it wound its away over the customs booth and into Alaska and the Yukon Charlie Wilderness Preserve.

This was wilderness in the truest sense of the word. No roads, no railroads, no houses. In the high country, the hills were covered with birch and aspen; at lower elevations black spruce, alders, and cottonwoods prevailed. Everywhere she looked, Lydia could see rivers and creeks, which provided the stitching on this crazy quilt of gray and green. But all too soon signs of civilization reappeared, first a paved road and electric poles, then a few scattered houses, and then a low skyline. The plane began its descent.

It was a perfect summer day in Fairbanks. Lydia was a couple of hours early for her appointment, so she decided to walk to the University. At the Chena River Bridge, she stopped to watch a boisterous group of teenagers messing around in two canoes. In one boat, two bikini clad girls were using their paddles to splash a boy, whose baggy trunks hung dangerously low on his skinny hips. He in turn was standing and rocking the canoe from side to side. Finally the canoe capsized. The trio righted the waterlogged boat, and the young man pushed it ahead him to shore. As he stood up in the shallows near the bank, he heard a chorus of shrieks from his female companions. That's when he looked down and realized that his trunks were around his ankles. He saw Lydia on the sidewalk and gave her a panicked look. He pulled up his trunks, ran up the bank, and disappeared up University Avenue holding his waistband tight in both fists. She grinned all the way to the campus.

CHAPTER 13

Lydia had no trouble locating the Biology Building but finding its denizens was more problematic. Even the secretaries seemed to have taken a holiday. In the far North a glorious summer day was not to be wasted working inside. Lydia finally found a student who could direct her to Professor Rudolph's office.

When Lydia knocked on the door, it was opened by a small, compact woman of about fifty who looked tense and harried. She was dressed in a silk shirt and a severely tailored, linen pantsuit. Her thick, salt-and-pepper hair was cut into a perfect cap. She didn't look like someone who ran with the caribou. "Ah," the woman said. "You must be Lydia Falkner. Excuse the mess, but I'm in the middle of packing." Lydia could see that the room was littered with half-filled boxes.

"Are you moving to a bigger office?" asked Lydia, standing in the doorway and surveying the chaos.

"No," replied Rudolph with bitterness in her voice, "I'm leaving U of A altogether. I've taken a job in the California system. I go at the end of next week." She drew her lips into a thin line and fixed her eyes on Lydia's. "My work isn't appreciated here. I was just turned down for full professor again, and I can't stay in a department that doesn't value my research. I'm sick and tired of being underappreciated."

Uh, oh, thought Lydia.

Rudolph barely stopped for breath. "You wouldn't believe it. Two of my colleagues were promoted last year with far fewer publications than I have. I've been published in some of the best journals in the field, but do they care? Nooo. They probably didn't even read my articles before they voted."

Finally Rudolph realized that Lydia was still standing in the doorway. "Oh, sorry, come on in." Rudolph climbed over stacks of books to sit in the battered office chair behind her desk; she waved Lydia into the student chair facing her.

As Lydia looked around the office, she noted the usual academic paraphernalia. There were shelves lined with books and journals, blue examination booklets were stacked on the floor, and the desk was littered with papers and pens. The four computers were a bit more surprising. Not wishing to unleash another torrent, she didn't ask about them but when Rudolph saw her glance at the networked machines, she pounced.

"Ah, yes, my modeling project. I spend as much time working on computers as I do in the field with the animals. Using data from previous migrations, I project the path of the herd in future years. My projections are very accurate and the state government and various Gwich'in tribes depend heavily on them."

Ah, thought Lydia. That explains it. She doesn't run with the caribou. She sits in front of a computer and crunches numbers.

"Say, would you like me to explain the modeling system to you?" Rudolph asked, smiling for the first time since Lydia had entered. "It's really fascinating. It wouldn't take long."

Lydia demurred. "No, I don't think so. I probably wouldn't understand it."

Rudolph's face fell. "That's too bad," she said. "It really is important work, even if these Neanderthals don't appreciate it."

Rudolph plopped both palms on her desk in a *lets get down to business* gesture. "Okay, what can I do for you?"

"Frankly," said Lydia. "I'm not quite sure. I need to learn everything I can about the Porcupine herd migration patterns in the Northwest Territories and the Yukon, and I gather you're the expert on that."

"Yes, I am," said Rudolph, "despite—." She stopped and shook her head with what appeared to be resignation. Lydia said nothing.

Then Professor Rudolph frowned and leaned forward. "Wait a minute. This is strange. You're the second person from Dawson who's asked me that question in the last few weeks."

Lydia sat bolt upright. "Who was the first?" She held her breath.

"Let me see if I can remember the name. I might have written it down." She paused for minute and shuffled through the papers on her desk. "No, I guess I didn't, but it sounded like an older man on the phone. He had a gruff voice. Fred something, maybe."

"Frank Johnson?" asked Lydia.

"Yes," she said. "That sounds right."

"Frank Johnson is dead," said Lydia. "He's the reason I'm here."

"What do you mean?" said Professor Rudolph with a look of alarm. "Why is he dead? What does it have to do with me? I've never even met the man."

Lydia raised her hand as if to reassure the other woman. "It really doesn't have anything to do with you. Frank Johnson was murdered and my friends and I think his murder is connected with his attempts to stop a tourist concession that somehow involves the Porcupine herd's migration."

Rudolph's eyes narrowed. "Now that you mention it, we spent a long time talking about what does and does not disrupt the migration. He wanted to know exactly what kinds of things would spook the herd."

"What did you tell him?"

"I told him that the herd can tolerate very small disruptions, a few backpackers and couple of bush planes. But a lot of human activity and a lot of noise is a problem. Mr. Johnson—was that his name?—asked me specifically about helicopters. Whether or not the noise of helicopters would be damaging."

Lydia grabbed the front of the desk with both hands. "Helicopters! They can come right in and hover over the herd." She recalled Jesse's words. *Rich tourists don't like to get their feet wet.* "That's the concession. Why in the hell didn't I think of that? Stupid, stupid, stupid!"

Lydia took a moment to compose herself before she asked, "So what did you tell him? About the helicopters, I mean."

"I told him that helicopters could be a disaster. A few intermittent flights wouldn't necessarily be a problem. We occasionally use helicopters in our research, but those flights are carefully scheduled to minimize impact. Bringing in helicopters over an extended period of time and hovering over the herd would do incredible harm. The animals would never be able to tolerate the noise, and if the machines flew low, the rotors would generate a lot of wind and dirt. All of it would disrupt the animals' feeding and traveling. And that's not the worst of it."

"What is?"

"Disrupting the herd in that way could seriously affect the breeding cycle. That would deplete the herd fairly quickly. Do you think this man Johnson was going to make a stink about these helicopter tours?"

Lydia nodded. "I think Frank Johnson was murdered because he found out about it, and somehow the tour company found out that he knew." Lydia reflected a moment. "Frank had a number of articles on the Porcupine herd's activities when it's south of Old Crow. That area was significant to him for some reason."

"The animals come back into that area in the early fall; some come even earlier. God, it would be awful if someone went in there with helicopters. Just awful." Rudolph's face reflected genuine sorrow. Lydia was glad to see that she was capable of looking at a world beyond her failed promotion.

The professor continued. "There's one thing I don't understand. The Gwich'in who live in Old Crow and the surrounding area are subsistence hunters. They depend on the animals for food, clothing, and tools; they even make thread from the sinew. I can't believe that they're not up in arms about this. The depletion of the herd would be a serious threat to their community."

"My guess is that they don't know," said Lydia.

Rudolph frowned. "They can't know or they'd be raising hell. When the oil companies started sniffing around the Arctic National Wildlife Refuge, the Gwich'in here in Alaska went ballistic."

"Once the helicopters start flying over the area, the Gwich'in will know," said Lydia. "Surely, they'll get it stopped then."

"Oh, maybe eventually," said Rudolph, sighing. "But, frankly, they could be tied up in court for years. Native people don't do very well in court against corporations. It's an on-going struggle. The Gwich'in don't have a lot of money to fight things like this. And in the meantime, the herd would suffer tremendous losses."

"What a horrifying prospect," said Lydia. "I assume that what you told me about the Porcupine herd applies to any caribou herd. The Bluenose herd might be involved, too."

Rudolph nodded. "The risks are the same. Fewer people depend on the Bluenose herd and it doesn't migrate far, but the risks to the animals are the same."

Lydia thought about her little ivory knife, which had been left on Al's dresser, far from the clutches of zealous TSA agents. Those scrimshaw antlers were more than mere decoration. This was a story knife after all. She took a deep breath and let it out slowly. "We think the big money for this project is coming from an outfit called Holiday Cruise Lines," she said.

Professor Rudolph's eyes grew large as she smacked the top of her desk hard with the flat of her hand. A pen jumped and rolled to the floor. "Holiday Cruise Lines! Those bastards!"

"You know about them?" said Lydia, pushing herself back into her chair as Rudolph's face went red.

"Know about them? Oh, I know about them. I know them all too well. They've already fouled the waters in Prince William Sound, then they moved into western Alaska, and now they want to bring small tourist ships to the north coast. I've heard they've been trying to buy their way into Barrow. It sounds like they've found another taker." She looked questioningly at Lydia. "But where will they bring the ships in? Most of the northern coast of the Yukon is National Park."

"They're going all the way to Nuvaktuk," said Lydia.

Professor Rudolph yelped. "Those people have no conscience at all. How can they take boatloads of tourists into that fragile little village?" She paused and frowned. "The grounds of the Bluenose herd aren't far from Nuvaktuk."

Lydia told Rudolph what she knew about Curtis Reston and his pier. Then she added, "It looks like the plan is to fly the ship's passengers over the herd in helicopters as part of the tour package. An extra added attraction. I found a letter that suggests that Reston has some members of the Nuvaktuk council in his back pocket."

"This is unbelievable," said Rudolph. She sighed deeply. "And yet it's not. Everything's for sale these days. Does this Reston character have any idea what this will do to Nuvaktuk or to the Gwich'in?"

"From what I've heard about Reston, he doesn't give a damn. All he cares about is making money. Do you have any suggestions as to how I should proceed?"

"I'm not sure I know," replied Rudolph. "I've dealt with Holiday before. I've testified against them in hearings on environmental impact. Holiday is second string as cruise lines go, but it wants to be a major contender in the industry and it plays hard ball. Its owner has a very shady reputation. I heard he was big in solid-waste management before he bought the fleet, and you know how crooked that sector is." Lydia didn't know but kept her counsel.

Rudolph continued. "Watch your step with these people. They're dangerous. A guy who was doing environmental impact studies in Glacier Bay tangled with Holiday Cruise Lines a few years ago. One night his trailer burned down. Arson. It was sheer luck that he wasn't in it at the time. He lost all his records."

Rudolph abruptly pushed her chair away from the desk and stood up. Her impatient, brusque persona returned. "I have to leave now. I need to go home and change my clothes. One of my grad students and I are flying to our caribou research site this afternoon."

Lydia stood, too. "How far away is that?" she asked.

"Not far."

"Is the herd aggregating there?" asked Lydia eagerly.

"Not the Porcupine herd. A smaller group called the Delta

herd. It's been losing an unusual number of calves over the last couple of years, and we're trying to figure out why." Rudolph was shoving books into a briefcase as she talked.

"Can I come with you?" asked Lydia, clasping her hands in front of her chest. "I would give anything to see the caribou." She felt like a kid who was asking to stay up late for the grownups' party.

Rudolph shook her head. "I don't think so. I won't have any time to explain things to you." She had grabbed her purse and was moving toward the door.

"Professor Rudolph, I promise not to ask a single question, and I'll stay out of your way. Please." She pressed her hands together in a gesture of supplication.

"Well," said Rudolph unenthusiastically. "There might be enough room in the plane, but you'll have to sit in the back. It'll be a very tight fit."

"That's fine," said Lydia. "I'll hang from a strut if necessary." She couldn't believe that she was begging. She doubted that this is what Anna had in mind when she urged Lydia to be more assertive.

Rudolph sighed. "Oh, all right. Meet me at the airport's east ramp in an hour and a half. Look for the University's Cessna 180. The pilot's name is Carol. She's one of my doctoral students. I'll let her know you're coming in case you get there before I do."

"Thank you so much," said Lydia, feeling at the same time exhilarated and a little guilty for horning in. "I really appreciate it."

"Okay, okay," said Rudolph impatiently. "I've got to leave." She opened the door and herded Lydia into the hall in front of her.

Lydia was surprised at herself. Making demands was not her style. But somehow she felt an urgent need to see this caribou herd, to experience first hand what Frank had died to protect, to understand what Curtis Reston was going to destroy.

Time was short, so Lydia took a cab back to the airport. To her relief, the driver knew the exact location of the east ramp. Thirty minutes later, a little red and white Cessna taxied up to the door of the tiny waiting room. A tall young woman climbed down from the pilot's seat. Lydia went out to meet her.

"Hi. My name is Lydia Falkner. Professor Rudolph said I could come along to see the caribou."

The other woman nodded and stuck out her hand. "I'm Carol Wood. I'm one of Rudolph's grad students, her pilot, and general gofer." Then she grinned. "You must be some sort of celebrity. Rudolph hates having outsiders at *her* research site." On the word *her*, Carol thrust her head forward and bugged her eyes out. "How did you convince her to let you come?"

"Oh, I begged and pleaded," said Lydia, laughing.

"Well, good. I'm glad you're coming. Maybe we can talk about something besides how much the U of A has screwed her over. It's probably true, but we're all tired of hearing about it."

"Yeah," said Lydia. "She is a bit obsessed."

"A bit?" exclaimed Carol. "Try totally, absolutely, utterly, and completely. Some of her students call her *Rudolph the Red F—*." Carol stopped mid-epithet and whispered, "Red alert. Here she comes."

Lydia turned to see Rudolph striding purposefully across the tarmac. Her linen suit had been replaced by khaki pants sporting a sharp front crease and a crisply ironed khaki shirt. Her broad brimmed canvas hat was clean and white. Only her scuffed hiking boots suggested that this woman had ever been in the bush.

Carol helped Lydia crawl into the small jump seat behind the two front seats. Suspended from the ceiling on cables, it was almost a hammock. Rudolph climbed into the passenger seat and handed her briefcase back to Lydia. "Stow this somewhere," she commanded. Lydia had to resist the temptation to say *Jawohl, mein Fuhrer* as she crammed the case into the small space next to her.

Carol finally climbed aboard, carefully scanned the runway, and yelled, "Clear prop," out the window. Only then did she start the engine. Soon they were taxiing down the runway and then they were aloft.

"Where are we going exactly?" called Lydia to the front of the plane at large.

Rudolph answered. "The site is about fifty miles south of here, about twenty-five miles east of Denali. It won't take long to get there." It didn't. Since Lydia couldn't see the ground from her seat in the bowels of the plane, she was startled when the wheels touched down, jumped, settled, and jumped again. The Cessna finally rolled to a stop. Straining to look out of a window, Lydia could see that they'd landed on huge gravel bar in what looked to be a dry river bed.

Carol killed the engine and she and Rudolph climbed out. Lydia tried to crawl around the passenger seat, but Rudolph had neglected to pull it forward. "Hey," called Lydia. "Hey, I'm still in here." Rudolph was already striding over the tundra toward a small cluster of nylon tents.

Carol came around to the passenger side and lifted the seat latch. "Sorry, but when the prof is on a tear, a nuclear attack wouldn't get her attention." She helped Lydia extricate herself and Rudolph's briefcase.

As Lydia tried to straighten her spine, she looked around in great anticipation. But there wasn't a single animal in sight, no antlers, no clumps of hair, no scat, nothing. "Where are the caribou?" she asked anxiously.

"They're on the other side of that ridge," said Carol. She waved her right hand as she took Rudolph's briefcase from Lydia. "Look, I have to go over to the camp and help Her Highness, but you don't need me. You can see a big piece of the herd from up there, and if you're not skittish, you can actually go down and walk among the animals."

"Really?" asked Lydia, her eyes widening. "It's safe?"

"It's safe," Carol assured her. "It's not rutting season and caribou are fundamentally gentle. Just walk slowly and don't make any abrupt motions. Stay downwind if you can. Be back by five-thirty. Rudolph can't abide tardiness."

"I'll be prompt."

"You better be," said Carol. "Rudolph wouldn't hesitate to leave you here." She grinned at Lydia and trotted off toward the camp.

Lydia checked her watch, turned, and began walking rapidly toward the ridge that Carol had indicated. Distances in the bush are deceiving. What had looked to be less than half a mile followed by a gentle climb was nearly a mile followed by a steep slope. By the time she was half way up the incline, Lydia was sweating and panting and trudging slowly.

But when Lydia reached the rocky crest, she gasped with pleasure. Below her was classic U shaped, glacial valley ringed with jagged white peaks. Patches of snow still clung to the shady sections of the lower slopes. She could see that a wide river braided with gravel bars meandered over the valley floor, but both the river and the tundra were rendered almost invisible by an undulating brown and white mass. Thousands of caribou were moving about in all directions. Most of them were walking slowly, long necks extended, heads down, searching for choice patches of lichen. A forest of antlers bobbed up and down rhythmically as each animal defoliated one patch of ground and moved on to the next. Every now and then, a phantom threat would spook a small group and, with tails raised and white rumps fully exposed, they would sprint a few hundred yards and then lower their heads again, all memory of the precipitating stimulus erased.

This was a mixed herd of bulls, cows, and calves. Most of the animals were eating but some of the largest bulls stood quiet but alert at the edge of the group, turning their heads this way and that, watching for wolves. Their only defensive weapons were sharp hooves and long curved antlers, which, at this time of year, were swathed in varying shades of brown velvet.

In the middle of the herd, countless knock-kneed babies leapt and pranced in the cotton grass and darted among the long legs of their elders. Periodically, a little one would thrust its fuzzy black muzzle between the hind legs of a cow to nurse. Lydia laughed silently as one calf attached himself to a teat and then was gently kicked and butted away when the female realized that somebody else's offspring was trying to score a free lunch.

As Lydia descended, she could hear huffing, snorting, and

splashing. When she reached the valley floor, some of the cows gave her a quick, curious glance and then lowered their heads to graze again. She walked into the herd a few short steps at a time. Slowly, slowly.

When Lydia was completely surrounded by caribou, she stopped and stood absolutely still, her arms at her sides. The animals ignored her. To them she was just another feature of the landscape, a strange, leafless tree perhaps. The caribou moved languidly as they grazed, as if pulling up and chewing the soft orange and yellow lichen was all they could manage. Every few seconds one would shake its head in an attempt to dispel the clouds of buzzing mosquitoes or to dislodge the flies that were trying to crawl up its nostrils.

Inside the herd there was a soft symphony of caribou sounds. The melody was carried by the snorting of the cows and the bleating of the calves. The click of hooves on hard rock kept the beat while the drone of insects produced a simple, hypnotic background theme. An occasional percussive interlude was provided by the hoarse croak of a raven who was exploring the entrails of a dead vole.

So entranced was Lydia by the sounds that it took her a moment to realize that a phalanx of cows was approaching, heads down, mouths working. Their coats were ragged checkerboards of dark brown and white as new hair replaced old. Lydia could see that the tundra was littered with tufts of stiff, white fur.

The animals kept coming, a few steps at a time. Periodically one of them would look up and fix her enormous, liquid brown eyes on Lydia's. A large cow grunted at her and pawed the ground. Lydia's breathing quickened, but she didn't move. When the front line was within six feet of her chest, the animals broke rank and flowed around her in a seamless, fluid motion. Lydia could hear them breathing; she could hear them chewing; she could smell the musky damp of their fur. She could have reached out and stroked the soft white hair on their necks, but she didn't. Time seemed to stop as the group of cows moved around Lydia and merged together again.

The wind began to drop and Lydia became aware that the mosquitoes were now swarming around her own head. Not wanting to alarm the caribou, she stoically refused to wave or swat. But when the insects began to buzz in her ears and crawl around her eyes, she lost control. As she brushed her left hand in front of her face, she caught a glimpse of her watch. "Dammit," she muttered under her breath. She had less than thirty minutes to get back to the plane. She was going to miss Rudolph's deadline. Lydia regretted having to leave these beautiful creatures, and she had to resist the temptation to wave goodbye. As she ascended the ridge, she quickened her pace. Almost en masse the caribou looked up, possibly baffled by the sight of that leafless tree moving swiftly across the tundra.

When Lydia reached the valley floor on the other side, she could see Professor Rudolph walking rapidly toward the Cessna. Carol was trailing behind, struggling with a large box. Lydia tried to run but soon realized that she was going to turn an ankle on a tussock. Walking as fast as she could over the uneven ground, she finally reached the two other women. Rudolph was standing at the passenger door tapping her foot and looking stormy. "You're late," she said through tight lips.

Lydia looked at her watch. "I'm really sorry," she said, "but only seven minutes."

"Late is late," said Rudolph as she removed her hat and hung it on her arm. Lydia nodded and tried to look contrite. Rudolph pursed her lips as she carefully adjusted her starched shirt collar, patted her hair smooth, and checked her boots for dust. As she turned away from Lydia and Carol, she pulled something from her pants pocket. Carol grinned at Lydia, raised her middle finger and pointed it at her professor's back. When Rudolph turned back around, she had something in her hand. She fixed her eyes on her graduate assistant. "Carol, you're a scientist. You've been trained to be an astute observer." She held up a small compact. "It's best to check for mirrors before you flip somebody off." For the first time that day, Lydia heard Geraldine Rudolph laugh out loud.

CHAPTER 14

Lydia was starved by the time her plane landed in Dawson, and she wanted a dinner companion. She knew Al wouldn't be home until late, so she headed for Anna's place. As she knocked on the door, she could hear voices inside. It took a long time for Anna to answer and when she did, she looked flushed and rumpled. Greg Rymer was sitting on the couch and he looked flushed and rumpled, too. His Toronto Blue Jays cap was on the floor and his shoes lay under the coffee table.

"I'm sorry," said Lydia with no hint of apology in her voice. "Did I interrupt something?"

"Yeah," said Anna with a silly grin, "but come in anyway. Do you want a beer?" Lydia nodded.

"So," said Lydia when Anna had left the room, "how's things going with the wife?"

Greg blushed. "Hey, I know what this looks like, but my marriage really is over. I moved out months ago. And, look, I really do like Anna. She's very sweet and a lot of fun."

"Well, I'll give you fun, but I'm not so sure about sweet," said Lydia.

Greg gave her a puzzled look. "Anna's very sweet," he insisted. Lydia grinned at him. He'd find out soon enough.

Anna returned from the kitchen carrying three opened bottles of Moosehead in a triangle between her hands. An unopened package of potato chips hung between her front teeth. She dropped it in Lydia's lap. "A nosh before dinner," Anna explained. "Sour cream and onion—." She stopped in response to Lydia's glare. "Like they serve in any bar." Lydia gave her a grateful smile.

Anna continued. "These are tonight's rules. No serious stuff. Let's laugh, drink, and be merry. Then let's go out and pig out."

As they drank beer and nibbled on chips, Lydia had to admit that Greg was okay. While she found his perpetual boyishness annoying, he *was* funny and had a real gift for mimicry. His Bogart was flawless, and he could also do Homer Simpson, Jay Leno, and Julia Child. He delighted Lydia with his full-body parody of former U.S. president George W. Bush—the thin lips, the cowboy swagger, and the endless malapropisms. "I am considerating peeling the laws that prevent our friends, the oil companies, from drillation in the Alaska Wildman Refugee," said Greg in a nasal Texas twang.

But Greg's entertaining antics did nothing to quiet Lydia's growling stomach. The three agreed they would take a short walk and then go to dinner. A pale sliver of moon hung high in the cloudless blue sky. Below it an enormous orange disk slipped slowly toward the horizon.

It was a busy night downtown, and the line at Dawson Dolly's snaked out the open restaurant door. Lydia, Anna, and Greg secured a spot in the queue which placed them directly across from the poem on the wall across the street. **I wanted the gold and I sought it.** Lydia had probably read that line a hundred times since she had first come to Dawson City. She had always written Robert Service off as a hack, a bad poet who could tell a good yarn. But now this piece of doggerel had taken on new life. For the second time in as many weeks, she considered the implications of those words. The gold rush wasn't a century old; it was happening now, again, maybe still. But no longer did impoverished miners ply picks and shovels to eke out a few ounces of ore. These days treasure meant oil, natural gas, salmon, timber, and tourism. The tools of the new Stampeders were far more effective and dangerous. They had in their service banks, multi-national corporations, courts, and even governments.

Greg pointed to the poem. "'I know what gold does to men's souls,'" he said softly. Lydia stared at him. It was as if he had read her mind.

"What are you talking about?" said Anna. "The gold rush has been over for over a hundred years."

"Walter Huston says that line in *The Treasure of the Sierra Madre*," Greg explained.

"Yes," said Lydia through tight lips, "I remember."

"Oh," said Anna.

The trio finally got a table.

During dinner, Greg mentioned that he had seen the account of Frank's murder on television. "I assume he's the old friend you told me about in the bar. How come you didn't tell me he'd been murdered? Finding the body like that must have really freaked you out."

"It did, but I really wasn't interested in talking about it, especially with strangers," explained Lydia.

"Do you have any idea why he was murdered? Was it because of his environmental activities, like they said?"

"I don't know. I hadn't seen Frank in three years. I was just going to visit an old and dear friend." Greg seemed satisfied and the conversation drifted on to other topics.

After dinner Anna and Greg set out to find a bar with music. Lydia returned to Al's place. She found him unloading the dishwasher.

"I hope your trip was productive," he said.

"Yes, indeed," said Lydia. "I have interesting news."

"I have news, too, but I'm afraid it doesn't amount to much. You go first. How about some Chianti while we swap information?" She nodded her assent and hoisted herself onto a tall stool at the counter as Al wiped down every square inch of the butcher block and then did it again.

"Enough cleaning," said Lydia. "You promised wine."

"So I did." Al threw his sponge in the sink and poured Chianti into two sturdy goblets. "So, what did you find out in Fairbanks?"

Lydia took a sip and launched into her tale. When she got to the part about the disrupted breeding and the Gwich'in's dependence on caribou, Al stared at her. "You mean to tell me that those people would jeopardize a caribou herd and an entire First Nation tribe just to make a few extra tourist dollars? Do you think they really understand the implications of all this?"

"Yes, I do," said Lydia. "Greed has eaten away their souls."

"But why kill Frank Johnson over it?" said Al. "Those tours might endanger the caribou, but I'll bet they're not illegal."

Lydia shrugged. "None of this makes any sense."

"On another note," said Al, "would you like to know who leaked the Falkner-Johnson environmental connection to the media?"

Lydia frowned at him. "Who?"

"Your old friend, Louie West."

"West! But why would he assume I was working with Frank?"

"Because of Frank's hat," said Al.

"What hat? What are you talking about?"

"It was a cap with a *Tree Hugger* logo. Inside it Johnson had written *from Lydia* in permanent magic marker. On the basis of that sterling piece of evidence, West leaped to the conclusion that you were an environmental activist, too."

Lydia banged her fist on the counter. "That goddam West is stupider than broccoli. He never even asked me if I worked with Frank. He's a lazy, unprofessional idiot." Al snatched Lydia's wine glass as she began to gesticulate wildly. "I could just kill him."

"Now, now," said Al, grinning and shaking his finger at her. "Killing a Mountie. Yikes! I couldn't bear the thought of visiting you once a month at the Edmonton Institution for Women. You wouldn't like the food and I hear the coffee's really lousy. But don't worry. Louie will be disciplined. The Assistant Superintendent is outraged."

"Okay. A public flogging then," said Lydia. "Downtown. In January. Naked."

"I'll see if I can arrange it," said Al.

Then he leaned over the counter and took Lydia's hand. His face grew serious. "I have some other news, too. We're sure we found the place that sold the green Mohawk canoe you saw on the river."

"My God, why didn't you tell me this right away," cried Lydia. "This is huge!"

"Not really," said Al. "It's not clear that it will get us anywhere."

"You don't think it'll lead us to the killer?"

"So far, it's not looking good. The outfitter is in Watson Lake. The canoeist bought the boat instead of renting one. He paid cash, American money. The clerk doesn't remember much about him, although she thinks he had brown hair and knows he had a beard. He was fairly young, late twenties or early thirties. She did remember that he was very excited about finding a Mohawk. It was used, a trade-in. She has a bill of sale on file with a name and address but unfortunately, they're both false."

"How do you know?" asked Lydia.

"The guy used the name Orlando Bosch with an address in Mosquito Bay, Florida. When we couldn't find Mosquito Bay on Google, Carmichael called someone he knew in the Miami Dade police department and asked them to check it out. The detective on the other end of the line laughed his ass off. Said the Mohawk guy was jerking our chain."

"How so?"

"The detective said Orlando Bosch was famous in Miami. Infamous, actually. He was a Cuban exile who was accused of blowing up a Cuban airliner in the seventies. No one ever went to jail for it though. Bosch was a member of some sort of fringe, paramilitary organization, but he's dead now. And there's no such place as Mosquito Bay."

"Cute," Lydia said grimly. Then her face brightened. "But it does reinforce the Miami connection."

"Yes, it does," said Al. "We're also hoping that the use of Bosch's name is significant, that maybe this guy is in some sort of paramilitary group, too. An organization like that might be a good place to recruit a killer. The Miami Dade police are going to pursue it. But since we don't have a real name or a good description, it's a long shot. I'm sorry my news isn't better."

"You'll find Mr. L. L. Bean." Lydia gave Al a small, tight smile and then raised her goblet in a toast. "Remember, the Mounties always get their man."

Al poured himself another glass of Chianti, but he didn't return the gesture. "We may not get our man, Lydia. And without the killer, we've got nothing linking Reston or Evangelist to Frank Johnson's death."

"I know," said Lydia, "and I hate it. Justice is too hard in coming."

"Yes," said Al, "it is." He stood and pulled Lydia off her stool. "Let's cease and desist. No more talk about greed or murder. I haven't even read today's paper."

"Me neither," said Lydia. Hand in hand they strolled into the living room and collapsed on the couch in unison. Al handed her the front section of the *Yukon News*. After reading about a mine closing and a rogue grizzly with a taste for cat food, Lydia's eye was drawn to a small picture of an old Inuit man. The photo was captioned *Still Missing*. Her eyes narrowed as she scanned the news story.

"Hey, Al, listen to this." She jabbed her finger at the paper and read aloud. "*Jacob Tingmiak of Nuvaktuk is still missing after disappearing over a month ago. There is no hope that Mr. Tingmiak is still alive and the search has been suspended. On June 8 Gerald Tingmiak reported the disappearance of his father, age eighty-five. According to his son, Mr. Tingmiak sometimes went hunting and fishing alone, despite his advanced age. Since his boat, rifle, and harpoon were also missing, authorities have concluded that Mr. Tingmiak had a marine accident. Mr. Tingmiak was a prominent Nuvaktuk elder.* Al, this guy was a prominent elder. Maybe he was a member of the council. Maybe he opposed the pier. Maybe Reston is responsible for his disappearance."

Al reached for the paper and examined the article for himself. "That seems like a stretch, but I'll have somebody check it out and talk to his son."

"It's not a stretch," said Lydia. "I saw Reston in action. He's a pig."

Al sighed. "Being a pig is not proof of murder."

Lydia threw the paper on the floor. "Proof is vastly overrated," she said. "I'm going to bed."

As she rose, Al picked up the newspaper and reassembled it. Then he smoothed out all the creases, folded it in half, and laid it in the middle of the coffee table. Lydia barely suppressed an urge to sweep the paper to the floor again and crumple every sheet with her feet.

Lydia awoke with her teeth clenched and a pain in her head. Three aspirin and two cups of strong coffee didn't remedy the situation. By lunch time she felt at the same time edgy and exhausted. She tried to nap in the afternoon but instead lay rigid on the couch, eyes wide open. When Al got home, he found her, remote in hand, cycling manically through sixty television channels. This pattern repeated itself the next day and the day after that.

Lydia was baffled by her own mental state. Her relationship with Al was going well. She was getting enough exercise, and it was too soon for menopause. Maybe she needed to cut down on coffee. Maybe her subconscious was anxious about her dwindling bank account. Maybe she needed to ramp up her job search.

Since colleges posted faculty positions on the Internet, it was easy to find out how many jobs were out there. Very few. Her only likely prospects were the state university in Grand Forks North Dakota, Western Nebraska Community College in Scottsbluff, and a Baptist college in Dallas. Lydia wasn't enthusiastic about Grand Forks, was even less enthusiastic about Baptists and Texas, and had never heard of Scottsbluff. But she was running out of options. So on a gloomy Tuesday afternoon, she pulled a thumb-drive out of her daypack and inserted it into a USB port on Al's computer. In a few minutes her standard application letter and curriculum vitae were in cyberspace, on their way to three departments of English, none of which she wished to join.

Lydia stared blankly at the monitor for a long time. Then she pushed herself away from the desk, jumped up, and headed for the front door. She jerked it open, slammed it shut, and began walking very fast. At first she moved aimlessly, up one street, down another, with no particular goal in mind. But after half an hour, she found herself on the floating dock of the Dawson pier. She sat at the edge with her legs dangling over the rushing brown water. The wind was strong and the river was in turmoil. The current seemed to be running in three directions simultaneously, and giant whirlpools appeared and disappeared at random. Lydia imagined a river bottom dotted with drains supervised by peripatetic river gods, who would periodically pull out one plug, then jam it back in the hole, pull out another and jam it back in, and then pull out another.

A water logged cottonwood trunk hit one of the moored boats with a sharp crack. It made an awkward, lumbering, horizontal arc and headed downstream again, riding the crest of a wave and disappearing into its trough. Lydia thought about the incredible journey this log would make as it floated past Eagle, past Fort Yukon, past Ruby and Galena, maybe even past Holy Cross and Russian Mission. She fixed her gaze on the current in front of her and followed it downstream until her eyeballs would turn no more in their sockets. Then she turned her eyes upstream and did it again—over and over and over.

This river, this magnificent 2,000 mile ribbon of water, was the reason she had come back to the North. She had come back to live on the Yukon's banks and, like the cottonwood log, to ride its currents. She had come back to fish its waters and hike along its banks. She had come back to confront her father's death and her own loneliness. She had come back to decide whether or not to sell the cabin and give up her refuge, her sanctuary. But all of her reasons for coming had been pushed aside with Frank's murder and its aftermath. Lydia now realized that his murder made it more important than ever that she come to terms with all this. She needed to live alone on the river; she had to know just how much she wanted that cabin; she had to accept the fact that her father would never share her life again and neither would Frank. Lydia liked Al a great deal; she could easily imagine loving him. But that didn't change the fact that she had to go back to her cabin and honor her commitments to herself. She couldn't live Al's life; she needed to live her own. She stood up, stretched, and smiled. For the first time in days, she felt normal.

That evening, before Al had even passed the threshold of his front door, Lydia greeted him with a serious face and a pronouncement. "I'm going home."

Al gave her a look that reflected both puzzlement and disappointment. "To Colorado?"

"No, no. Just back to the cabin." She put her hand on Al's arm. "Al, as much as I enjoy being with you, I can't hang around here forever. Who knows when you'll find Frank's killer. There are so many things to do before I can even think about selling my place. I have to get started. And," she paused and took his face in her hands, "I came to the Yukon to be at the cabin, to see how it feels to be there without Dad, to find a piece of myself that I lost three years ago. I have to go back." She dropped her arms but her eyes locked on his.

Al rubbed one of his temples and sighed. "I was expecting this. I can't really blame you for wanting to go home." He dropped his briefcase and put both hands on her shoulders. "But I am sorry to see you go." He took a deep breath and let it out slowly. "And I can't pretend it doesn't worry me, you being up there with a killer still on the loose. You do have to promise me that you'll be extremely careful."

"I'll be careful. I promise not to move three feet without the shotgun."

"I'll have the patrol boat stop at your place regularly, just to check on you."

"That would be great," said Lydia and she meant it.

Neither of them had moved from the doorway during this exchange. Al put both arms around Lydia and pulled her close. "I have to say that it's been so nice to come home every night, knowing you'd be here. I've got used to that." He rested his chin on the top of her head.

"Me, too." Lydia's voice was muffled by the folds of Al's shirt. She pushed away slightly and looked up at him. "I really do care about you. This was a hard decision to make and I'll miss you a lot, but it's something I have to do. I promise that I'll come back to Dawson regularly and you could come up on your days off."

"Oh, I will, I will," said Al fervently. Then he smiled and looked down at her. "How's the fishing up there anyway?"

Al reclaimed his briefcase and led Lydia inside by the hand. He closed the door with his foot and said, "I guess we should make the most of our last few nights in civilization together."

"I guess we should," said Lydia. "Do you have champagne and bubble bath?"

"No, but how about Boone's Farm Apple wine and a hot shower instead? I'll get the wine."

Lydia addressed his retreating back. "As I recall from my college days, apple wine is always accompanied by Hostess Twinkies." She heard mock retching from the kitchen. When Al returned with two stemmed glasses filled with wine the color of garnets, Lydia knew that she had been spared Boone's Farm.

The next day Al and Lydia drove south to go canoeing. It was an exquisite day, seventy-five degrees, sunny, and just enough wind to keep the bugs down. Al had promised Lydia that he was taking her to a pretty, secluded spot where a river gradually widened into a vast wetlands filled with ducks, raptors, and even coots, a bird rarely seen in the Yukon.

They parked in a small gravel lot just off the road and unloaded their supplies. Al loosened the straps and ropes and they lifted the canoe off the SUV. Flipping it right side up, they lowered it into shallow water and loaded it. While Al held a line, Lydia rolled up her pants, pushed the bow into the current, and stepped over the side. When she was seated, Al shoved the boat forward and got into the stern on the fly. Lydia executed a cross bow sweep and the canoe turned smoothly into the downstream current. It was at this point that the river spread out and the canoe floated lazily toward a maze of narrow channels and small islands.

Lydia and Al were both experienced canoeists and, although they had never paddled together before, they had no difficulty matching their strokes. Al counteracted the tendency of the canoe to steer toward Lydia's bow side by inscribing a fluid J on every second stroke. At each sharp turn in the river, he reached out and drew a perfect C in the water, a classic stern sweep. Lydia provided the power as she leaned forward, thrust her paddle into the water just behind the bow, and pulled back. She also watched for submerged logs and rocks and when she spied an obstacle, she yelled "pry" as she planted her paddle parallel to the gunwale and pulled the canoe toward it. The boat slipped smoothly sideways.

There is something sensual about paddling a canoe when everything is working right. A canoe is a sensitive craft. It responds dramatically to the slightest movement of its occupants, the distribution of the load, the wind, and the waves. When two people paddle together, they are playing a duet. A miss-timed stroke or a sudden shift of weight and the whole thing becomes discordant, but when everything is synchronized, it's the *Moonlight Sonata*. Simultaneously, a paddle on each side of the canoe cuts the water; simultaneously, two paddlers lift and feather their paddles, carrying them forward just a few inches above the water; simultaneously, the two paddlers reach forward and thrust their paddles into the river once more. Thrust, pull, feather, thrust, pull, feather. The rhythm is hypnotic. As the canoe cut smoothly and silently through the riffles made by the wind, Lydia felt that she could do this forever.

After about five minutes on the river, all signs of civilization disappeared. The only persistent sound was the rustling of alder leaves and the hissing of the tall dried grass as the stalks moved against each other in the breeze. Even the ospreys were silent as they sat motionless in the highest branches of the dead cottonwoods and waited for an unsuspecting grayling to dally in a pool or a spawning salmon to leap in a fit of sexual irritation.

Every now and then the canoe startled a flock of coots, and the rotund little birds would emit loud, raucous squawks, flap their wings, and run across the surface of the water on their chicken feet. They'd settle again about thirty feet in front of the canoe and when the bow approached, the whole scenario would be reenacted. The small flock of blue winged teals floating in the shallows seemed to disdain the company of the noisy, flighty coots. Periodically a teal would upend itself, driving its bill toward the bottom as its tail feathers waggled in the air. Lydia chuckled as one duck butt after another presented itself to the approaching canoe. "That sure is an undignified way to get lunch," she said over her shoulder.

"Speaking of lunch," said Al, "let's eat. I'm faint from hunger."

Lydia snorted. "Yeah, I don't know how you expected to get through the morning on three eggs, six pieces of bacon, and two pieces of toast."

"Hey," said Al, "no fair keeping score."

They steered the canoe to a large island. Al secured the boat while Lydia hunted for a suitable picnic area. She found a dry spot bisected by a large downed tree trunk, the perfect back rest. She motioned to Al, who grabbed the cooler and the thermos. Together they spread out a small tarp. Sitting cross-legged on the plastic, Lydia unpacked the goodies. As usual, Al had produced a feast. There were corned beef sandwiches on rye bread, cartons of potato salad and coleslaw, and four kosher dill pickle spears. Two amber bottles of Bass Ale lay in the melting ice at the bottom.

Twenty minutes later, all that remained was two plastic bags, two empty cartons, and two empty beer bottles. Lydia and Al sat side by side, lounging against the big gray log. Al picked up Lydia's left hand and kissed the palm. "You know," he said, "there's no one around. We're alone in paradise."

"Uh huh," responded Lydia with a slight smile.

"We could do it here," he said.

"Do what?" asked Lydia.

"It," said Al.

"*It* has no antecedent," said Lydia primly.

"God spare me from English teachers." Al grabbed Lydia and

pulled her down on the tarp. They wrestled for a minute and then Al propped himself on one elbow and began to unbutton her shirt with the other hand. After each button he lightly kissed the exposed skin working from the hollow of her neck, to her shoulders, to the tops of her breasts.

"Is this *it*?" asked Lydia.

"Not yet," said Al.

He reached down and unzipped her jeans. There was urgency in his movements as he sat up and grabbed the waistband of her Levis pulling them over her thighs and down to her knees. She could feel him tugging at the denim when suddenly he stopped and put his mouth to her ear. "Shoes," he whispered. She opened her eyes and looked at him quizzically. "I can't get your pants off. You have to take off your shoes."

Using her toes, Lydia flipped off her sandals without loosening the toggles. Al on the other hand was forced to sit up and untie and unlace in order to remove his shoes from his size fourteen feet. Then he stripped off his own blue jeans and threw them over the log. Lydia grinned when she saw that he was wearing his favorite boxers. They were covered with fish, but these fanciful creatures had never been studied by any ichthyologist except Dr. Seuss. Some were red with blue polka dots, others bore purple and yellow stripes, a few sported a red and black checkerboard, and one was Scotch plaid. The fish were heading in all directions simultaneously and one particularly psychedelic specimen appeared to be swimming into the fly.

Before he could take off his shorts, Lydia grabbed Al and pulled him to the ground. "I love necking in my underwear," she said as she ground herself against him. "It's like high school."

"God," said Al as he slipped one hand under her bra and brushed her nipple. "I hope not. I never got laid in high school."

He locked his mouth on hers and their tongues met and circled. Al slipped one hand into her panties and began stroking. Lydia's breath grew ragged. As she arched her back to meet his fingers, she reached past the psychedelic fish and into the fly of Al's boxers.

He groaned softly and pressed himself into her hand. He groaned again and then pulled back.

"Wait a minute," he mumbled. He got up on one elbow and frantically removed his underwear and helped her remove hers. As he lowered himself again, Lydia spread her legs, raised her knees, and guided him into her with one hand. When he reached full penetration, he lay still for a moment and then began a slow and rhythmic motion. "This is it," whispered Al into her ear. "This is most definitely *it*." Lydia was too far into the moment to respond.

Just as Lydia was ready to climax, she heard an annoying buzzing in her ear. She waved her hand and the noise faded, but it resumed in treble on the other side of her head. It was then that Al seemed to lose concentration. She could feel his lower body tighten and flinch. He supported himself on one forearm and slapped at his backside with the other hand. He tried to maintain his strokes but his rhythm had been broken.

"Goddam," he muttered as he abruptly moved one hand to his butt and then the other, pressing his entire weight into her. "I'm sorry," he whispered as he withdrew. He rolled off Lydia and immediately began to clutch his backside.

"What's wrong?" said Lydia. "What happened?"

Al began rubbing frantically. "The goddam black flies found me. They're eating me alive. Talk about lousy timing."

"Let me see," said Lydia. She rolled Al rolled over on his stomach and inspected his butt; it was dotted with small, bloody bumps.

"Oh yeah," she said. "You definitely have fly bites. We need to get some cortisone cream on these. I don't suppose you brought a first aid kit."

"There's one in the car," said Al morosely. He rolled over again and sat up. He looked like a little boy who'd lost his bicycle. "I'm so sorry. I feel so stupid. We were so close."

At that moment the flies found Lydia. "Get away!" she yelled as she swatted her neck, then her shoulders, then her lower back. "Let's get dressed before we're hamburger."

There was very little breeze now and the black flies had been joined by a squadron of mosquitoes. Virtually every inch of exposed skin was being attacked. As they scrambled into their clothes, Lydia looked over at Al and grinned. "Hey, I'll bet this happened to the cave men and women all the time."

Al chuckled. "Yeah, maybe that's why the Neanderthals died out. Vermin during intercourse."

"Hey," said Lydia, "the anticipation will only heighten the experience."

"Promise?" said Al.

Lydia interrupted the zipping of her jeans to give him a lingering kiss. "I promise."

When they got to the car, Al extracted a small first aid kit from the glove compartment. Since the parking lot was bordered by trees and brush, the Explorer was completely invisible from the road. Lydia had Al drop his pants and lean over the hood of the car. She had just begun applying the cortisone cream when a pickup truck full of teenagers roared into the tiny gravel lot and pulled up right next to them. Al grabbed for his pants, but it was too late. The kids were hooting and hollering before the truck had come to a stop.

"Hey, man," called one kid, "that was one fine moon shot."

Another one yelled at Lydia. "Hey, baby, would you do that for me?"

A third said, "I'd rather see her bum than his."

"Time to get out of here," said Al softly. "I don't want to get into a thing with a bunch of punks, especially when I'm the one guilty of indecent exposure."

The kids laughed as Lydia and Al scurried into the Explorer and peeled out of the parking lot. Lydia grinned.

"What are you smiling about?" asked Al.

"I was just thinking how much fun it is to catch a guy with his pants down."

"Screw you," said Al sweetly.

"Later," said Lydia. "Later."

CHAPTER 15

On the day Lydia was to return to her cabin, she awoke very early in the morning. Slipping quietly out of bed, she grabbed her clothes and left the bedroom, closing the door softly behind her. She dressed in the gray light coming in through the living room window. When she sat on the couch to put on her hiking boots, she looked around with a sense of regret. She liked this house. It was attractive, cozy, and comfortable. The well appointed kitchen was a joy to work in. It was nice to be able to walk to the grocery store, to peruse books in the public library, to stroll into a bar and have a drink with a friend. Above all, seeing Al everyday and sleeping with him every night was a special gift. There was a piece of her that couldn't believe that she was leaving all this. But she knew she had to go.

By the time Al arose, she had set the table, brewed a pot of coffee, and poured two tall glasses of orange juice. As she bent over to open the oven door, he walked into the kitchen and sniffed the air appreciatively. "I smell a peace offering," he said as Lydia removed a platter of *huevos rancheros* swimming in green chili.

She carried the plate to the table and directed him into a chair. "I wasn't aware that the peace had been breached," she said.

"Only my peace of mind," he countered, but his smile was relaxed and Lydia knew he had come to terms with her leaving.

Two hours later Al drove Lydia and her duffle bag to the pier to meet Anna, who had agreed to ferry her up to the cabin. Their first stop, however, would be Frank's homestead. After returning to Inuvik with Buck, Jesse had called Lydia and asked her to pick up his treasured Jack London books and a set of wood planes that had been made by his grandfather. Anna had promised to send them up to Jesse.

Lydia was surprised to see Greg standing next to Anna on the pier. Anna introduced him to Al and then said, "Greg wants to come along, if it's okay. He's never been on the river. And that way I'll have someone to ride back with tomorrow." This explained why Greg was wearing his Toronto Blue Jays cap bill-forward and was carrying a tube of sun screen.

"Yeah," said Lydia half-heartedly. "Greg can come." She wasn't in the mood for Greg, but Anna deserved to have company on the return trip.

Al kissed Lydia and headed down the pier. Lydia was throwing her pack and duffle bag into the boat when she noticed a waterproof gun case under the middle seat. "Hey, I hope that's your gun, Greg, and not Anna's." Anna rolled her eyes.

"It is," replied Greg, smiling proudly. "It's my new Marlin forty-five-seventy. Anna said that your gun was still at your cabin, and I don't think it's safe to be in the bush without one. Would you like to see it? It's a work of art."

"Sure."

Greg kneeled, extracted the gun case, and pulled out a lever-action carbine. The wood was a dark, deeply grained walnut. The stock and forestock were checkered with hundreds of tiny triangles, some of which had been included in an even larger triangle, almost a Navaho motif. The breech and the barrel were a deep matte black. The gun was equipped with iron sights but no scope.

Greg handed Lydia the rifle. "Be careful. It's loaded but there's nothing in the chamber."

"Wow. This really *is* beautiful," she said, caressing the stock. She checked to see that the chamber was indeed empty and that the safety was on. Then she raised the gun to her shoulder and sighted in a sea gull perched in a tree across the river. There was a loud shriek from a woman standing at the other end of the dock. Lydia jumped and almost dropped the Marlin. "Jesus! Put this away before I scare somebody to death." Greg gently placed the gun in its case.

They all piled into the boat and Anna headed upstream. Greg was an eager tourist. He was fascinated by the boiling currents; he waxed poetic about the cliffs; he was fascinated by the fragile cutbanks hanging out over the rushing water. Lydia concluded that having him along was okay after all. She had grown weary of these journeys, but Greg's enthusiasm made it all fresh again. While Anna steered from the stern, Lydia pointed out interesting landmarks to Greg, explained the histories of the ruins they passed, and described some of the old homesteaders she and her dad had known.

At noon they hauled the boat onto the flats of an island in preparation for a lunch break. As they waded through the mud toward the island's center, Lydia realized that the place looked familiar. Then she saw the bleached log on which she had spread out her lunch on her first trip upstream. Before she could think, she had blurted out, "My God, Anna, this where I saw the guy in the Mohawk!"

"No kidding! That's too weird for words." Lydia could see Anna shudder slightly as she glanced around.

Greg frowned. "You saw a guy in a Mohawk out on this island?"

"Yeah," said Lydia. "A green Mohawk. Actually, he was on the river."

"What was he? Some sort of punk rocker or something?"

"Not a Mohawk haircut, you idiot," said Anna. "A Mohawk canoe."

"Oh," said Greg, grinning. "So what's the big deal? I assume a lot of people canoe this river."

Lydia answered before Anna could elaborate, "Oh, it was interesting just because Mohawk canoes aren't common up here." Greg nodded and turned his attention to his tuna fish sandwich.

Two hours later Anna steered the boat toward Frank's sandy boat ramp, killed the engine, and lifted it up. With a satisfying crunch the bow slid up the bank. Lydia jumped out and held the bow rope while the others clambered over the gunwale; then she pulled the boat further onto dry land and tied the rope to an alder. They made their way up the bank through the horsetails and cotton grass toward the cabin. Greg stopped when he saw the gazebo. "Man, what a cool place. Lydia, you need to put a hammock and a wet bar in there. It would be the perfect retreat."

"This isn't my place, Greg," said Lydia. "It's Frank's. We passed my place twenty miles ago. Didn't Anna tell you that we were coming up here to pick up some books and tools for Frank's son Jesse?"

"Frank? That old guy who was murdered? That Frank?" Lydia nodded. Greg gave Lydia a long look. "Man, that's heavy. Doesn't it bother you to come back here?"

"Not really," said Lydia. "I've been back a couple of times. It spooked me the first time, but it doesn't now."

Greg seemed fascinated by the fact this was a genuine murder scene. He couldn't stop talking about it. "This is spooky. I feel like I'm in one of those TV mystery shows. So do you guys have any idea who killed the old guy? I know there aren't very many people out here, but you'd think somebody would have seen *something*."

"Lydia did see something," said Anna. "The guy in the Mohawk." Lydia glared at her but it was too late.

Greg's eyes narrowed. "The guy Lydia saw from the island?" He turned to Lydia. "You saw the actual murderer? Do you know who he was?"

"No, and neither do the Mounties. And we don't know for sure that he *is* the murderer."

She pushed open Frank's front door and led Anna and Greg over the threshold. Greg squinted into the gloom. "Man, what a mess. That guy needed a wife."

So much for Greg's feminism, thought Lydia as she lit the Coleman lantern.

"Where did you find the body?" asked Greg.

Lydia was irritated by his voyeurism but pointed toward the back door. "Out in back, in a trash pile."

Greg opened the door and stepped outside. He reentered a few minutes later. He was scowling. "I looked all over the place, but I couldn't find a trash pile."

"The Mounties hauled it all away," said Lydia.

Greg's scowl deepened. "You could've mentioned that fact." Lydia didn't reply. Greg shrugged. "Oh, well. Where are those books we're supposed to get?"

"We're not sure," said Lydia. She waved her arms around the room. "Somewhere on these shelves."

"Damn," said Greg. "There's thousands of books here. It'll take forever."

"Nah," said Lydia. "This is a leather bound set of four. You shouldn't have any trouble spotting it."

"Me?"

"Yeah, you. You're the tallest. Besides, Anna and I have to look for some things out in Frank's shop."

Greg wrinkled his nose as he looked around the room. "I'll never find anything in here."

"Sure you will," said Lydia. She went to the kitchen and retrieved Frank's step stool. "Here you go," she said. "Four books, green leather, should say Jack London on the spine. You better get started. It might take awhile."

Lydia was enjoying ordering Greg around and he knew it. He glowered at her. "Man," he said, "you sound just like my wife."

Anna glowered at Greg. "And you sound just like the late, unlamented Bryan." She opened the front door and stalked out. Lydia followed her.

"Hmmm. Do I detect trouble in paradise?" asked Lydia as they approached the workshop.

"Oh, he gets to me sometimes," said Anna. She opened the shop door and Lydia followed her into the building.

"I was deliberately pushing his buttons, you know," said Lydia.

"I know," said Anna. "But he makes it so easy. Frankly, I'm not sure he's any more mature than Bryan. I sure know how to pick 'em." She shook her head ruefully. Then she grinned. "But, hey,

I'm not in this for the long haul. It'll be a good time while it lasts."

"Words to live by," said Lydia. She cast her eyes around the shop and spotted the six antique wood planes sitting on a shelf, neatly arranged by blade width. "I'll find something to carry those in," she said. As she rummaged through a small collection of empty cardboard boxes stacked in one corner, Lydia's eyes fell on a piece of plastic PVC pipe propped next to them. She stood silently and stared at it.

"What's the matter?" asked Anna, peering at her intently.

"See that length of plastic pipe?"

"Yeah. I see it."

"Frank was carrying plastic pipe and some hacksaw blades the last time I saw him. I'll bet this is a piece of that pipe. It looks new." Lydia paused and peered at the pipe more closely. "And look, it's capped at both ends."

"So what?"

"Why would Frank cap an empty piece of PVC. I'll bet there's something in there."

A knot formed in Lydia's stomach as she walked over and grabbed the pipe with both hands. When she picked it up, she heard a dull thud inside. She looked at Anna and exhaled. She laid the pipe on Frank's workbench and began to pull at one of the caps. "It won't come off." She opened a tool box and found a claw hammer. After a couple of hard pries, the cap popped loose. Lydia put one hand inside the pipe and pulled out a piece of crumpled newspaper. She inserted her hand again and frowned.

"For God sake, what is it?" asked Anna.

"I'm not sure," said Lydia as she pulled gently on the contents of the pipe. Slowly a cylinder wrapped loosely in more newspaper emerged. Lydia pulled the paper away and laid the cylinder on the workbench. It was white, about eight inches long, and tapered toward a blunt point at one end.

"What in the hell is *that*?" asked Anna.

"Oh, my God," said Lydia, her eyes wide, "it's a tusk. It's a walrus tusk. It can't be anything else."

Lydia picked up the tusk in one hand and ran the other over its surface. It was rough, pitted, and covered with long, thin cracks. Part of the tusk was pale yellow and the small ridges that ran along its length ranged from deep gold to tan. Lydia had always assumed that a walrus tusk would be pure white and smooth—like ivory.

"I wonder why Frank had a walrus tusk," said Anna, as her finger joined Lydia's in tracing the cracks and ridges, "and why would he hide it?"

"I have no idea," said Lydia, laying the tusk gently on the bench.

"Is there anything else in there?"

Lydia picked up the tube and peered into it. "Yeah, there's a piece of paper."

She found a thin piece of welding rod and put a hook in one end. She stuck it down the pipe and managed to snag the paper and extract it. The sheet was badly crumpled. When Lydia finally ironed it flat with her hands, she could see that it was a business letter badly typed on crisp, new bond. She read for a few seconds and then reached out and steadied herself on the bench, her face drained of all color.

"What's wrong?" asked Anna. "What's wrong!"

"*We* were wrong. We've been wrong all along. Frank wasn't killed because of caribou or cruise ships or loan sharking. He was killed because of ivory." Lydia picked up the tusk and pointed it at the door just as Greg was about to step over the threshold. "This is our smoking gun,"

Greg was looking straight at Lydia when she pulled an imaginary trigger and said, "Bang!" He failed to negotiate the step and fell into the room. He was able to catch the doorframe with one hand, but the books he was carrying in the other arm went flying. One of the volumes slid under the workbench and a second fell upside down on the floor, badly creasing a page.

"Jeez, Greg," said Anna. "Watch what you're doing. Those are beautiful, old books."

Greg pulled himself upright but made no move to retrieve the Jack London collection. His eyes were locked on the tusk. He walked over to the bench and touched the tip. "This is a walrus tusk, isn't it? Did it belong to that old guy?"

"Not exactly," said Lydia.

"Where did it come from then?"

"Yeah," said Anna. "Where *did* it come from?"

Lydia laid the tusk on the workbench. "Oh, it came from him but it wasn't exactly his. This is piece of smuggled ivory."

Greg scowled. "What do you mean it's smuggled? How could you possibly know that? It looks like any walrus tusk. Maybe somebody gave it to the old guy."

"The old guy was Frank Johnson, Greg," said Lydia sharply. "Try using his name."

"Sorry."

"But Greg's got a good question, Lydia. How *do* we know it's smuggled ivory?"

Lydia picked up the badly crumpled piece of bond. "This is a letter that Frank wrote to the Director of the Canadian Wildlife Service in Ottawa. It's dated June fifteenth." She closed her eyes a moment. When she opened them, she said, "That's two days after I saw him in the cafe and two days before he was killed. He says that Holiday Cruise Lines and Aurora Tours are smuggling new walrus ivory out of Alaska into Canada. He lists some dates. He says that he has a witness who is willing to testify and he gives a name and a phone number. He says this is a piece of the smuggled ivory. This, my friends is a motive for murder."

"So you think the ivory smugglers are the same people that killed the old g—, uh, Frank Johnson," said Greg as his eyes moved to the tusk again.

"Oh, I know they are," said Lydia. Greg responded with a grunt as he dropped to one knee and began collecting the Jack London books from the floor.

Anna picked up the crumpled sheet and perused it. "Frank says these people were smuggling new ivory. What you think that means?" Lydia told her what she had learned from the artist in Inuvik.

"So this is big business," said Anna, who was now helping Greg brush dust off the books.

Lydia nodded. Then her hand went to her belt and she pulled the knife Frank had made her from its sheath. She held it up. "Frank told me this knife would speak to me but I was only listening for one story, not two. I heard the story about the caribou, but the ivory story went right over my head." She collapsed on a stool and began to shout at the ceiling. "Damn you, Frank. Damn you. Why couldn't you just tell me? Why did everything have to be a scavenger hunt or a riddle?"

Anna walked over and put her arms around Lydia. "But we did it. We not only have the smoking gun, we have Curtis Reston by the balls."

Lydia looked up at her. "Yes, we do. And I would like to cut them off with my own little ivory knife." She stood up and shook it threateningly. Greg backed away.

Lydia ran her finger over the tusk again. Then she began to grin. "Oh, my God," she said. "This is Rosemary's baby."

"What are you talking about?" asked Greg.

"Anna, remember that empty file folder we found in Frank's cabinet? I just remembered that the Latin name for walrus is something *rosmarus*. This is a small tusk. A baby rosmarus. I'll bet Frank had this letter in that file folder before he packed up the tusk."

"You actually know the Latin word for walrus?" said Greg. He sounded annoyed.

Anna shook her head and sighed. "You have no idea how hard it is to be best friends with a know-it-all."

"Hey, give me a break," said Lydia. "That artist in Inuvik gave me a pamphlet on walrus and ivory. It mentioned the Latin name. I just remembered the *rosmarus* part."

"So I guess Frank didn't have time to mail the tusk before he was killed," said Anna.

Lydia nodded and then gave a low groan. "When I saw Frank in the cafe before he died, he was tense. I've always assumed that it was because he was mad about my selling the cabin. But he had just bought that pipe. That must mean he already had the tusk. He was upset about the cabin, sure, but he must have been far more upset about the ivory and nervous about what he was going to do."

"If only he'd told you then," said Anna.

"Yeah," said Lydia. "If I'd forced him to talk to me, maybe he'd be alive today." She lowered her head, then snapped it up again. "Damn it. I'm sounding like Jesse." She hopped off the stool. "Look, we've got to get this back to Dawson. Right now."

They returned to the cabin, where Anna refilled her canteen and Greg put the Jack London books in the waterproof bag Lydia had brought for that purpose. Lydia wrapped Frank's letter in plastic and buttoned into her shirt pocket. Then she waved Anna and Greg out the front door, turned off the lantern, and followed them down the bank to the boat.

They had been barreling down the river at full throttle for about an hour when Greg said, "I need to stop. I've gotta go."

"Why didn't you do that at Frank's place for God's sake?" asked Lydia. "You knew we were in a hurry."

"Sorry," said Greg. "I didn't realize it was going to be a problem then." He turned to Anna and pleaded. "Just land at the next island. I'll be quick."

"Come on, Greg, just go off the side of the boat," said Anna.

"That's not what I have to do," he mumbled.

"Shit," said Anna as she turned the tiller handle sharply.

"Exactly," said Greg.

Anna steered the boat toward a large island that was heavily wooded at the center. She found a narrow channel and was able to nose the bow onto the mud flats without picking up the engine.

"I'm going to take the rifle," said Greg, glancing around. "This looks like prime bear territory. You guys might as well pee while we're here. That way we won't have to stop again." He stood up.

"Not a bad idea," said Lydia. "I don't want to stop twice."

"I don't have to pee," said Anna. "I'm staying here."

"You'll have to pee in half an hour," said Greg. "Come on." He sounded like he was talking to a six-year-old.

"Schmuck," muttered Anna, but she stood up and made her way to the bow end, where the water was shallowest. She lowered herself over the side. Lydia and Greg followed her, the rifle clutched in Greg's hand. The water came up to Lydia's shins. When the three reached land, the mud was ankle deep and Lydia could hear a familiar sucking sound every time she raised a foot. Finally the elevation rose a few inches and the terrain grew drier. As they walked, they scanned the area for bear prints.

It was clear that this was a popular camping spot for canoeists and boaters. Lydia saw evidence of old camp fires—charred logs, partially disassembled rings, large rocks cracked from heat. She found an abandoned spoon sitting on a stump and stuck it in her pocket. There were less savory signs of human use as well. A snarl of monofilament line was caught in a bush, its red and white treble lure hanging at knee level. A cheap plastic lighter and a small pile of spent wooden matches indicated that someone had struggled to light a fire or a stove.

When the trio reached the middle of the island, they separated. Greg headed for a patch of alders on the left and Lydia and Anna walked toward a stand of small birch trees. As they passed a big wad of half-buried toilet paper, Lydia paused to glance at it, frowned, and said to Anna, "That's odd."

"What is?"

"Greg didn't ask if you have any toilet paper on the boat."

"Maybe he's planning on using leaves or something," said Anna.

"Maybe, but wouldn't you have asked for toilet paper?"

Anna nodded vigorously. "Absolutely. I've never wiped my ass with leaves. Never have, never will."

"Well, I hope he's careful," said Lydia, smiling broadly. "It would be a shame if he used poison hemlock or cow parsnip by accident."

"Yeah," said Anna, grinning back, "then he really would be a flaming asshole."

Lydia stepped behind a tree, dropped her pants and crouched, steadying herself with a low hanging branch. Anna crossed her arms and remained standing. "I don't have to pee and I'm not going to."

"Suit yourself," said Lydia, who was now using her free hand to swat at the horde of mosquitoes zeroing in on her bare butt.

Since backwoods etiquette requires that one be allowed to urinate in a modicum of privacy, Anna stood at the margin of the grove and faced the center of the island. "Hey, I thought Greg had to go really bad. But he's just pacing back and forth over there. He hasn't gone into the woods at all."

Lydia peered through the trees. Anna was right. Greg seemed to be wandering aimlessly over the sand. He clutched his rifle in his right hand, then his left, then his right again. Each time he lifted it a bit, as if measuring its heft. Then he stood still, grabbed the Marlin in both hands, and held it waist high. He bowed his head for a moment. When he raised it, he fixed his eyes on Anna and began walking toward her. His gait was stiff and his steps erratic, as if he were being propelled against his will.

"Hey, Greg, Lydia's not done yet. Give us a couple of minutes," yelled Anna, cupping her mouth with her hands. Greg kept coming.

Greg was about fifty yards away now and had raised the rifle to his shoulder. He was peering at Anna through the sights. Anna yelled at him again. "Stop it, Greg. This isn't funny!" But Greg didn't lower the gun. Instead Lydia heard the unmistakable sound of a bullet being racked.

"Jesus," she said softly, scrambling to get her pants back up. She hissed at Anna. "Move! Stay behind the trees but keep moving!" Lydia was still buttoning her pants as she began to dart from tree to tree. Anna followed. Lydia's heart was pounding so hard she could hear it in her ears. She couldn't catch her breath and she felt a chill crawl down her back.

There was an explosion and a small tree directly behind Anna splintered into kindling. Anna screamed and her knees buckled. Lydia grabbed her elbow, pulled her upright, and said in a harsh whisper, "We've got to run for the boat. If you get there first, start the engine. Stay in the trees until the very last minute. Don't run in a straight line. Go!"

Anna ran. Lydia ran, too, but in a different direction, hoping to distract Greg. It was hard going; the ground was very soft and it was littered with tangles of brush and downed logs. In the meantime, Greg had lowered the gun to see what damage his bullet had done. It took him a moment to realize that his targets were fleeing. Anna had been the 400 meter champ at her high school and she was still very fast. She ran in a short, random, zigzag pattern. Greg saw her first and took off after her. Periodically, he would stop running and put the rifle to his shoulder, but Anna's path was so erratic, he couldn't keep her in his sights.

Soon it was clear to Lydia that he wouldn't catch Anna before she reached the boat. It was also clear to Greg. As Anna broke into the open, he slowed to a walk. When she reached up to pull herself over the gunwale, Greg began to raise the rifle. Lydia stopped dead and screamed, "No!" at the top of her lungs. Just then Greg's right foot sank into the mud and he went in up to his knee. The sudden cessation of forward motion threw him off balance so abruptly that he toppled sideways, driving the barrel of the Marlin into the muck. His Toronto Blue Jays cap spun off his head and landed upside down in a puddle. As Greg struggled to free his weapon, Lydia sprinted past him for the boat. She could hear Anna's frantic attempts to start the engine.

But then Lydia, too, went down into the mud, first one foot and then the other. She cried out in frustration as she felt herself go. She fell backwards into a pile of brush, not ten yards from where Greg lay. Her entire torso was ensnared by gnarled and twisted branches. The sharp end of a broken limb was sticking into her right shoulder blade, a bundle of small sticks was poking her in the neck, and the handle of the spoon in her pocket was digging into her thigh. She struggled to get up but with every movement, she sank deeper into the pile. Panic seized her; she began to thrash aimlessly around in the brush. It finally occurred to her that she had to free her feet before she could do anything else. She reached down and grabbed her left knee with both hands. As she tried to pull her foot out of the mud, she looked to the side and saw Greg yank the carbine free. She could actually hear the *foop* as the suction broke.

Greg's foot was still pinned. He got up on one knee, put the gun to his shoulder, and turned to her. She could see him clearly at this distance, the sky blue of his eyes, his boyish round face, his pretty blond hair. This can't be happening, she thought. Cherubs don't kill people.

Greg racked a bullet. Lydia tried to scream, but she could only emit a raspy croak. Her hands remained locked around her leg. She looked straight at the carbine and in her mind's eye it was transformed into a gun in a Yosemite Sam cartoon—its bore a gaping hole and its barrel absurdly long, tapering back and back and back like an image in a fish-eye lens. She could see a strand of mud hanging from the muzzle. At ten yards Greg couldn't possibly miss. She was going to die and she was astonished that all she felt was a great hollowness in her chest, a touch of nausea, and that damn spoon poking her in the leg.

As Greg squinted through the rear sight, Lydia closed her eyes tightly, screwed up her face, and held her breath. Time seemed to stop. A mosquito was buzzing in her ear and Emily Dickinson's famous line, *I heard a fly buzz when I died*, flitted across her consciousness. Then she heard a loud and at the same time strangely muffled *kaboom* and a blood curdling scream. The scream wasn't hers. She opened her eyes, raised her head, and looked in Greg's direction. Greg was still on the ground but now he was lying flat on his back and was thrashing around; his bare arms were bloody and he was yelling something she couldn't understand.

Lydia closed her eyes again and tried to breath. Her heart was pounding wildly. She was shaking violently. She was afraid she was going to throw up. She couldn't move and she couldn't think. Then she became aware that Anna was kneeling over her, grabbing her shoulders, and screaming into her ear. "Are you okay? Are you hurt? Answer me."

Lydia shook her head, trying hard to focus. She took a couple of deep breaths and the nausea began to subside. "I'm okay," she gasped. She gulped more air. She held Anna's hand until the shaking stopped. "What just happened?"

"I don't know. I thought Greg was going to kill you and then he was on the ground, screaming."

Anna helped Lydia extricate her legs from the mud. She got up slowly, hanging onto Anna for support. Her head was swimming. When the dizziness finally passed, she fixed her eyes on the figure writhing on the ground. "It looks like his gun blew up. I think he's really hurt."

"Good," said Anna. "I wish he were dead. Why in God's name was he shooting at us?"

Lydia took a deep breath and exhaled slowly. "I think it has something to do with ivory," she said, her voice flat. "Let's go see what happened."

Anna nodded and the two women walked slowly toward the fallen man. Greg was alternately moaning and crying. Now Lydia could make out his words. "Help me, help me. I think my hands are gone."

Greg's body was rigid, and his hands and arms were covered with mud and blood. The right side of his face was a deep red. The Marlin lay about five feet away, its sleek, black barrel peeled back like a banana. It was clear that the barrel had become obstructed when Greg's fall had jammed it into the mud. When he had fired his weapon, the bullet was unable to pass through the mix of mud and gravel and it had burst the barrel. Both Greg's hands and his left forearm were full of small metal shards and the heat of the explosion had burned his face.

"I need a doctor," Greg whispered.

"Shut up, you coward," said Anna through clenched teeth. She turned to Lydia. "So what are we going to do with my ex-boyfriend and attempted murderer?"

"We're going to take him back to Dawson. The Mounties will be very interested in him." Greg moaned.

Lydia tapped him on the hip with the toe of her boot. "So,

Greg," she said, "to quote Sam Spade, 'You're not exactly the person you pretend to be,' are you?" Greg didn't respond.

"I'll bet he's not hearing so well at the moment," said Lydia. She squatted next to his head and said loudly, "You work for Curtis Reston, don't you?" He nodded ever so slightly. "Were you the one who murdered Frank? Were we wrong about the guy in the Mohawk canoe?"

"No, no, it wasn't me. It wasn't." His voice was shrill.

"Who did it?" yelled Anna.

Greg spoke slowly through clenched teeth. "I don't know."

"I don't believe you," hissed Anna.

"I really don't know," Greg repeated. He looked at Lydia, his eyes pleading. "You have to believe me. I didn't even know the old guy had been killed until I heard about it on the radio."

"But Curtis Reston had him killed, didn't he?" said Lydia.

"I don't know. He never talked to me about it." A flash of anger passed over Greg's face. "There was a lot Curtis didn't tell me. I was just hired help." Greg went silent. He seemed to be considering his words. When he finally spoke again, his voice was strained. Lydia had to lean forward to hear him. "I'm sure Curtis was involved in that murder somehow. He had to be. He was completely obsessed with the old guy. He wouldn't do the dirty work, but he was involved." Lydia turned and looked up at Anna. Anna nodded and gave her a small, tight smile.

Lydia turned back to Greg. "So I'll bet Reston sent you to Dawson to keep an eye on us."

"Just you," said Greg. "But when I met Anna, I realized that she could get me close to you."

Anna took a sharp breath and her eyes grew large. "You worthless piece of shit," she screamed. She kicked Greg hard in the ribs. Lydia could hear the thud as Anna's boat-shoe met bone and muscle. Greg whimpered and tried to roll.

Lydia stood up and pulled Anna away. She waited until Greg had stopped groaning before she crouched again. "See, Greg," she whispered into his left ear. "Anna's not so sweet after all."

Greg turned his face away. Lydia grabbed his chin and turned it back. "I'm not done. Why did Reston want to keep an eye on me? You started hanging around before that TV special linked me to Frank. Why was I a threat then?"

Greg grimaced and then continued. "Curtis met some guy who's a Dawson Mountie. He told Curtis about how you found the body, how you had worked with the old guy and everything. Curtis thought you could be a problem." He moaned again and then said softly, "He was right."

Lydia looked at Anna. "Louis West!" She spat out the name. Then she turned to Greg again. "Why did you come up here with us?"

"I really did want to see the river. That's the only reason I came."

"Bullshit," yelled Anna. "You planned all along to kill us."

Greg shook his head. The motion obviously caused him pain. "No, no. I didn't. It wasn't until you read that letter that I had to."

"Had to! Had to!" Anna's voice was trembling with rage. She raised her foot.

"Anna," said Lydia, grabbing her friend's arm, "we need to get going. Would you go get the duct tape out of the utility kit? And see if you can find a couple of clean bandanas in my duffle bag. We have to get our boy ready for the trip back to Dawson." Anna nodded, took a deep breath, and began quick stepping over the mud toward the boat.

Lydia squatted down next to Greg again. "Just between the two of us, why *did* you have to kill us? Why was Frank's information worth a double murder?"

Tears came to Greg's eyes. His chest began to heave. His voice was hoarse. "I had to stop you because I knew Curtis would kill *me* if the Mounties got their hands on that stuff. He'd hold me responsible and he'd kill me."

"Why would he hold you responsible?" asked Lydia.

Greg emitted a sound between a dry laugh and a sob. "Curtis always knows everything. He'd find out that the evidence came from you, and he'd find out that I was with you when you discovered it.

He'd find out I didn't do anything to stop you. And then—."

"But did you really think you could get away with killing us?"

Greg touched Lydia's hand lightly with bleeding fingers. He spoke in a whisper. "I don't know. I was so scared. Oh, God, I don't know. I don't know." Greg closed his eyes, turned his head away from her, and began to cry.

When Anna returned, she had a large silver roll in one hand and two bright red bandanas in the other. Lydia pulled her little ivory knife out of the sheath. She cut and ripped the bandanas into strips and gently wrapped the strips around the worst of Greg's wounds. It was clearly a painful operation.

"Put your wrists together, Greg."

"No," he whimpered. "It hurts."

"Do it," said Anna. She raised her foot over Greg's testicles. Greg did it.

Lydia took a three foot length of duct tape and wrapped it around his wrists four times. "Okay, let's help him up."

They each hooked an elbow under one of Greg's arms and pulled. His leg remained mired up to the knee. Lydia reached down with both hands and grabbed Greg's thigh. After two sharp yanks, the muck gave up its hold on his leg but kept his shoe. The two women raised Greg's torso again, this time hauling him to his knees. Greg groaned. Then they yanked him to his feet. Greg groaned again. With Anna holding one arm and Lydia the other, they walked him to the skiff. His teeth were clenched and his breath was rapid and shallow during the entire operation.

After much lifting, pushing and pulling, they got Greg into the bow seat facing backwards. Lydia taped his ankles together. "I hope you're not prone to motion sickness," she said.

Greg simply closed his eyes and let his chin sink to his chest. His taped wrists hung between his thighs. Anna climbed into the stern.

"Wait a minute," said Lydia as Anna pressed the starter. Lydia jumped out of the boat, slogged through the water, and made her way gingerly over the mud toward the Marlin. She picked the gun up in one hand. "Evidence," she called out to Anna, holding the curled barrel aloft. She also retrieved the Blue Jays cap.

Before Lydia headed back to the boat, she took a minute to look around the island. There was nothing left to hint at what had just transpired. Birch leaves rustled in the warm soft breeze; little rivulets of water meandered over the sand; a couple of sea gulls screamed overhead, and a flock of tiny sandpipers bobbed up and down on the shore. She shook her head hard as if trying to exorcize the images of the last—what had it been anyway—twenty minutes, an hour, an eternity?

She returned to the boat and climbed in. She jammed Greg's soggy cap on his head and thrust the Marlin in his face. "'My, my, my!'" she said in a deep nasal voice, "'such a lot of guns around town and so few brains.'" In her own voice she added, "Humphrey Bogart, *The Big Sleep*, 1946."

CHAPTER 16

First time tourists in the far North can't get enough of the midnight sun, so it wasn't surprising that there was group of people milling around the Dawson pier at 11:30 PM. None of them paid much attention to the boat that had landed at the end of the dock. A few of the guys glanced with some appreciation at the attractive, curly-headed woman who jumped up on the pier and secured the stern line, but they quickly returned their attention to their companions. But when the woman who had remained in the boat took the bow passenger by the arm and pulled him to his feet, one of the tourists did a double take. "Hey, that guy's tied up and he's all bloody," he said. "What in the hell's going on?"

Soon all eyes were on Lydia and Greg. Lydia grabbed Greg by the elbow and helped him hook his upper arms over the bobbing pier. Anna grabbed him under the arms while Lydia lifted his torso. They carefully rolled him onto the dock where he lay silent, his eyes closed. The red bandanas were weeping blood again, staining his pants and shirt. The group of tourists, mouths agape, walked slowly and apprehensively toward the bizarre spectacle.

Lydia addressed the group. "This guy just tried to shoot us." There was a collective gasp. One woman covered her mouth and backed away. "I need to call the Mounties. Does anyone have a phone." In an instant five cell phones were thrust in her direction. Lydia chose one with a conventional keypad, punched in Al's work number, and spoke briefly to the constable at the main desk. As she returned the phone, she said to all assembled, "They'll send someone right over."

"Is Al coming?" asked Anna.

Lydia shook her head. "He's not there."

The tourists began to pepper Lydia and Anna with questions. Lydia shook her head and waved them off. She was not the least bit interested in discussing the recent events with retired orthodontists and vacationing school teachers. But no one made a move to leave. Instead, the group stood gazing in near silence at Greg, who kept his eyes tightly shut and his teeth clenched.

Ten minutes later, two Mounties trotted onto the dock and pushed their way through the little crowd. She recognized the older one as the cop she had talked to after Frank's murder, the one with the Mont Blanc pen. He smiled with recognition. The other was a stranger, blond, buff, exuding machismo.

"What's going on here?" the blond asked. He squatted next to Greg. "A woman said something about attempted murder. Is this the perp?" He stuck his index finger into Greg's chest. Lydia explained the situation as briefly as she could.

"So this is connected to Frank Johnson," said the blond. "That's West's case. We should call him." He looked up at Lydia. There was suspicion in his eyes.

"No," said Lydia emphatically. "Do not call West. He's a screw-up. Call Cerwinski. He knows a lot more about it than West does."

The two cops looked at each other. The blond narrowed his eyes and started to speak, but the other Mountie interrupted him. "She's right about West and we both know it. Besides, West's down in Alberta. I'm calling Al." He walked away from the crowd, removed a radio from his belt, and spoke into it. He returned and said, "We should wait. Al will be here shortly."

Greg groaned and opened his eyes. "Hospital. Take me to hospital."

The Mont Blanc Mountie looked down at Greg and snorted. "We'll get you to hospital soon enough, buddy. But I'd say you need a lawyer a lot more than you need a doctor." Greg whimpered and closed his eyes again.

Less than five minutes later, Lydia heard the roar of a motorcycle going much too fast down Front Street. She watched as Al turned sharply into the gravel parking lot, braking so hard he almost dropped the BMW. He cursed out loud as his left toe fumbled to locate the sidestand. He hurled himself off the bike and ran for the dock. He was dressed in shorts, sandals, and his *Fish Worship: Is It Wrong?* T-shirt. He was even more rumpled than usual, his mouth was set in a grim line, and his face bore a look of near panic.

When Al reached Lydia and Anna, he put an arm around each of them and pulled them close. "I can't believe I let you go off with a killer. How could I have been so stupid?"

He exhaled and looked down at Greg. His look of disgust turned into a grin when he saw the duct tape. "You two are damn resourceful." He turned to the other two Mounties. "Let's cut the tape on his legs and take him over to the detachment." He pulled a jackknife out of his pocket, opened the blade, and made a slashing motion between Greg's ankles. With a groan of relief Greg spread his legs apart.

The blond Mountie reached down, put his hands under Greg's armpits, and pulled him upright. "Let's go, asshole," he said as he grabbed Greg by the upper arm. The Mount Blanc cop took Greg's other arm and picked up the Marlin with his free hand. They walked Greg down the dock so rapidly that his shoeless foot barely touched the planks. The excitement over, the tourists drifted away.

Al shook his head and closed his eyes for a moment. "I just can't believe this happened," he said softly. "I didn't give a second thought to that guy. I knew he was Anna's boyfriend; it never occurred to me that he might be involved in any of this."

Anna grimaced. "Imagine how I feel. He seemed like a nice enough guy. He's got an estranged wife, a couple of kids, a regular job. He seemed so normal." She put her face in her hands and said in voice full of self-recrimination, "I slept with him, for God sake."

Lydia put her arm around Anna's shoulder and gave it a squeeze. "None of us had any idea. Besides, nothing terrible happened. We're both okay, Greg's in custody, and we know why Frank was killed."

"What do you mean?" asked Al. Lydia knelt down and reached into the boat. When Al saw the piece of PVC pipe, he frowned. "What's that?"

"This is your smoking gun," said Lydia, handing him the tube. "A veritable cannon."

"That's just a piece of plastic pipe."

"No," said Lydia, "it's not. But we shouldn't open it here. Let's take it to the station. This is what we've been looking for all this time. We just didn't know it."

Al gave Lydia a broad grin. "And Louie West is out of town again. He's going to miss the whole thing."

"Don't mention that name to me," said Lydia, growling. "He's screwed up yet again."

The look of surprise on Al's face couldn't have been more gratifying. "What did he do?"

"It'll be part of my official statement," said Lydia primly as she strolled down the dock, carrying the bag of books.

Al gave Anna a look of exasperation. She grinned, took the plastic tube from Al, and put it in the box with the antique planes. "No way am I entrusting this to a motorcycle luggage rack," she said as she picked up the box. "We'll walk. You ride."

Three and a half hours later, Lydia, Anna, and Al collapsed in Al's living room, each clutching a cold bottle of Extra Special Bitter. Despite the fact that the sun was rising, no one was ready for sleep. Lydia and Anna had each given a tape recorded statement and Greg had been taken to Dawson's small nursing station. While his wounds were in no way life-threatening, the extraction of the metal pieces had been a painful operation, and he had been heavily dosed with painkillers. The Mounties had asked a few preliminary questions but were waiting until morning to get a full statement from him.

Anna was still in the throes of self-recrimination. "What I don't understand," she said for the fourth time, "is how I could have been so wrong about him. Sure, he was immature, but I never imagined anything like this. And he was so damn cute."

Lydia said, "I guess cute guys are just as likely to be scum as the Peter Lorre types. Greg got on my nerves, but I never would have pegged him for a criminal."

"I wonder how Rymer thought he was going to get away with this," said Al. "He knew that I saw you guys go upriver with him. How in the hell did he expect to dispose of two bodies and a boat? It's insane."

"Greg told me he was sure Reston would kill him if he allowed the cops to get hold of that letter. He probably wasn't thinking at all."

"And he wasn't the brightest bulb in the package on a good day," said Anna.

Al turned to her. "Did Rymer know that I'm a Mountie?"

Anna shook her head. "No. It never came up."

Finally the adrenalin wore off and exhaustion set in. Anna couldn't face the short walk to her apartment and took the guest bed in the study. Al and Lydia retired to the bedroom. Al fell asleep immediately, but Lydia kept replaying the day's events in her head. Every time she closed her eyes she saw Greg's soft blond curls inscribing a halo above a sleek black barrel; she watched one blue eye focus on a rear sight; she held her breath as an index finger crooked and moved toward a trigger. When Al got up to answer the doorbell at 10:00 AM, Lydia was too tired to drag herself out of bed.

It was almost noon before Lydia managed to shower and dress. When she opened the bedroom door, she could hear two men talking. One of the voices was Al's, but she couldn't identify the other one. She crept quietly up the hall. Someone she had never seen before was sitting at the dining room table with Al. He was a distinguished looking man of about sixty and he was wearing a RCMP uniform. Lydia was hoping to slip into the kitchen for a cup of coffee before she had to be civil to a stranger, but Al waylaid her as she darted past. He introduced the officer as Assistant Superintendent Walter Carmichael from Whitehorse. Carmichael had just finished questioning Greg and had come to debrief Al, who was in charge of the Dawson detachment given West's absence.

After the introduction, Carmichael pushed his coffee mug to the middle of the table and rose. "I really have to get back to the nursing station. We're hoping the doctor will release Rymer early this afternoon so we can take him to Whitehorse." Al saw the Assistant Superintendent to the door and then turned to Lydia. His eyes were dancing and he gave her a triumphant grin.

"What?" said Lydia. "What!"

"Sergeant Louis West has just put the last nail in his coffin. Seems that he did share his boneheaded theories about how you and Frank had worked together with Curtis Reston. I suspect that my esteemed colleague will be spending the next ten years patrolling the Canol Road."

Lydia grinned back and then her face grew serious. "Do you think Greg killed Frank?"

"No, I don't," said Al. "He claims that he was at a construction site in Inuvik with six other guys during the period in question. We'll check it out, of course, but I still think that our killer is the guy in the canoe. I believe Rymer when he says he didn't know anything about the murder."

"Did Greg tell the Mounties that Reston sent him down here to keep an eye on me?"

Al nodded. "That was a result of Reston's conversation with West. But the whole thing was serendipitous, for Reston anyway."

"What do you mean?"

"Your first encounter with Rymer on the Dempster Highway was a complete accident. He really was on his way back to Inuvik with building supplies. But Reston had already told him about this woman who was supposedly working with Frank Johnson and Rymer recognized your name. But since you told Rymer you were going to Eagle Plains to see a friend, it never occurred to him that your trip had anything to do with Frank Johnson. When Rymer got to Inuvik, he told Reston about meeting you. Reston instructed Rymer to come back to Dawson immediately and engineer another meeting. Rymer did. He bought you a beer and hit on Anna and the rest is history."

"Most expensive beer I ever drank," said Lydia grimly. "So what else did Carmichael tell you? I won't tell a soul."

"Actually," said Al, "you already know most of it. Let me get the coffee and I'll tell you what there is to tell. Sit." Lydia sat. Al went into the kitchen, grabbed the insulated carafe and two large mugs, and placed them on the pass through. He came back around and poured each of them a cup of steaming coffee. Then he inserted a CD into the player and turned the volume low. Lydia smiled when she realized it was Dave Van Ronk singing *The Teddy Bears' Picnic*.

Al sat down directly across from Lydia and leaned forward on his forearms. "Carmichael didn't get quite as much from Rymer as he thought he would."

"You mean he wouldn't talk?" asked Lydia, her heart sinking.

"Oh, no. He talked. He talked endlessly. He just doesn't know as much as we'd hoped."

"But he knew about the ivory smuggling," said Lydia with exasperation. "He admitted as much to me. And what about that witness Frank mentioned in his letter?"

"Let me explain," said Al. "I'll start with the witness. According to Rymer, Tillie Nesbitt is a clerk who works for Aurora Tours. She's an older woman, widowed, who has been at Aurora maybe three or four years. One of the constables has been trying to find her."

"She's missing?" asked Lydia, her eyes narrowing.

"We don't know. One of the constables called Aurora Tours and asked for her. The secretary said that Mrs. Nesbitt had requested her week of holiday time and three additional weeks of unpaid leave. They say they haven't seen her since and have no idea where she went. We've checked her house, left phone messages, checked all the airlines. There's no sign of her."

"So she disappeared about the time Frank was murdered," said Lydia. Al nodded silently.

Lydia pressed her fingers into her temple and swallowed hard. "So what about Greg? How much does he know about the ivory smuggling?"

"He was involved but at a fairly low level. According to Rymer, Reston has been smuggling ivory from Alaska for about three years. At first he carried it overland in camper vans, but the border really tightened up about two years ago and Reston got nervous. Last summer he started smuggling it around the north coast by fishing boat. Frank Johnson's letter was referring to those shipments. The boats come up the Mackenzie River and then Greg Rymer takes the ivory from Inuvik to Whitehorse in his truck."

"Wow," said Lydia.

"Wow is right. That's a long boat trip, and there's only about three months when those waters are navigable," said Al. "They were lucky this year. Breakup came very early. But even so, this strategy isn't going to be cost effective in the long run; the boats are too small. Reston was looking for a way to bring in really large shipments. That's how Evangelist got involved."

"The cruise ships," said Lydia.

"Exactly," said Al. The lilting strains of *Green, Green Rocky Road* wafted softly from the speakers. "He brought Evangelist in on the ivory action, and they hatched a plan. The pier is the only piece of the plan already in place, but the rest goes like this. On the way up the west coast of Alaska, Evangelist's cruise ships stop at a couple of different villages. The poachers deliver the ivory to them there. None of the local governing boards will know what's going on, and Holiday Cruise Lines won't build docks in those villages. The ships anchor off shore and a few Zodiacs go into town, ostensibly to get supplies. Some hardware or staples are purchased, but most of the boxes put on the inflatables contain ivory. By the time the cruise ship gets to the Northwest Territories, it's carrying a good sized cache. The ivory is offloaded at Nuvaktuk and flown to Inuvik in Aurora's planes. Then Rymer continues to do what he's been doing; he carries the ivory from Inuvik to Whitehorse in his construction truck."

"Why not fly the ivory straight to Whitehorse?"

"Aurora's planes don't operate out of Whitehorse."

"Greg told you all of this."

"Yeah, after we offered him a plea bargain. Carmichael told him he'd try to reduce the charges from attempted murder to assault with a deadly weapon, if he'd testify against Reston and Holiday Cruise Lines. Rymer agreed. He's scared to death."

"So you do have something! You've got Reston and Evangelist both," said Lydia.

Al's face was grave. He shook his head. "Not exactly." He lowered his eyes as if he couldn't quite meet Lydia's gaze.

"Why not? You've got Greg's testimony."

Now Van Ronk was exhorting his sister to "stop that shaking your yas, yas, yas."

"We've got Reston, but Evangelist hasn't done anything illegal yet," said Al.

Lydia exploded. "What are you talking about?" She jumped out of her chair and stood in front of him, her arms stiff at her sides, her hands clenched. "He's the one who hired Frank's killer. You know the killer came from Florida. Evangelist had Frank killed!"

"We believe that, Lydia, but we've got no compelling evidence to prove it. The plantain chip bag, the Orlando Bosch alias, and a fake Miami address–that's all that links this murder to Miami. There's nothing linking it to Herman Evangelist."

"I hate this!" said Lydia. Dave Van Ronk began singing *He was a Friend of Mine,* one of Otto Falkner's favorite songs. It was a lament, a eulogy, made all the more poignant by Van Ronk's raspy, nasal voice.

"He died on the road," croaked the bluesman. "He died on the road. Never had no money to pay for his board. He was a friend of mine." Lydia looked down at Al with quivering lips. "He never done no wrong," insisted Van Ronk. "He never done no wrong." Lydia collapsed in her chair and put her face in her hands as the singer intoned, "When I hear his name, well, you know I just can't keep from crying."

Al jumped up and turned off the CD player. Then he put both arms tightly around Lydia. She was silent for a moment and then raised her head. "I'm okay," she said. Her eyes were dry, but they reflected sadness bordering on hopelessness. Al released her but kept one hand on her shoulder. She swallowed hard and then she asked, "But you can nail Reston, right?"

"Oh, yeah. We've got plenty of witnesses on the loan sharking, and we've got Rymer's testimony and Johnson's letter on the ivory." Al paused. "However, you need to know that Rymer's testimony is somewhat problematic."

Lydia sighed deeply and started to speak. Al put a finger to her lips. "Let me finish. Rymer knew what he was carrying, but he never saw any of the ivory. The boxes were nailed shut before they were put on the boats, and they weren't opened until they left Rymer's custody. We don't want to raid Reston's office because, if that storeroom is empty, we've got zilch. According to Rymer, the ivory is never on the premises for more than a day or two. Finding Reston in possession of smuggled ivory would cinch the case against him, but we don't have much time. Word of Rymer's arrest is bound to reach him."

"Oh, Jesus, these guys are going to get away with everything. I just can't believe it." Anger replaced sadness and Lydia's face went red.

"They'll blow it somehow," said Al, but his voice lacked conviction.

Lydia scowled. "Wait a minute. How did Reston know that Frank had found out about the ivory?"

"Reston might not have known. Rymer sure didn't. He was shocked as hell when you found that tusk. He thinks Johnson was killed because he was going to make a stink about the pier and the helicopter concession."

"That doesn't make any sense. You yourself said that the helicopters flights probably weren't illegal."

"Yeah, but all of Reston's schemes are tied together," said Al. "The ivory smuggling was the lynch pin of this operation, and that depended on the pier at Nuvaktuk. In order to off-load the quantities of ivory a cruise ship could bring in, they needed a real dock. No pier, no ivory. But the pier was more than just a cover for the ivory smuggling. Evangelist really did want to bring tourists to Nuvaktuk. Those cruises would be a very lucrative sideshow. Evangelist and Reston were going after high-end, exotic tourism, people who'll drop two hundred thousand dollars or more on a two month cruise to the Arctic Ocean on a very small but very fancy ship.

"And they really wanted that caribou gig, too. It would have been a unique opportunity for the tourists, a chance to see the caribou without having to endure the discomforts of a wilderness backpacking trip or even a day hike. Rymer says the plan was to helicopter tourists over the Bluenose herd during the summer since it's close to Nuvaktuk, and then in the early fall they'd fly them over the Porcupine herd as it moves into the Yukon. That was supposed to be the big draw, seeing the Porcupine herd."

"At least the caribou and the walrus will be spared now," said Lydia.

"Yeah," said Al, "until the next unscrupulous lowlife comes along. It'll never end. Greed rules."

"It's worse than greed," replied Lydia. "It's betrayal. Like Frank said the last time I saw him, it's the betrayal of everything and everyone. That's what Curtis Reston did. He betrayed the people in Nuvaktuk, the Gwich'in, the caribou, and the walrus. He even betrayed his father's vision for Aurora Tours."

Al nodded, but it was clear that his mind was somewhere else. He was quiet for awhile and then he spoke. "Rymer said that another ivory shipment is scheduled this week. The dates in Frank's letter confirm that. I wish to God we could figure out where they're bringing it in. If we could catch Reston at the drop off site, we really would have him by the short ones. The problem is that we don't know *where* it's coming in. The Mackenzie River delta is a big place. There's a lot of spots for a boat to land. Too many."

"So Greg doesn't know."

"He says he doesn't. All he knows is that it's somewhere fairly near Inuvik. Someone else who works for Reston picks up the boxes, and later they load them into Rymer's construction truck. It's clear that Reston wanted Rymer to know as little as possible."

"There can't be that many places to come ashore by boat," said Lydia, squeezing her eyes shut as she tried to recall the delta landscape. "The landing site has to be accessible by vehicle," she noted, "and it's very, very wet up there, so I'll bet there's a road. Very few vehicles could handle that kind of muskeg. An ATV maybe, but you can't carry much on those."

Al brightened. "A road. That would certainly narrow things down. How many roads can there be up there anyway?"

"Very few," said Lydia. She put her hands on the table grew quiet for a few moments. Then she looked intently at Al. "That letter Frank wrote included shipment dates, right?" Her face was animated again.

"Yeah. He said two shipments were due in June and two in July."

"What were those dates?" asked Lydia. "Do you remember?"

"No, but I have my notes here," said Al, getting up and heading for the bedroom and his briefcase.

"Get me a calendar, too," called Lydia.

As Al walked back into the living room, he was flipping pages in a loose leaf notebook. "Here it is," he said. "The first shipment Frank mentions was due June seventeenth. The next one was due on June twenty-eighth. The two others are scheduled for July fifteenth and July twenty-sixth." Al slammed the notebook shut. "Damn, if we could just figure out where they're landing, we'd still have two chances to nail 'em."

"Let me see the calendar," said Lydia. "I need June."

Al pulled a small daily planner out of his shirt pocket and opened it. "Here," he said, splaying two pages flat with his thumb and little finger.

Lydia looked closely at the right page. She held her breath as she placed her index finger on one numbered box and then another. Then she closed her eyes and counted on her fingers. She sat back in her chair and breathed out. She began to smile. Her smile got bigger and bigger. "Holy shit! I think I know exactly where that ivory's coming in."

"No," said Al. "How could you possibly know *that*?"

Lydia moved to the edge of her seat and explained, tripping over words in her excitement. "When I went up to see Jesse, up to Inuvik, I didn't want to stay with him and Evelyn because his apartment's too small, so I went back to a campground that's off the highway a few miles south of town and there were a lot of people in the campground and there was a volley ball game and—."

Al interrupted her, laughing. "You can slow down. We've got plenty of time here."

Lydia grinned again and took a deep breath. She remained perched on the edge of her chair as she described her campsite and the three men she'd seen unloading boxes from an open boat. "It seemed a little odd, but it was the middle of the day and they weren't acting furtive, so I didn't think too much about it. This was June twenty-eighth. I'm sure of it."

"My God," Al breathed. "This is incredible. Did these guys see you? Did you get a good look at them?"

"I was standing in the woods, so I don't think they saw me at all. I remember that one of them was tall and thin and another one was short and fat. I don't remember much about the third guy accept that he had a Slavic accent of some kind. And I really couldn't see their faces. They were all wearing hats."

"Did anybody pick the boxes up with a vehicle?"

"They were still unloading the boat when I left. I didn't see a vehicle." She paused. "Wait a minute. An old RV was pulling into the campground just as I was driving out. I remember it because that idiot was driving like he was at Indy."

Al jumped up and started pacing. "It fits. It works. It's an overnight campground without any on-site tourist activities. Right?" Lydia nodded. "So the smugglers could be sure it would be fairly empty during the day. Right?" Lydia nodded again. "And nobody would notice people loading stuff into an RV in a campground. Right?" Lydia nodded a third time.

"This is it!" said Al. "This is it." He grabbed Lydia, pulled her to her feet, and gave her loud kiss.

"But wait," said Lydia as she wriggled out of Al's embrace. "What about Greg's truck. If they're making another pickup, they'll need Greg and his truck for the trip to Whitehorse. If he's not there, won't they get suspicious?"

"Not a problem. Rymer wasn't scheduled to make the next pickup because Reston had sent him down here to keep an eye on you."

Lydia shivered. "Oh, yeah."

"If this pans out," said Al, "you will be a hero. I gotta call Carmichael and tell him. I need to make some notes too, so I'm going over to the detachment."

As he walked toward the hall, Lydia followed him with her eyes, her expression solemn. He had just reached for his briefcase when she called to him. "Wait. Come back a minute." Al obeyed. "Sit down." Al lowered himself into a chair and gave Lydia a wary look as she resumed her own seat. She took a couple of very deep breaths, steeling herself. "I have something to say."

"Yes?" said Al expectantly.

"If you go up there to get those guys, I'm coming."

"No," said Al. "It's not safe. I can't take you along on a bust."

"You're not taking me, and I'm not asking your permission," said Lydia flatly. "I'll fly up on my own if need be. Pay my own way. Just a civilian flying to Inuvik and looking for a nice place to camp. But I *am* going. I want to get the bastards who had Frank killed and who tried to kill me. I want to see it happen. I can't just stay here and read a magazine."

"How can I do that, Lydia? It violates every rule in the book. And I don't like it. If you got hurt, I'd never forgive myself. Never!"

"Look, Al, I don't plan on playing cop. I won't get hurt. But I need to be there and, frankly, you need for me to be there. I know the campground; I know exactly where the boat came in. And I saw the guy in the green canoe. If he's there, I might recognize him. You need me, Al. I'm your informant."

Al groaned and put his head in his hands, "Damn," he said softly to the floor. Then he looked up at her. "Okay, I'll talk to Carmichael. At the very least, I'll see if he'll agree to you flying up there with us so you can show us the spot."

Lydia smiled at him. "Great," she said. "You won't regret it."

"I sure as hell hope not."

"One more thing," said Lydia. Al fell back into the chair with a sigh. "Relax," she said, "I'm not going to make any more demands."

"Thank God."

"I want to understand how you'll set this thing up. It's a public campground. That's going to be a problem, isn't it?"

Al thought a moment and then spoke. "We'll reserve all the campsites for the day before, the day of, and the day after the drop is scheduled. That way there won't be any civilians in the place." He grimaced. "Except you, maybe."

"Yes," said Lydia. "The Mounties could set up camp, make everything look as routine as possible. It could be one of those business retreats. That would explain why everybody knows everybody."

"Good idea," said Al, growing excited at the prospect of planning the operation. "We'll have food and beer and everything."

Lydia laughed. "You're planning a bust and your thoughts immediately turn to food."

"Sure," said Al. "We'll have to keep our strength up."

At that point, the study door opened and Anna stuck her head out. Both Al and Lydia jumped when they heard the click of the latch. They had forgotten she was in the house.

"Not a word to Anna," whispered Al. "Not a word to anyone." Lydia nodded.

Anna's curls were askew and her face still bore creases from her pillow. She peered at them as if she couldn't quite focus her eyes. "Is there any coffee?" she moaned from the doorway. Al nodded and headed for the kitchen.

"Coffee! You don't drink coffee," said Lydia as Anna crept into the dining room and collapsed in a chair.

"Not true," said Anna. "I always have a cup or two after someone tries to kill me." She stretched and yawned. "Who knew that facing death would be such an exhausting experience."

After downing a large mug of Columbian Supremo, Anna perked up. She turned to Al. "So, how much does Greg know? What all did he tell you? Does he know who murdered Frank? Was he involved in the ivory smuggling? Does he know the witness?"

Al gave Anna a rueful smile and said, "You know I can't discuss police business with you, Anna." Her face dropped and she glared at him. He laughed and said, "Okay, okay. I can tell you this much. Greg helped Reston move the ivory from Inuvik to Whitehorse and he's cooperating with us. He'll be a very important witness."

"Good," said Anna. "I'm glad that schmuck has some redeeming social value."

"No more questions, please," said Al, waving his hand in front of his face. "I can't tell you anything else."

"All right, all right," said Anna. "I get it. I've gotta get home anyway. I'm in desperate need of clean underwear." She swallowed the last drop of coffee, collected her fanny pack from the couch, and walked out the door with a wave. A few minutes later Al left for the station.

At first Lydia was glad to be alone, glad to have a chance to digest the events of the last twenty-four hours in peace. But she soon found that solitude was the last thing she wanted or needed. Her euphoria over identifying the pickup spot was replaced by apprehension and a series of *what ifs*. What if Al got hurt during the arrests? What if Reston didn't participate? What if the smugglers didn't even show up? The very fact that she couldn't discuss any of this with anyone only heightened her anxiety.

She began a set of yoga stretches in an attempt to calm down. She was in the middle of *gomukhasana* when the phone rang. She nearly dislocated her shoulder trying to untangle herself and then banged her elbow on the counter when she reached for the phone. "What?" she barked into the receiver.

"It's me," said Al. "I have some interesting news. Your

speculations about Jacob Tingmiak were right on the money. Gerald Tingmiak said that his father was a council member and did oppose the pier. He not only wanted to stop construction, he wanted Reston's entire operation out of Nuvaktuk. He lost the original vote on the construction issue, probably because three council members were in hock to Reston. But then somehow Tingmiak found out about the helicopters. That had been a closely held secret. He was outraged and vowed to take the whole thing back to the council. He went missing before that happened, but the son is sure that the council members would have shut Reston's operation down had they known about the helicopters. Gerald Tingmiak also thinks that if Frank Johnson was in Nuvaktuk asking about the pier, someone would have steered him to Jacob."

"Didn't the younger Tingmiak think his father's disappearance was suspicious?" asked Lydia.

"Not really," said Al. "Old Mr. Tingmiak's memory was failing and sometimes the lapses were severe. Gerald Tingmiak assumed that his father simply forgot how to get back to the village and died at sea."

"Didn't it occur to Gerald that Reston might be really angry about his father's public opposition to Aurora's enterprises?"

"Sure. But he never imagined that Reston would harm the old man. Jacob Tingmiak was Curtis Reston's great-uncle."

"My God," said Lydia softly. She was silent for a moment and then added, "Ernest Hemingway once said that some people show evil like a great racehorse shows breeding. I think Curtis Reston fits that description."

"That's because you're not in police work," said Al. "Curtis Reston is a nag when you put him up against the worst of the worst."

"Thanks, that really cheers me up," said Lydia.

"There's nothing cheery about any of this," said Al. "We have no body, no murder weapon, and no evidence of foul play. All we have is a missing old man and some very suggestive connections."

"This whole saga is a giant roller coaster ride," said Lydia. "We can't have an up without a down. It's wearing me out."

"It seems that way, doesn't it? Well, I do have an up for you. Carmichael has agreed to let you fly to Inuvik with us and spend a few hours out at the campground while we set up. The people from Yellowknife and Whitehorse will arrive in the late morning, along with two Dawson constables. You and I will leave tomorrow afternoon with the remaining Dawson contingent."

"Yes!" said Lydia, making a triumphal fist. "And maybe when I get there, I can convince Carmichael to let me spend the night at the campground."

Al's voice communicated both annoyance and resignation. "You're going to pain in the ass about this, aren't you?"

"That remains to be seen," said Lydia.

Al sighed dramatically. "I give up," he said. "By the way, I forgot to tell you something. The Assistant Superintendent has asked me, as the ranking officer in Dawson, to coordinate this action with the other detachments."

Lydia nodded at the phone, and then her eyes widened as she actually processed what Al had said. "Wait a minute. Ranking officer? What happened to West?"

Al was gleeful. "Louie got back into town this morning. That's when he found out that he's being suspended without pay. He screwed up once too often. There'll be an internal investigation. He'll be fired."

Lydia gave the telephone receiver a broad smile. "A morsel of justice at long last."

CHAPTER 17

Al, Lydia, and three constables touched down at the Inuvik airport in the afternoon before the anticipated ivory shipment. Two vehicles awaited them at the small rental car office. Lydia drove the bright red Jeep Cherokee out of the parking lot, while Al hung out of the passenger window and admired the landscape.

"I can't believe how wooded it is up here," he said. "I was expecting treeless Arctic plain. This isn't how I imagined it at all."

"Jesse told me it's the river that does it. It's huge and it affects the local climate."

The trip to the campground was quick and within fifteen minutes Lydia was steering the Jeep down the well maintained park service road. She was astonished at how utterly normal the scene appeared. A large sign reading *Campground reserved by Porter Electronics July 14-July 16* had been posted on the message board. Four rental RVs were parked in pull-through sites randomly situated throughout the campground. Four other sites were occupied by tents varying in style and size. The empty spots bore RESERVED signs. Picnic tables were littered with thermos bottles, camp stoves, and coolers. Someone had even erected a volleyball net and two very fit constables were batting a ball back and forth. The woman was wearing short-shorts and a shirt that ended just above her midriff to expose her belly button ring. The guy was dressed in tight jeans and a tank top and had an orange and black Harley Davidson tattoo on his right bicep.

"Well, those two certainly are undercover," said Lydia, grinning.

Al had chosen to sleep in a tent, since tent camping would

maximize his opportunities to be outside and would make it easier to hear any unusual noises at night. He had also brought fishing gear, which would give him a good excuse to hang around the river bank for extended periods of time. He asked Lydia to show him the site nearest the putative landing area. Lydia pointed it out and pulled the Jeep into the gravel parking space.

Al got out and turned around very slowly taking in the scene. "What a beautiful spot," he said. "It's a shame we can't just sit back and enjoy it." He pulled a long duffle bag from the back of the rental vehicle and removed three stuff sacks. He pulled his tent from one sack and laid it in a rectangle on the ground. Then he removed three flexible tent poles from the long thin bag. In less than three minutes he had erected a perfect taut, green dome.

"They sell this as a two-man tent," said Al, "but there's barely room for me in there."

"Well," said Lydia. "You are sort of a man and a half."

"Okay, okay, I'll lay off the Nanaimo bars," he said, laughing as he tossed his sleeping bag inside. Then he plopped himself down on the bench of the picnic table and leaned back. "Now what?" he asked.

"Now," said Lydia, throwing her shoulders back, "I'm gonna go convince Carmichael to let me spend the night here."

"Of course, you are," said Al through his teeth. He emitted a huge sigh. "If it really means that much to you, go ahead. But this you do without my blessing."

"I know," said Lydia. "I can live with that."

Lydia approached the largest RV and knocked on the door. Carmichael called, "Come," and Lydia entered.

Carmichael was making himself a cup of coffee in the little kitchenette. He was tall, straight, and moved with military bearing. Every thing he did was slow and deliberate. When he turned toward Lydia, he didn't smile. She felt like a ten-year-old in the principal's office.

"Sir," she said. "I have a favor to ask."

Carmichael raised his eyebrows and looked at her expectantly.

"Yes?" he said.

"I'd like to stay here in the campground at least until tomorrow morning. I want to watch you set up for this bust. Frank Johnson was a dear friend of mine and these people almost killed me. I need; I need." She stopped not knowing how to communicate a need that she couldn't even articulate to herself.

Carmichael raised his hand. He finally smiled. "I understand Ms. Falkner."

"You do?" said Lydia, incredulous.

"Yes, I do. You can stay. But you have to be out of here by six in the morning. We think the smugglers will come later when the campground is relatively empty, but we can't be sure. I don't want to endanger a civilian, even one with a vested interest in the outcome."

"Thank you, sir. Thank you so much." When Lydia exited the RV, she jumped to the ground and ran to Al who was still lounging against the picnic table.

"I can stay! I can stay!" she cried.

"Your powers of persuasion are truly frightening," Al said as he hauled himself off the bench. "Okay, I lose. Let's go set up your tent."

In hopeful anticipation of this development, Lydia had insisted that Al bring an extra tent and sleeping bag. He had borrowed the gear from a fishing buddy. Unlike Al's tent, this thing was not a simple dome affair. It had more poles, stakes, and guy ropes than any tent Lydia had ever seen. The nylon itself was a crazy quilt of stitched together triangles and rectangles. The overall geometry of this pile of nylon seemed utterly untent-like and utterly unworkable. Finally, after many false starts and much cursing, they got the thing upright. The roof sagged, the walls were flaccid, and the door was askew, but it was at least a mosquito barrier.

"If there's wind or rain tonight," Lydia said to Al, "I'm sleeping with you."

"No fraternizing on the job," said Al. "It would be unseemly and distract me from my work. You know the drill; no sex before the big game."

"Yeah, yeah, yeah," said Lydia, throwing her borrowed pad and bag in through the lopsided doorway. "We women know where you guys keep your brain cells."

"Hey," said Al, "show some respect to the second in command here."

"I promise to respect you in the morning," said Lydia. "So what are we going to do now? How does one prepare for a bust?"

"We're going fishing," said Al.

"Fishing? Isn't there stuff to do—plans to plan, strategies to strategize, operations to operationalize, procedures to, uh, proceduralize."

Al laughed. "Stop. Enough. Fishing *is* an operation. I want to check out the area around the landing site thoroughly so we don't have any surprises. Fishing'll give us a good reason to be wandering up and down the river bank."

"Can't argue with that," said Lydia. "It'll be the first time I've actually fished since I got to Canada."

They walked back to the SUV and Al pulled two graphite rods from the cargo area and handed one to Lydia. Then he grabbed the large green tackle box.

"Okay," said Al. "Show me exactly where that boat came in."

Lydia led him into the grove of alders and cottonwoods. "Here's where I was standing. The boat came in over there." She pointed to a spot about twenty yards away.

"I'm going to stroll in that direction and do some casting. You go the other way and do the same. Keep your eyes open."

"For anything in particular?"

"No, just for anything unusual."

"Give me a lure," said Lydia. "I won't be a very convincing fisherwoman without a hook on my line."

Al put the tackle box down and opened it. It was a deep rectangle and, as he raised the lid, a series of compartments unfolded to reveal a comprehensive collection of lures. They were neatly organized by hook size, number of barbs, color, and body type—popper, pixie, spoon, plug, spinner, rooster tail.

"If I'm going to pretend to fish," Lydia said to Al, "I'm going to pretend to catch something really big."

Al smiled as she chose a yellow plug with enormous red eyes and matching red eyebrows. She attached it to the swivel on the end of her line. "Good luck," he said as she turned and strolled toward the river.

For two hours Al and Lydia alternated casting their lines and walking along the river bank. In that time Lydia found nothing unusual, saw no one at all except Al, and didn't get a single nibble. Strolling in the damp sand and muskeg was tiring and not catching fish was boring. To make matters worse, the smell of searing meat was wafting over the breeze. She turned to look at Al. His nose was straight up in the air.

"Please," she implored, "I'm bored and I'm hungry. Let's go back."

"You betcha," said Al. "I'm starved."

When Lydia and Al emerged from the woods, they could see Assistant Superintendent Carmichael hunched over a Park Service grill, a long fork in his hand, his head engulfed in smoke. Four large sirloins sizzled on the grate and a pile of raw steaks sat on a plate on the picnic table behind him. One of the other picnic tables was loaded with cartons of potato salad and coleslaw, a stack of cardboard plates, and a pile of plastic silverware.

"Whoa," said Lydia. "This is a very well organized operation."

"A well greased machine," said Al prophetically as a morsel of beef fat hit the coals and flared up. Carmichael doused the conflagration with a splash of water.

Lydia was famished by the time she plopped a perfectly grilled sirloin and a mountain of coleslaw on her plate. She found herself seated next to Constable Marie Moreau, one of the volleyball players. Marie had swapped her short-shorts and tank top for mosquito-proof cargo pants and a long-sleeved T shirt. As the two women explored their mutual Dawson connections, Lydia learned that Marie had once dated one of Anna's old boyfriends. Lydia and

Marie spent a pleasant forty minutes gossiping about Hank and chatting about other inconsequential things.

Marie was about thirty-five and an experienced police officer. With her cropped blonde hair, fit lithe body, and long purposeful stride, she looked like a teenage boy from a distance. Up close her ample breasts and pretty, round face gave her gender away. But neither Marie's boyishness nor her prettiness undermined her quiet authority. She was self-contained, utterly focused, and supremely confident. Al said that the other constables called Marie *Nerveless Nelly*.

At one point in their conversation, Lydia mentioned the impending operation. Marie shook her head. "I don't like to talk about actions in advance," she said. "It weakens my effectiveness. I prefer to just put it out of my mind until the time comes; then I can focus like a laser beam."

"God," said Lydia. "I wish I were like that. I have to over-analyze and spell out every worst case scenario. How did you learn to put things out of your mind?"

Marie shrugged. "I don't think I did. I've always been like that. I just don't worry about things."

"You have a rare gift," said Lydia with envy.

But much to her own surprise, Lydia did not spend the night stewing about the next day's events. When she crawled into her cockeyed tent and her musty sleeping bag, she felt calm and relaxed. Maybe it was the prospect of finally getting Curtis Reston; maybe it was knowing that the campground was guarded by well-armed sentries; maybe her subconscious had taken Marie's as its role model. In any case, she slept well. She didn't awaken until 5:30 AM when Al called to her through the screen.

"Time to get coffee. We've gotta get ready and you need to leave."

When Lydia crawled out of her tent, the campground was already abuzz with activity. Two Mounties were hunched over a map of the Mackenzie River that was spread out on a picnic table. She could hear faint static from an RV as someone tested electronic equipment. Carmichael was talking to Marie Moreau, who was wearing a fishing vest and carrying a rod and reel.

Last night's calm dissipated. Lydia could feel her jaw tighten and her back muscles tense. She joined Al at a picnic table and poured herself a cup of coffee from a big, blue enamel pot. Two boxes of doughnuts lay open on the table. She reached in and snagged one covered in chocolate. "I knew you cops couldn't do this without doughnuts," she said to Al, but there was no levity in her tone.

Al wasn't in a joking mood either. "Look," he said. "I want you out of here in twenty minutes, no *ifs*, *ands*, or *buts*."

"Okay," said Lydia. "Let me get caffeinated, get my blood sugar up, get washed, and I'm gone."

Marie walked up to the picnic table and grabbed a doughnut. "So," said Lydia, "do you still feel calm this morning?"

"Oh, yeah," said Marie. "I'm pretty nerveless, just like they say."

"You know about that?"

"Sure, I do. I'm not ashamed of it. Frankly, I couldn't stay in this line of work if this stuff freaked me out." Lydia knew Marie was armed but the gun was invisible. She could, however, see the faint outline of a radio in the pocket of Marie's vest.

"Gotta go watch the river," Marie said over her shoulder as she strolled off toward the woods, fishing rod in one hand, doughnut in the other.

"Good luck," called Lydia in parting. Under her breath she added, "And be careful."

Lydia finished her doughnut and coffee, pulled her toiletry kit out of the tent, and headed for the bathroom. Not wanting to stand around doing nothing and yet not wanting to leave a minute sooner than she had to, she dawdled over the sink. She brushed her teeth twice and then flossed. She brushed her hair and then braided it. She washed her face, her hands, her arms.

When Lydia finally emerged, she was surprised to see how quiet the campground was. Al was sitting at a picnic table alone. "Where is everybody?" she asked him.

"In position. It'll probably be a tedious wait, but we want to be ready when the boat arrives. Three of the constables are in the Winnebago. Moreau is fishing over there," Al waved his arm toward his own tent site, "and Peters is fishing at the other end of the campground. Urniq's in the trees up by the road picking wild strawberries."

"Yum," said Lydia.

"He won't be bringing any back, and you need to leave right now. The smugglers could come any minute."

"Where shall I go? What shall I drive?"

"Take the red Cherokee," said Al. "The keys are in it. Wait at that service station up the road. There's a little restaurant there." He handed her a radio. "Keep this with you. I'll call you on it when it's all over. Keep the radio volume very low though. We're all on this channel and I wouldn't want anyone in the place hearing anything. Here's how it works." He touched each button on the radio in turn, explaining the functions as he went.

"Okay," said Lydia. "Got it." She attached the radio to her belt and pulled her shirt over it.

"I have to get into position now," said Al. "Get your butt out of here." He began walking toward the woods, and Lydia headed for the Cherokee.

When she was less than five feet from the vehicle, her radio emitted a soft crackling sound. Lydia unclipped it and held it to her ear. She turned the volume up until she could hear Marie's voice, faint but clear. "A fishing boat is headed my way, registration impossible to read. Moving slow. Three men on board." Al broke into a run and disappeared among the trees.

Then Lydia heard Carmichael's voice over her radio. He was almost whispering. "Moreau, make sure you're out of sight. I'm sending Kuptana, Leonard, and Rogers into position." Three Mounties, one carrying a rifle, two carrying shotguns, burst out of the Winnebago and disappeared among the trees.

Someone said softly, "Damn. I didn't think they'd be here *this* early."

It was then that Lydia became aware of the distant purr of an outboard on her radio. The sound grew louder and louder as the boat approached the campground. Lydia's heart began to pound. She knew that she should leave immediately; she had promised Al. She knew she was the only unarmed member of the party. She knew that her presence could endanger the others. But she couldn't take her ear from that tiny speaker.

Then Lydia heard the faint sound of the boat hitting the gravel shore. Someone killed the engine and the air grew silent—no voices, no birds, no wind. She opened the Jeep door and slid into the driver's seat. She kept the radio plastered against her ear as she inserted the key into the ignition. Just then an old battered RV drove into the campground fast, sliding a bit as it turned the sharp corner by the bathrooms. Its windows were rolled up and tinted dark gray. The vehicle passed the registration booth with its CAMPGROUND FULL sign and slowed as it rolled toward the river. She could hear Constable Urniq's soft radio transmission. "Suspects in white Ford RV heading for boat ramp."

Al's going to kill me if I don't get out of here, thought Lydia. She laid the radio on the passenger seat and turned the key in the ignition, praying for a quiet exhaust system. The engine purred softly as Lydia kicked the transmission into drive.

That's when a brand new VW camper turned into the campground. It still had a remnant of the dealer sticker on the front window. Lydia could see only one person in the vehicle, a male driver. This was not in Carmichael's script. The vehicle pulled up to the closed registration booth and the driver got out and began perusing the notices on the bulletin board. Urniq relayed this development to the Mounties hidden in the woods. In the meantime, however, the side door of the van had opened and a small boy peered out and then jumped to the ground. Lydia realized that the VW camper was blocking Urniq's view of the road, that he couldn't see the child. The little boy's companion was so engrossed in reading the fishing regulations for the Mackenzie delta that he didn't even notice when the child took off running down the gravel road toward the river.

"Oh, God," said Lydia out loud. She grabbed the radio from the passenger seat and had just raised it to her mouth when all hell broke loose at the river's edge. Three voices yelled, "Stop! Police!" in unison while another voice screamed, "You motherfucker!" There was more yelling which Lydia couldn't make out. All the voices sounded hollow and tinny.

Then Lydia heard scuffling, running feet, and the sound of a shotgun being racked. Frantically she screamed into the transmitter. "There's a child in the campground; he's running toward the river. Don't shoot. Don't shoot."

She could hear Carmichael yell, "Hold fire," just as Marie muttered, "Shit," into her radio.

Upon hearing Lydia's voice, the man at the registration booth turned around, screamed, "Billy," and began running down the road after the child.

Lydia heard an engine crank hard and the sound of tires spinning in gravel. Within seconds the old RV was roaring into the camping area. The vehicle passed the boy just as one of the Mounties reached him and scooped him up in his arms. The instant the child was safe, three Mounties raised their guns and fired at the retreating RV. One blast blew out a back window, but the vehicle kept coming. Lydia's Jeep was the only thing between the ivory smugglers and the road.

"Oh, shit," she whispered. "Shit, shit, shit."

She clutched the steering wheel hard in both hands as she tried to control her shaking. She was about forty yards beyond the RV, very near the campground entrance. If she could time it right, she could block the vehicle before it reached the gate, which was fenced on either side. Lydia gritted her teeth, peered through the windshield, and pressed firmly down on the accelerator. The SUV spun gravel and lurched forward. That's when she saw the passenger in the RV lower his tinted window and rest a shotgun barrel on the glass. She saw the slide move forward and back. She saw the barrel aim for her head.

"No!" Lydia screamed. She ducked down on the seat just before her windshield exploded, sending glass all over the interior of the Jeep. Blood rushed to her head. "Fuck you," she screamed. The Jeep was still moving forward. She wedged herself between the seat and the dashboard. Then she reached for the accelerator with both hands and pressed down with all her might. She was going over twenty miles an hour when the Jeep smashed into the front end of the moving RV.

CHAPTER 18

When Lydia awoke, she was in a bed, covered by a crisp white sheet. She looked around and saw a bedside table, a cheap plastic pitcher and glass, and a high-backed vinyl chair with wooden arms. A young woman wearing pink scrubs was gazing down at her with a concerned look. "Ms. Falkner, how are you feeling?"

"I feel fine," Lydia said, looking around with a puzzled expression. "Why am I here?" She got up on one elbow and then fell back on the pillow groaning. "Actually, I don't feel fine," she said softly. "I feel like a horse kicked me in the head."

"Well," said a booming voice from the other side of the room, "that's not far off." Lydia heard the scrape of a chair and then Al was looming over her. He grabbed her left hand and held it in both of his. "You scared the hell out of me," he said. "I thought you'd gone and killed yourself. You're making a habit of getting shot at."

"I seem to be alive," Lydia said, wiggling her fingers in front of her face. Then she looked around the room again. "And this doesn't look like heaven, although I'm not wearing my glasses." She paused. "But I don't remember what—." Lydia stopped talking as a series of disconnected images flashed through her mind—an explosion, glass flying, her hand reaching for the floor of a car. "Oh, lordy," she moaned. "I remember now. I hit that RV, didn't I?"

"Indeed you did," said Al. "You rammed those sons-of-bitches right in the engine compartment. They couldn't go another foot. We got 'em, Lydia. We got 'em all. And you did it."

"I did? Wow. Am I okay?" She flexed her elbows and then threw off her covers and wiggled her feet and raised each leg in turn. "Nothing broken, I guess."

"The doctor says you're fine," replied Al. "The impact knocked you out. You've got a cut on your forehead and you might have a headache for a couple hours is all. Maybe some bruises."

Lydia reached up and lightly fingered the bandage in the middle of her forehead. "Stitches?" she asked.

"Just a few," said the nurse. "It wasn't bad."

Lydia raised herself up on one elbow again. She grimaced as something throbbed inside her skull.

"Let me raise the bed for you," offered the nurse. She pushed a button, a motor whirred, and Lydia's head and torso rose. The nurse poured some water into the little plastic cup and handed it to Lydia.

Lydia took a small sip and then asked, "Can I get a cup of coffee?"

"Okay," said the nurse dubiously, "but wouldn't you rather have a glass of ginger ale or some fruit juice?"

"No," replied Lydia firmly. "Coffee."

The nurse shrugged and left the room, her soft-soled shoes squeaking rhythmically on the highly polished vinyl tiles. In less than a minute she returned with a steaming Styrofoam cup. Lydia took a swallow and made a face. "Whoops, maybe this *was* a mistake," she muttered.

"I tried to warn you," said the nurse, grinning as she headed for the door. "This is the crap I have to drink all day."

Lydia put the cup on her tray table and turned to Al. "Find my glasses for me and then tell me exactly what happened."

Al reached into his shirt pocket and removed her wire rimmed spectacles. He carefully hooked them over her ears. Then he pushed one of the guest chairs next to the bedside and settled into it. He took her hand again. "We couldn't have asked for more," he said. "Curtis Reston was in that RV; he was in the back along with twelve crates of ivory. We caught him red-handed. The three guys in the boat are probably the three you saw in June. The fat one is named Henry Hock and the tall one is Robert Lucas. They're both local.

The third guy was Boris Oblonsky. He works with Reston on the Alaska side. Mr. Oblonsky walks with a slight limp."

Lydia smiled with recognition. "Oh, yeah. The guy who had a crate drop on his foot. Is this Oblonsky Russian?"

"Born in the Ukraine, lives in Alaska now," said Al. "These guys have already started to talk. They're not the least bit interested in taking the fall for Reston. We've got him, Lydia." He squeezed her hand.

"What about Frank's murderer, Al? Do we have him? Is it one of them? Do they know who it is?"

Al released her hand and touched her face with his fingers. He sighed and shook his head. "No. We don't. None of these guys comes close to matching the description of the guy in the Mohawk. We'll check them out and show the outfitter pictures, but I'm certain none of them is our murderer. They don't seem to know anything at all about Frank Johnson."

Lydia picked up her cup again and peered into it. An oily blue swirl danced on the surface of the now lukewarm coffee. She put the cup back on the table. There was nothing to say.

Al stood up, leaned over, and kissed her gently. "I'm really sorry to leave you," he said, "but there's a lot I have to attend to. I need to go over to Aurora and help them seal the office and I want to find Jesse Johnson. Take a nap and I'll try to spring you later this afternoon."

"That would be great," said Lydia. "I think the headache is going away, and I'm pretty sure that I don't want to eat the food in this place."

After Al left the room, Lydia, removed her glasses, lay back on her pillow, and gazed at the ceiling. "I'm sorry, Frank," she said aloud. "I'm really, really sorry." Then she reached for the down switch on her bed, and slowly lowered herself. She was asleep before the motor went silent.

After what seemed like minutes but was probably hours, she heard voices in the hall and a fumbling at her door. There was a knock and she recognized Al's voice as he called, "Can we come in?"

"Sure," mumbled Lydia, forcing her eyes open. Three blurry figures entered the room. She reached for her glasses and put them on.

There next to her bed stood Al, Jesse, and a wiry Inuit woman with iron gray hair and a weathered face. The woman was a complete stranger.

"Jesse," said Lydia. "It's great to see you." Jesse leaned over and kissed Lydia on the cheek.

"We have a story to tell, Lydia. Are you up to it?" asked Al.

"Absolutely." Lydia was wide awake now. As she pushed the button to raise the bed, Al put his hand on the older woman's shoulder.

"This is Mrs. Tillie Nesbitt, Frank's witness," Al explained.

"Thank God you're all right," said Lydia.

Mrs. Nesbitt grinned. "I'm just fine, dearie, just fine." She was dressed in blue jeans, a classic western style shirt with pearl buttons, and leather boots. She was about seventy and had the gravelly voice of someone who had smoked for decades.

Al pulled up the two visitor chairs and motioned Jesse and Mrs. Nesbitt into them. He sat on the edge of the bed and turned to Lydia.

"After I left you, I went to Aurora to help one of the constables close the place and seal all the records. Jesse was in the office and so was Mrs. Nesbitt. Believe it or not, nobody at the office had heard about the arrests yet. Anyhow, Jesse introduced me to Mrs. Nesbitt. As soon as I heard her name, well, uh," Al gave Mrs. Nesbitt a sheepish grin, "I hugged her, which, needless to say, surprised the heck out of her."

"Actually," said Mrs. Nesbitt, "it was lovely."

Jesse picked up the story. "Tillie drove down to B.C. about a month ago. Her brother was real sick and needed someone to take care of him. She hadn't even heard about Dad. I told her about him when she came in this morning."

"Frank was the only person who knew where I was," said Mrs.

Nesbitt. "That's why nobody could find me." She paused and blinked hard. "He was a wonderful man. I'm going to miss him a lot."

"Me, too," said Lydia. "How did you meet Frank?"

Mrs. Nesbitt's eyes lit up at the recollection. "I met him a couple of years ago when he come up to Inuvik to see Jesse. Me and Frank, we met one night at the Mad Trapper and we got along real well. When he come up this summer, we spent some more time together. We even made plans to go camping together in September. We were pretty close." She offered Lydia a small, sad smile.

"My friend and I found a Holiday Cruise Line brochure in Frank's cabin," said Lydia. "Did you give that to him?"

"Yes, indeedy. I found a stack of them on Mr. Reston's desk and figured he was in cahoots with those people. When I saw the ivory tusk on Mr. Reston's desk, I knew it for sure."

Lydia gaped at Mrs. Nesbitt. "You saw a tusk on Reston's desk?"

"Yup. The same tusk you found at Frank's place. Corporal Cerwinski told me about that."

"But how did Frank get hold of it?"

"I bought it from Mr. Reston." With that Mrs. Nesbitt laughed out loud.

"Nooo!" exclaimed Lydia. "You didn't!"

"I did," said Mrs. Nesbitt. "One day I walk into his office and this little tusk is just sitting there. I ask him where he got it. He hems and haws and says he got it from a friend who hunted walrus up in Nuvaktuk, that this fellow gave it to him as a present." She paused and looked at Lydia expectantly.

"So what happened then?" asked Lydia.

"Dearie, there aren't any walrus in Nuvaktuk. You gotta go to Herschel Island or Nunavut to find walrus up here. He was lying through his teeth."

"Not a very informed tour operator, is he?" said Lydia.

"No," said Mrs. Nesbitt. "Mr. Reston isn't very smart. Anyhow, I knew that one of the back rooms at Aurora had been turned into sort of a warehouse and that they stored wooden crates in there sometimes. I also knew that Mr. Reston was the only person who had a key to that room. I put two and two together and it added up to ivory smuggling. So I asked Mr. Reston if he'd sell me the tusk. I told him I always wanted one. Mr. Reston, he'll do anything to make a buck, so he agreed. Frank and me, we split the cost. But we knew that this tusk wouldn't be enough to get Mr. Reston in real trouble. I had to find more."

"So what did you do?" By this time Lydia was sitting up on the bed in her skimpy hospital gown, her feet dangling over the side, her eyes fixed on Mrs. Nesbitt.

"I snooped in Mr. Reston's mail and listened in on phone calls. Our phone system has caller ID, so I tried to keep track of everyone that was calling him from Nunavut or Alaska. One day, I hit pay-dirt. I see this Alaska number flashing. I pick up the phone and hear some man say, 'We'll make contact with the poachers through our man in Point Hope.' I got the phone number and I got pickup and delivery dates. I wrote it all down and gave it to Frank. He said he'd take care of notifying the authorities, that it was too risky for me since I lived in Inuvik and all."

"Do you think someone found out that Frank knew all this?" asked Lydia.

"I'm afraid so." Mrs. Nesbitt lowered her voice. "Frank got real tipsy at the Mad Trapper one night. He might have said something to somebody he shouldn't have. Frank would still be alive if I hadn't told him about that tusk." She looked down at the floor.

Lydia reached over and touched the older woman's hand. "Mrs. Nesbitt, we all feel that way. We all have things we wish we had or hadn't said to Frank. We're all connected in this thing."

"You're right about that, dearie, you're right about that."

"It's so ironic," said Lydia to Al and Jesse. "Curtis probably fired Evelyn so she wouldn't see anything in the files and Mrs. Nesbitt had complete access."

"It's because I'm old," said Mrs. Nesbitt, grinning. "I'm sure Mr. Reston just saw me as a dithering old fool. But he was the fool," she added with satisfaction.

"I have to get Mrs. Nesbitt to the airport now," said Al to Lydia. "She has to be formally interviewed in Whitehorse, and I have a ton of paperwork to do to wrap this thing up. I'll probably be there all day tomorrow and maybe the next day. Marie's coming over to the hospital to take you to the airport when you're discharged." Al checked his watch. "The nurse told me they'd let you out around four so you can catch the five-thirty flight."

Lydia nodded. "Go ahead. I feel fine."

Mrs. Nesbitt stuck out her hand and vigorously shook Lydia's. "Bye, dearie, I hope I see you again sometime."

"I hope I see you, too," said Lydia.

"I've gotta go, too, Lydia," said Jesse. "I promised the Mounties I'd help them with the office."

"That's fine, Jesse. Will you come down to Dawson soon?"

"I will. I promise." He gave Lydia a hug.

After Jesse left, Lydia got up and went into the bathroom. She peered at herself in the mirror. The only outward sign of her ordeal was the small bandage in the middle of her forehead and a scrape on one cheek. She splashed cold water on her face and wiped it with a thin hospital towel. She returned to the room and pulled open the little closet door. Her toiletry kit and belt sat on the shelf and there were clothes hanging on the large metal hook, but they weren't hers. She pulled the unfamiliar cotton shirt and khaki pants out of the closet. There was a note pinned to the shirt. *Your clothes were full of glass. Hope these fit. Marie.*

Lydia stripped off the pink and blue hospital gown and donned Marie's clothes. The pants were a bit snug but the shirt fit fine. Before running a comb through her hair, Lydia checked her scalp for glass. Thank God she'd been wearing a hat when that windshield exploded.

A few minutes later, the nurse brought Lydia a clipboard. The Inuvik hospital was small and discharge was a relatively simple affair. Shortly thereafter, a local constable and Marie Moreau collected Lydia and whisked her off to the airport. The plane touched down in Dawson at 8:00 PM. Marie had left her car at the airport, so she drove Lydia into town.

"You know," said Marie, as she sped down Highway 2, "you were Nerveless Nelly yourself this morning. That was pretty amazing what you did."

Lydia shook her head. "Are you kidding? I was terrified. I was shaking so hard I could hardly hold the steering wheel. And I just dove when that blast hit the windshield."

"You sell yourself short," said Marie. "Pressing on the accelerator and ramming those guys took real presence of mind. We all owe you a lot. You saved us a nasty chase and maybe a gun fight. That would have endangered civilians on the highway. Mounties, too."

Lydia grinned. "Thanks," she said. It was at that moment that the realization hit. I'm not afraid of fear anymore, she thought. Fear is a perfectly rational emotion when someone's shooting at you. She pumped her fist in the air. "Eureka," she said out loud as Marie turned into Al's driveway. Marie gave her a puzzled look but Lydia didn't explain.

It was late the next morning when Lydia threw her legs over the side of the bed, sat up, and assessed her body. No headache and no dizziness, although both her shoulders ached. One of her wrists was tender and the cut on her forehead felt tight and sore beneath the bandage. Her most overwhelming physical sensation, however, was hunger. She realized that she hadn't eaten since breakfast the morning before. As she started for the door, the phone rang.

"Hey," said Anna, "I haven't seen you in days. What's up?" When Lydia told her, all Anna could muster was an incredulous, "*Oy vey*!"

"Look," said Lydia, "I'm half-starved. I'm going over to the cafe. Join me."

"Brad Pitt couldn't keep me away," said Anna.

Lydia reached the cafe's front door at the same time Anna did. The room was almost full when they entered its air-conditioned splendor. As Lydia passed the old fashioned cash register, she noticed the top of a very distinctive head tucked behind an open newspaper. "Dammit," she whispered to Anna, "that's Sergeant West. Let's eat somewhere else." She turned back toward the door.

Anna grabbed Lydia's sleeve. "No way. That asshole almost got us killed. I'm gonna have some fun with him."

"No, Anna, don't." But it was too late. Anna was already striding toward the hunched figure.

When she reached his booth, Anna pushed West's newspaper paper down with both hands. "Hey, it's Sergeant West of the Royal Canadian Mounted Police," she said in a loud, jovial voice. "How the hell are you, you incompetent son-of-a-bitch?"

West gave a startled squeak and then sputtered. "What the—? Who are you?" With a big smile on her face, Anna slid into the booth across from him and pulled Lydia in next to her. West's eyes widened when he recognized Lydia. "You!" he said.

"Yes," said Lydia. "It's me."

"Go away. I don't want to talk to you. Leave me alone." West tried to wave them away with one hand.

"We don't feel like going away," said Anna. "We'd like to take this opportunity to tell you what a pathetic creep we think you are. You didn't give a damn about Frank Johnson, and you endangered Lydia's life and mine. You're poor excuse for a cop. Hell, you're a poor excuse for a human being."

West clenched his teeth and his pale gray eyes darted around the cafe. "Stop it right now," he said, his voice low and sharp. "Everyone in the place can hear you. You're embarrassing me."

"Oh, I have every intention of embarrassing you," said Anna. Then she knelt on the bench and pointed dramatically at the Mountie. "Hey, everyone, listen up. This guy is a bad cop, a really bad cop. Because of him, my friend and I were shot at. If you ever need a Mountie, make sure they don't send Sergeant Louis West."

The other patrons began to murmur and stare at West. A few of them giggled. The Mountie's face turned deep red and he hissed, "Shut up. Just shut the fuck up." Then he picked up his paper and ran for the door. As it banged behind him, a waitress looked up from the counter where she had been doing a crossword puzzle, oblivious to Anna's exposé.

"Hey," she yelled. "That bum didn't pay for his breakfast. He stiffed me!"

"Don't worry," said Lydia. "We'll take care of it. Just put it on our tab." Then she leaned back on the bench and breathed out. "That was quite a performance, Dame Anna."

"Are you pissed at me?"

Lydia grinned. "I'm ashamed to say I loved every minute of it."

Anna snorted. "Ashamed! God, you are so small town."

"I know. My mother has *What will people think*? tattooed on her forehead."

"It's curable," said Anna, "but I may have to take you back to Brooklyn for treatment."

CHAPTER 19

When Anna and Lydia finally got back to Al's, the red message light was flashing on his answering machine. Lydia pushed the button. Al's booming baritone sounded thin over the tiny speaker. "Hey, it's me. I'll be in at three this afternoon. Pick me up at the airport."

Al arrived at the Dawson airport at three on the dot. He looked tired as he ambled across the tarmac. He squeezed himself into the passenger seat of the Corolla, and Anna and Lydia whisked him home. By the time he entered the front door, he had already extricated himself from his uniform coat and tie. He threw the clothes in a heap on a footstool. With a groan he flopped on the couch, removed his shoes and his gun, and put his stocking feet on the coffee table. Lydia fetched him a beer and Anna plied him with cheese and crackers.

"Whewww," he said, sending a spray of crumbs into his lap. "I'm glad that's over. As the interrogations wore on, more and more crap kept coming out. You would not believe what a sleazebag Reston is."

"Tell us," demanded Lydia. "We won't spill the beans."

"No problem," said Al. "This'll be all over the local news by tomorrow." He leaned forward. "We got the details on the loan sharking. Turns out Reston targets people in trouble, people with gambling debts primarily, and loans them money. Sometimes they can pay it off, but in most cases they can't and then he uses them. Usually it's Reston himself who gets them into debt. He runs a stick gambling game somewhere in Inuvik. The game is fixed. When

Reston's marks lose, he offers them loans. That's what happened to Moses Charlie. He got sucked into the game and couldn't dig his way out. It wasn't just his wife's illness that got him into trouble."

"God, I hate Curtis Reston," said Lydia, grinding her teeth.

"This is how Reston got to some people on the governing council in Nuvaktuk," said Al. "It was all very carefully calculated. He brought them down to gamble at high stakes; they eventually lost, of course, and when they couldn't pay up, he extracted a deal. Support the pier and I'll forgive the debt. Don't support the pier and I'll hurt you. It was that simple. Apparently, Reston was going to try to snare some council members from Old Crow, but he hadn't approached anybody there yet. Technically, he didn't need the tribe's permission for the fly-overs, but he knew there'd be a huge stink once the Vuntut Gwich'in got wind of the project. He wanted to cover his ass, but he also knew that the Old Crow council would be a tough nut to crack."

"Is that how Curtis sucked Greg in?" asked Anna. "Gambling?"

"No," said Al. "Reston and Rymer had been friends years ago in Edmonton. When Reston moved to Inuvik, he looked Rymer up. Reston concocted the ivory smuggling plan and immediately thought of Rymer and his construction truck, the perfect way to transport the contraband. He offered Rymer good money."

"So they were old friends," said Lydia. "That's why Greg was so angry at being treated like hired help." Al nodded.

"Does Greg really have a wife and kids or was that story all part of the scam?" asked Anna.

"Yeah, he really does," said Al. "Kuptana talked to his wife. He said she was a nice woman. He's convinced that she had no idea what was going on. She did say though that over the last year and a half, Greg had been buying stuff he couldn't afford. She wondered where the money was coming from, but they were already estranged so she never tried to find out. She was just grateful that he was helping her out financially."

"What about Frank's killer? What did Reston have to say about that?" asked Lydia.

Al studied the label on his beer bottle a moment and then responded. "Reston continues to maintain that he had nothing to do with the murder. The DNA on that chip bag wasn't his or Rymer's. Evangelist voluntarily gave DNA evidence and it wasn't his either. Evangelist insists that he's never heard of Frank Johnson and knows nothing about a smuggling operation. We can't touch any of them on the murder. I'm not sure we'll ever find the shooter, Lydia."

"So justice is blind in more ways than one," said Lydia bitterly.

Al's face tightened. "When I was a rookie, I once complained to my superior about somebody getting off on a technicality. He responded with this line that he'd read somewhere. 'You get justice in the next world; in this world you have the law.' We do the best we can with the law."

Lydia did not respond. There was a long silence. Anna glanced at Lydia, then at Al, then back at Lydia. She looked at her watch and jumped to her feet. "Hey, I've gotta get to work," she called as she dashed for the front door.

Lydia and Al sat in silence for a moment longer. Then Lydia, too, jumped up and headed for the door. "I'm going for a jog," she said. "I need to air out my brain. It's too cluttered to function."

The silence was broken and Al's face relaxed. "I understand. I'll make some phone calls while you're gone."

Lydia's frustration began to ebb as she trotted through town toward the park. When she approached the playground, she was surprised to hear singing. Two young women were perched one above the other on the kiddie slide. The woman on the top step was playing acoustic guitar and the two were harmonizing in high clear voices.

As Lydia approached, a group of small children wandered over to the slide, entranced by the music. One by one they sat in the sand and gazed up at the performers. With an elaborate flourish on the guitar and two wide grins, the women launched into a rapid fire version of *Old MacDonald Had a Farm.* The kids were ecstatic and soon the entire playground had erupted into *moo moo here* and *baa baa there* and *woof woof everywhere*. The mother of one of the kids contributed a verse about a model T that involved a lot of animated coughing and sputtering; a passing mail carrier with a deep basso added one about a Harley Davidson with an unbaffled muffler. But when one of the local hippies sang, "and on his farm there was there was a patch of pot," the chorus being two sharp intakes of breath, the singers chastised him and shut the performance down. The diminutive audience was crestfallen. One of the kids, a boy about five, walked over to the offending librettist and kicked him in the ankle.

As Lydia turned to leave, she felt a tug on her belt. She looked down into the big brown eyes of Molly Maguire. Lydia knelt down and gave the child a hug. "It's so good to see you, Molly." She looked around. "Where's your daddy?"

"He's away," said Molly. "He went to his *ammy*."

"His ammy?" said Lydia. "What's that?"

Molly shrugged. "I dunno. I'm staying with Grandma. She's over there. Come on. I'll *inaduce* you." She grabbed Lydia's hand and led her across the playground to where a plump, auburn-haired woman was sitting at a wooden picnic table, drinking a Diet Coke and eating chips.

"Grandma, this lady's name is Lydia. I met her when Daddy and I were in the storm. This is my grandma, Lydia. Her name is Mrs. Maguire."

"Nice to met you," the woman said. "Please call me Maeve."

"You have a delightful granddaughter, Maeve."

Maeve nodded happily. "Isn't she a doll? She looks a lot like I did at that age although I was a little butterball. She's got her father's build." Then Maeve held out her cellophane bag. "Would you like some chips?"

Lydia reached in and snagged a couple. She ate them and frowned. These weren't potato chips. They were sweet and tasted like crystallized fruit. When Maeve offered the bag again, Lydia took a small handful and shoved them in her mouth. Her eyes widened as she finally identified the taste. Bananas. Maeve Maguire was eating banana chips. Lydia took a sharp breath.

"Can I see the bag, please?" she asked. Maeve looked perplexed but handed it over. The crinkled cellophane read *Plantain Chips* in bold green letters. Lydia scanned the fine print—*Distributed by International Products, Miami Florida.* It was the same kind of chip bag the Mounties had found in Frank's trash pile. Then Lydia looked down at Molly. Her daddy had gone to *his ammy.* Molly had heard *my ammy.* Miami. Then Lydia remembered that Molly had met the real live Mickey Mouse. This was not Tom Maguire's first trip to Florida.

Lydia's hand was unsteady as she handed the bag back to Maeve. She cleared her throat as she tried to compose herself.

"Do you have a cold, dear?" asked Maeve.

"Allergies," responded Lydia. She pointed to the bag. "These are very unusual. Where did you get them?"

Maeve laughed. "Oh, you can't buy them up here. My son Tommy gets them from his boss."

Lydia knees gave way; she sat down so abruptly, the picnic table shook. "Where is Tom?" she croaked as she tried to catch her breath.

"He's in Florida. That's why I have Molly. He's away on business a lot, and when he's gone, he sends Molly to stay with me. Tommy's wife died four years ago. It was an asthma attack. Awful. Simply awful."

"I'm so sorry to hear that," said Lydia. She immediately turned the conversation back to Tom. "As I recall, Tom's from Alaska."

"Yes," said Maeve. "Anchorage."

After exchanging a few comments about the economic and cultural advantages of Anchorage over Dawson, Lydia decided to take a chance. "Didn't Tom tell me that he works for an outfit called Holiday Cruise Lines?"

Maeve nodded. "It's a great job. He loves it."

"What does he do there?" Lydia's throat was tightening and she had to work to keep her voice low.

"Frankly, I'm not sure. I think he works on their reservation system. Tommy's a computer whiz. I don't understand any of that stuff myself."

"How long has he worked for Holiday?" asked Lydia.

"About two years," said Maeve.

"Did Tom ever tell you that he and Molly spent the night at my place on the Yukon?"

"Tommy didn't but Molly did. She couldn't stop talking about Lydia and her cookies." Maeve laughed and chucked Molly under the chin. Molly giggled.

Lydia's mind was racing. She hoped that Maeve didn't notice that she was leaping from topic to topic. "Does Tom own a canoe?" Lydia asked. "I'm putting together a group canoe trip in a few weeks and maybe he'd like to come."

"I'm not sure if he has one right now," said Maeve. "But he knows how to canoe. He's canoed every inch of the Yukon and most of the other rivers up here. Once he canoed right over a waterfall. On purpose! It's a wonder he didn't kill himself."

"My God," said Lydia. "Why did he do *that*?"

"Just for the thrill of it. He didn't need a reason. He never needs a reason. Tommy has always loved to take risks. The closer to the edge, the better, in his opinion. And if something was forbidden, that made it even more attractive. He likes a challenge."

"Like what?" asked Lydia, trying hard not to sound eager.

Maeve put her finger to her chin and thought. Then she grinned. "When he was really little, he would take candy from the mercantile and then put it back the next day. He just wanted to see if he could get away with it. He never ate it."

"Did he get caught?" asked Lydia.

"Oh, yes," said Maeve. "He was pretty obvious about what he was doing. The owner watched him do it three or four times and then called me. Tommy's dad tanned that kid's behind, let me tell you."

"That's a great story," said Lydia. "Tell me more."

"Well, when Tommy was in sixth grade, he made a ramp and tried to jump his BMX bike over our car. Broke his leg and two ribs and smashed the windshield on the Chevy. Claimed a bear picked him up and threw him." Maeve howled at this. "He was grounded for about a year." Then her face grew serious. "That wild streak got Tommy into a lot of trouble as a teenager. I had some sleepless nights. But after high school he joined the military and that straightened him right out. Then he married Gretchen and they had Molly. He's done very well ever since. I hope Tommy can find another woman like Gretchen. She was the best thing that ever happened to him."

Lydia stared at the ground and attempted to blush. "Well, I'd like to see Tom again, Maeve. Can you give me his phone number and address?"

Maeve grinned conspiratorially. "Sure can, hon. You two would make a great pair and Molly really likes you." She peered closely at Lydia. "But isn't he a little young for you?"

"I like 'em young," said Lydia. "Guys my age can't keep up with me."

Maeve roared. "You're a gal after my own heart." She rummaged around in her purse for a pencil and paper and scribbled for a moment. "Here you go. But Tommy won't be back home for four or five days.

"That's fine," said Lydia. She shoved the paper into her pants pocket. "Thanks a lot." She paused and frowned. "By the way, has Tom ever had a beard? He looks like somebody I met awhile ago, but that guy had a beard and mustache."

"Tommy did have a beard. He shaved it off about a month ago. I don't know what possessed him to grow it. He's got such a handsome face and to cover it up with all that hair." She shook her head and clucked.

Molly, who had been standing patiently throughout this entire exchange, jumped up and grabbed Lydia's hand. "Swing me," she demanded. "Pleeease."

Lydia was dying to get back to Al's with her bonanza, but she couldn't bear to disappoint Molly. "Just for a minute. Then I really have to get home."

Molly ran for the swing set. She crawled into a fake rubber tire, grabbed the chains, and stretched her feet straight out in front of her. Lydia pushed Molly from behind until the swing gained altitude. Then she grabbed the tire and ran forward, ducking under it as it sailed into the air. Molly squealed with delight. The arc gradually decreased and Lydia repeated the operation. While Molly was still high in the air, Lydia called to her. "Molly, I really have to run. I'm sure I'll see you again." And then with a wave to Maeve, she ran.

Al was at the kitchen sink when Lydia burst through the front door. She left it open as she sprinted into the kitchen and grabbed his arm. "I've found the murderer," she shouted. "I've found him. You won't believe it." She dragged Al into the living room, pushed him onto the couch, and began to pace across the floor in front of him.

"What in heaven's name are you talking about? You've only been gone thirty minutes."

"I know who killed Frank, Al. It's the guy who stayed at my cabin with his daughter. Tom Maguire. I just talked to his mother."

"Wait, wait," said Al, holding up his hands, palm out. "Start from the beginning." He stood up, took Lydia's arm, and pulled her down on the couch beside him.

Lydia caught her breath, told him about the plantain chips, and recounted her conversation with Maeve. "Her son was the guy I saw in the Mohawk canoe on the river. I'm sure of it now. When I first saw him in the meadow at my place, I thought he was that guy. But then when I saw him up close, he didn't look right. He was clean-shaven and his hair was too short. He seemed bigger, too, but he was wearing a loose jacket. Maeve Maguire said that Tom used to have a beard. Tom Maguire is Mr. L. L. Bean, Al. I know he is."

"Unbelievable," said Al. He stared at the wall for a long time. Then he said, "I wonder why he stopped at your cabin. Was it really the storm or did he come to check you out— or worse?"

Lydia covered her face with her hands and shook her head. "I don't know," she said, her voice muffled by her palms. She dropped her hands and looked up at Al. "But he knew that there were at least two people in the cabin. Anna's boat was there next to mine. It wasn't late at night. And he had his little girl with him. What kind of man would bring a child if he meant to cause harm?"

"What kind of man commits murder?" said Al grimly. "The child was the perfect cover. How could you refuse her shelter?"

"I couldn't," said Lydia, swallowing hard.

"Besides," said Al, "why would Maguire stop at a place just twenty miles from the scene of his crime unless he had business there."

"Because a storm was coming up," said Lydia. "Al, I want to believe that, no matter how evil he is, he stopped for Molly's sake."

Without warning, Al kicked one leg of the coffee table. Two soapstone figures fell over. "I can't believe we were all so stupid," he growled through clenched teeth. "Even though we knew the name and address on that bill of sale were fake, the guy managed to con us. It was no accident that he bought a Florida built canoe. The Orlando Bosch thing wasn't a joke; it was a clever, false lead. Maybe Maguire dropped that chip bag on purpose. We kept on assuming that the killer came in from Florida. He outsmarted us."

"Is this enough to arrest him?" asked Lydia softly.

"Maybe," said Al. "I'm calling Carmichael." He stood up and went into the kitchen. Lydia could hear the rise and fall of his voice as he talked to his supervisor. She picked up the fallen carvings and arranged them neatly on the coffee table.

It took the Mounties two days to convince the Anchorage police department that there was probable cause to search the home of Thomas R. Maguire on East Northern Lights Boulevard. It took another two days to obtain a search warrant. Lydia and Al were sipping coffee in the kitchen on a quiet Sunday when the front door knocker rattled violently. Al hadn't even reached the door when Assistant Superintendent Carmichael pushed it open.

"We got him," said Carmichael, slamming the door behind him. "Anchorage just called. The house was full of great stuff." He carefully draped his suit coat over the back of a chair. He sat on the couch and slowly crossed his long, lean legs.

"Jesus, man, don't keep us in suspense," said Al.

"Well," said Carmichael, "for starters, Maguire has a pantry full of plantain chips."

"And?" said Al impatiently.

"We found a handmade knife. A large one. It was lying on Maguire's coffee table. Frank Johnson's name, *Yukon Territory*, and a date were inscribed on the blade."

Lydia put her hand to her mouth. "Another story knife," she said.

"How did he explain the knife?" asked Al.

"Oh, he had an elaborate tale about how he'd had a little engine trouble and stopped at the homestead to borrow some tools. He said he helped Johnson with some chores and Johnson gave him the knife."

Lydia shook her head emphatically. "Frank would never have done that," she said. "Every knife he gave away was custom made. Look." She took her own ivory knife from its sheath. "This was shaped for my hand. See how it fits me perfectly?" She wrapped her fist around the handle and then handed the knife to Carmichael. It disappeared in his large paw. "Frank hasn't given away more than ten or twelve knives in his entire life and they all went to close friends or family members."

"That's good to know," said Carmichael. He handed back the knife and made his fingers into a tent. "There were a couple of other interesting items in Maguire's house." He paused again.

"Like what?" said Al. He was getting testy.

"Maguire had a real Inuit harpoon hanging on his wall," said Carmichael. "An old one."

"Jacob Tingmiak," said Al. "Maguire killed him and took his harpoon as a trophy, just like he took Johnson's knife."

"Yes," said Carmichael. "Maguire claims he bought it in a pawn shop, but we're sure it's Tingmiak's. His son is coming to take a look at it. Unfortunately, the harpoon doesn't do us a lot of good since

Tingmiak's body has never been found. Man and boat are probably two hundred meters under water. The Beaufort Sea doesn't give up its dead. Maguire has no reason to admit that he killed Tingmiak.

Lydia reached for a carving sitting on Al's coffee table. She cradled the tiny seal hunter and his four inch kayak in one hand.

"But why would Maguire display trophies from the men he's killed?" asked Al. "That seems incredibly stupid."

"I agree," said Carmichael. "It's strange."

"I think I know," said Lydia. Both men turned and stared at her. "Tom Maguire's mother told me that he's a risk taker, that he likes to court danger. I'll bet that taking and displaying those things gave him a thrill."

"Interesting," said Carmichael. "You may be right. That might also explain the matched set of walrus tusks prominently displayed on a living room shelf. New ivory."

"Wow," breathed Al.

"And," said Carmichael, his eyes dancing, "the DNA on that chip bag—it's Maguire's!"

"Holy shit!" exclaimed Lydia. Al grinned when Carmichael threw her a disapproving glance.

"But if Maguire did help Johnson with some chores, couldn't that explain the presence of the chip bag?" asked Al.

"No," said Carmichael. "Maguire got his dates wrong."

"What do you mean?" asked Lydia.

"Maguire maintains that he stopped at Johnson's cabin on June first. He was very insistent on that date. Said he remembered it because it was his mother's birthday. We checked; it is, in fact, his mother's birthday. Maguire also said that he remembers throwing the bag on the trash pile that day, but he's lying."

"Yeah," said Al. "But how can we prove it?"

Carmichael smiled. "Archeology."

Al groaned. "What does that mean?"

"The constables excavated Mr. Johnson's trash pile very carefully," said Carmichael. "Layer by layer. There was a June third issue of the *Yukon News* in the pile. It was under a big mound of rotting cabbage leaves and potato peels. Maguire's chip bag was found on top of that mound, and Frank Johnson's right thigh was on top of the chip bag. Maguire couldn't have dropped that chip bag on June first. It would have been buried under all the vegetable matter along with the *News*."

"So what did Maguire say when you pointed out this gaping hole in his story?" Al asked.

"He didn't say anything but he turned shamrock green. So did his lawyer. There was a lot of sputtering and backpedaling but, to make a long story short, a deal is in the works. He gives up Evangelist and Reston, he gets a speck of leniency from the prosecutor."

"Since Maguire works for Holiday, I assume Evangelist hired him." said Al.

"Oh, yeah," said Carmichael. "Evangelist chose Maguire because he was a river rat, knew every turn, every channel, every island. And the fact that he doesn't live in the Yukon anymore made him even more attractive."

"So what happened to the Mohawk canoe?" asked Lydia.

"Maguire says he paddled it up a remote tributary and hid it. A bush pilot picked him up. That's the reason he used a canoe instead of a boat. It allowed him to simply disappear." Carmichael smiled at Lydia. "And if it hadn't been for you and those plantain chips, he would have. Some constables are out looking for the canoe now. We'll find it."

Lydia shook her head sadly. "Tom's mother said that he got into trouble when he was in his teens, but she also said that the military and his late wife had straightened him out. I guess Maeve was wrong."

"Oh, she was wrong, all right," said Carmichael. "Turns out the military reinforced his worst tendencies. He was in Joint Task Force Two."

Al groaned. "Another JTF Two cowboy, eh?" Carmichael nodded.

"What's JTF Two?" asked Lydia.

"It's Canada's counter-terrorism security force," said Carmichael. "Its activities are highly secret, and its men are trained to operate in violent environments. Over the years a few of them have run amok after leaving the force. Maguire didn't wait. He was dishonorably discharged for beating up another commando. He nearly killed him."

"It's so hard to believe," said Lydia. "He seemed so gentle; he was such a loving father." She turned to Carmichael. "Did you ask Tom Maguire why he stopped at my cabin that night? Was it really the storm?"

"Yes and no," said Carmichael. "We checked with the weather service. That storm was predicted. Maguire was on the river precisely because he knew the storm was coming. His plan all along was to seek refuge in your cabin. He knew what Louis West had told Reston—that you and Johnson had worked together. He wanted to find out what Johnson had told you. You were a problematic loose end. He had no plans to hurt you though, or so he says."

Lydia frowned. "You know Tom did quiz me about Frank that night." She paused, trying to remember the conversation. "I told him that I didn't have a clue about the murderer or the motive. I told him that I had just returned to the Yukon and had seen Frank just once, briefly. He didn't pursue the issue after that."

"But Curtis Reston wasn't convinced and decided to sic Greg Rymer on you," said Carmichael.

Lydia grimaced. "Ah, yes, my second lapse in character judgment." Then she smacked herself on the forehead. "Damn it. I should have been suspicious of Tom Maguire from the start. He told me he was taking Molly to Fort Selkirk. But that's silly. What six-year-old girl is interested in historic cabins and old graveyards? I completely missed that." She bit her lip. "It's just incredible that he deliberately exposed Molly to that storm."

"Well," said Carmichael, "his mother did tell you he was a risk-taker. I guess he was willing to risk his little girl, too." Carmichael lifted his shirt cuff to check his watch. He stood up. "It's getting late and I have a plane to catch." To Al he said, "I'll keep you posted."

Al retrieved Carmichael's jacket from the back of the chair and helped him into it. Then he and Lydia walked the Assistant Superintendent to his rental car. After offering each of them a quick handshake, Carmichael ducked his head and folded himself into the cramped driver's seat. He started the engine, methodically checked each of the dashboard gauges, adjusted his mirrors twice, and tuned the radio to a classical music station. Then he slipped the car into gear and, driving well below the speed limit, headed down the street.

Lydia watched the squat, purple compact until it turned the corner and disappeared. She felt spent. Every muscle in her body was turning to gelatin. She walked back to Al's front yard and collapsed into one of the canvas lawn chairs under the cottonwood tree. Al lowered himself into the chair next to hers and took her hand. Across the street a neighbor's toddler was playing in a rotating lawn sprinkler. As the baby tried to catch rainbows in the dancing water, Lydia thought about Molly—motherless and soon to be, in effect, fatherless.

"I betrayed her," Lydia said softly.

"Who?" said Al.

"Molly Maguire."

"You know you didn't have any choice," said Al.

"I know. But a piece of me actually believed that justice would be pure or at least—." She paused searching for the word. "Comforting. It's not, is it?"

"No," said Al, "almost never."

"At least it's over," said Lydia. She raised her eyes to the clear blue sky. "Goodbye, old friend. Rest in peace."

CHAPTER 20

A week later, Jesse Johnson held a memorial service for his father at the homestead. Frank had been cremated and his ashes placed in beautiful birch box that Frank himself had made years before. Seven boats were required to ferry everyone up the river. They had all assembled at the gazebo. Al, Anna, and Tillie were there and so, of course, was Evelyn. Lydia was astonished at the physical transformation in the young woman. Evelyn's hair was still brick red but with her lovely eyes devoid of makeup, one dainty pearl earring in each ear, and dressed as she was in a simple cotton shift, she looked like a child.

Jesse had invited as many of Frank's old cronies as he could find, and they were an interesting and colorful lot. Nigel Jones must have been almost ninety; he was stooped and arthritic, as brown and wizened as prune. He had donned an ancient smoking jacket for the occasion, gray tweed with patches on the sleeves. He wore it over a pair of bib overalls and a work shirt. Mick and Mack McDougal were both there, giant, gentle identical twins, whose luxuriant gray beards hid their dress shirts and nearly obscured their suit coats. Moses was there, too, in a beautiful beaded caribou skin jacket that had been made by his father fifty years before. He wore it, he said, in honor of Frank's commitment to the caribou and to the Gwich'in people. Buck panted and strained at the leash that Moses held in his hand. Jesse hated restraining his pet, but Buck, joyous at having so much company, had run amok. He had already dug a large hole beside the porch, had muddied one mourner's Sunday dress, and had clawed two runs in the pantyhose of another.

A number of townspeople had come up for the service, including most of Dawson's bartenders, Crystal and Ray, who owned the cafe, and the lady who played the organ at St. Paul's Anglican Church. The organist sobbed noisily as she walked up the bank to the gazebo and kept dabbing her eyes with tiny lace handkerchief. Anna whispered to Lydia, "Maybe Frank was more of a lady's man than anyone imagined."

Lydia had agreed to give the eulogy. As she walked to the bank of the river and turned to face the crowd, she fought back tears. All the people Frank loved had assembled here to say goodbye. Lydia had to clear her throat twice before she could trust her voice. Then she began.

"Frank Johnson was a man of the Yukon. He was of this place and this place shaped him, made him the man he was. Frank cared about this river, these cottonwood trees, the black spruce, and the wildflowers. He cherished the salmon, the moose, and the caribou; but he also enjoyed a big bowl of moose stew or a nice piece of smoked fish." Lydia could see Al smile at this. "Frank cared about these things more than anyone I have ever known. He spent his life challenging those who wanted to destroy or damage this beautiful place. Frank died protecting something that mattered, something that he loved as much as he loved his family and friends. In a way, he died protecting his family and friends because, without all this, we wouldn't be who we are."

Lydia stopped a moment as her own words lodged in her consciousness. Without this place, she would not be who she was. How could she even think of giving up this piece of herself? She went on. "Frank touched every one of us in countless ways. He built our cabins, made us homebrew and cookies, told us stories, and protected our forests. Frank's legacy is all of this," Lydia stretched her arms wide as if to embrace the entire riverbank, "and all of us."

With that Lydia reached down and picked up the birch box, which had been sitting on a low stool next to her. She walked over to Jesse and handed it to him. Then hand-in-hand Jesse and Evelyn walked down the bank to the river and scattered Frank's ashes in the current.

After much eye-wiping, hugging, and hand-shaking, everyone trooped back to the cabin for coffee and a buffet. The place was spotless. Jesse and Evelyn had spent four entire days picking up and putting away, washing dishes and windows, scrubbing floors, and dusting bookshelves. Mason jars filled with wild flowers adorned every bookcase and every table top.

Crystal had handled the food and she had outdone herself. Even the spread was a tribute to Frank. There was an enormous pot of moose stew with potatoes, onions, carrots, and morel mushrooms. Slabs of sourdough bread were stacked next to a crock of sweet butter and a platter of smoked lake trout. Jars of Frank's dill pickles anchored the table cloth at either end. Dessert was a double-header, rhubarb pie and molasses cookies. A few people got tipsy on Frank's homebrew and others got wired on Jesse's strong, dark coffee.

Jesse filled a plate for Frank and put it on the cherry desk. "Dad was never one to miss a party," he said with a smile. "He'll turn up in his own due time."

"Like Elijah," said Anna.

Lydia was reminded, as she looked around the cabin, of the real function of wakes. Wakes were for the living, not the dead. They brought together people who loved each other but hadn't seen each other in years, people who had parted in anger and couldn't remember why they were mad anymore, people who didn't know each other but would like each other and did as soon as they met. Wakes were an affirmation of life, love, and commitment. They were also part of the process of healing and Jesse was starting to heal. He could laugh now, relax with his friends, and had even made plans to go fishing with Al and Ray the next day.

As the wake reached a crescendo, Lydia slipped out the front door and headed for the gazebo. She plopped in Frank's old rocker and put her feet up on the bar that ran around the circumference of the structure. It was strange sitting here in this familiar place, a place where she had spent so many hours with her dad and Frank, both now gone. Every other summer on the river, she had known exactly what she was going to do come September. Not this year. It was strange not having any idea what the future held. But Lydia was at peace. For the first time in months, she wasn't worried about finding a job; she wasn't speculating about her future with Al; she wasn't even anxious about her dwindling bank account. No longer did she feel that compulsion to be in control of every corner of her life. As Al was fond of saying, "Something will happen." Something would.

When Al found Lydia half an hour later, she was half asleep in the rocker, her legs tucked under her butt, her chin on her hand. She stirred when the door creaked and opened one eye. "Hi," she said. "How's it going in there?"

"It's winding down," Al said. "People are starting to pack things up."

Lydia sat up and rotated her shoulder blades while Al massaged her neck. "We gave Frank a good send off, didn't we?" she said. "He would have loved the party."

"Oh, Jesse assured me that he did," said Al.

Al and Lydia walked back up the slope to the cabin just as the guests were beginning to stream down the embankment toward their boats. Soon Lydia heard the cacophony of four different outboards being fired up almost simultaneously.

When they reached the cabin, Crystal and Ray were emerging, carrying casserole dishes, pots, and a big garbage bag apiece. "That's it," said Ray. "Everything's cleaned up."

Lydia and Al entered to find that all traces of the wake had disappeared. Lydia stood in the middle of the living room and looked around at a space devoid of grime, clutter, and debris. She could hear the sound of outboards receding in the distance. "You know," she said. "Frank wouldn't recognize this cabin. It doesn't look like his anymore."

"It's not his anymore, Lydia," said Jesse gently, walking in from the kitchen. "It's ours now. Evelyn and I are getting married next month and we're moving up here."

Lydia rushed Jesse and gave him a hug that almost knocked him flat. "Oh, my God, that's wonderful." Evelyn beamed and Buck danced around the embracing couple, yapping and trying to jump between them.

"We'll be neighbors," said Lydia, stepping back and glancing over her shoulder at Al. She smiled at the look of surprise on his face.

"Does that mean you're keeping the cabin?" asked Jesse, fixing his eyes on hers.

"Yes," said Lydia, "I'm keeping the cabin. I'm going to manage it somehow. I have to stop being afraid of the future."

"Hooray!" cried Jesse.

"Hooray," said Al softly as he grabbed her hand.

"But, Jesse," said Lydia, "how will you and Evelyn survive up here without any kind of employment? What will you do for money?"

"We're not sure what we're going to do, but we'll think of something. Dad managed; we can manage, too. Maybe we'll put in a little campground, sell baked goods and coffee to passing canoeists. Hey, maybe I'll become the Yukon's new Coffee John." He thought a second and then broke into a grin. "I'll call myself Java Jesse."

"The passing of the torch," said Lydia, squeezing his arm.

As Jesse and Evelyn left the cabin carrying the last few odds and ends to their borrowed boat, Al grew pensive. "How about you?" he asked. "You're unemployed, too. Dawson is as good a place as any to be unemployed in. You could live with me in the winter and get some sort of job in Dawson and then come back up here in the summer."

Lydia took both his hands and looked into his eyes. She was silent for a moment and then spoke softly. "A couple of days ago I decided that to the best of my ability I would live life one day at a time. I need to do that for awhile. I came back to the Yukon to sit quietly by the river, drink a cold beer, and sort out my life. The only piece of that I've accomplished is the cold beer. I care for you a lot. I don't want our relationship to end— ."

Al interrupted. "It doesn't have to."

Lydia put her fingers on his lips. "Shhhh. Let me finish. This is hard." Al nodded and tightened his grip on her hands.

"Right now I don't know what I'm going to do. I haven't ruled anything out. I need some time to figure things out. I had always assumed that I'd just get another teaching job in the States, but having you in my life makes the idea of leaving the Yukon for nine months a lot less attractive. On the other hand, to stay, I'd probably have to give up teaching and I'm not sure I'm ready to do that. It's a big step for me. I'm not saying I won't stay. I'm saying I don't know."

Al released Lydia's hands and took her in his arms. He rested his chin on the top of her head. "I'll give you time. As much time as you need. Believe me, Lydia, you're worth waiting for." Lydia buried her face in Al's shirt.

They were still standing locked in each others arms when Jesse burst in through the front door with Buck at his heels. They separated with a start and Jesse whooped. "Caughtcha! Come on, Lydia. You need to help me and Evelyn with something."

"Where is Evelyn?" asked Lydia. "What's going on?"

"Come with me," commanded Jesse. He grabbed Lydia's hand and pulled her toward the door. Al followed as Jesse led Lydia down the path toward the river. Then Lydia saw Evelyn emerge from the woods, straining as she carried a long flat stone across her outstretched forearms. She carried it to a high bank about fifty feet from the boat ramp. Anna was waiting there. Lydia, Al, and Jesse scrambled up the sandy incline. When they reached the top, they were greeted by half a stone man. He already had two sturdy legs and a lower torso. Evelyn's long rock was the arms and she gently laid it in place.

"This is a memorial inukshuk," Jesse said. "It's for my father and yours. They both died on the Yukon, and their ashes are in the Yukon. So, Evelyn and I agreed that they should have a memorial on the banks of the Yukon." Jesse picked up a large round stone which was flat on one side. "This is the head, Lydia. Would you do the honors?" Fighting back tears, Lydia took Jesse's rock and carefully placed it on Evelyn's.

"It's perfect," said Evelyn, "absolutely perfect." Lydia nodded but she was too choked up to speak. Even Anna was a little misty. Lydia looked over at Al and realized that he had tears in his eyes, too.

Jesse turned and sprinted for the cabin. "I'll be right back," he called over his shoulder. A few minutes later he climbed up the embankment with a fishing rod in his hand. "Hey," he said, "neither one of those guys would have wasted an afternoon on a river bank, doing nothing. This inukshuk is going fishing." Jesse rested the rod on one of the stone arms. A piece of monofilament hung down about six inches and one of Frank's handmade flies danced in the breeze. Everyone laughed and cried at the same time. Buck barked and ran circles around the inukshuk. Frank's wake was over. It was time to go home.

Jesse and Evelyn rode straight back to Dawson, while Anna and Al dropped Lydia off at her cabin. When Anna's boat roared off, Lydia stood and watched the spray of water until the craft rounded a bend and disappeared from sight. Then she sat on the bank next to her own skiff. With her elbows on bent knees and her chin in her hands, she fixed her eyes on the river. The sun was low and had turned the brown water shades of gold and amber. The noise of the rushing current was hypnotic, and in a few minutes Lydia had slipped into a state that was somewhere between reverie and dozing. She sat stock still for a good fifteen minutes. But then her half opened eyes caught a slight movement on the other side of the clearing. She slowly turned her head in that direction.

There, standing not thirty feet away, was the magnificent black wolf. He was looking straight at her, but this time his gaze was neither remote nor disdainful. He watched her with interest as his tail moved slowly back and forth through the cotton grass. Then slowly he approached. Lydia held her breath and didn't move a muscle. When he was within fifteen feet of her, he stopped, sniffed the air, looked left and right, and lowered himself to the ground. Lydia could see his haunches relax as he sank into the sand. He stretched his front legs out in front of him and put his nose on his paws. The two watched each other for awhile, and then both woman and wolf turned their eyes to the mighty Yukon and watched the water rush by on its long journey from Lydia's cabin to the Bering Sea.

Acknowledgments

Many thanks to all those friends who read the manuscript, provided helpful critiques, and cheered me on. Special thanks go to Jim Hall, who offered invaluable advice and encouragement early on, and to Mary Jane Elkins, who is the most careful and thoughtful reader I know. Most of all, I am grateful to my husband Toby, who served as my sounding board, plot consultant, tech support, graphic designer, fact checker, and morale officer.

Made in the USA
Coppell, TX
16 September 2021

62377716R00154